By Christopher Dow

FICTION
Effigy
  Book I: Stroud
  Book II: Oakdale
The Books of Bob
  Devil of a Time
  Jumping Jehovah
The Clay Guthrie Mysteries
  The Dead Detective
  Landscape with Beast
Roadkill
The Werewolf and Tide, and other Compulsions

NONFICTION
Lord of the Loincloth (nonfiction novel)
The Wellspring: An Inquiry into the Nature of Chi
Circling the Square: Observations on the Dynamics of Tai Chi Chuan
Elements of Power: Essays on the Art and Practice of Tai Chi Chuan
Alchemy of Breath: An Introduction to Chi Kung
Book of Curiosities: Adventures in the Paranormal

POETRY
City of Dreams
The Trip Out
Texas White Line Fever
Networks
Puzzle Pieces: Selected Poems

EDITOR
The Abby Stone: The Poetry of Bartholo Dias
The Best of Phosphene
The Best of Dialog

EFFIGY

BOOK I: STROUD

EFFIGY

BOOK I: STROUD

CHRISTOPHER DOW

Phosphene Publishing Company
Houston, Texas

Effigy: Book I—Stroud

© 2018 by Christopher Dow
ISBN 13: 978-0-9986316-5-3

Published by:
Phosphene Publishing Company
Houston, Texas, USA
phosphenepublishing.com

1.1

For Michael Reyes

EFFIGY

BOOK I: STROUD

PROLOGUE

THE OPPRESSIVELY DAMP breathlessness permeating the dimness of the rain forest gave lie to the diffuse, cool green light that filtered through the thick canopy above. Nothing stirred in the dense underbrush, most of the animal inhabitants having gone to ground, waiting for dusk to bring respite to the thick atmosphere. Even the gaily colored birds of the higher reaches, where the merest hint of a breeze wafted a few cooling degrees, were as motionless and silent as paintings by Audubon. The whole jungle seemed to hold its breath.

At the edge of a rare clearing, broad-leafed fronds parted silently as a small brown-skinned man slipped into view. His straight black hair was bobbed in a bowl cut, and he wore nothing but a G-string. His left hand clutched a bow and five broad-bladed arrows, all longer than the man was tall. His right hand rested for a moment on the knife hilt protruding from a leather sheath at his hip. The knife was special among his people. It was made by inki—the white men from outside the forest—from across the sea, some said. Somehow, it had found its way inland. Pataxó had taken it and tsantsa from a Cahuarano when he was still a youth. Many of Pataxó's enemies coveted the knife as well as Pataxó's arutam and muisak.

Pataxó's sharp, dark eyes glittered as he glanced quickly around the clearing. Then with a stealthy tread, he slid across to the wall of vegetation on the other side. Half way there, he suddenly halted and snuffed at the heavy, still air, a slight frown creasing his brow. He turned around, nostril flexing, trying to catch the direction of the spoor he smelled, but the still air disguised the odor's bearing.

11

The smell wasn't particularly strong or foul, but Pataxó didn't like it. He'd detected the scent several times since midday, and the fact that there was no breeze to bring it from a distance told the Indian that its origins were close. Too close, considering the distance he'd traveled since he first caught whiff of it. Almost as if it was following him. It made him nervous to think he was being stalked, especially since he was the best stalker among his own people. That was why he was currently the tip of the spearhead of an Aragaruna raiding party.

Usually, intertribal warfare among the Shuar was not over territory but over tsantsa, the trophy heads taken during skirmishes and later shrunken. But time had changed things. Now, the Aragaruna were looking for anything they could acquire, but especially territory. They had recently been pushed west by the Achuar, who were being driven out of their own hunting grounds by Aymara who were being pushed in turn by the inki.

Pataxó had never seen an inki, though he'd heard they were giants with pale skin and had weapons that threw thunderbolts. He valued the knife they'd made, but he wasn't afraid of their other weapons. His arrows were accurate as far as the eye could see in the forest. They were quick and deadly and nearly silent, unlike thunderbolts, which would give away one's presence. In fact, two of Pataxó's arrows were especially toxic, smeared with a dose of curare guaranteed to bring down any white giant he might run across.

And Tuchaua. The Huambisa wawek was a man to be feared and killed as quickly as possible. A powerful bewitching shaman like Tuchaua could almost instantly unleash his tsentsak, his invisible and deadly spirit darts, and it would take an equally powerful pener uwisin, or healing shaman, to undo the damage.

The Huambisa were a problem for the Aragaruna. The only lowland forest that remained lay just before the land lifted into the highlands and impassable mountains to the north and west, and it was home to the Huambisa. Until now, the Aragaruna had only rarely seen a Huambisa. That might have simply been because the Huambisa were reclusive, though Pataxó's people had fought scattered skirmishes with them over the years. Pataxó had even taken one Huambisa tsantsa during the last battle.

But the few people who ventured deep into Huambisa territory never came out again. Stories were told around the campfire. The Huambisa were fierce and implacable warriors who lived forever and could melt through the forest like the morning mists. They possessed a secret dart poison more potent than any known to other Shuar tribes. More important, it also was said that Tuchaua not only had powerful tsentsak, but that he controlled a demon warrior, called the manin-pasuk. No one had ever seen the manin-pasuk, but supposedly it was a tsantsa that embodied the muisak of a powerful rival wawek.

Pataxó wasn't sure he believed that. Everyone knew that upon a slain foe's death, his arutam—his spirit's vision and power—immediately became one with the victor's own spirit. And with the taking of the tsantsa, the foe's muisak—his vengeful spirit—was prevented from destroying the victor's life, family, and ancestors.

Taking the tsantsa not only harnessed a slain foe's muisak, it also guaranteed the loyalty of the enemy's women to the will of the victor. Once the head was severed, the muisak was bound, and shrinking the head was more to have something to gloat over later and to insult the foe's family than for any practical purpose. Pataxó had collected many tsantsa over the years in skirmishes with the Karijona, the Ashuar, and others, though most had washed away in last year's unexpectedly high floods. No matter. He would replace at least one this day with Tuchaua's head.

But even Tuchaua's tsantsa would be a lifeless husk of no real value once it was taken. Tsantsa were not alive, therefore, there could be no manin-pasuk. Besides, Pataxó couldn't imagine what such a tsantsa might look like. Would it be like a big head that floated in the air? Maybe Tuchaua had taken the tsantsa but not shrunken it. Would it be as large as a white giant's head? Pataxó chuckled silently.

Then he sobered. The Huambisa were no laughing matter. For a single hunter to run into a party of them would be worse than death, for some said that the Huambisa were eaters of human flesh, like those filthy Yanomami he'd heard lived far to the northeast. And Tuchaua, their most powerful shaman, was their protector. He was the reason that Pataxó and the eight other warriors arrayed some distance behind him were here. This was not the typical mission of vengeance that Pataxó and his people knew all too well. It was what other warriors in distant countries might call a preventive surgical strike. Tuchaua simply wielded too much power on behalf of the Huambisa, and his tsentsak and the stories of the manin-pasuk were preventing the Aragaruna from advancing further into Huambisa territory.

When Pataxó first detected the odd odor, his initial thought was that it might be a band of Huambisa. But he soon realized it wasn't they who followed him. Huambisa would have encircled and attacked him long before now. And the Huambisa, even if they were unusually large for Shuar people, smelled just like other men, as Pataxó knew from the skirmishes he'd had with them.

Now the odor had vanished, and Pataxó slipped almost silently through the low foliage, senses on high alert, reminding himself that his people needed territory and that he was the tip of the spear. The Aragaruna tribal council had decided that the Huambisa reclusiveness was because there really weren't all that many of them and that the manin-pasuk was just a story told to mask their weakness. It would be relatively easy to take their land and either force the Huambisa to move farther west, into the foothills or higher, or let them die by Aragaruna arrows or poison. Maybe that would be best. The Aragaruna would take the Huambisas' arutam, bind their muisak, and give their tsantsas to the children and dogs.

A sudden rustling of branches in the jungle beyond the edge of the clearing from which Pataxó had just emerged caused him to freeze like a deer poised on the brink of flight. His sharp eyes and ears sought evidence that something approached, but the sound ceased as quickly as it began, and his eyes didn't catch any movement. The smell, though, returned, slightly stronger than before.

Pataxó nocked one of the arrows he'd made to kill white giants, then he turned, eased through the wall of vegetation, and disappeared into the forest.

Whatever was following him, the Indian mused as he glided through the underbrush, wasn't a jaguar or puma, the only two predators in the jungle, aside from another man, large enough to be a threat. Pumas were too cowardly and retiring to attack a full-grown human where other, easier prey was readily available. Nor was it a jaguar, for he'd heard none of the hunting jaguar's characteristic *uh uh uh* grunting. Besides, he knew well the musky, slightly carrion-scented odors of both animals. Whatever followed him had a dully tangy aroma that faintly reminded him of the steam bubbling from a pot of cooking curare mixed with the smell of old wood.

He moved on quickly, and soon lost the scent, though that might have had something to do with the gentle breeze that was just now beginning to waver through the trees. Pataxó recognized the current as the breath of night beginning to stir the depths of the rain forest a couple of hours before sunset. Disappointed that his search for Tuchaua's hut had so far been fruitless, he decided to press on a few miles farther before returning to the rest of the raiding party coming up cautiously behind him.

They would find a good place to spend the night, and their search would continue in the morning. This far inside Huambisa territory, it would be a night of light sleeping alternating with guard duty, but that was a routine Pataxó and his companions knew well.

He slid on silently for another few hundred yards, when a wash of his stalker's dull, tangy odor caught him by surprise. And he heard a rustle in the brush close to one side. The stalker was too near for caution or stealth. Pataxó bent his head, dove through an opening to his other side, and darted, dodging and ducking, through the brush.

Maybe it *was* Huambisa. It had to be. Maybe they could change their smell. There was no telling what the Huambisa could do. The Aragaruna tribal council had discounted the stories as tales to scare the children, and Pataxó had gone along, but now he wasn't so sure. It had to be Huambisa. There was nothing else. He just didn't know how many.

But numbers didn't matter right now. Right now, he just ran as fast as he could. He needed to find a way to circle back to his own band and warn them. And above all, he needed to avoid being caught. The result would be short but painful, his arutam and muisak would be taken, and his tsantsa would adorn the huts of the enemies he'd sworn to kill.

Alarm and the need for speed made silence impossible. For several minutes, all he could hear was the sound of his own footfalls, his own breath panting hard with exertion and fear. Then another sound intruded: that of a compact but heavy body rushing after him through the growth.

All thought of Huambisa vanished. It is a jaguar. It must be. But why does it make no sound? Why does it smell so strangely?

He had no chance against a jaguar if it caught up with him in the midst of the brush. The only way he could stay alive was to meet it in a clearing where his curare-tipped arrow might pierce its hide before it could leap and fell him with a crippling blow or ripping claws. Pataxó poured on extra speed, trying to stay ahead of the creature until he could find a clearing in which to make a stand.

Then, miraculously, there it was! An open space, maybe twenty-five feet across, filled with thigh-high ferns mixed with broad-leafed plants. Not much, but enough for the Indian, whose breath blasted through his lungs like fire, whose limbs quavered with exertion. He lunged to the far side of the clearing, feeling safe in the knowledge that his arrow, bearing a heavy dose of poison brewed especially for large animals, would paralyze a full-grown jaguar in mid-spring even if the arrow did not kill it outright. He drew the bow and waited, almost unbreathing, as the animal that had been chasing him sped to the edge of the clearing.

But then, terribly, horribly, the thrashing stopped before the animal emerged into view. Pataxó, shaking with fatigue and fear and the effort of holding the drawn bow, sucked in a few gasping breaths. The last caught in his throat as the branches shook and parted.

Though Pataxó was a hunter and warrior who had bravely faced death in the jungle and in battle and accrued much arutam, his eyes now opened with vibrant terror as the creature that emerged from the brush moved toward him with inexorable steps. Only its chest, shoulders, and head showed above the foliage.

Pataxó had heard the legends, and now he knew....

"Manin-pasuk," he breathed. With a lightning movement, he released the arrow—the arrow designed to kill white giants. It sped straight at the thing and embedded with an audible thunk in the bare, mahogany-colored chest. But the rictus leer of the thing's ragged fangs did not alter one bit, though it had taken a dose of curare strong enough to instantly paralyze any normal animal a dozen times its size.

A taloned hand reached up, wrenched out the arrow, and cast it aside with a contemptuous gesture. The gash left by the bladed tip did not bleed. Then the thing stalked toward Pataxó, who could only cower back, as paralyzed by fear as if he'd been the one pierced with the arrow.

But then Pataxó managed to move. He dropped everything except the remaining arrow with the extra curare and rammed its blade into his own chest. He went rigid, his knees buckled, and he toppled into the brush. The incredibly powerful dose of curare so paralyzed his nervous system that he felt nothing as the manin-pasuk pounced on him, ripping and tearing with razor-sharp claws, its teeth seeking the last faint beat of Pataxó's heart.

After the demon warrior left Pataxó, shredded and rent, it went looking for the rest of the raiding party.

1: BOARDER

THE ROOM WASN'T much. Smaller than what he'd had at home.

Home.

The thought of it turned Stroud's stomach.

"It's thirty dollars a month," Mrs. Dewitt said. "That includes dinner, but not breakfast or lunch. You share the upstairs bathroom with Mr. Hudson and Mr. Leaton."

"That's fine, Miss Agnes," he said without looking at her. He didn't need to look at her. He'd known her all his life. All eighteen years of it.

"Your mother told me you have a job at the mill," she said. "You can pay me after your first payday."

He looked at her then. Rawboned and graying, she had every reason to be bitter. Her husband had worked at the sawmill until a log slipped from a conveyor and rolled across his legs and hips, crushing him. He'd taken four days to die. That had been eight years ago—too late for her to find another man and too early for her to lay down and die with him. But if she was bitter, she didn't show it, and her eyes held kindness.

"That's okay," he told her, digging a wad of crumpled bills from his pocket. "I can pay you now."

He started to count out the amount, but she stopped him.

"I like to collect at the first of the month. Keeps things simple. That's about ten days away. You only owe me ten until then."

"Thanks, Miss Agnes." He handed her two fives.

She folded the bills and slipped them into the pocket of her faded apron.

"It that all you brought?" She nodded toward the battered suitcase and canvas duffel he'd dropped on the floor by the door after she'd let him into the room.

"That's all." He started to think about all the things he'd left at home: his bike, his collection of rocks, the model airplane he'd crudely carved from balsa, the.... But none of it mattered now. All of it was part of his childhood, and there was nothing about his childhood that he wanted to keep.

"Well," she said. "You know the rules. You're a man now, and you can come and go as you please, but I go to bed early, so if you come in late, come in softly. I don't allow liquor in the house, and there's no cooking in the room. And I'd appreciate it if you keep the room clean."

"I'll do that, Miss Agnes."

She handed him two keys.

"This one is for the front door and this one is for your room. Don't lose 'em or I'll have to charge you to get new ones made."

"Thank you."

"You're welcome," she said. "Well, I got a chicken in the oven I gotta tend. Dinner's at six during the week and at five on the weekend. Come in promptly, or Mr. Hudson will eat your share."

She smiled and her eyes twinkled, and he couldn't help but smile back, but then her face grew serious.

"When do you start at the mill?"

"Tomorrow."

"You be careful, Johnny. You know I lost my Frank down there."

"I know. I'm sorry."

"Long time ago," she said with a shrug. "And there ain't been an accident there since then. But that don't mean it can't happen, and logs are unforgiving. You watch out for yourself."

"I will."

She nodded then went out of the room, and a few seconds later, he heard her footsteps going down the stairs. He waited for the sound to fade, standing by the door, looking into the room but not really seeing it. Thinking of the one thing this miserable town of Woodville, Louisiana, had that he wanted. At last he closed the door.

It didn't take him long to hang his few shirts and trousers in the narrow, musty closet and to empty the rest of the contents of the suitcase and duffel into the simple pine dresser coated with chipped green paint. He folded the duffel into the suitcase and slid the suitcase under the bed, then he lay on the mattress, the springs creaking beneath his weight. His eyes roamed the room as if seeking some way out, but the wallpaper's faded pattern of pale green vines and faded yellow flowers against a background of darker green was as ensnaring as the pine forests around Woodville and as dull and monotonous as the life here.

For a time, he wondered why the hell he was staying. He'd like to have thought that his mother loved him and couldn't do without him or that he reminded her of his father, whom she missed terribly. But all that would have been a lie. Jenny Stroud had had a long time to forget all about his father, who'd gone off to die at Pearl Harbor two years after Stroud was born.

The thought struck him then that maybe he reminded her too much of his father. Stroud's tall, lanky frame, dark and unruly hair, and big hands certainly hadn't come from her side of the family.

But did reasons really matter? He'd come to the realization two or three years ago that his mother didn't really love him all that much and couldn't wait for him to move out of the house. And she'd made it plain just last week.

"Now that you're out of high school, Johnny," Jenny Stroud told him, "it's time for you to get out on your own." She had it all worked out. "Agnes Dewitt has an empty room in her boarding house, and Andrew will give you a job at the mill. You go talk to him tomorrow, and he'll tell you all about it."

Begging that bastard for a job was almost the last thing Stroud wanted to do, but he didn't have much choice. Not if he was staying in Woodville. Andrew Buchman was manager and half owner of Richmond Lumber Company, which was the one big employer in this backwater of a town. If you lived in Woodville, Louisiana, one way or another you worked for Buchman.

But the fact that Buchman was top dog in Woodville wasn't what riled Stroud. What he hated was Buchman's relationship with Jenny Stroud. During the war, she taken a secretarial job at the mill and stayed on afterward to support herself and her son. Back then, the mill had been owned and run by the Richmond family, who'd started it in the late nineteenth century. But the same war that killed Stroud's father also reduced the Richmonds to a brother and sister. After Elsa Richmond's husband died of a heart attack in 1946, she wanted nothing more than to sell off her half and retreat to her fading Victorian mansion, which, even then, was slowly crumbling into the Louisiana loam two blocks off Main Street.

But James Richmond couldn't afford to buy out his sister's half of the mill. The war had demanded metal, rubber, and food, but not much wood. And it demanded able-bodied men, which left the mill with a skeleton crew of men too old or infirm to endure the hard labor.

By the end of the war, Richmond Lumber was in dire financial straits. So when Buchman showed up in Woodville a year later, waving enough money, Elsa Richmond saw her chance and sold out her share, much to James Richmond's displeasure. He had a pair of sons he wanted to bequeath the place to, and while he didn't have enough money to buy out Elsa, he had offered to keep her in the mansion as long as she lived. In the end, Buchman's cash trumped blood, and James Richmond found himself with a partner, whether he liked it or not.

Buchman was a widower with a young daughter. He hadn't grown up in Woodville. He said he was from Lafayette and had served in the infantry in Europe during the war. His wife had died in an automobile accident while he was helping storm Berlin, and when he came home, he wanted to start somewhere new, somewhere fresh. He'd saved a lot of his military pay and there was an insurance payout on his wife's death, which gave him enough to go into business.

He was, as it turned out, pretty good at it. Being younger than James Richmond, he took over the daily operations at the mill, and in the end, James was glad his sister had turned him down. Buchman ran the place better than the manager he'd displaced, and he had good business savvy that took advantage of the post-war building boom that was making the nearby towns and cities—especially Houston—grow like patches of mushrooms on the forest floor. Business was good, and Richmond sent his sons off to LSU where they could make something more of themselves than lumbermen. One of them became a doctor and the other a lawyer, and Richmond had hopes the latter would go into politics.

Buchman did more than take over the operations of the mill. He also took an immediate interest in the widow Stroud and made her his personal secretary. John Stroud, who was eight at the time, was well aware of the change in the family income, because Jenny quickly moved them from the shabby old frame house they'd been living in to a new brick ranch home on the edge of town. Stroud had a larger bedroom, more toys at Christmas, and better food. There even was a middle-aged Negro woman named Gladys who came in to clean up and do the cooking.

What Stroud wasn't aware of for a couple of years—at least until Wally Leavon and Jimmy Shorter made it clear—was the change in his mother's personal status. He knew she had an important job at the mill and worked long hours. That was why she'd hired the maid. He just hadn't understood how important Jenny Stroud had become to Andrew Buchman or exactly what work she was doing during all those late hours.

Stroud hit Wally almost before the word "whore" had completely left his mouth. But Wally and Jimmy were both twelve, and that was the last blow that Stroud landed, though Wally and Jimmy landed plenty. All Stroud could do was ball up and wait, hoping they'd get tired. They did soon enough, swaggering off, laughing and trailing more epithets about his mother. Stroud didn't understand all of what they were saying, but he knew what they meant.

Shamed, he went home. It was easy enough to hide his bruises from his mother since she rarely came home until well after Gladys had fed Stroud and he'd taken his bath. He pretended to be asleep when she came in to check on him, but what he was doing was trying to ignore her and the things Wally and Jimmy had said by thinking of ways to get back at his tormentors.

In the end, it had been easy, and all it took was to turn his disadvantage into advantage. Maybe his mother was Buchman's whore, but it paid well, and before long, the Strouds had gone from being one of the poorest families in town to being one of the best off. Stroud learned that if he couldn't beat Wally and Jimmy with his fists, he could use his economic advantage over them. Both their fathers worked in Buchman's mill, and Stroud would have gotten them fired if he could. But if that was beyond his influence, flaunting his advantage wasn't.

By now, Stroud knew that his mother didn't really care about him, but she wanted to pretend she did by filling the emptiness between them with just about anything Stroud wanted. It was a weakness Stroud learned to exploit. If Stroud saw one of his tormentors with a toy, he soon had a better one. The bikes they had were heavy old clunkers with rusty handlebars and loose fenders, but Stroud rode to school on a sleek, brand-new red J.C. Higgins with a tank-shaped top bar, chrome fenders, and a real headlight attached to the handlebar post. And as the years passed through junior high and into high school, Stroud could go to the soda fountain in Lampson's Pharmacy every night if he wanted to, where the poorer kids like Wally and Jimmy might go only once a week.

Stroud didn't really give a damn about hanging out at the soda fountain. Mostly he didn't say much because he never really felt comfortable socializing, and he didn't really care about Saturday night football or the rock-n-roll music that was beginning to blare from the new jukebox's tinny-sounding speakers. He just did it to give Wally and Jimmy a rise. At first. But before long, there was something there that kept bringing him back every weekend night.

Someone.

Claire.

He'd known her since she'd moved to town back when Stroud was in grade school. A year younger than Stroud, she'd been a shy little girl—the new kid in town. Stroud still remembered the way she'd looked then: her blond, shoulder-length curls and the bright, cotton-print dresses and white socks she always wore. The blond curls were still there, but the shyness had long since worn away as she grew into the most beautiful and popular girl in town. She was why Stroud endured the other kids in the soda shop as they nattered on about the football game or watching Buddy Holly sing "That'll Be The Day" and "Peggy Sue" on *The Ed Sullivan Show* just before Christmas.

It was about that time, nearly half-way through Stroud's last year of high school, that he realized he loved her. He thought he'd probably always loved her, but the feeling had been so foreign to him that he hadn't recognized it until now. He knew he had to say something to her, but his feelings made it almost impossible for him to approach her, even though he'd never before had trouble talking to her. And he'd talked to her a lot through the years because they had a special connection. And that connection was the real problem.

Claire was Andrew Buchman's daughter.

Stroud often wondered if she knew that their parents were more than boss and employee, and back in junior high, he broached the subject as circumspectly as he knew how, asking if his mother ever came over to the Buchman house.

"Of course she does," Claire had said. "She works for Daddy."

The innocence of her demeanor told Stroud that Jimmy and Wally hadn't taunted her with the truth, and apparently neither had anybody else. And no wonder. Stroud might not have any power to convince Buchman to fire anybody, but Claire sure did, and every kid in school knew it. And since most of their families were dependent on the mill for their economic survival, they were discreet with Claire where some, like Wally and Jimmy, could say what they wanted to Stroud.

But finally, Stroud couldn't hold himself back. The longer he sat in the soda shop watching her, hearing her bright laughter and seeing her figure bud and flower before his eyes, the more he had to have her. He fondled and jerked himself at night, imagining her with him and groaning with a release that was as much frustration as satisfaction. He had to do something to make her see him as he saw her: as more than just another one of the kids at the soda fountain.

He contrived to sit next to her when a group of them would go to the movies at the Woodville Drive-in Theater, and once, when they saw *20 Million Miles to Earth*, she clutched at him when the monster ripped through the canvas covering its cage and clawed at the heroine. Stroud wanted to clutch back, but all he could manage was a gruff, "It's just a movie."

But it was another movie, *The Horror of Dracula*, that finally drove her into his arms. They were sitting in the back of Eddie King's old Dodge, wedged in with Tim Mercer and Martha Short, while Eddie and Janet Evers sat up front. Tim and Martha had been making out since the first reel, and Stroud had been trying since then to figure out how he might casually drape his arm on the seat above Claire's shoulders without seeming obtrusive. Then, as Dracula sucked Lucy dry, Claire laid her head against his shoulder. Thinking she'd gone to sleep, he glanced down to see that she was far from asleep. Her eyes were looking right into his, and her lips were slightly parted.

The way his arm slipped around her shoulders was as natural as the warm press of her lips against his. He felt clumsy, but at the same time, a great power surged through him. And then he felt embarrassed as his crotch tightened with the the most profound erection he'd ever known.

Stroud never did see the end of the movie, but whatever happened, it was all too short. And then they were leaving the drive-in, Eddie easing his old Dodge over the tire spikes at the exit and roaring off down the highway. They dropped off the girls one by one, then, with Tim riding shotgun, the three boys drove around the back country roads, drinking whiskey from a fifth that Tim had gotten somewhere.

"You were making out pretty good, back there," Tim commented as he handed the bottle to Stroud.

"Yeah," Stroud said, feeling himself reddening and thankful for the darkness. "I guess I got lucky."

"Prettiest girl in town, and he says he got lucky," Eddie laughed. "Pretty good luck."

"Yeah," Stroud said, trying to deflect the turn of the conversation. He handed the bottle over the seat to Eddie. "Y'all weren't doin' too bad yourselves."

"I'm gonna get in Martha's britches if it's the last thing I do," Tim vowed.

Stroud had the same plan for Claire, but when the words came out of Tim's mouth, they sounded crude and far from the other feelings that welled confusedly in Stroud's breast. He thought of Claire as a destination, not as a goal or prize to be attained.

The next afternoon, when he went into the soda shop, Claire was already there at a small table, surrounded by her friends. She didn't look at him as he came in, but she didn't *not* look at him, either. She just sat there, enclosed in a little bubble of talk and laughter, seemingly unaware of anything that was outside its range. Which was where Stroud found himself.

He went over to the counter and sat on a stool by himself, although Tim came in a few minutes later and sat next to him. Tim was looking pretty peaked.

"I think I drank too much of that rotgut last night," he admitted to Stroud. "A Coke," he told Reggie, the soda jerk. "Did you say anything to Claire today?"

"Not yet. Haven't had a chance."

"Don't mess up," Tim warned. "You got to first base, which means she's interested. Keep her interested, and you might score a home run."

Stroud had never like the metaphor, but Tim was right in principal. Claire wouldn't have kissed him if she wasn't interested, would she? Wasn't that how these things worked?

Maybe, but they sure didn't work smoothly. After half an hour, Claire left with her friends, and he didn't see her until the next day at school. But even then, he couldn't find the right time to approach her. It wasn't until Tuesday that he managed to catch up to her when she was walking alone between classes.

"Hi Claire," he said.

"Hi, Johnny." She smiled at him but kept walking.

"I…. I was wondering if you and me might go to the movies sometime."

She looked at him, her smile twisting ever so slightly.

"I don't mean the drive-in," he said quickly. "The Palace."

"I don't know, Johnny. Let me think about it."

And then Martha came up, and the two girls hurried off to class, leaving Stroud in a funk.

And when she kissed him again the next time a bunch of them went to the drive-in, he was more confused than ever.

And so it went until one Saturday things changed. Before Claire got out of the Dodge, she leaned close. He thought she was going to kiss him again, but instead she whispered in his ear.

"Meet me in the old garden shed behind my house in one hour."

That hour seemed like an eternity. When he sneaked down the alleyway that ran behind the Buchman mansion and went into the shed, he found it lit by a pair of candles. Claire lay on a pallet of blankets, another blanket pulled over her, her shoulders bare above its top edge.

"Take off your clothes," she ordered.

Stroud stripped, embarrassed by his growing erection.

27

But he needn't have been. As he lowered himself to the pallet, she pulled back the blanket with one hand, revealing her perfect and lush body. Her other hand held a rubber.

"Make love to me, Johnny," she breathed.

The first time was short. Too short. But they did it again soon after, and Stroud felt gratified in a way he couldn't explain to feel her body stiffen and arch beneath him, to hear a moan escape her lips as he came.

The rest of Stroud's senior year was a blur of school punctuated by Claire melting in his arms on Saturday night and turning a cold shoulder in the light of the weekdays. But despite the fact that she often ignored him, in his growing obsession with her, Stroud thought she was weakening, feeling something for him that was akin to what he felt for her. Thinking it would further his cause with her, he began to confide his ambitions to her, though he could barely articulate much less formulate them. All he really knew was that he felt an emptiness that need fulfilling, and he was smart enough to know he wasn't going to find it here in Woodville. But he didn't know how to get out, where to go, or what to do.

"College," Claire said. "That's the only way, these days. Daddy's sending me to Tulane."

College. Stroud had thought about it already. Old man Richmond's sons had gone to LSU, and one was now a heart specialist in Houston and the other was a lawyer turned Louisiana state legislator. Stroud wasn't sure what he wanted, but even if he didn't want to be a doctor or politician, college was the way. And if he went to Tulane, too, then he could be near Claire until they both graduated.

He talked to one of his teachers about it, and learned the harsh truth. His grades weren't good enough to get him into Tulane or LSU, but he probably would qualify for one of the smaller state universities. And then came the worst news of all: money. Or the lack of it. High school was free, but college cost a bundle.

"I'm sorry, Johnny," his mother said when he approached her about financing his education. "I have a good job, and we do all right, but I don't have enough to send you to college."

Yeah, Stroud thought that night. Rich folks like Richmond and Buchman could send their sons and daughters on to a better life, but the rest of us just have to sit here and suffer. He knew it might be possible to work his way through school, but how long would that take? Ten years? Claire might be tempted to stay with him if he did well and got out as soon as she did, but he doubted she'd wait ten years. *He* certainly couldn't wait that long. Besides, down in New Orleans, she'd be meeting future doctors and lawyers, and what chance would Stroud have to compete with that if he was stuck in some Louisiana backwater town no better than Woodville?

He had to have money. But where was he going to get it? The only other person Stroud knew who was going to college was Tim, who was moving up to Shreveport. What Tim told him turned his heart black.

Like Stroud, Tim's father had been killed in the war, only in Europe instead of the Pacific.

"I'm using my dad's pension," Tim said.

"Pension?" Stroud was puzzled. "How could he have a pension if he was killed?"

"That's *why* he has a pension," Tim said. "My mom got a check every month from the government until she married Larry. Part for her and part for me. She worked and saved most of it so I could go to school. Your mom probably has the same deal."

Stroud's mom had a deal, all right, but it wasn't the same.

Stroud had never known about the government check, but he was determined to find out. He began scanning the mail every day, and sure enough, a little more than two weeks later, there it was. He steamed open the envelope, read the amount, then resealed the envelope and went to his room to put the math he'd learned in school to real use for the first time in his life. He multiplied the amount on the check by twelve to get the total for the year, then by sixteen for all the years the checks had been coming. The final total staggered him. Even if only half of it was his, his share was more than enough to send him to school, house and feed him for four years, and buy him a car to boot.

Why had his mother lied? He didn't want to think it was because she didn't care. Maybe she'd used the money to buy the house. Wondering what the house cost them every month, he rooted around in his mother's desk until he found the deed, and what he saw there was as staggering as the pension money. The house was owned by Andrew Buchman.

Jenny Stroud hadn't had to spend one red cent on it.

Where had the money gone, then?

A little more detective work gave him the answer. It hadn't gone anywhere. It was sitting in a bank account, collecting interest. Most of it, at least.

That night, he confronted her. At first, she was angry.

"How dare you look through my personal things?" she demanded. "I give you a nice home and everything you want, and this is how you show your gratitude?"

"But what's it all for?" he pressed. "You can't give me some of it to better myself?"

"What did I have? A woman without a husband and a wild boy to raise all alone?" She looked away, then, unable to meet his eyes as she worked out the lies in her head. Or maybe she'd told herself the lies enough times that she already believed them. "You're young, and a man. You can make your way. You don't think I'm getting any younger, do you? I need something to support me when I retire."

Stroud stared at her with almost clinical disbelief. Jenny Stroud was only thirty-eight and far from retirement. Besides....

"What about Mr. Buchman?" he sneered. "Won't he support you?"

"What's that supposed to mean?" Her mouth set in a grim line, but her eyes looked defensive behind their defiance.

Stroud couldn't bring himself to say what he wanted, so he said what he could—something he knew would defuse her.

"Won't he give you some sort of money when you retire?"

As he said the words, a new emotion flooded through him. At first, he didn't recognized it, but it was too powerful to ignore, and as it turned over and over in his mind like an earthworm on hot pavement, he saw its kinship with what he'd felt for Wally and Jimmy when they'd called his mother the name he dare not. He saw it was what he'd felt for his mother and for Buchman since that day. It was hate, but now it was nearly overwhelming in its power and frightening in its aspect, and it withered something inside him.

He hated himself. He hated himself for being unable to stand up to his mother, and he hated himself for loving the one girl who was most dangerous and impossible for him to love.

If his mother sensed any of this going on inside of him, if she had an inkling that he knew about her relationship with Buchman, she either ignored it or wrote it off as inconsequential to her. Just as Stroud was inconsequential.

"The mill doesn't pay retirements, Johnny," was all she said, but as the words emerged, the defensiveness in her eyes shifted subtly to something else, something he could not read.

But he understood less than two days later when she told him it was time for him to move.

He went up to the mill the next day to talk to Buchman—not out of a sense of duty, but because there didn't seem to be anything else he could do.

"Hi, Johnny," Buchman said from behind his big desk. Stroud noticed it was made of mahogany—a strong wood that grew far from the pine forests that surrounded Woodville and spread across the South. "Have a seat." He waved to a chair with short arms and red leather upholstery held in place with brass tacks.

Buchman wasn't a big man, but he radiated self-assurance. His fair hair was thick on his head, and the forearms protruding from his rolled-up sleeves were hairy and muscular. Stroud knew that Buchman, despite his money, power, and influence, wasn't all that old. Maybe forty-five. He'd done well since he'd moved to Woodville.

Stroud sat. He'd been told to, and he did, like a puppet directed by unknown forces. The chair wasn't comfortable, or maybe it was, and he just wasn't comfortable being in it.

"So," Buchman said. "You're all grown up and ready to leave home."

It wasn't a question, but Stroud replied, "Yes, sir," his voice flat in his own ears.

If Buchman noticed, he gave no indication.

"Your mother asked me to give you a job." Buchman paused, and Stroud understood that he was waiting for Stroud to say something, as if they were engaged in some sort of call-and-response thing like they did at those Negro churches.

"Yes, sir. I need a job."

He was shocked at how easily the self-hatred had settled comfortably around his shoulders like a leaden overcoat and allowed him to say what he did not want to say, to act as he did not want to act.

"We all got to work, boy," Buchman said. "Know anything about the lumber business?"

"No, sir. Not really."

"That means you're unskilled." Buchman leaned back in his chair and folded his hands across his slightly thickening stomach. "You know what that means?"

"I guess it means I'm not worth much."

Buchman laughed.

"I'm glad you see it that way, 'cause it's a fact. Tell you the truth, I don't really need any more help right now. I'm just doing this as a favor to your mother, her being such a good employee and all."

And all.

"Yes, sir. I appreciate whatever you can give me."

"I don't give nothin', Johnny. You want something, you gotta work for it. Work hard. I've worked hard to get all this," Buchman waved around the room but taking in the entire mill—and maybe Woodville, too—with the gesture.

"Yes, sir," Stroud said, thinking, yeah, getting hold of your dead wife's insurance money sure was hard work. "I don't expect something for nothing. I can work."

"I'm sure you can, Johnny. You're a strapping young fellow. Just so you know: You're the new man around here, and new men with no experience start at the bottom."

"I understand."

"Good. Your mother tells me you're going to move in at Mrs. Dewitt's."

"Yes, sir."

"Fine woman. Her husband was killed here a few years back."

"Yes, sir. I know."

"Log rolled right off the conveyor and crushed him." Buchman shook his head, and he actually looked saddened at the memory. Then he stared at Stroud, his eyes hardening. "That was the last big accident we had here, and I want it to stay that way. If you make a mistake, it might be you that's killed, but it might be another man. That's not something you want to live with."

"I understand, sir. I'll be careful."

"Good." Buchman nodded, his mouth taking on a satisfied line. "All right. You're on. Shift starts at five sharp. See the foreman, Denny Miller. He'll tell you what to do."

"Thank you, sir."

"Give me good work, and that'll be thanks enough."

Stroud understood that the interview was finished. He rose awkwardly, and with Buchman's eyes on him, he shuffled to the door and went out past his mother's desk.

"What did he say?" she asked.

"I start tomorrow."

"Good. Go down to Mrs. Dewitt's. She'll set you up."

"Okay."

He paused for a moment, half-heartedly expecting her to say something more, but she just shooed him with her hand.

"Go on, now. I have work to do. I left some money for you with Gladys."

He went on. There was nothing else to do. At the house, he packed up the ratty suitcase his mother had given him and the Army surplus canvas bag he used to tote his gear when he went camping in the woods. After collecting the money from Gladys, he trudged across town to Mrs. Dewitt's

And now, here he was, staring at the old wallpaper and listening to the ticking of the wind-up alarm clock, waiting for it to tell him it was time to go down to the mill.

2: SAWDUST

THE RACKET WAS enough to deafen. It ranged up and down the register without cease, from the dull rumble of the logs rattling down conveyors and tumbling into cutting cradles to the clatter of rough boards being shuttled off to the planer. In between, there was the roar of diesel engines and the shouts of men, and above it all was the incessant, shrill, grinding whine of saw blades cleaving heavy timbers lengthwise.

Stroud hated it. Among all the sounds of the mill, the only one he ever wanted to hear again was the blast of the whistle signaling it was time to quit.

Right now, that moment was unmercifully far off. Stroud bent and used the broad blade of the coal shovel to scoop wood chips and sawdust from the floor and dump them into the hopper. From there, they were funneled onto a conveyor that eventually dumped them into a huge pile behind the mill. The pile would quickly have grown impossibly large, but every day, one of the mill employees hauled it off, bit by bit, in an old flatbed truck with rickety staked-panel walls. Stroud heard that most of it went to local farmers, who used it as a cheap and crude fertilizer to enrich the meager sandy soil from which they scratched a living.

Stroud scooped, swung the shovel, dumped. That's all he did, every hour of every day, and that's all it seemed like he would ever do. He looked up at Roy Tobin, who operated the saw Stroud was assigned to and envied the ease with which Tobin grasped and manipulated the levers that controlled the saw blade and the conveyor.

Then he caught himself. Was that all he aspired to? To jerk levers this way and that all day? In the hierarchy of the mill, what Tobin did was near the top, but when Stroud thought about it, it seemed pretty measly compared to other things a man could do. To what Stroud could do, given half a chance.

Not that he'd have sneered at being taken on as Tobin's apprentice. The work sure would be easier and the pay better. But that job had been offered to, of all people, Wally Leavon. Wally's father, George, operated one of the other saws, and that gave Wally a step up.

What about me? Stroud thought. If Wally's father could keep the job in the family, shouldn't Stroud be working in the office? That's where he belonged, not down here on this dusty floor, shoveling a cheap but better-smelling substitute for manure. But there was a difference, and it was that George gave a shit about Wally, even if Wally was a shit, unlike Jenny Stroud, who was all too happy to have Stroud out of sight and out of mind.

So Stroud shoveled, and the only compensation, besides his meager pay check, was the way his tall, lanky body filled out with muscle and his big hands grew callused and powerful. But there were problems, too. Problems that had nothing to do with the harsh and exhausting work. Problems with Wally Leavon.

"Not so high and mighty, now, eh, Johnny?" Wally had sneered at him on Stroud's first day. "Doing nigger work for me."

Stroud would have beaten him there on the spot, but with Roy looking down on them with a jaundiced eye and the realization that he needed this job, measly as it was, he swallowed his pride and turned back to his shoveling.

"Hey, nigger," Wally shouted, leaning over the railing of the platform on which he stood with Roy. "I'm talking to you."

"Shut up, Wally," Roy said. "Keep your eye on the timber, or you'll be down there shoveling along with him."

That kept Wally off Stroud's back while the work was going on, though it didn't stop the jeering after the quitting whistle blew. If there was any consolation, it was that Jimmy Shorter wasn't there to back up Wally. Both of them had dropped out of high school at sixteen, but they'd soon after split up as friends when Jimmy went to work for his father at Shorter's Texaco. Then the social code of

Woodville took over, separating the mill workers from everyone else in town.

But the consolation was small. Wally had new friends at the mill, and even if they didn't have his history with Stroud, they followed Wally's lead in taking every opportunity to torment Stroud and make his life miserable.

That kept Stroud away from the usual haunts frequented by the mill workers after hours: either Shanks' Ice House or the El Dorado, Woodville's only real bar, where a perpetual card game went on in the back room, as ignored as the legal drinking age by the local authorities. Everybody figured it was better to keep the mill workers happy, even the ones who hadn't yet reached twenty-one. Maybe especially those.

Stroud didn't dare go to the El Dorado. That's where Wally and his friends hung out. And while he didn't doubt he could beat Wally to a pulp in a fair fight, he wasn't sure Wally's friends would allow the fight to be fair. And the repercussions at the mill would be worse than a beating.

He ventured into Shanks' a few times and had a few beers. The folks were friendly enough, but Stroud didn't make enough money to go there often. So most nights, he just went back to his room at Mrs. Dewitt's, read books, and sipped cheap whiskey he bought at the package store on Ogden despite his landlady's prohibition against alcohol in her boarders' rooms.

In their own way, the books made him feel as bad as his job did. They taught him a lot about life outside of Woodville, but, fueled by the whiskey, they brought dreams he knew he'd never find on the streets of his insulated hometown or fulfill shoveling sawdust at Richmond Lumber. Dreams of more. With Claire.

On Saturday nights, he went down to the soda shop, but now that he was out of high school, it wasn't the same. Or maybe it was, just more so. He'd always been on the fringes, and now, he felt like a complete outsider. There might have been something pathetic about it, but he knew he had purpose in coming here, and it wasn't to continue to revel over Woodville football victories or to wallow in the latest song on the jukebox. It was because this was the one place he could see Claire and signal to her that he was still there.

If Stroud was increasingly the alien among the high school crowd, Claire was its reigning queen. Now a senior, she was more gorgeous than ever. He knew she was going out with Mike Rogers, the captain of the football team, whose father owned a furniture store down on Main Street. He hated that, hated the thought that she might be giving Mike what she gave him. But he said nothing. What could he say? What demands could he make unless they were married?

So far, he'd kept from her that one wish, though she must have known. He wanted to cement their relationship before he asked her, wanted to make sure that the asking was not a question but a statement of inevitability. He contented himself with showing up at the soda shop, and later, after Mike dropped her off, meeting with her for an hour of fleshly release before she had to be inside Buchman's palace.

"That was wonderful," she'd say afterwards, her face and breasts sheened with sweat.

"I love you," he always told her. She'd never said it back. Not yet. But she would. He was convinced she would, so he wasn't worried.

Not about that. But he was bothered by the fact that she had said nothing to her father about Stroud. That was worse than the way she kept their relationship secret even from her own friends. They didn't matter, but Buchman did. He practically owned the town—certainly he owned Stroud.

But I'm cheap, Stroud realized, thinking of how hard he worked for the pittance he earned.

He had to find a way up the ladder, a way to prove to Buchman that he was worthy of Claire. Or, barring that, a way to convince Claire to elope. Once the deed was done, Buchman—and Stroud's mother—would have to accept him. But he didn't want to do it that way. Proving himself was better.

But how? Shoveling sawdust wasn't going to cut it. He suspected that working in any capacity in the mill would automatically lower Buchman's opinion of him. But what else could he do in Woodville? Sack groceries in the Piggly Wiggly or serve up burgers and shakes in the new Dairy Queen? He had to get out of Woodville, go to college, make something of himself.

Stroud began applying to colleges, starting with Tulane and LSU. He had to know if he could get in before he worried about how to pay. He was working hard now. He could take some job that would eke him through. He'd do whatever it took.

Both of the big universities turned him down, but a couple of other schools accepted him, and miraculously, one was Nicholls State University in Thibodaux. That was just south of Baton Rouge and it had just instituted a four-year degree program. He could prove himself there, and transfer to Tulane or LSU, and in the meantime, he'd be close enough to see Claire on the weekends.

He needed her promise that she'd stay true to him, even if he was down in Thibodaux most of the week, and he tried to tell her of his plans during one of their all-too-brief trysts, but she just averted her face and pulled him closer.

"Oh, Johnny. Let's not talk about that now."

"When?" he asked, thinking, all we have is now.

"Later. We have all the time in the world."

The glitter of lust in her eye wouldn't be denied. He, at least, could not deny it because it was all she offered. So he lost himself in her desire and forgot the statements he hadn't made and the questions he hadn't managed to ask.

Money remained an issue, though. He had to save up enough for that first year, when he'd probably be unemployed but would still have school fees and living expenses. The mill took up so much of the day that he didn't have the time or the energy to find a second job much less work one, and he despaired of being able to save enough to cover his first year of school no matter how frugally he lived.

Then one day, as the first touches of spring were coaxing early blooming flowers from their buds, Denny Miller, the foreman, took him aside.

"I been watching you," Miller said. "You come in on time, do your work right, and you even take all Wally Leavon's guff."

Stroud bristled, unable to help himself.

"Now, don't go raisin' yer hackles," Miller said. "I seen the hate in your eyes when he lays into you. I guess you got some sorta past. Fact is, Wally's mighty good at throwing words, but I ain't never seen him offer to come down off that platform. I think, deep down, he's scared of you. I don't care about that. Alls I care about is that you keep your mind on the work and don't let him goad you into a fight."

"Yes, sir. I try."

"You don't try," Miller said. "You do. I admire that. When Mr. Buchman told me to give you a job, he said to make it at the bottom. I done that, but I figured eventually he'd tell me to put you on as a sawyer's apprentice or over on the planer, but he's let you sit down here for a long time doing what we usually hire niggers to do. I guess there's some sorta history there, too. I don't know. But I do know that you ain't never caused trouble when you had call to cause plenty, and I appreciate that."

"I just want to make my money," Stroud said. "I got plans, and I need money more than I need trouble."

Miller nodded.

"Smart boy like you oughta have plans. But sweeping this floor ain't givin' you much money."

"No, sir."

"Like to make a little extra?"

"How?" Stroud had to fight to keep his voice level. He could feel his heart beating in his chest.

"Charlie Folger is feelin' poorly. He ain't said so to me, but I hear he's got the cancer. I guess admitting it would seem like losing, and he don't wanna lose. He ain't showing his pain much, but fact is he can't do nearly as much as he used to do."

Charlie was the worker who trucked off the sawdust from the pile behind the mill.

"I reckon you might like to drive a truck for a change," Miller said. "Haul off all that dust you've been shoveling for the last year. If it works out, we can make it permanent. Maybe deliver lumber, too."

"What about Charlie? Are you going to fire him?"

"Hell, I wouldn't do nothin' like that. Charlie been with us near his whole life. He can ride with you for a week or so, show you the ropes, then I'll make him night watchman. Don't really need nothin' to be watched, but it'll give him a paycheck, and he can sleep if he needs to." Miller stared at Stroud. "Whatcha say? Pay's about twice what you're makin' now."

There wasn't much Stroud could say but, "Yes. Thank you, sir."

"Thank yourself, son, and quit sirrin' me. Finish out your shift, and see me tomorrow after the starting whistle."

Stroud went back to work, feeling Wally's hate palpable on his back, but he found it easier than ever to ignore because he also could feel that the hate was now fueled by curiosity as much as it was by fear.

In the morning, Miller set him up with Charlie, who told him to ride shotgun.

"Glad you're taking this over, kid," Charlie said, "but let me drive it one more time."

Stroud watched the older man climb up into the cab. He was favoring his left side, and he grimaced as he slipped behind the wheel.

Charlie drove the truck behind the mill to the pile of sawdust. More dust and wood chips were cascading from the mouth of the vent above the pile, which was nearly twenty feet high. Stroud stared, thinking of how much of his own sweat was mixed into that pile. Of course, it didn't all come from the saws where he worked. There were three other saws and six planers, and a lot of it had come from them.

"How long did it take to build that?" he asked as Charlie backed the truck up to the pile.

"They just about build it up faster than I can haul it off," Charlie replied with a chuckle.

"How do we load it?" Stroud was attempting to calculate how much sawdust he'd shoveled during the past year, and failing. However much it was, he didn't want to shovel any more.

"We don't have to shovel it, if that's what you're getting' at," Charlie said. He blew the truck horn. "Zeke'll come out directly and load it with that little ol' steam shovel over there."

Charlie pointed to the rusty machine that rested in the shade of the mill next to the pile. If he hadn't said it was operational, Stroud would have taken it for junk.

Zeke came out of the building, went over to the shovel, and climbed into the cab. A second later, black smoke belched from the shovel's stack, then the arm swung as Zeke operated the controls, and the shovel's scoop dug into the pile. It didn't take long to fill the truck, which settled on its springs, and when it was done, Zeke shut off the shovel and disappeared back inside the building.

"Come on," Charlie slapped Stroud on the arm. "We gotta get out and cover the load or it'll blow everwheres before we get it anywheres."

A ratty canvas tarp was rolled up in the space between the cab and the bed, and Charlie showed him how to unroll it and tie it down. Then they were off.

"We're goin' to McCutcheon's today," Charlie said.

"Just one load?"

"Hell, no, boy. He's gonna take that whole pile."

McCutcheon's farm was about five miles outside of town, and although it didn't take long to get there, it was one of the best rides of Stroud's life. He couldn't believe he was sitting here, looking at the scenery roll past, and earning twice what he had swinging a shovel on the dingy, noisy mill floor.

They stopped at the farm house, and Mrs. McCutcheon told them to take the load out to the cow pasture, where her husband was waiting.

"Do we have to shovel it out?" Stroud asked.

"Naw, he's got them for that." Charlie waved at a handful of Negro field hands armed with shovels and hoes and a couple of rough wooden wheelbarrows. "We just gotta wait."

He got out of the cab, grunting as he did, and Stroud followed, coming around the front bumper just as McCutcheon strode up.

"Howdy, Mr. McCutcheon."

"Howdy, Charlie," the farmer said. He was an upright, middle-aged man with thinning gray hair and thick forearms.

"This is Johnny Stroud," Charlie said, waving in Stroud's direction. "He'll be taking over for me after this week."

McCutcheon looked past Charlie at Stroud and nodded. "Howdy, Johnny." Then he looked at Charlie. "I hear you're doin' poorly."

"I guess so," Charlie said. "Leastways, that's what Doc Thomas claims. He wants me to take it easy, and Denny Miller's givin' me the night watchman's job."

"Well, you take care of yourself, hear? When those boys're done with this load, you can bring two more back here, then take two to the cow pasture out past the barn, and the rest to that ten acres I just cleared down by the crick."

"Yes, sir. We can have all that done by dark. Right, Johnny?"

Stroud, not knowing what to say, just nodded.

Under McCutcheon's watchful eyes, the field hands quickly unloaded the sawdust, then Charlie and Stroud got back in the cab. Waving to McCutcheon, Charlie backed up the truck, and turned around, then and pulled out of the field and onto the dirt track that lead back to the farm house.

"Thing to remember is not to go out on one of them fields if the ground's soggy, or you won't never get out until things dry up."

Stroud nodded. He didn't have any worries about the job. Everything so far had been simple, and he didn't doubt that he could do the work. All he had to do was remember the people and locations, and that would be easy enough since he'd grown up around here.

They went back to the mill, Zeke filled them up again, and this time, Stroud drove. Charlie told him about the way the gear shift lever sometimes got a kink between first and second and showed him the best places to stop if he had to take a piss—bleed the lizard, as Charlie put it. And so the day passed, and for Stroud, it was almost like a vacation after shoveling sawdust off the mill floor.

That night, as Stroud lay in his room, he felt the best he had since he'd moved into the boarding house. Physically, that is. But mentally, he was in a funk. He was thinking about Charlie and the way he favored his side and grimaced when he got in and out of the truck. About the cancer that was eating him up inside.

Charlie was dying. And the horrible thing was, he knew it. Yet he was going on as if nothing was wrong. He was "doin' poorly" and taking a physically easier job. Was he trying to deny he was dying? Stroud didn't think so. He was just facing it as an inevitability.

For the first time in his life, Stroud realized on a visceral level that *he* was going to die. It wasn't like he was unfamiliar with death. His father had been killed before Stroud had ever really known him. Mrs. Dewitt's husband had died, and so had Claire's mom. Lots of other people who'd once lived in the town now didn't live here or anywhere else. But all that was in the past. Abstract, somehow. Not real. Or expected, like grandparents and other old folks. They just sort of grew old and frail, and eventually they faded away and you never heard about them any more.

But Charlie wasn't old. Maybe in his late fifties. He still had some time. Or should have. He had a wife and his two sons who worked at the mill. And he was facing death, facing….

What was death?

Like most folks in Woodville, the Strouds had gone to the Baptist Church on Main Street, but Stroud had never really believed in all the stuff they taught in Sunday school. Hell, some of it didn't even make sense. But he realized that religion had a way to look at death by saying that after it was over, things got better for good people and worse for those who were bad.

But Stroud had done enough reading to know that there were other ways to look at it. From what he could tell, there were two possible outcomes: Either there was something after death or there was nothing. If there was something, then maybe the churches were right about Heaven and Hell. Or maybe it was like the way those people out in India and China thought: that you kept coming back in a new life and forgot all about the old ones you'd already been through.

Stroud liked that idea a lot better than winding up in Heaven or Hell since it seemed unlikely that anybody could go through their life without committing acts that would make Heaven a hopeless dream. But he liked contemplating a death that was just nothingness even less. He couldn't bear the thought of living an entire shitty life only to have what little hope you might possess cast into oblivion by some bullet or disease or accident—or worse, creeping decrepitude and a slow fade into nonexistence. It just wasn't fair.

He strove to put the thoughts out of his mind. After all, he was in a hell of a better position now than he'd been yesterday. Another year of living carefully, and he might be able to afford that first year of college. He could start when Claire did. Things were good, he was young. He didn't need to be thinking about death now.

But seeing Charlie the next day brought it all back. Stroud managed to keep his demeanor straight, realizing it wasn't really Charlie's fault that he was dying. But when the week was out, and Stroud knew most of the farmers he'd have to deal with, he was glad to have the bastard, and his stoic complacency, out of the damn truck and out of his life.

The relief, palpable in his chest on Friday night, turned into something akin to joy on Saturday as he anticipated seeing Claire and telling her the good news about his promotion.

"I got a new job at the mill," he told her, pulling back from her hungry mouth.

"You did?" She didn't seem surprised.

"Yeah. Truck driver."

"Doesn't seem like much of a promotion," she said, chuckling.

"It would if you knew what I've been doing for the last eight months. Takin' the kind of guff...."

"Don't get mad, Johnny," she said, smiling at him. "Kiss me."

"Don't you want to hear about my job?"

"You just told me."

"It's more than the job," he said. "It'll mean I can save up enough to start school."

"Down in that little town?" She frowned. "What was it?"

"Thibodaux."

"You ought to go to Tulane," she said. "Or at least LSU."

"I can't afford those." He'd never admitted to her that he hadn't qualified. "But after I get on my feet...."

"We can talk about it then," she said, drawing him to her.

"But we need to talk about it now."

"Why now?" She sat back, the sparkle of lust in her eyes flashing into peeved anger.

"We gotta talk about things before they happen," he said. "So we can plan."

"Well, it seems to me you already have it all planned."

"But what about you?"

"What about me, Johnny?"

"Don't you want to make plans?"

"I have plans," she said. "I'm going to Tulane next fall. What other plans do I need to make?"

She must have sensed his hurt, for her eyes and voice softened.

"Look, Johnny. What we have is now. We're still young. We've got a whole life ahead of us."

"I just want to make sure," he said lamely, when he really wanted to grab her by the shoulder and stare deeply into her eyes and tell her he wanted them to be together for that whole life ahead of them.

"Who can tell about the future?" she asked. "My mom died young. Who can be sure of anything?"

I'm sure I love you, he thought, but he didn't say it, because another thought came to him, making him suddenly afraid. There was something else one could be sure of, and that was death. He'd just spent a whole week riding around in a truck with it.

"Now, Johnny," she was saying. "That's all we can be sure of. Now. That's all that matters."

She pulled him closer, mouth raised hungrily.

Now, he thought as he lost himself in her kisses and tried to forget the way Charlie favored his left side and grimaced when he got in and out of the truck. Now.

3: CARNIVAL

IF STROUD'S RELATIONSHIP with Claire remained maddeningly un-certain, his new job made daily life considerably easier. As the low-est-level truck driver employed by the mill, he mostly hauled sawdust to the local farmers, but a day or two every week, they loaded up his rattletrap old truck with lumber slated for delivery to nearby towns. He wanted to step up to a better truck that could make the longer hauls to Baton Rouge, Shreveport, New Orleans, and even Houston, but that would have to wait. He still had to prove himself.

And so the weeks went, the job taking on a familiar routine as the days edged through spring. Then one Friday afternoon, Denny Miller met him at the truck when Stroud came in from his last haul.

"Got a change in schedule for next week," Miller said. "Starting on Wednesday, everything we've got's going out to that big field Warren Byrum's got out east of town. Know the place I mean?"

"Yeah," Stroud said, though he was puzzled. Byrum never did anything with that field except grow grass for mowing and bailing. Didn't seem like he'd need any sawdust there, much less a whole week's worth, and he said so to Miller.

"You're forgetting something, Johnny. Warren does do something else with that field every April."

"That's right," Stroud said, nodding now with understanding. "The carnival." He laughed. "You know, I never thought about the sawdust they put down in the tents and where people walk. Where it came from."

"Now you know," Miller said with a smile. "This year, it's coming from you."

Like just about everybody in Woodville and the surrounding area, Stroud had gone to the carnival every year—usually more than once, especially when he was younger. And he couldn't help but think of last year, when Claire had ridden some of the rides with him. So, as he drove out to Byrum's field early Tuesday morning, he had an image etched in his mind about what the carnival looked like, how it smelled and sounded. It had always stirred an excitement in his breast mixed with a vague trepidation at the foreign and exotic atmosphere. What went on in those tents? What wonders lurked just around the next corner? It never mattered that the petrified giant turned out to be a crude papier-mâché prop or that it was hard as hell to win a prize at the arcade, and when you did, it wasn't the giant plush teddy bear but a plastic Kewpie doll. What mattered was that here, for a few hours, you could be some place that wasn't Woodville.

The reality, at least this early in a Wednesday morning, was a lot different. Maybe that was because the carnival had just rolled into town the afternoon before, and while most of the tents were up, some of the rides were only half-assembled, giving the place an air of incompletion. He wondered if he'd see any of the few freaks that traveled with the show, but the only people who were up and about were roustabouts who didn't look much different than most of the employees at the mill.

Stroud parked the truck on the edge of the cluster of tents, got out of the cab, and went up to a couple of men bolting together a teacup kiddie ride. Somewhere nearby a generator gave out a muffled roar.

"I'm from the mill," he said. "I got your sawdust."

"Go see the manager," the older of the two men said, pointing down the midway. "Dixon. Last trailer on the left."

Stroud walked down the aisle between the tents. Some were open-air, where men and women were setting up games that could not be won and stocking shelves with prizes that would never be given away. Others were closed-in, with signs advertising an Alligator Woman, a Lobster Boy, a midget couple, a fat lady, a strongman, and a mentalist. At the end of the midway was the large, false-front wall of the haunted house ride, and beside and beyond it spread the larger rides: the Ferris wheel, a small roller coaster, bumper cars, and others.

The manager's trailer sat just off the last intersection before the big rides. Stroud mounted a pair of wooden steps sitting on the ground beneath the door and knocked. The door opened a moment later to reveal a barrel-chested middle-aged man with blunt feature and a bald head fringed with salt-and-pepper hair.

"I'm from the lumber mill," Stroud said. "With your sawdust. Where do you want it?"

"Pile it up out there," the man waved toward the south. "Out past the tents. Don't put it too close."

He started to shut the door.

"Who's going to unload it?" Stroud asked quickly.

"What the hell are you for?" the man asked.

"I'm just the driver. I don't do the unloading."

"I got a whole outfit to set up and not much time to do it in," the man said. "I ain't got anybody to spare, so you have to do it this time."

"I don't have a shovel."

"Well, hell, boy. That's pretty half-ass."

"I told you I don't usually unload."

"All right, all right," the man said, then he stepped down from the trailer, nearly knocking Stroud over. He went to the corner of the trailer and bellowed down the midway, "Hicks!"

A few seconds later, a man wearing a white undershirt, stained gray trousers held up with suspenders, and a porkpie hat emerged about half way down the aisle and came toward him. The manager turned to Stroud and said, "See Hicks. He'll get you a shovel."

Then the manager brushed past Stroud and went back into his trailer.

"He told me to get a shovel," Stroud said, walking toward Hicks. "I have your sawdust."

"Okay, follow me."

Hicks led him between a ring-toss game and the tent for the Alligator Woman. Behind the tents was a row of trailers. As Hicks pulled a flat-bladed shovel from where it was fastened to the side of a trailer, the door of the next trailer to the right opened, and a midget woman, dressed in a nightgown and robe, emerged and came down the steps. She barely came up to Stroud's waist, and he tried hard not to stare at her, though he'd paid to do so for the last six years.

"Be sure you bring this back to me," Hicks said, thrusting the shovel at Stroud. "Dixon tell you where to put the stuff?"

"Out that way," Stroud gestured.

"All right. Don't take too long. We need it right away."

"I could drive the truck down the midway and dump it there," Stroud suggested.

"Now why the hell would I want you to do that if Dixon wanted you to put it over there?"

"Well, the first load, at least," Stroud said. "You wouldn't have to haul it so far. You said you're in a hurry. I could put the rest where Dixon told me."

"Yeah," Hicks said, thinking. "Might not be a bad idea. Go ahead and do that. And the second load, too. After that, put it where Dixon told you."

Stroud went back to the truck, tossed the shovel into the cab, then carefully pulled the truck into the midway and stopped about half-way down. He got out, rolled the tarp back, and started shoveling. At first, he felt disgruntled in having to do this shit work again, but before long, his muscles fell back into the familiar rhythm, and the work felt good.

As long as he didn't have to look forward to it permanently.

By the time he'd emptied the bed, three men had showed up with their own shovels and wheelbarrows and were working at the pile Stroud had left behind the truck. He took the shovel back to where Hicks had gotten it, hoping to get another look at the midget woman, but she wasn't there. He tied the shovel in place and turned to go back to his truck when he saw a couple of women looking at him. They were sitting in the shade of an awning set up over the door of the second trailer to the left, drinking coffee. They smiled at him and went back to their conversation.

Stroud returned to the truck, pulled out of the midway, and drove back to the mill. While Zeke was filling the truck, he got a shovel and put it in the cab, and after the truck was full, he drove back to the carnival.

He'd unloaded about half the sawdust when Dixon came up, face frowning.

"I thought I told you to put that stuff over there," he said, gesturing angrily but vaguely.

"Yes, sir. But I thought if you were in a hurry, putting a couple of loads here might save time. Hicks said it was okay."

"Oh, he did, did he?" Dixon reared back and bellowed, "Hicks!" Hicks appeared.

"I said for him to do it, boss. It's saving us time."

Dixon looked back and forth between Stroud and Hicks for a few seconds, then threw up his hands.

"Just so long as the fucking thing gets done." He stalked off.

"It's okay, kid," Hicks said. "Don't worry about him. And you can bring your next load here, too."

By the time the third load was on the ground, Stroud was sweating. Digging out whole piles of damp sawdust all at once was a little harder than scraping it dry off the mill floor. He was sitting on the rear edge of the bed, watching the carnival roustabouts haul it off to various tents and resting and catching his breath, when a woman came up to him bearing a glass of water. She was young, but a little older than Stroud.

"Here, honey. You look like you could use this." She was one of the women who'd been drinking coffee under the awning when he'd returned the shovel. She'd been wearing a heavy cotton nightgown then, but now she was dressed in dark trousers and a baggy brown shirt.

"Thanks." He took the glass, drank it down, and handed it back.

"I'm Sara."

"I'm Johnny."

"You ain't no Johnny," she said with a chuckle. "Johnny's a boy's name. You're doing the work of a man." She looked him over. "You live around here?"

"Yes."

"Too bad."

He couldn't help but laugh.

"That's the truth."

"Well," she said. "Don't want to keep you from your work." She turned to leave.

"Thanks for the water," he said, and she waved over her shoulder without looking back.

* * *

By the time Friday rolled around, Stroud had been to the carnival a dozen times a day, and he'd gotten used to seeing it as it really was: a business whose employees lived where they worked. Funny that he'd never really thought of it like that. If you only came on a weekend night, when the place was lit up and smelling like carnival and all the rides were going and the barkers were hawking their wares—human, inanimate, or somewhere in between—you only saw the business part, not the people who gave life to it. At night, the people were just part of the background. You stared at the barker as he harangued his audience, but did you ever really see him as more than a costume and a voice that eventually would fade into a distant wash of sound? Did you ever really see the women behind the concession counters as anything more than hands that served and took your money? And did you ever see the freaks as anything other than their freakish traits?

Stroud had to admit that he'd been coming to this carnival his whole life, but he couldn't remember a single face from year to year. Sure, he remembered the midget couple, but only as short people with blurry faces. Now he knew he'd never forget their faces. One morning, as he and a couple of roustabouts were shoveling sawdust between the tents and trailers, the diminutive couple had an argument as big as anybody's. It started as a flurry of high-pitched voices then erupted from their trailer as the midget man came out in a hurry, half-dressed, a scowl seaming his face. She, in her nightgown and housecoat, followed close behind shaking an empty gin bottle at him. They disappeared around the corner of a tent, and there was the sound of breaking glass. The woman reappeared a few seconds later, tears streaking her face, which was set in a stoic frown. She went back to her trailer, shoulders tense, and slammed the door.

One of the roustabouts chuckled, but the older one, a man named McGuire, just shook his head. Stroud couldn't really tell what had happened, though he was definitely curious. He'd never in a million years thought he'd see a midget couple fighting.

"Don't mind them," McGuire said. "Happens all the time."

"What's wrong?" Stroud asked. "Did he get drunk or something?"

"*She's* the drunk," laughed the younger man.

"Marital trouble ain't nothin' to laugh about, Mouton," McGuire said, but the other man just shrugged and went back to shoveling. "He's right," he said to Stroud. "She's the one that does the drinkin', and it makes her see things that ain't there."

"You mean like pink elephants?" Stroud asked, feeling like an idiot as the words came out of his mouth.

"Nothin' like that. Not things or animals. I mean like intentions that ain't there. She gets afraid that Wee Willie is having the time of his life with every lot lizard he sees."

"Lot lizard?"

"Yeah," Mouton said, leaning on his shovel, his face twisting into a leer. "Townie women who got the hots for carnies." He stared at Stroud, the leer growing wider. "You ain't never heard of that?"

"No," Stroud said slowly. He was trying to picture Woodville women sneaking up to the carnival for a late-night liaison with a carny. "Why? Why would they do that?"

"Look at it this way, John," McGuire said. "We're here today and gone tomorrow. Some gal's got a little screwing on her mind, she don't have to worry about us blabbin' or the neighbors findin' out."

"And they come to screw Wee Willie?"

All three of them took in the irony and burst out laughing.

"Naw," McGuire said. "Mary just thinks it happens, but that don't mean it does. Maybe it has, but I couldn't swear to it. And sure, there's some who go for the special people. Lottie gets her fair share." Lottie was the fat lady. "I guess some guys wonder what it would be like crawling all over a mountain of woman flesh."

"See if they can find the door," Mouton said.

"What the hell do you know?" McGuire snapped.

"I had me some of...."

"You wish your peter was long enough," McGuire said, then he turned back to Stroud. "If Mouton had any sense, he'd know he don't got no sense. Like I said, there might be some lot lizards got a hankerin' for the special people, but most of them just want a good roll in the hay. But they favor the guys like me who run the arcade games, not roustabouts like Mouton."

"None of that free town stuff for me," Mouton said. "I gotta pay like everybody else." He looked at Stroud. "Bet you get you some. Big handsome fella like you."

Stroud felt an irrational urge to hammer Mouton's head with the flat of his shovel, but McGuire just said, "Mouton, if you had a lick of sense, you'd use it to clean your own ass like a good dog. Now we done enough jawin'. Let's get this shit onto the ground. We gotta fix the gears on the merry-go-round, and John, here, gotta go back for more of this sawdust."

They finished shoveling in silence, then, as the two carnies went off toward the midway, Stroud climbed into the truck and drove back to the mill, his brain ringing with new thoughts. The carnival had always seemed exotic—a doorway through which peeped a world of wonders that existed beyond the pine forests surrounding Woodville —but while that was true, he'd seen that the reality was much more complex. Wee Willie and Miss Mary may have been funny little freaks on stage, but in their own world, they were just another couple suffering marital discord. And she had a drinking problem.

And there were lot lizards. He'd never imagined that such a thing existed, and he couldn't help but wonder if there were any in Woodville. According to McGuire and Mouton, there probably were. But who? Smiling, he vowed to keep an eye out to see if he could spot any.

* * *

Denny asked Stroud to work half a day on Saturday since Dixon wanted all the sawdust he could get. Stroud was reluctant because he wanted to approach Claire about going to the carnival with him on Saturday night, but in the end, the offer of time-and-a-half pay persuaded him. He could stop by the Dairy Queen every run to see if she was there.

He did, but she never was. Stroud finished his last run just after one, and he went home to rest and clean up, but he was feeling restless at not having talked to Claire about tonight. At last, he did what he rarely did because she didn't like it: He called her from the pay phone in the boarding house's downstairs hallway. If Buchman answered, he'd just hang up. If the Buchman's maid answered, she wouldn't know who he was, and he could just ask for Claire.

Thankfully, the maid answered, and a moment later, Claire was on the line.

"It's me," Stroud said.

"Oh. Just a second." Her voice grew slightly fainter on the word "second," as if she'd turned away from the phone, and there was a short pause before she said, "You know I don't want you to call here."

"I know," he said. "But I didn't see you at the Dairy Queen."

"I've been busy, today. Daddy had some papers for Tulane that I had to fill out."

Tulane, he thought. I'm going to school, too.

"I was wondering about tonight. The carnival. I was wondering if you'd like to go."

He knew it was a ridiculous question. Everybody went to the carnival on Saturday night.

"I'm sorry, Johnny. I can't go with you."

Can't.

"Aren't you feeling well?"

"It's not that, Johnny. I'm going, but I just can't go with you."

"Why?"

"Mike already asked me, and I said I would."

"But Saturday is our night."

"Not this time," she said, a peeved tone sliding into the words. "Besides, Daddy'll be there, and I'm not ready for him to know about…."

She let the words trail off as if she was reluctant to say them.

He could have pressed her, asked her, "Know about what?" But he knew, and he was afraid that if he pushed her, that peeved tone would grow into something more frightening.

"Okay," he said. "I'll see you next week?"

"Yes," she said. "Next week. Same as usual."

Stroud replaced the receiver on the hook, trod the stairs to his room. Then he lay down on the bed and stared at the dull brown wallpaper with its venous pattern of pale green vines and yellow flowers repeating itself all around the four walls like some encompassing jungle that he could never escape.

He was still lying there an hour later when Mrs. Dewitt knocked on his door. He knew it was Mrs. Dewitt because Hudson and Leaton never knocked, and no one else ever came to visit him. He got up and opened the door.

"Hi, Johnny," Mrs. Dewitt said. "I hope you don't mind, but I'm serving dinner at four tonight instead of five." She must have misinterpreted his expression of blank ennui for puzzlement. "The carnival," she explained. "Are you going?"

"I'm not sure," he said.

"I never miss a year," she said. "It ain't much to look forward to, but when you live in Woodville, you grab what you can get."

"I guess so," he said.

"I got to tell Mr. Leaton, now, and get back to the kitchen."

She hurried off, and Stroud shut the door. As he lay back down, he heard her knock on Leaton's door and the muffled sound of her voice as she told him of the change in dinner time. Then Leaton's door shut, and her footsteps receded down the stairs, leaving the second floor in silence.

He dozed for half an hour then woke with a start from…it wasn't a dream, exactly. More a series of images in which he was shoveling sawdust into large holes in the ground, and from each hole sprang a tree that was then felled and hauled to the mill and cut into lumber, leaving more sawdust for him to clean up.

He rose, the old bedsprings squawking beneath his shifting weight, and went to the door and glanced down the hall toward the bathroom. The door was open, which meant it was unoccupied. He ducked back into his room, gathered a fresh set of clothes from his closet and chest of drawers, carried them to the bathroom, and shut the door.

A hot bath didn't soothe his bruised emotions, but it made him feel better to have all the sawdust and sweat washed down the drain. He combed his tousled hair and took the dirty clothes back to his room and put them in the wicker hamper that stood next to his closet door. Then he went down to dinner.

Leaton and Hudson were already there as Mrs. Dewitt bustled about, practically tossing the plates and bowls of food onto the table. Her hair was in curlers and there was rouge on her cheek and lipstick on her thin-lipped mouth. She was wearing a bright print dress. Stroud had never seen her look like this, or if he had, he couldn't remember when.

"You fellows go on and eat," she said. "Just clear off your plates as usual and leave 'em in the sink. I'll take care of them later."

And then she was gone, the swinging kitchen door flapping vigorously behind her.

The three of them stared at the door until it stopped moving, then Hudson said, "Well, boys, I guess we'd better dig in."

Stroud hadn't thought he was hungry, but he was. All the shoveling he'd done the past week had sharpened his appetite. He loaded his plate with a second helping, and as he did, there came the sound of the front door slamming and footsteps hurrying down from the porch.

"There she goes, boys," Hudson said around a mouthful of pie. He glanced at the others as he chewed and swallowed, then he asked, "You boys going to the carnival, too?"

"Not me," Leaton said as he scraped his plate into the garbage can. "I just got in from a haul up to Shreveport, and I'm beat. Got to go back Monday, too. I'm hittin' the sack early." He set his plate in the sink, rinsed his hands, and headed for the door. "See you boys tomorrow."

"What about you, Johnny? Carnival?"

"I hadn't planned on it," Stroud answered.

"Young fellow like you? You need to get out. See what's what." Hudson got up, emptied his own plate, and set it in the sink on top of the one Leaton had left. "Me, I'm going on down there. Might as well have a little fun before the starting whistle on Monday."

Instead of leaving, though, he sat down, pulled a flask from his pocket, and took a hefty swig. Pulling his lips back from gritted teeth, he sucked in a breath, then held out the flask to Stroud.

"Care for a snort?"

"Sure." Stroud took the flask and drank a swallow that burned all the way down.

"Pretty good, huh?" Hudson said, taking the flask back. "That's ain't no store-bought. Know a fellow outside of Jameston who makes it somewhere back in the woods." He drank again, and passed the flask back to Stroud. "Go on. Don't be bashful. I got a whole jug up in my room." He winked. "But don't let on to Miss Agnes."

"I won't," Stroud promised, then he took another slug. This one went down easier. He returned the flask to Hudson and got up to deal with his plate.

"Thanks for the drink," he told Hudson as he headed for the door.

"Where you off to in such a hurry?" Hudson asked. "Thought you wasn't goin' nowhere."

"I changed my mind," Stroud said. "I think I'll go to the carnival after all."

"Well, if you'll give me half a minute to fill this up," Hudson lifted the flask, "I'll mosey on down there with you."

Stroud wasn't sure he wanted the company, but the moonshine was sitting mellow in him, and he wouldn't mind a little more if Hudson offered.

By the time the two of them reached the carnival grounds, Stroud was feeling pretty good. He hadn't been here at night this year, and seeing it all lit up, with its odors and sounds wafting in the balmy night air, gave him a sense of dislocation even more powerful than he'd felt when he'd hauled his first load of sawdust here on Monday morning.

"Hey," Hudson slapped his shoulder and pointed toward the meager stage in front of a colorful tent where a woman dressed in a harem outfit complete with veil was shimmying. "Get a load of that. Come on."

He hurried off through the milling bustle toward the hoochie-coochie tent, but Stroud lingered, and in a moment, Hudson was lost in the crowd. Stroud angled off and headed slowly up the midway.

He found McGuire in his ring-toss booth.

"Hey, John," the man said, giving his gap-toothed smile. "Hanging out with the rubes?"

"I guess so," Stroud said. "Not much choice since I was born among them."

"You ain't no rube, young feller, even if you live among 'em."

"I don't know about that, McGuire."

"Ring toss," McGuire barked out. "Three rings for a dime. Look at the wonderful prizes. Ring toss. Ring toss." He glanced back at Stroud. "You'll find your place," he said gravely. Then he turned to the people strolling by. "Ring toss. Ring toss. Three tries for a dime. Hey, you, young feller." He beckoned to a pimply high school boy holding hands with a plain girl in a print dress. Stroud didn't know them. "Bring that gal over here, sonny, and win her a great prize. Show her what you're made of. Three rings for a dime."

Captured, the teenagers came over, and while McGuire took the boy's dime and handed him the rings, Stroud waved and wandered on down the midway. Last year, it would have been him being lured to the game or into the tents. But now, none of it held the same sort of attraction. He'd spent too much time here during the past week. Seen it during full light. Seen the Lobster Boy eating breakfast, just like anybody. Seen the midgets quarrel. Seen the Alligator Woman laughing at a joke the fat lady told while she curled the golden ringlets atop her plump head.

Stroud wasn't part of this world, but he knew it better now. He'd seen behind the exotic façade that the carnival presented to the rest of the world and glimpsed a life full of real people. Now, the façade was back, and he no longer knew which was more true: the exotic ambience or the real people. And how did the real people behind the exotic ambience create it? Was it something that was just mechanical, like the rides? Did you just set up the mechanism, usher people into its seats, and push a button that changed the lighting and the smells? The atmosphere? Or was it something that they exuded from themselves, and the mechanisms of the rides and games and food were just by-products?

About ten-thirty, he saw her. He was standing in the shadows where two tents came together to form a narrow canvas alley when she came by with her friends, including Mike Rogers. Stroud couldn't help but see how Mike ached to touch her or how she favored his attentions.

They went up to Dan Masiello's milk bottle booth, where fools tried to knock over lead-weighted wooden "milk bottles" with soft, lopsided softballs. Mike plunked down a dime, while Claire clapped excitedly, he bounced the ball in his hand for a moment, then reared back and let go.

All the bottles went down.

He was the football quarterback and had a good arm.

The teenagers around him cheered while Masiello—a man Stroud had only briefly talked to—pulled a bear off the shelf and handed it to Claire. The group, clustering around her and Mike, wandered off toward the Ferris wheel.

Stroud followed and watched as the big wheel took Claire and Mike high over the carnival grounds. Watched as, high up there, Mike kissed her, and she kissed him back.

Stroud hung his head and turned to go. Back up the midway.

Back to the small, empty world of his room with its dull, entwined wallpaper.

"She's pretty."

He hadn't heard her come up behind him. Her footsteps had been muffled by the sawdust that lay all over the ground, now trodden and damp.

"Hi, Sara." It took him a second to recognize her; he'd never seen her in anything but the plain trousers and shirt she wore during the day. Now, her face was heavily made up, and her lean body was dressed in a short, tight silver lamé skirt, a matching top that clung tightly to her breasts, and a glittery headdress that looked like it was made from pink and blue tinsel.

"She your girl?" Sara nodded toward the Ferris wheel as it carried Claire and Mike back down then up the backside.

"Not really."

"No?"

"No. I just…." He shrugged. "I just thought we had something, but I'm not sure, now."

She nodded, a wistful smile on her face. It made her look older.

"I've had a few thoughts like that," she said.

"Well," he began, embarrassed. "I guess I'd better go." He started to move off, but Sara's voice stopped him.

"Go? Go where?"

"Home, I guess."

"If you're just guessing, it can't be very urgent," she said. "You leaving because of her?" She nodded toward the Ferris wheel, where Claire and Mike were now debarking.

"I guess," he started to say, then changed it to, "Not much to keep me here."

"I'm on my way over to relieve Lou in the Kiddie Playland ticket booth. Come on over and keep me company for a while." Your friends won't come over there if you're worried about them seeing you."

"I wasn't worried," he said, hating the defensiveness in his voice.

"Sure," she said as if she hadn't noticed. "Come on around this way. It's quicker. Won't have to work our way through all the rubes out there."

She led him around a generator truck then through a narrow alley between tents and trailers, toward the south end of the carnival where all the kiddie rides were set up. The alleyway was mostly dark, lit here and there with slashes of light from between the tents, and every time they went through the light, Stroud's eyes were drawn to the glittery roll of Sara's rump beneath the short lamé skirt.

Claire, he thought guiltily, forcing his eyes to look at Sara's back.

When they got to the Kiddie Playland ticket booth, Lou levered her bulk out of the box.

"'Bout time you got here," she said without malice. "I'm ready to bust."

"Take your time," Sara called after her as she hurried off toward the trailers, her flowery muumuu swirling around her.

Sara slipped into the booth and sold tickets to the families in line while Stroud leaned against the edge of the open doorway.

They didn't talk much. Mostly Stroud watched her take the money, tuck it into a metal cash box beneath the window counter, make change, and tear the tickets from a large roll that hung on a ten-penny nail to the right of the cash box.

"So," she said when a break in the traffic came after about ten minutes. "You just drive a sawdust truck?"

"Right now," he said. "It's not permanent. I'm just saving up."

"What for?"

He was embarrassed to tell her he was going to college.

"Just trying to establish myself," he said instead.

"Got plans for the future, is that it?"

"Yes. I guess I do."

"They include that blond miss back there on the Ferris wheel?"

They did, he thought.

"Maybe. Maybe not. I don't know."

"Hard to plan for the future if you ain't sure about it," she said, turning to the window to take care of a man with two boys.

Yes, Stroud thought.

Lou came back a few minutes later.

"Dix needs you to take over for Marty," she said as she wedged herself back into the booth. "Tell Marty to get over to the Yoyo. Some mechanical problem."

Sara led Stroud back around the tents toward the other end of the midway. There, Sara circled behind the large tent at the end. From behind, Stroud couldn't read the sign on the tent's huge false front, but he knew what it said. Fright House. Thrills, Chills, Delights.

He'd been in it often enough. Just last year with Claire.

Sara went through a flap door in the rear, and Stroud followed. A single bulb lit the small area: in front of them was a wooden wall that circled the inside of the tent, leaving a gap of about three feet between it and the canvas. A plank walkway angled off into the darkness around the curves to both sides.

"This way."

Sara went to the left, and a moment later, they came into a small room lit with another bare, dim bulb. A man sat on a folding wooden chair, desultorily watching through a slot of a window set in the wall.

"Yoyo's broken down, Marty," Sara said. "Dix needs you over there."

"Right."

The man got up and left, and Sara took his place on the chair and peered through the window.

"What are we doing?

"Watching," she said. "Lot of these kids like to try to get out and mess with the props. If one does, we just push that button, and it stops the ride. Don't want anyone to get hurt."

"I probably tried that," he said.

"You probably did. You want to look?"

She got up, and he took her place. Through the slot, he could see a section of the ride where the car came into a little room where a skeleton popped out of a niche as an evil laugh bellowed out. While he was watching, a car came through bearing a pair of teenagers. The girl was leaning against the boy, a look of mock fear on her face, and he was looking steadfast, his arm draped around her shoulders. Then, as the booming laugher subsided, they were gone on down the tunnel. A minute later, a second car came along, this one with two laughing teenage boys. One of the boys threw an empty drink cup at the skeleton.

"This must get boring," Stroud said.

"Yeah, it does." Her hand ruffled through his hair, and he looked up at her. She was standing between him and the bulb, her face obscured by shadow. Then he blinked as she sat sideways on his lap, blocking his view of the window. "But there are ways to pass the time."

She leaned against him, and as his left arm went around her shoulders, she lifted her face and he kissed her. He could feel himself growing erect beneath her, and at first it embarrassed him, but when she squirmed against him, all his self consciousness fled and he groped at the tight mounds of her breasts beneath their sheath of silver lamé.

Minutes passed, and the jacket's buttons yielded to his clumsy fingers. Beneath was a lacy white bra. Funny how he'd never thought about her wearing a lacy white bra when she was giving him water, dressed in her simple clothes. As he touched her, he couldn't help but notice how different she was from Claire. Claire was all soft curves that melted against him hesitantly, while Sara's lean body was harder, more vibrant and assured beneath his hands.

"Let's get out of these," she said, standing up, shrugging off the jacket, and dropping it carefully on the floor.

"What about Marty?"

"He won't be back for a while. Long enough."

He watched as she unzipped the skirt and let it fall next to the jacket. Her white lace panties matched the bra, which she reached up behind her back to undo.

"I don't have a…a…. You know." He shrugged helplessly.

"A rubber? Forget it. I'm barren. Can't have kids."

"Oh." He didn't know what to say. "I'm sorry."

"Don't be. I'm not."

Not knowing what else to do, he stood and began to remove his clothes. She was done before he was, and when he finished, he looked at her in the dim light. Again he was surprised at how different she was from Claire. Smaller breasts tipped with darker buds, lean torso sweeping down to narrower hips framing a wedge of hair that was dark instead of blond. She even smelled different. He felt angular and gawky in comparison—and somehow smaller, though he stood more than a head taller than she.

She stepped up to him, slid one hand behind his back and the other behind his head and pulled his face down to hers. As she pressed lithely against him, he felt her tongue seek his, and he ran his hand down her back and over her buttocks. Her hand left his back and reached down between them, her fingers finding his scrotum. As it tightened at her touch, his erection grew again, pressing against her stomach.

Soon his hand reached for her crotch and was rewarded with slippery wetness. They kissed and stroked each other for several minutes, then she pushed him onto the chair and straddled him. As his cock slipped deep inside her, she moaned, and her nails raked his back.

So different, he thought as she began rocking her hips rhythmically against him. He and Claire had done it only in the shed out behind her father's house, lying on that pallet they'd made from old blankets. And now here he was, having sex with a strange woman on a folding chair in a barren little room where the air shook once a minute with booming, sarcastic laughter.

Then all thought fled as her rhythmic rocking grew more urgent, stiffening his cock to the bursting point. She cried out gaspingly as he came, and a second later gave a deep moan as her body stiffened then released.

Gradually, her rocking subsided, and spent, he softened and finally slipped out of her. She leaned against him, her body relaxed. Her hair tickled his cheek.

"That was nice, John," she said after a few minutes.

"I...," he hesitated. "I don't love you." He was thinking of how the slipperiness of her vagina had felt on the skin of his penis. With Claire, he'd never felt that, only rubber.

Sara laughed gently and sat back so she could look in his face.

"Didn't expect you did." She laid her fingers on his cheek. "It don't have to mean anything more than it was," she said. "Just another amusement park ride."

"Does this mean I'm a lot lizard?"

She laughed again.

"I don't think you'll ever be a lot lizard, John." She stared hard at him. "But what, John? What *will* you be?"

"I don't know," he admitted. "I know I want to be somebody. I'm just not sure how to go about making it happen. But I'll think of a way."

"It's hard," she said, nodding and pursing her lips. "A fellow once told me that a man can think with three things. He can think with his head, with his dick, or with his heart. If he's thinking with his head, he's probably thinking too little, and if he's thinking with his dick, he's probably thinking too much. But if he's thinking with his heart, he's probably thinking about things that are important."

"What about women?" he asked.

"The recipe ain't so easy there," she chuckled. "It's probably best not to try to figure women. Even other women can't do that. Best you can do is put up with them or not."

Is that what he was doing with Claire? he wondered. Putting up?

"Why are you here?" he asked. "In the carnival, I mean. Is this what you wanted?"

"This?" She laughed. "Oh, hell, no. I just fell into this. I wasn't looking for nothing but a way to get away from home. My ma was a drunk and my old man was a mean drunk. Soon as I turned sixteen, I lit out at the first opportunity, and this was it. Didn't plan on it lasting this long, but what the hell. Coulda done a lot worse. Could be walking the streets in New Orleans or Houston or somewhere. Didn't want nothing like that, though. This is poor living, most times, but it's cleaner than the streets. And you got friends around all the time to help take care of you."

She kissed him once more, then stood, her inner thighs glistening.

"Best get dressed," she said. "Marty'll be back soon, and we don't want to embarrass him."

They dressed quickly, the Sara gave him one last kiss and pushed him toward the door.

"Better run along, John. I got to finish out tonight and then pack up. We're headed to Oakdale tomorrow. It's gonna be a long night. But thanks for making it a good one, too." She smiled.

"Yeah," he said. "Me, too. I mean, thanks."

He didn't want to go. Didn't want to face the town outside this dim room. Face Claire or his mother or the men at the mill. But that was his life. "See you around."

"Sure you will," she said.

He left, working his way back through the narrow passageway to the flap at the back of the tent and out into the night. The carnival was in full swing, now, though many of the families with younger children had already gone home, leaving the grounds to adults and teenagers. He stopped at a concession booth to get a Coke, and he stood there, sipping it and looking around, trying to spot Claire and Mike and their friends. He didn't see them, but he did notice Mrs. Dewitt.

She was at the ring-toss game, talking to McGuire, but she wasn't tossing any rings. Or maybe she was—both of them were smiling.

Chuckling, Stroud went back to the boarding house, let himself in, and went upstairs and lay on the bed. At last, he dozed, but a sound somewhere woke him. It was Mrs. Dewitt letting herself in. Stroud glanced at the clock. One-thirty.

In the nine months he'd live here, he'd never known Miss Agnes to go to bed later than ten.

But he hadn't known she was a lot lizard, either.

Smiling, he rolled over and went back to sleep.

In the morning, the carnival was gone.

4: UPROOTED

STROUD SHIFTED INTO reverse and carefully backed the truck down the main aisle of Monroe's Lumber Yard. Monroe's was in Alexandria, but it could have been anywhere in the state. In the month since the carnival had left Woodville, he'd graduated from hauling sawdust to driving loads of finished lumber to lumber yards across Louisiana or to the port in Baton Rouge. He'd even driven all the way to Houston several times. The city impressed him more than even New Orleans. There was a sense of simmering purpose there, and he never tired of seeing the huge orange eye of the Gulf sign atop the Gulf Building keeping watch over downtown.

He liked seeing the world as it existed outside the small town he'd grown up in. It made his mind seem small just being from Woodville. But he was learning. And gaining confidence. He could succeed. Given half a chance, he could succeed.

He'd have to if he expected to have half a chance with Claire, he thought as he climbed down from the truck and walked toward the office. Especially with a rival like Mike Rogers, who already was several rungs up the success ladder thanks to his father's furniture store.

Stroud hated Mike. Not that Mike had ever done anything to deserve Stroud's enmity aside from being a rival for Claire's affections. In truth, Mike probably barely knew Stroud existed. Certainly Claire wouldn't have said anything, and their relationship, if that's what you could call it, was about as low-key as you could get. Stroud doubted if Claire even told her best friends about him.

But Mike had Claire's interest, and that was enough for Stroud.

And to make matters worse, Mike was going to Tulane on a football scholarship. He'd be around Claire all the time—and a football star—and Stroud would be down in Thibodaux, stewing in his own juices.

It was a hard idea to take, and it plagued him constantly during the hours he was on the road between Woodville and what he'd come to consider as the "real world"—the large towns and cities he visited. It kept him awake at night, no matter how many miles he'd driven that day or how tired he was. And it weighed more heavily as the days passed. Claire would graduate soon, and after the summer, she'd be gone to New Orleans.

In the office, he handed the bill of lading to the man behind the counter, who assigned a couple of stevedores to unload the truck. While they did, Stroud meandered over to the coffee pot and poured himself a cup.

He knew that matters were coming to a head—that he'd have to get Claire to promise to be with him—but he didn't know how to do that, didn't even know how to broach the subject. And with Claire's graduation approaching, time was running out. The cup of bitter coffee tasting of paper cup didn't help. At last the man at the counter signed the paperwork and beckoned Stroud over. Then suddenly, Stroud saw the solution, plain as day. It circled the ring finger of the counter man's left hand, winking dully as Stroud took the paperwork from him.

They could get married. Isn't that what he wanted? Wasn't that what women wanted? A proposal and a ring and pledges of love for eternity?

They would have to elope, of course. Certainly her father wouldn't condone their union. But once it was done, he'd have to assign Stroud to a better position—have to see Stroud's worth and ambition.

The thought of asking Claire to marry him made him more nervous than the possibility of Buchman's anger. He pondered it all the way back to Woodville, feeling more and more confident that this was what he had to do, yet fearing it in equal proportion.

He meant to bring it up on Saturday night, but she brushed him off when he called her, saying she was spending the night with her girlfriends. Suspicious that she might be going out with Mike, instead, he followed her, but she went straight to Janet's house, and while he watched, a couple of other girls showed up. He went back to the rooming house, feeling better but also disgruntled that she'd chosen them over him.

The week that followed was a hard one. The scenery that passed for hours on the other side of the truck windows gave his mind more room than it needed, and he found himself unable to stop thinking about asking Claire to elope. He rehearsed it over and over, expanding and elaborating the scene until he woke up in a sweat early Thursday morning, realizing he'd completely forgotten about a ring. Did he need to give her a ring when he asked her?

How much did a wedding ring cost?

He knew he had enough money in the bank to pay for a ring, even if it was $200, though he hated to part with that much of the savings he'd so dearly earned and stashed away to pay for school. School was the future. Their future together.

That evening after work, he went to Bailey's Pawn Shop over on Lang Street, a few blocks off of Main, and looked at rings. Simple wedding bands were within his budget, but he saw several rings there sparkling with diamonds that he couldn't have afforded even if he spent everything he'd saved.

He didn't know what else to do, so he did the only thing he could: He bought a thin, plain gold band for $120. He'd give it to her when he proposed, and he'd tell her that he'd buy her a fancier one later if she wanted.

After leaving Bailey's, he walked back toward Main Street, thinking he'd stop in at Shanks's Ice House for a beer before going back to Mrs. DeWitt's. As he rounded the corner and turned left onto Main, he saw Andrew Buchman come out of Wilson's Jewelers across the street and half way up the block. He was slipping a small package into his jacket pocket. Stroud faded into an open doorway and watched as Buchman strode across the sidewalk, got into his Buick—the Special Skylark edition in dark blue—which was parked at the curb, and drove off.

Seeing Buchman soured Stroud's already ambivalent mood, and, thinking he'd already spent enough money for one day, he decided against Shanks's and went on home.

There, he lay on the bed, took the ring from its little, felt-lined box, and held it up to the light.

Such a small thing, he thought. A hole, really. Nothing but a portable hole that you carried around on your finger. How could this little bit of emptiness stand for so much?

He put the ring back into it's little box and put the box into the drawer in his bedside table. Eventually he went to sleep.

Friday morning, a nip of chill was in the air as he left the boarding house and walked toward the mill. Even so, he felt warm inside. He had the ring. He would propose on Saturday. He would insist on seeing Claire—wouldn't have it any other way. Her girlfriends could wait. Mike could wait. Forever! Saturday would be his moment. He thought of how warm her body felt next to his and how she cried out when she came. She wouldn't say no.

He knew something was up as soon as he arrived at the mill. The absence of the roar and clatter of machinery and whine of saws and planers made that obvious as soon as he entered the grounds. Nor did he see any of the other workers. Denny Miller was standing by the entrance to the building.

"What's up, Denny?" This came from Eddie King, one of the planer operators, who was walking a little ahead of Stroud. "Something happen?"

It was a question fraught with meaning at a sawmill, where the slightest error could cripple or kill a man.

"Don't know," Miller said. "Boss wants everybody over at the loading docks. Says he's got an announcement. Clock in first."

The loading docks were on the other side of the building. When Stroud arrived, he could see most of the other employees standing around on the paving in front of the loading docks. Most wore puzzled looks, but no one knew of any accident, so whatever Buchman had to say, it wasn't that one of their fellow employees wouldn't be coming back.

Over the next fifteen minutes, the rest of the workers arrived, and ten minutes after that, Buchman appeared on the center loading dock. Stroud's mother was there with him. It looked like they were standing on a stage.

"I know you're all wondering why you're out here instead of inside, cutting lumber and helping America grow," Buchman said. "It's because I have something important to tell you." He turned, held out his hand to Jenny Stroud, and pulled her up next to him. "*We* have something important to tell you." He faced the crowd again. "Last night, I asked Jenny Stroud for her hand in matrimony. Can you guess what she said?"

There was a scattering of laughter, and Jenny, a big smile on her face, raised her left hand and dangled it so her fingers were visible. Sparkles jumped from the ring there as it was hit by the morning sunlight. The crowd cheered.

"This is truly a joyous occasion for both of us," Buchman said, draping his arm around Jenny and giving her a quick hug.

"Shit," somebody behind Stroud muttered. "I been married sixteen years, and I can tell you it ain't all that joyous."

A couple of other men nearby chuckled.

"I want to tell you one more thing," Buchman said, holding up his hands to subdue the noise. "As soon as the nuptials are complete, Jenny and I will be buying out James Richmond's share of the mill."

The cheering broke out again, a little more subdued this time.

"Jenny and I want to share our happiness with you," Buchman went on as the sound subsided. "At her request, I'm giving everyone the day off with pay."

The loudest cheer of all rose, and the man behind Stroud said, "Now that's what I call a joyous occasion."

"If you've already clocked in, go clock out," Buchman went on as the cheer subsided. "Have a good weekend with your families, and we'll see you back here bright and early on Monday."

He and Jenny disappeared into the mill, and the workers headed for the time clocks.

Stroud, numb, let himself be carried along, almost oblivious.

"Hey, Johnny," Eddie King said, jostling up to him. "How come you didn't say nothin'?" King grabbed Stroud's hand, and pumped it, a big smile plastered on his face. "Congratulations."

Congratulations.

The word seared across Stroud's realization that his mother and Buchman were buying out old man Richmond after they were married. That's when what was hers would become his. When the government money—the money that rightfully should have gone to Stroud's future—would be going, instead, into Buchman's pocket to help him buy the mill.

Stroud would have walked into Buchman's office and killed him right then, but the thought of Claire stopped him. She was the one, thin thread of his life that hung tenuously intact. How could he hope to win her if he murdered her father?

Stroud left the mill without clocking out. Unlike the men around him, who were happy to have the day off with pay, he wished he had work to preoccupy himself and keep his mind from brooding on this new turn of events. It seemed that everything was conspiring to beat him down and take what was his so others could have more than their share.

It's not fair, he thought, and in the same instant, he realized that the concept of fairness was as bogus as the colorful photographs of food on the Dairy Queen menu. It was a sham. The reality was that all the traits that the teachers and preachers said were important—honesty, good will, and fairness, included—were tools that men like Buchman used to make themselves wealthier and more powerful. If you wanted to move up in the world, the only reality that counted was ruthlessness. Take what you want, and the hell with anyone who got in your way.

But two could play that game. Stroud smiled, thinking of Claire. For once he wasn't thinking of her pretty face or lush breasts or even of how he longed to be with her. In his mind, he now saw her as a little girl being dragged away from her horrified father.

Taking her, he realized, would be the best revenge. And it would force Buchman and his mother to accept him into the family.

Not knowing what else to do, where else to go, Stroud went back to Mrs. Dewitt's. The landlady was surprised to see him, but when he told her the reason he wasn't at work, her long face broke into a smile.

"Imagine that," she said, wiping her hands on her apron. "Your ma and Mr. Buchman. When's the big day?"

"They didn't say."

"Well, it's sure to be a whoop-tee-do. I guess you'll be getting a promotion, soon."

Not likely, he thought.

"I think I'll go on up to my room for a while," he said.

Mrs. Dewitt headed for the telephone in the hallway as he trudged up the stairs. It was ringing.

News travels fast in a small town, he thought, then it struck him for the first time that Buchman's public announcement was the first Stroud had heard of the pending marriage. Not that it was a surprise, but his mother could have at least told him herself and not let him hear it along with everybody else in town.

That depressed him even more than the loss of his father's pension. Money might be hard to come by, but it could be found. A mother's love had to be freely given.

To hell with her, he thought as he lay down on his bed and stared at the familiar brown wallpaper with its serpentine vines and fading flowers. Focus on what's important.

Claire.

No. Money and Claire.

But after a few minutes, all he could think about was Claire, and the more he thought, the more restless he grew. At last, he got up and left the house, passing Mrs. Dewitt in the hall. She was on the phone with one of her friends, talking about the big news, and she barely saw him brush by and out the door.

Every phone in town must be off the hook by now, he thought bitterly as he went down the steps. At the bottom, he stopped, suddenly realizing he was moving without thought of direction. But where was there to go, really? It was nine o'clock on a Friday morning in Woodville, and a lot of the shops and eating places were open, but he didn't want to go to any of them. H couldn't just stand here, though. At last, he turned to the right, went down to Main Street, turned right again, and walked over to Phillips Cafe.

He sat down at the counter and ordered a cup of coffee from the blowzy waitress. She set a white mug in front of him and filled it from a stained glass pot then went back to her conversation with a man at the far end of the counter. They were talking about Andrew Buchman and Jenny Stroud.

Stroud drank his coffee, put a quarter on the counter next to the empty cup, and left, feeling desperate.

Wasn't there any place in this whole damn town he could go without being reminded of how his life had fallen apart at nineteen?

He needed to be alone, and the only place he knew of where that could happen today was the mill.

He was so used to the racket that permeated the building, that the eerie quiet laying over it was unnerving. He walked around to the loading docks, where he sat on the top step and stared, unseeing, at the fringe of trees on the far side of the loading yard.

After a few minutes, a noise behind him startled him from his reverie. He turned to see Charlie Folger shuffling out of the building and coming across the loading docks toward him.

Shit, he thought.

"Johnny? Is that you?"

Charlie didn't look good. His face was thin and gray, and the corners of his eyes and mouth were pinched.

"It's me, Charlie."

"Whacha doin' here? Ain't no work today."

"Yeah, I know. I just needed a quiet place to sit for a while."

"Well, you got the right place. It's as quiet as Sunday around here today." Grimacing, Charlie settled next to him on the step. "So, your ma's marryin' Mr. Buchman." His breath smelled of whiskey.

"Looks like."

"Guess you won't be driving a truck no more."

"Don't know, Charlie." He wished the sick old man would get up and leave him alone.

"Hell, Johnny, you're a smart young feller. You'll be running the mill before you know it."

At this rate, Stroud thought, I'll be where you are in forty years.

"Nice day, ain't it?" Charlie asked after the silence between them had grown.

Did such silences always have to be uncomfortable, Stroud wondered. Could he and Claire sit alone together and say nothing and not even notice?

"I got to go, Charlie."

Stroud stood and started across the lot.

"Good seein' you, Johnny," the old man called out behind him. "Best wishes to your ma and Mr. Buchman."

Stroud just walked on, feeling Charlie's eyes on his back until he rounded the corner of the building. As he strode back to town, he thought of where he might go, but there was no place to go, nothing to do, and no one to do it with.

He went back to Mrs. Dewitt's.

That night, he called Claire's house.

"You know I don't like you calling me here," she said after the maid had fetched her.

"I know," he said. "It's just…. I really need to see you tomorrow night."

"I'm supposed to go to the Palace with Martha and Janet."

"But you did something with them last Saturday." He hated the whine he heard creeping into his voice, and he roughened it as he said, "I really need to see you. It's important."

"All right, Johnny," she said. "But I'm not going to break my plans. You'll have to meet me at six. It'll still be light out. Don't let anybody see you."

"I won't."

She hung up, and Stroud did, too, then returned to his room. Sitting on the bed, he opened the drawer in the bedside table and took out the little black box. The ring sat there in its black felt bed, gleaming dully like a promise in the night.

"After tomorrow," he told it, "I won't have you. Your emptiness will be filled with Claire."

If waiting through Friday had been hard, enduring Saturday was excruciating. He went out, looking for something to do, and not finding it, he returned to his room. There, he had to put his wind-up clock into the bedside table drawer to keep from glancing at it every minute. He tried to read, and couldn't. Tried everything he knew and always found himself staring at the wallpaper, rehearsing what he would say to Claire over and over again.

Mrs. Dewitt served dinner at five on Saturdays, but Stroud was so nervous, he could barely eat.

"You feeling poorly, Johnny?" Mrs. Dewitt asked.

"No, ma'am. I guess I just haven't got an appetite today."

"That's what comes of not working yesterday," she said firmly. "Man's got to work to keep himself in the mood to eat."

"I guess so, ma'am." He got up. "It's a good meal, Miss Agnes, but I'm just not hungry, and besides, I have to meet someone in a little while."

"Well, you run along, then, and have a good time with your

friends. But you better bring home a good appetite for tomorrow. I'm fixin' ham and yams and green beans."

"I will," he promised.

Friends, he thought. What are those?

The question left him puzzled. Sure, he knew guys from school and at the mill, but he never did anything with them any more, never went fishing or hunting or drinking and playing cards down at the El Dorado.

It struck him then that he'd never had a real friend, just acquaintances. He'd always been alone. Felt alone.

Except for Claire. She was his friend. Wasn't she?

He went upstairs and put on clean trousers and his best shirt, then he opened the drawer and took out the little black box. His fingers fumbled at the lid, then ceased. He didn't want to look at it now. He'd see it soon enough when he gave it to Claire.

The shed, hidden behind a bank of oleander bushes, wasn't hard to get to unseen from the house, though Stroud hated sneaking up on it from the access alley that ran behind the Buchmans' and adjacent properties. One day, he promised himself, he'd be walking in Buchman's front door without knocking.

He was there ten minutes early, and he waited in the dim light, nervously fingering the box in his pocket and watching for Claire through the single dirty pane. He'd never noticed how dingy the shed really was.

And then he saw her hurrying toward the shed, and a moment later the door opened then quickly shut behind her.

"Johnny?" She peered around in the dim light, blinking.

"I'm here, Claire."

He stepped forward, took her by the shoulders, and kissed her. She returned the kiss perfunctorily, then pulled back, not quite looking into his eyes.

"You said you had something important to say."

"Yes." His hand slipped into his pocket and fingered the little box. He felt uncertain than ever. And rushed. And awkward. He wanted this moment to be better than it was turning out. He felt too rushed. He wanted to make love to her and, in the afterglow, ask her.

"Can we sit down?"

"All right," she said.

They went to their pallet. It seemed like so many rags in the dim light coming through the dirty windowpane.

"What is it, Johnny?"

"I've saved up enough to start school this fall," he said, his carefully worked-up script abandoned in the awkwardness of the moment.

"That's good."

"Yes." He hesitated, looking at the floor between his feet and feeling her eyes on him. "I'll probably go down there in a couple of months to look for a place to live and maybe a job. I…. I was hoping…."

"What?" she prompted after a few moments of muddled silence.

"Look, Claire," he said, digging in his pocket and pulling out the little box. He opened the box and showed her the ring. "It's for you, Claire."

She stared at the ring for a few moments.

"Are you asking me to marry you?"

"Yes, Claire. I want to be with you more than anything in the world."

She flinched away from him.

"Weren't you at the mill yesterday?" she asked. "Don't you know?"

"About our parents? I know. But what does that have to do with us?"

"I'm sorry, Johnny," she said, shaking her head and abruptly getting to her feet. "I can't do that."

"But why?" He stood and faced her, though she half turned away.

"I don't know, Johnny. I guess it'd be too much like marrying my own brother." She shivered. "I'd just die from embarrassment."

"But I don't understand," he said. "I thought you loved me. Wasn't that what all this is about?" He waved around the shed. "Meeting here and making love?"

"I don't know," she said, staring at the floor. Tears streaked her cheeks.

And she never had, he realized suddenly.

"So all this was just a game to you?" Unnoticed, the little box slipped from his fingers. It bounced on the floor, and the ring popped out and skittered into a dark corner.

"Not a game." She finally looked at him. "I don't know what it was, but it wasn't a game."

"Yes, it was. That's why you never let me take you out. That's why we always meet here. You let Mike take you to the movies, but I was always your dirty little secret."

Her eyes flared, and her beautiful, sensual lips curled in a snarl.

"Don't you ever tell about us, Johnny." Her voice had a dangerous edge. "If you do, I'll swear you raped me. You hear? You tell, and you'll be in real big trouble." She stood up quickly and pointed to the door. "Now, you get out of here."

He stood, his legs nonexistent, his head filled with fog and turmoil. At the threshold, he paused and looked back at her. Her scowl was angry, but her eyes were afraid.

"I'll always love you."

"Get out," she snarled. "Don't come back, and don't call me. I never want to see you again."

Only later, after he was almost home, did he remember the ring. In his mind, he could see the little black box lying on the floor of the shed where he'd dropped it, the ring vanished through some crack in reality.

He put it out of his mind. It meant nothing.

Feeling drained, he fell asleep.

* * *

In the morning, the world looked different. Everything seemed flatter and had less color. The people seemed more like cardboard cutouts instead of beings of three-dimensional flesh, and he walked among them like a breeze that bends the stalks of grass in a fallow field but remains unseen.

When Monday came, it was a blessing, for he had a run to Alexandria, and the only people he had to deal with were the gas station attendants where he fueled up, the waitresses in the greasy spoons where he stopped to eat, and the manager at Monroe's Lumber Yard. Tuesday and Wednesday, he drove to the port at Baton Rouge, and Thursday, he hauled another load to Alexandria. Friday, was the best because he made a long run to Shreveport, from which he returned at dusk. And that was when Charlie Folger unflattened the world, and Stroud again saw people as flesh and blood.

Charlie emerged onto the loading docks when Stroud backed the truck up to the one on the far right.

"That you, Johnny?" Charlie said as Stroud climbed down from the cab.

"Yep," Stroud said, trying not to look at the older man. "Long haul today." Stroud had his own damn problems, and he didn't want to get involved in some pointless conversation with someone who was bent over with pain and reeking of alcohol.

Who was dying.

That fact didn't ease Stroud's pain any, but it suddenly made the world pop back into perspective. Dying. Charlie was dying, and when you got right down to it, everyone was dying. Stroud, Claire, their parents, everyone. It made everything seem like dying was the whole point of living. "I'd just die from embarrassment." Wasn't that what Claire had said? All the work of living was just a way to keep from dying, all the love was just an attempt to pretend it wasn't going to happen, and all the sex was for kids who'd supposedly live on for you after you croaked.

"I'll always love you." Isn't that what he'd said? Love eternal. That was living, not dying.

Bullshit. When had he seen love be anything more than ephemeral? Lovers were taken in death, lovers were separated, lovers forgot their love. Love withered on the vine. Love was just a way for people to forget that this miserable existence was all that was real, and that even the real was transient.

Stroud didn't know what lay after death, but right now, he didn't give a crap because he suddenly understood that his whole life up until now had been an empty promise, and if that promise had remained unfulfilled, he had only himself to blame for believing that fulfillment was possible. How *could* it be when everyone was going to end up like Charlie, bent with pain, eyes staring into the growing dusk, trying to discern some flicker of light in the greater darkness as it descended on him.

"Care for a snort?" Charlie asked, pulling a flat bottle of cheap whiskey out of his pocket and holding it out toward Stroud.

"No thanks." Stroud had to keep himself from flinching away, as if the old man's touch might infect him with the aura of death that lingered around him more strongly than the alcohol fumes. "Got to get going."

But the truth was, he did want a drink, wanted a drink more than he ever had in his life. Wanted it for the same reason that Charlie did—to chase away the demons and to help him forget the disaster his life had become.

He didn't go home. Instead, he walked to the El Dorado. There was drink there, and noisy people who would help him forget.

There was drink, and the people were noisy, but they didn't help him forget. No sooner had he bellied up to the bar and ordered a beer, than someone jostled him.

"If it ain't the nigger who sweeps our floor," a nasty voice said.

Stroud turned to see Wally Leavon standing there, flanked by a couple of men Stroud knew only by sight.

"Hey, Frank," Leavon called to the bartender. "I thought you didn't serve no niggers."

"I don't want trouble, Wally," Frank said, sliding Stroud's mug onto the bar. "Take it outside if you have to, but if you start something in here, it'll be the last time you come in."

Leavon didn't back off, but his eyes shifted a little. The El Dorado was the only real bar in town, and he didn't want to be banned.

Stroud didn't need Frank's threat to stare Leavon down. He felt cold inside except for a molten core in his belly that was just itching to explode. And, he suddenly realized, he stood a head taller than Leavon.

"Who gives a shit about some fuckin' nigger floor sweep?" Leavon spat. Then he turned and stalked over to an empty table, followed by his friends.

Stroud picked up the mug and drained about half of it, feeling Frank looking at him.

"I'm here for this," he said, hefting the mug and looking Frank right in the eyes. "I don't give a shit about him." He jerked his chin toward the table where Leavon and his friends had settled and were grousing among themselves.

"Okay," Frank said. "Long as we're clear."

Stroud drained the mug and set it on the bar.

"I'll have another."

Frank set it up and went to serve another customer down to the right. Stroud turned, leaned against the padded edge of the bar, and surveyed the room.

It wasn't the first time he'd been in the El Dorado, but he didn't come here often. It was a simple, one-story cement block building enclosing a couple of dozen round tables and a modest dance floor overseen by a new juke box. The long bar ran along the wall adjacent to the entrance, and in the back right corner were two pool tables. It was still early, but the place was about half full, though no one was dancing yet.

Stroud picked up his beer and went over to watch the men shoot pool. The two at the first table worked at the mill, but the two at the other table were strangers to him. They were playing straight pool at a dollar a game.

After a while, one of the strangers racked his cue.

"I've had enough," he said, and he headed toward the bar.

The other man looked at Stroud and nodded toward the table.

"Play?"

Stroud had never shot pool, but it looked interesting.

"Okay," he said. "But I never played before."

"It ain't hard," the man assured him. "First, put down your dollar." He laid a bill on the edge of the table, and Stroud followed suit.

The man told him the rules, and they flipped for the break. Stroud called the flip right, but it was the last thing he won as his dollar, and eight more, vanished from the table.

"That's all for me," he said, putting his cue back in the rack.

"Don't worry about losing," the man said. "Takes practice."

"I'm not worried about anything," Stroud said.

And he wasn't, he realized as he went back to the bar for another beer. Losing at pool, having a shitty job, and least of all, being rejected by Claire. He thought about college, and it wasn't important, now, either. He'd been so directed toward his goal of winning Claire that, now that she was out of reach, the whole edifice of his hopes had come tumbling down. But he was still standing amid the rubble, and he didn't know if it was just the rush of alcohol in his head or something else, but he felt free for the first time since he'd realized back in junior high that his mother didn't care about him.

He had another beer at the bar, then left the El Dorado. He wasn't tired, really. He was just tired of the smoke and noise and sad country songs whining from the jukebox. And, by now, he was a little drunk. Not drunk enough to stagger, or even waver, but drunk enough to know he'd had enough. The cool night air felt good on his face as the door shut behind him, muffling the sounds from the bar. A few people were in the parking lot, but Stroud paid them no mind as he headed across the asphalt.

"Hey, nigger."

Wally Leavon and the two men who'd been with him in the bar were leaning on Wally's pick-up. Leavon levered himself upright and swaggered toward Stroud. "We got something to settle."

"That mean me and you, or me and all of you?" Stroud looked at the two men then back at Leavon. "If they step in, Wally, you'd better kill me, because when I recover, I'll hunt you all down and cut your throats."

"Won't be no cuttin'," Leavon snarled. "Or recoverin'."

Leavon swung at Stroud's head, and when Stroud swayed back, he aimed a punch at Stroud's gut. Stroud let him connect, tensing his stomach. Nine months of shoveling had given him hard abdominal muscles, and helping the carnival roustabouts spread sawdust had renewed their vigor. He could see that Leavon's punch hurt his own wrist more than it damaged Stroud. Stroud took another punch to his chest. By now, the other people in the parking lot were gathering around, and he wanted to make sure that everybody was clear who started the fight and that Stroud was simply defending himself.

He let the fourth punch take him in the gut. He barely felt it and cared even less if it hurt. He balled his own fists, then, thankful for the first time for the large, meaty hands that were his father's meager legacy. When Leavon stepped in with a straight right to Stroud's jaw, Stroud slammed his left fist against Leavon's elbow and heard it snap. Then the ball of his right fist hammered into the left side of Leavon's head, and Leavon went down like dead meat.

Stroud turned to the other two.

"Anybody else?"

One of the men backed away, but the other stepped forward. Stroud readied himself, but it was unnecessary. The man knelt down beside Leavon and rolled him onto his back. Leavon groaned.

"He's alive," the man said.

"Too bad," Stroud replied, letting his fists turn back into hands. "You going to give me any trouble?"

"It was fair," the man said, looking up at Stroud. "I told him to leave you alone, but he went for you, anyway, and he went down. I don't want no part of it."

Stroud turned, walked across the parking lot, and headed for the boarding house.

* * *

The weekend seemed to stretch interminably. There was simply nothing for Stroud to do and nowhere to go. At midday on Sunday, sick of his room and the boarding house, he went over to The Palace. They were showing *North by Northwest*, which might have interested him two days ago. But half-way through the movie, Stroud realized he didn't really care what happened to Cary Grant and Eva Marie Saint. The only thing that sparked his interest was the scenery as the couple was pursued across America by the evil agents. Wide open plains, mountains, the huge heads at Mount Rushmore. They all seemed so foreign in this dingy little theater in this dingy little town stuck in the middle of an interminable pine forest where you couldn't see for more than half a mile except on the roads or across an occasional farm field.

How he hated this place. How he longed for something more. What, he wasn't sure, but he no longer thought it was anything college could offer. He'd thought that school would give him Claire, but he'd been wrong. His whole life had been wrong, and now he didn't know what to do, and worse, right now, he didn't particularly care. He could have killed Wally Leavon and gone to prison or the electric chair, and it would have made no difference.

On Monday morning, when he went in to get his driving assignment, Denny Miller was waiting for him.

83

"Mind stepping in here for a minute, John?"

Stroud followed Miller into the foreman's tiny office, and Miller shut the door.

"I'm afraid I have some bad news for you, John. I'm going to have to let you go."

"You mean I'm fired? Why?"

"Wally Leavon says you attacked him down at the El Dorado on Saturday night. He's in bed with a broken arm and a concussion."

"He started it," Stroud said. "Everybody there saw."

"I don't doubt it," Miller said. "But Wally's father's been here a long time, and he has a lot of sway with the other saw operators. They want you gone."

"Or what? They're all going to quit?"

"I don't like it," Miller said, and he looked like he meant it. "But I can't help it. They went to Mr. Buchman, and he says I have to let you go." Miller hung his head for a moment then looked up at Stroud. "Can't say as I'm surprised at the way this turned out," he said. "You're too smart for this job." He waved around, taking in the expanse of the mill beyond the walls of the tiny office. "You'll find your place somewhere." He picked up an envelope from his desk and handed it to Stroud. "Here's your pay."

"So, that's it?"

"Can't do nothin' else, John. I got to follow Mr. Buchman's orders."

"I suppose you do," Stroud said with disappointment. He pocketed the envelope and left without another word.

But he didn't leave the mill. Instead, he went upstairs to Buchman's office. His mother was at her desk in the outer office, and when she saw Stroud come in, her face turned red with anger.

"I knew it would come to this," she said. "You're just like your father...."

"Shut up, you thieving slut," Stroud said. "I want to see Buchman."

"How dare you! You get out!"

"Not until I see the great master," Stroud said.

"I'll have you thrown out!"

"I'm sure you would. You always have. But Buchman better see me, or there'll be trouble that's a whole lot worse than a fight."

The door to Buchman's office opened, and Buchman stepped into the room.

"What's this, John?" His face was set in an angry scowl, and his eyes held contempt.

"I want to talk to you about being fired."

"All right." Buchman turned to Jenny. "It's all right."

He led Stroud into the office and sat behind his desk.

"I suppose you want your job back," he said. "Fighting is a serious offense, and I can't…."

"I don't want my job," Stroud said.

"You don't?" Buchman seemed surprised. "Then why are you here?"

"I want $5,000 in cash and your Buick." The amount wasn't calculated. It just popped into his head.

Buchman blinked then burst into a laugh.

"You have your pay. Why would I give anything more to you, much less that kind of money and my car?"

"You may be the richest man in town, but I can ruin a lot of things for you?"

"Are you threatening me?"

"I don't have to. The damage is already done, you just don't know it. But if you don't give me what I want, everybody will find out."

"What the hell are you talking about?"

"For the last year, I've been fucking Claire every week in the shed behind your house."

Buchman surged to his feet and looked like he was going to come over the desk at Stroud.

"I'll kill you, you little bastard."

"Not only am I'm fucking your daughter while you're fucking my mother, you're about to marry my mother and buy out old man Richmond with money my mother is giving you—money that rightfully is mine. How's all that going to sound if I start talking? Will your money buy back your reputation? My mother may be a whore, but maybe even she won't want to marry you if people find out how you and she cheated me. Then what'll happen to your deal with old man Richmond?"

"I have a lot of influence," Buchman said. "I can have you put away for a long time. Rape is capital crime."

"That's what Claire threatened. But we've done it a lot of times, and all her girlfriends know. Do you think they'll all lie for you?" It was a bluff, but apparently it worked.

Buchman sat down, tense and scowling.

"Give me what I want, and I'll be gone," Stroud pressed. "Try to cheat me again, and I'll hurt you bad."

"I can't just give you the keys to the car," Buchman said. "I have to sign it over."

"You have the registration in the car, don't you? And you have a checkbook up here. Write the check and we'll go down to the car."

Buchman reluctantly opened a drawer and took out a checkbook. After he'd filled out a check and handed it to Stroud, they left the office. Stroud's mother obviously had been listening at the door, and when they emerged, she spit in Stroud's face.

"I hope you rot in hell, you little bastard."

"As long as I'm not in Woodville with sluts like you," Stroud said, wiping off the spittle.

As they walked out, he made sure that he was ahead of Buchman all the way to the parking lot. Nobody was going to think he was the boss's toady.

"This better be the last time I see you," Buchman said, handing over the title to the car.

"As long as you don't try to tell the cops I stole this, you have nothing to worry about. I never want to see this shithole town again."

Without another word, he got into the Buick, started it, and drove away from the mill. In the rearview mirror, he could see Buchman staring after him, but the man, and the mill, were soon lost around a tree-lined bend.

It didn't take long to visit the bank, cash the two checks, and withdraw his savings. When he arrived at Mrs. Dewitt's, the widow was surprised to see him.

"What's wrong, Johnny?" she asked as he came into the kitchen. "You not feeling well?"

"I'm feeling fine, Miss Agnes," he told her. "Really fine. But I have to tell you that I'm leaving town."

"Leaving?" She wiped her hands on her apron. "What about your job? Your folks?"

"Don't have a job. And the folks can…."

He'd just about said, "shove it up their ass," but Miss Agnes had been pretty decent to him, and his personal hatreds and pain were not her fault.

"They don't need me around," he finished. "I need to go out and find my own way."

Mrs. Dewitt nodded.

"Sometimes a young man's got to do that. What you aim to do?"

What was he going to do? He hadn't thought about it. Hadn't had time. Had just been reacting to what had been thrown at him. But now the future was open. He had a car and money. It was a start, whatever he decided.

"I'm not sure. Maybe go to Baton Rouge, find a job down there."

"Just don't you go to New Orleans," she warned. "The people down there's bad, and the cops are worse."

"I won't," he promised. "I guess I better go pack." He turned to leave the kitchen, then faced her again. "I know I already paid for the month and there's still a couple of weeks to go, but I don't need the money back. You keep it. You might not find another roomer right away."

"You're a good boy, Johnny," she said, laying a hand on his arm. "I'm sorry to see you go."

"Thanks," he said, thinking, you're the only one.

He went up to his room and packed. When he'd moved into the rooming house the year before, all he'd brought were the battered suitcase and the duffel bag, and now, moving out, he didn't have much more, just a couple of dozen books, which he left where they were, lined up on the dresser top. He was done learning from books. Life was going to be his teacher, now.

He toted his suitcase and duffel downstairs. Mrs. Dewitt heard him trudging down beneath their weight, and she came out of the kitchen to tell him goodbye.

"You take care of yourself, Johnny," she said. "It's a mean world out there."

Can't be any worse than Woodville, he thought.

"Goodbye, Miss Agnes."

She saw him out the front door, and she seemed surprised when he put his suitcase and duffle into the Buick, but she didn't say anything. A minute later, the boarding house was out of sight, and two more, he was on the road heading out of town.

It didn't take long to get out of Woodville, once you set your mind to it, he thought.

At first, he drove mindlessly, just feeling the breeze coming in the windows and enjoying the blue sky with its dappling of clouds. After a time, he came to a fork in the road, and although he knew it was there, it shocked him when he came up on it. It was nothing but a fork he'd taken dozens of times since he'd been driving the truck for the mill. The left fork led to the road to Baton Rouge and the right toward central Louisiana and more towns like Woodville.

For a time, he didn't understand why he chose the right fork. It seemed natural, somehow, as if it beckoned and turned the steering wheel for him. But after half an hour, he realized why he'd come this way. This road would lead him to Oakdale. Wasn't that where Sara said the carnival had headed?

When he arrived in Oakdale a couple of hours later, he learned that the carnival already had moved on. Eunice, somebody thought. It wasn't there, either, but a man at a gas station said the caravans had come this way, gassed up, and had gone off toward Crowley. And that's where Stroud caught up with it.

He parked the Buick in the makeshift lot off to the side and walked down the midway. Hicks saw him first.

"The sawdust man, right?" Hicks said.

"John Stroud."

"I recall. What you doing down here? Weren't you in Woodville?"

"Not anymore."

Hicks eyed him.

"I know that look, boy." Hicks shook his head. "You don't know what you're getting into."

"You don't know where I've been," Stroud replied, and Hicks laughed.

"Yeah, I do. That's why I ain't still there. But I ain't the one that does the hirin'. You'll have to see Dixon. Good luck."

Stroud went on down the midway to Dixon's trailer and

knocked on the door. It opened a few moments later, and Dixon stuck his scowl through the opening.

"What?"

"I'm John Stroud. I brought the sawdust when you were in Woodville."

"Yeah, I remember. What you want?"

"I want a job."

"What makes you think I'm hiring?"

"I was hoping...."

"Hoping won't get you anywhere," Dixon said. "If it did, I'd be running Ringling Brothers."

"I can work hard."

"You and every other rube who thinks he wants to run off with the carnival."

"Ask Hicks. He'll tell you. And McGuire and Mouton." For some reason, he didn't mention Sara. "I had a good idea that saved time. Brought the sawdust truck right onto the midway and dumped it there."

"I remember." A thoughtful look crossed Dixon's thick features. He leaned out of the door and bellowed, "Hicks!"

Hicks showed up seconds later. He must have been waiting right around the corner.

"You know this rube?" Dixon demanded.

"John? Sure. He's no rube."

Dixon looked appraisingly at Stroud. "What can you do?"

"I can drive, I can shovel. Whatever you want. I have a car."

"He's got a car." Dixon snorted. "What kinda car you got, kid?"

"A Buick Skylark."

Sudden suspicion crossed Dixon's eyes.

"Where you get that kind of car, boy? You didn't steal it, did you?"

"No, sir. I inherited it."

"You an orphan, is that it?"

"I guess I am." I guess I am.

Dixon glanced at Hicks, who nodded almost imperceptibly.

"All right, John. I'll take you on, provisional like. You do good, you stay. You screw up, I'll leave you by the roadside. Can't afford trouble with the law."

"You won't get any trouble from me, Mr. Dixon."

"Hicks'll show you what to do."

Dixon retreated into his trailer and slammed the door. Stroud looked at Hicks, who grinned.

Welcome to Hanley Brothers Attractions," he said.

5: CARNY

"STEP RIGHT UP, young fellow. You look like a ball player. Knock down all the milk bottles and win your little lady her choice of any of these big teddies. Don't want her to go home empty handed, do you? Three balls for a quarter." Stroud bounced a softball in his hand.

The boy tried to ignore Stroud, but Stroud saw the girl give a sneaking glance at the huge plush bears perched on shelves above the ranked row of wooden milk bottles sitting in pyramids of three. The bears looked ready to leap happily into the arms of some teenage girl, but they were well out of reach of anyone who might walk by and try and snatch one without paying for the privileged.

They'd have to pay a lot. The "milk bottles," lathed from wood and stuffed with lead, weighed about four pounds each and were pretty hard to knock over. Especially since, of the eight pyramids, four had one of the bottom bottles glued to the shelf on which they sat. Only the second pyramid from the right had bottles made solely of wood. In the six years Stroud had owned this game, he'd lost only a handful of big prizes.

"Come on, young lady," Stroud said. "I know you want one of these big, beautiful teddies. Look how easy it is."

Stroud tossed the softball he was bouncing in an easy, under-handed toss at the second pyramid, which collapsed in a clatter.

"Easy as pie," Stroud proclaimed. "Be the envy of all your girlfriends."

The girl whispered something to the boy, who reluctantly approached. Stroud quickly set three balls on the counter. Unlike the ball he'd tossed, which was a regulation softball, the ones for the rubes were lumpen, light-weight, and soft-covered, with off-center bags of lead shot buried in their hearts. Even Stroud couldn't throw one of the damn things straight.

"Three balls for a quarter," Stroud said. "Knock all the bottles down, and take your pick of prizes." He didn't reset the pyramid he'd knocked down.

The boy brushed a lock of long hair from his face and dug in the pocket of his bell-bottom jeans. The girl, somewhat pretty, had long reddish hair and was dressed in a loose blouse and long skirt and wore granny glasses. They both smelled of marijuana.

"Can't tell the boys from the girls, these days," McGuire frequently complained, but Stroud didn't give a shit how people dressed or wore their hair, as long as they gave him their money and didn't win any of the stuffed bears.

The boy put down a quarter and picked up one of the balls. Predictably, he missed on his first two throws, but the third tipped a bottle off the top of one of the pyramids, and it thumped into the sawdust behind the shelf.

"Good try," Stroud praised, picking up the fallen bottle and putting it back on its pyramid, careful not to reveal how much it weighed. "I thought you looked like a ball player. Give it another shot."

The boy put down another quarter, and Stroud gave him three more balls. The kid managed to bowl over two bottles on the same stack—one where the third bottle was glued down—but his third ball missed entirely.

Stroud coaxed another seventy-five cents from him before he gave up and wandered off with his girl toward the rides. Not too bad. Stroud began pitching the stream of people walking by the tent, but his mind was only half on what he was saying. Instead, he was trying to figure out how he could get out of the arcade games entirely. He was sick of squeezing quarters from the rubes. He knew he was more than that.

"I don't know why you're complaining," Sara said that night as they lay in the little bed in the trailer they pulled behind their pick-up truck. "We're doing okay."

No, Stroud thought. Maybe okay for you, but not for me.

"You could still be doing menial labor with the roustabouts."

"Don't remind me."

He'd done that for three years after joining Hanley Brothers Attractions. The work was hard, the hours long, and the pay low. At first, he'd slept in the back seat of the Buick he'd blackmailed from Buchman, but big as the car had been, it wasn't big enough for his long frame. After about six months, it became clear he couldn't continue to live out of the car, especially if he and Sara were going to stay together. At the time, she was sharing a tiny trailer with an older woman named Carol who ran one of the concession stands. The trailer belonged to Carol, and there was no chance that Stroud could move in.

So Stroud traded in the Buick on the pickup, and using some of the cash he'd weaseled out of Buchman, bought the modest trailer. But even that was barely adequate, and Stroud longed for a place he could completely stand up in and stretch—at least a big trailer like Dixon and most of the acts had.

"We're still young," she said. "There's time to do better."

Young? he thought looking at her. I'm young, but I'm not sure about you.

He'd known from the beginning that she was older than he was, though she'd never told him by how much, and he'd never asked. But he was almost twenty-eight, which certainly put her over thirty. And by the way the wrinkles were creeping into the corners of her eyes and her breasts were beginning to sag, she was probably mid-thirties, at least.

Fuck it, he thought. She was still good enough in bed, and she brought in her fair share of cash.

"We're never going to do better if we keep doing what we do," he said. "We're just going to scrape by."

"We have each other."

"Yeah."

He could tell that the flatness of his tone hurt her, but he didn't care. He was thinking of Buchman and everything that Buchman had, and of how little he'd accomplished in the nine years he'd been with the carnival. He'd come in expecting to eventually work his way up to be Dixon's assistant or some such position of authority and power, but all he'd managed was to pool his money with Sara's to buy the ball-toss booth from Dan Masiello when Dan quit the circuit for good. And it was clear that Dixon would hand off to Hicks, not Stroud, when he retired. Hicks had been with the carnival for more than twenty years, and Stroud supposed he'd earned the privilege of buying the place.

Stroud didn't know what he was grousing about, really. He'd become complacent, falling into the carnival's routine and mindset, and he barely saw the towns they visited, though he knew them as well as he'd known Woodville. As well as he still knew Woodville.

The carnival, being on a regular circuit, passed through his hometown every year. While there, Stroud did his best to keep in the background, and he wore a straw boater and grew a handlebar mustache and long sideburns to help disguise his features so that people who knew him then would not know him now. But he knew them. Watched them. Watched Mrs. Dewitt and the other lot lizards. Watched Wally Leavon who, after a few years, looked wretched and friendless. Watched Andrew Buchman and Stroud's mother play royalty, at least for a time.

But there was no Claire to watch. She had gone off to New Orleans, which was just out of the carnival's range. Not that Stroud could have found her, though he supposed he could just go hang out at Tulane, pretend to be another student, and ask a few discreet questions. But after a few years, that was no longer possible or necessary. He heard enough of the town gossip to know that Claire had graduated and married Mike Rogers right afterward. The wedding was the talk of Woodville. It was billed as a high-school romance. The happy couple stayed in New Orleans, where Mike was going to law school, and Claire was…. Well, she was just Mrs. Rogers.

Once Stroud wanted nothing more than to go back to Woodville a rich man—to show his mother and Buchman and Claire that he'd been more than they imagined he could be. But the funny thing was, it didn't matter any more. Stroud was no longer doing the things he did to be able to one day lord it over the people in Woodville. Somehow, the resentments he'd once harbored and cherished had vanished. Even Buchman didn't matter. He'd served his real purposes in providing the role model Stroud needed and the means he required to break free.

As for Jenny Stroud, Buchman had divorced her last year, a

spare decade after their nuptials. She must have gotten something out of it since she moved into a nice house not far from the old Richmond manse and always drove a new car though she never worked again. But then, she probably owned half—or a good part—of the mill, thanks to the money that rightfully belonged to Stroud.

Maybe, but she was, Stroud learned, a lonely, broken woman whose liquid diet ensured that she'd stay that way. Stroud didn't care one way or the other. He might have stopped giving a shit about the past, but that didn't mean he was about to drop by to cheer her up with light talk about the good old days and words of forgiveness.

In any case, Stroud had more than enough troubles to stew on right now. He'd learned he needed more than the carnival could offer, but he felt as stuck here, as unable to break away as he had been in Woodville. Even if the towns were all podunk jerkwaters filled with rubes living rube lives, sometimes he envied the rubes. Not their complacency or small-mindedness, but their stability and the opportunities that offered to someone with enough drive to go after and take what he wanted. Stroud had the prime example of Andrew Buchman to prove that point. Buchman essentially owned Woodville and the surrounding portion of the parish, and his influence extended well beyond, into the state capitol, and even into Houston.

The problem was that the kind of wealth and power Stroud desired could be found only in a town, and he felt like a perpetual outsider who could never break into the social structure of any town. Hell, he'd been more of an outsider in Woodville, the town of his birth, than Andrew Buchman, who was the true outsider.

That's what cemented Stroud to the carnival—not the camaraderie, exactly, but the shared alienation. The special people were outsiders for obvious reasons, but even the so-called normal people working the game booths and rides and concessions were, beneath the skin, as different from the townies as the special people were.

But being more comfortable in this environment didn't mean that Stroud wanted to stay here. He figured that a man with enough money could be as alien as he wanted, and no townie could do a damn thing about it. The question, though, when he was honest with himself, was: What the hell did he really want? He wasn't sure. Wealth? Power? Sure, those would do. But that left him with a new and more involved conundrum. In the words of one popular musician the teenagers were listening to: He knew what he wanted, but he just didn't know how to go about getting it.

Whatever it was, he certainly wouldn't be getting it from running the ball-toss concession or just about anything else at the carnival. Dixon would be able to retire with some money, and the special people might, too, if they were careful with their funds, since they brought in more than anybody else except a few of the normals with top acts.

That's what Stroud needed. His own act. But what? He wasn't like Dr. Presto, the magician and mentalist, who did even better than the special people, or Madam Curie the fortune teller, or Bull Martin, the strong man, who competed against the rubes in feats of strength for a buck a shot. Even the hoochie-coochie girls made more if they turned tricks on the side.

Stroud didn't have the talent, training, or body to do any of those kinds of things. What he needed was a gimmick, something like Ed Crocker's petrified giant, which was a ten-foot-long papier-mâché figure that never fooled anybody who saw it, even in the dim light of Crocker's tent. But by the time they'd seen it, Crocker already had their fifty cents, and most just came out chuckling at being had. What was important wasn't the giant, but Crocker's spiel about how the giant had been dug up from the center of Stonehenge in England—proof positive that the Anglo-Saxon race was superior to the giants they slew and replaced. The rubes loved that fiction, and it drew them right in, and Ed did all right for himself without having to work too hard.

That's what Stroud needed. Something that would bring in easy bucks and give him time to develop something on the side to augment his income. Hell, he could buy up several concessions like the ball-toss. Jim and Marge Evans, owners of the rifle range, would be retiring in a couple of years. He could buy their outfit, and no telling how many others. He might even be able to force Hicks into a partnership after he bought out Dixon.

"I'm going out for some fresh air," he told Sara. She rolled over in the bunk as he got up.

"Don't wake me up when you come back," she said, her voice muffled and stiff.

Stroud ignored her. In the early days, that would have been impossible, but now it came easy. He pulled on his slacks and shoes then opened a cabinet, took out a bottle of whiskey, and went out into the night. They had a little canopy that rolled out from the side of the camper to roof over a sort of open-air living room with a card table and a couple of folding chairs. He sat, took a swig from the bottle, and stared out across the dark field where the carnival had set up.

What town was this? He couldn't remember. Did it matter? Every place they went was the same—hick towns filled with ignorant fools just waiting to be had. Stroud was only too happy to accommodate them. He just wished he earned more than the penny-ante take from the ball-toss.

The mid-summer air was muggy and still. The tops of the tall pines surrounding the field were unmoving silhouettes against the light of the nearly full moon.

Fucking pines, he thought, taking another slug from the bottle. His whole fucking life, and nothing but those goddamn fucking pines. Would he never be rid of them?

He'd have to leave the carnival for that. Its circuit took in almost all of Louisiana, East Texas, western Mississippi, and southern Arkansas, and only when they traveled through the latter did the pine forests begin to thin as the land rose toward the Ozarks. Of course, there was always southern Louisiana, where the pine forests melted into cypress swamps, but even there pines dominated any land dry enough to hold a town. Besides, there was nothing to look at in the swamps except murky water infested with snakes, alligators, and mosquitoes.

Not that there weren't enough of those anywhere you went in this godforsaken armpit of the world. He slapped one that landed on his arm into black and red pulp then raised the bottle again before putting it down and lighting a pair of citronella-oil lamps that sat on the table. They weren't always enough to keep off bugs, especially if a breeze blew the scent away. But the night was still, so he didn't have to rub any of the oil on his exposed arms, neck, and face.

He sat there, drinking and pondering the knot of his life and squashing the occasional mosquito that dared approach close enough to think it could take even the tiniest amount of his blood. It was ironic that he had fled the entrapments—social and familial as well as economic—of Woodville, only to become equally ensnared by the carnival. Even the apparent freedom of travel and not having to clock in every morning at Buchman's mill was an illusion. He still had to clock in, still had to pay obeisance to the society in which he lived, still had to pay rent, although it was to Dixon instead of Miss Agnes. The only difference was that he now had to buy gas for his truck, make repairs to his booth, and restock the prize plush animals when some occasional rube with a good arm and a lot of luck took one away from him. It was a pitiful fucking existence, but he couldn't see any way out of it.

And there was Sara. He'd been intrigued by her in the beginning and flattered by her attentions. She was, for him, the experience of the world in one gypsy package. Plus, she was a far more enthusiastic and inventive partner in bed than Claire had ever been, and for the first couple of years, the trailer had been filled almost nightly with the scent of their lovemaking. But as time passed, he began to see that her exotic exterior was simply that—a veneer beneath which lay the heart and soul of a small-town girl who was content to just get along. Her ambition, even if she couldn't see it herself, was to have a cottage in a small town and marry a small-town man who worked a steady job. Like Stroud, she had seen the carnival as a way out of an intolerable situation, but now she was just using it as a way to get back to the same place.

Stroud was looking for a way completely out, a way to move beyond not just the small town but the idea of small, be it town or anything else. It wasn't that he didn't want stability, he just didn't want to be one of the fools upon whom the stability rested. He wanted to be on top. Like Buchman. And he couldn't see working as hard as the rubes did just to be satisfied with less. Sara didn't understand that. She wasn't dumb, but she was limited.

And her limitations were affecting him. She was saving as much as she could for that little cottage dream, and Stroud found himself anchored to that dream by association. She saw him going back to mill work or clerking in a store. She didn't dream of one of the largest houses in town bought with money Stroud made as the owner of the mill or store.

And Stroud didn't know what he could do about it. He didn't

want to loose the things he wanted from her—the sex and companionship and income—but he found that all were trickling through his fingers like sand the longer they were together and the more their dreams diverged. But he wasn't yet ready to make a break because he had nothing better to break away to.

He took a last slug from the bottle, then, tired of slapping mosquitoes and looking at the black pines fringing the field, he went inside.

Sara was already asleep, half turned on her back. Her nipples showed dark beneath her sweat-dampened cotton top, but the sight, which once would have tightened his groin, now brought no desire. He took off his shoes and trousers, lay down beside her on the narrow bunk, and tried to sleep.

* * *

The carnival moved on two days later, and on again and again through the season—movement that used to be exciting for Stroud but now was little more than a headache since he had to break down the ball-toss booth and pack it into the pickup bed, only to unpack it all and reconstruct it a day or two later. It was hard work, even with Sara's help, and after years, it seemed almost as pointless as the movement of the carnival itself as it retraced its annual path.

He tried to think of the carnival as some sort of nomadic tribe—Indians or Laplanders or some such—following the herds through the seasons. At least that would lend the life some semblance of design, give the movement some sort of meaning. But a more apt analogy was that the carnival was a flock of vultures descending on a carcass to pick it clean before moving on to the next. The fact that the towns regenerated themselves each year to be consumed anew only highlighted their immobility and deadened nature. Herds of animals at least had the sense to run when predators appeared in their midst.

The season finished at the end of October, following the harvest and after all the county fairs had played out their repetitive little dramas of biggest bull, best pie, and prettiest face. After that, the cold fronts of November began to wash across the land and everyone retreated indoors and planned for holidays that didn't include carnies. During the winter, Hanley Brothers Attractions took up residence in Kirby County, Texas, where Dixon had a one hundred and twenty acre tract. Most of the carnies stayed there until the season resumed in March. The wintering grounds were less than a hundred miles west of Woodville, and the land wasn't any different. Although Dixon's acreage was cleared, it was surrounded by forest.

More fucking pine trees.

The southern half of the property had an old farm house, a barn, and a handful of outbuildings. The northern half was occupied by the carnies' trailers and campers, all drawn together into a little ramshackle town complete with a main street and side alleys. Dixon lived in the house, and one of the outbuildings had been converted into a communal kitchen and another into a communal bathroom with showers. The rides were stored under tarps around the barn, the interior of which was the shop where Dixon employed mechanically and artistically inclined roustabouts to repair the rides, tune up the generators, and repaint the signs.

They were just about the only ones who made money directly from Dixon during this fallow time. Some of the other roustabouts found work as laborers in the small Texas towns that lay nearby or across the state line in Louisiana, and some emigrated seasonally to Houston, and even Baton Rouge and New Orleans. Almost everybody else lived on their meager savings. Sara took a job as a waitress in a diner in Dunnison, a little town half-an-hour's drive north of the wintering grounds. Luckily, she could catch a ride with Carol, her former roommate, who was clerking in a dry goods store, so Stroud didn't have to drive her to work every day.

For his part, Stroud wasn't inclined to do much of anything but sit under the canvas veranda, drinking cheap whiskey, brooding on the encircling pines, trying to figure a way out, and dreading the time Sara would come home and start talking about settling down in a podunk place like Dunnison where she could wait tables while he started some sort of half-assed business with money from the sale of the ball-toss. That wasn't what he considered a way out.

And so things dragged through a soggy, defeated Christmas and into a cold, dreary January that kept him cooped up inside the trailer. By the end of the month, even the books he'd bought had begun to bore him more than they frustrated him with their visions of something better out in a world where the closest thing to a forest of pine trees was stacks of lumber in a lumberyard.

* * *

In the middle of February, when Stroud was ready to kill anyone or anything that crossed him, a brand new Pontiac towing a nice new Airstream trailer pulled up in front of Dixon's house.

The weather had warmed a bit under a bright sun, and Stroud was sitting under the awning, drinking at regular intervals from a bottle of Wild Turkey when the car and trailer came into sight where the dirt road to the property emerged from the forest.

Another act, he thought. And not a bad one, judging from the car's sparkling newness and the trailer's neat deportment as it bounced through the dirt road's potholes. Airstreams weren't cheap. He watched with curiosity as a woman emerged, went up the steps to Dixon's front door, and knocked. The distance was too great for Stroud to be able to see any details besides her dark hair, but she didn't seem like she was a special person. In fact, it looked like she was a pretty well-built female person. After a moment, the door opened, and Dixon ushered her into the house.

That was Stroud's first introduction to Denise Campbell, though he didn't know her name then. Or for some time after. And even when Dixon finally relented to repeated questioning from the carnies, he just said her name was Seraphina Campbell and that she had some sort of burlesque act. Denise—or Seraphina—drove off right after meeting with Dixon and didn't return until March, when Hanley Brothers Attractions went back on the road.

By then, Stroud and practically everybody else at the carnival were wondering about her. None of the carnies had ever heard of a Seraphina Campbell, nor was her name known to carnies in other regions. Dixon was closed-mouthed about her, and most of the carnies figured they'd find out about her soon enough. If she did have a burlesque act, how she managed to make a go of that in this growingly permissive environment was a mystery to Stroud.

But then word came up from New Orleans that just last year, a stage performer named Slinky Sal had quickly left town after her boyfriend was knifed to death in an alleyway. Some said it was the police who'd wielded the blade then passed it off as just another mugging. The boyfriend, it seemed, had been involved in a prostitution ring that was resisting police muscle who insisted on collecting protection money to do the opposite of what the taxpayers were already paying them to do.

Stroud wouldn't have minded some of that illicit loot, but he could understand why Slinky Sal, aka Seraphina, aka whatever other names she might have, would want to put New Orleans behind her. And, he wanted to see her act. Seems like Slinky Sal got it on with a pet python five nights a week at the Gator Club before she'd had to flee the city.

He caught her show at the first town they set up. Hell, half the audience in her modest tent were roustabouts at loose ends until they struck on Sunday night. She called her show "Seraphina and the Serpent." She didn't exactly get it on with the snake, which was a pretty big one, though Stroud wasn't sure it really was a python. Maybe it was a boa. Instead, she just suggested getting it on after letting the serpent slither all over her richly endowed and scantily clad body. It was definitely a show for the men-folk only, but although it was lewd, there also was a crude artistry to Seraphina's sensuous counterpoints to the serpent's writhing.

Or maybe he was just horny for new flesh. Sara certainly had grown unresponsive enough....

Their curiosity satisfied, the carnies tended not to come back, but Stroud wanted to. He was fascinated with Seraphina and the fact that she'd come from New Orleans. And she had a pretty good act. It wouldn't be long before she was pulling in good dough. He managed to keep himself away for a week, but that was mostly because he needed to find a way to watch Seraphina's show without arousing Sara's suspicions. Not that any such suspicions would have a real foundation, Stroud told himself. He was just curious about Seraphina's act. After all, he was looking for his own gimmick, wasn't he? He needed to learn from those who were successful.

Really though, there was little he could learn from Seraphina. The painted sign depicting her figure was all the advertising she needed, and her show didn't have a story. She just put some whiny Eastern-sounding music on a portable phonograph and sashayed out onto her small stage wearing a gauzy harem outfit. Center stage was a large ottoman upholstered in black leather whose hinged seat pad concealed a box holding her python. She called him Peter.

Before long, Peter the python was crawling around all over her, disarraying the gauzy outfit, which gradually seemed to disintegrate as its various diaphanous pieces were displaced by the snake's movements and fluttered to the floor like leaves from an autumn tree. Eventually all that was left was a G-string and pasties and the snake held in a suggestive pose while Seraphina said breathily, "Oh, Peter."

But even if Stroud had nothing to learn from Seraphina, he kept returning. He knew she'd seen him standing at the back of the audience, but she never acknowledged his presence. Didn't acknowledge the presence of anyone in the audience. Only the snake.

He wanted to say something to her. Catch her in the daytime, introduce himself. But she tended to keep to herself at first. She was a stripper, not a real carny, and carny society wasn't the type to welcome new folks with open arms. It had taken Stroud three years of manual labor to become one with the rest of the people in the carnival, and though it would take a moneymaker like Seraphina a lot less time, it would take more than one season.

Eventually he managed to catch her as she was on her way back to her trailer from Dixon's office.

"Hey," Stroud said. She'd been about to go on by without a word. He had to say something. "You're the snake act." She stopped and looked up at him, but not too far up. She was a tall woman, only a few inches shorter than Stroud. "I've caught the show a few times. You have a good gimmick."

"Thanks." She gave no sign that she'd seen him at a performance.

"I'm John Stroud. I run the ball toss down the midway."

"Yes," she said. "I've seen it."

Game operators like Stroud were one step down the social ladder from the carnies with acts, but Seraphina might not yet know that.

"Well, nice meeting you, John. You'll have to excuse me. I have to get back to my trailer."

"Sure," Stroud said, stepping aside, wondering what the hell for? he thought. You gonna play with that snake? "See you around."

"I'm sure," she said, and she moved past him and out of sight around a corner.

After that, Stroud saw her more frequently, and occasionally he managed to catch her eye. She always smiled and nodded, but that was it. No suggestion of anything more.

*   *   *

And so the spring and summer progressed until the oppressive heat and humidity of August permeated the pine forests that lay around the towns of the carnival's circuit. By now, Stroud and Sara habitually watched the news on TV on while they ate dinner. Even if the news was bad, it was better than any conversation they might have. One night, about two weeks into the month, the screen showed a huge mass of hippies who were camping out at some place up in New York called Woodstock.

"Looks like a gigantic carnival without the rides and games," Sara said.

"Looks like a filthy mess to me," Stroud said.

Sara looked at him.

"Yes. It does."

"What's that supposed to mean?"

"Tell me, John. Are you happy being here. In the carnival? With me?"

"What the hell kind of question is that?"

"Just a simple one."

"Well, yeah, I guess so. Happy as I'd be anywhere."

"Happy to be living in the mess?"

"I don't know what you're talking about."

"I'm looking at all those kids," she waved at the TV, "and thinking that they're like the rubes we deal with every day. They get to leave the mess whenever they want and go home. We have to stay right in the middle of it. We work in it and eat in it and make love in it."

"Your point being?" he asked impatiently, knowing already.

"I'm thinking about a home, John. One away from the mess."

"You want to leave the carnival? Settle down?"

"I've been thinking about it." She clutched at his arm. "It wouldn't be so bad. The folks who own the diner in Dunnison said they'd take me on full-time. I've spent a lot of time in that diner every winter, and it's a real nice town."

"So you waitress in a dump diner, and what do I do? Twiddle my thumbs?"

"That's just it," she said urgently. "I heard the man who owns the auto parts store is fixin' to retire. We could sell the ball toss and use the money for a down payment…."

"You want me to run an auto parts store? While you waitress." Stroud snorted and shook her hand off his arm. "You can forget that shit."

"I know it's a small place, John, but it's a real nice town."

"Maybe. It's not the size, it's the position you imagine for me. If I move anywhere, it's not going to be near the middle. I only want the top spot."

"Sure, John," she said, turning away. Bitterness was in her voice. "And just how does someone like you get that top spot?"

"I don't know," he admitted.

Gimmick, he thought. I need a gimmick. Like Seraphina. Without that snake, she was nothing but a hoochie-coochie dancer.

But a pretty good looking one. As the season progressed, Stroud found it harder and harder to keep her out of his mind. On the increasingly rare occasions when he and Sara broke down and stroked each other out of pure lust and physical need, Stroud tried to imagine Sara's lean, hard body transformed into Seraphina's sumptuous curves. He wondered how those curves would feel beneath his hands and pressed against him. He tried to imagine himself the snake, probing her every desire. But it was always Sara who cried out beneath him, or worse, who didn't cry out at all.

A week after the news broadcast about the big music festival, Stroud found he could no longer contain himself. He wanted Seraphina badly—worse than he'd wanted Claire—and she was never far from his thoughts. Like Claire, Seraphina was above Stroud's level, but Stroud knew that he could bridge that gap by making himself more valuable in the carny world. He didn't have the gimmick right now, but he had no doubt that he'd know how to exploit it when he did.

And he knew that he could manage Seraphina and better exploit her potential. She needed a partner. Someone who could help shape her act, and Stroud could be the man to do it. He could give her some ideas so she would understand his value.

Determined to make a play for her before the season was out, Stroud waited for the right opportunity to approach her, and one day, he thought he found it. He'd noticed that Seraphina left the carnival every day in the early afternoon to go into whatever town the carnival was playing to have a meal in the local diner or café. Stroud guessed that she probably wasn't much of a cook. He planned to be in the diner the next time Seraphina came in. He could join her for lunch, chat her up, maybe make a proposition.

He made sure to arrive at the diner a little earlier than she usually did, and he sat on a stool at the counter, nervously and impatiently sipping coffee and wishing she'd get her ass in here. Then, there she was. It was funny how, dressed in street clothes and without her make-up and snake, she looked pretty much like any other attractive, youngish woman. She glanced around at the tables, not paying attention to the people at the counter, and found an empty table near the windows. Stroud let the waitress take her some silverware, water, and a menu before he rose from the stool and ambled over to her table.

"Hello, there, Seraphina."

She'd seen him approach, and while the expression in her eyes wasn't exactly welcoming, it wasn't hostile, either.

"Hi, John. I didn't expect to see you here."

Her delivery was innocent enough, but the implication still lay there between them: Stroud just ran a game booth and couldn't afford to eat in town. At least not often.

"I like a good meal now and again," he said. "Mind if I join you?"

"Actually, I do," she said. "I'm meeting someone for lunch."

Meeting someone. For lunch. Everyday?

"Too bad," he said. "I thought we might get to know each other a little better."

"Maybe another time," she said, picking up her menu.

"Yeah, another time," he said. "See you around." He turned,

went back to the counter, and ordered another cup of coffee. He wasn't leaving until he saw who she was meeting.

He should have expected it when Bull Martin, the strongman, pushed through the door a few minutes later. Bull went to Seraphina's table and sat down. Stroud saw the way Seraphina looked at Bull. Noted the slight flush on her cheek when he came in and the lust in her eyes as he sat.

Bull Martin was the only carny in Hanley Brothers who gave Stroud the slightest bit of worry. Stroud was as tall as Bull, but packed about half the strongman's muscle. Worse, Bull had never liked Stroud. Stroud didn't know why. Maybe it was the difference in carny social class, or maybe it was because Stroud was a heavy drinker and Bull considered him to be just another lazy bum. Whatever it was, it didn't really matter since Stroud didn't like Bull Martin, either. He found the strongman to be a sanctimonious fitness buff as well as an obnoxious, loudmouth bully who thought he could say anything he wanted because no one dared challenge him.

Bull didn't notice Stroud sitting at the counter, but Stroud noticed the way Bull tenderly patted Seraphina's hands and the way the two of them leaned intimately across the table. They're cooking up something, Stroud thought, but he had no idea what. Disappointed and disgruntled, he left the diner. Neither one of them saw him go.

Stroud was right. Seraphina and Bull were cooking up something, and that something became evident during the waning months of the season when they moved in together, combined their tents, and displayed a new, brightly painted sign. The act was still called, Seraphina and the Serpent, but now the picture showed the python wrapped around Seraphina while a heroically posed Bull Martin wrestled it off of her. The sign looked like a cheap imitation of those Conan book covers Stroud was seeing on drugstore paperback racks.

Stroud caught the act during its first week and was amazed. Seraphina and Bull had created a kind of sexual drama in which Seraphina was drawn down into the underworld and fondled by the snake until she was just about nude. Then in came Bull, dressed in a loincloth, and he spent a lot of time writhing around with Seraphina and the serpent as he pried it off her. In the process, he managed to do more fondling than the snake did. The little drama ended when he'd completely separated the snake's coils from Seraphina's curves, and the final pose, just before the lights went out, had the strongman and the beauty facing each other, their sides to the audience. Bull would reach up with his left hand to hold Seraphina's shoulder, while his right arm, with the snake wound around it, held the snake's head and neck at groin height so that, in silhouette, it looked like a huge penis writhing toward Seraphina's crotch.

It was the kind of gimmick that nobody in the carnival could match. By the end of the first month, Bull also was hoisting Seraphina about while she played slinkily with the python, and they were raking in the cash. Stroud could only watch from the sidelines, hating Bull and aching for the right gimmick as much as he ached for Seraphina.

Then one Saturday night, toward the end of the evening when the townies were crawling back to their houses and the carnies were getting ready to count the take and relax, Stroud's aches became real. He'd just sneaked out of Seraphina and Bull's tent after catching their show for the twentieth time. He didn't want Sara to know where he'd been, not that it really mattered. They were barely speaking, and Stroud didn't think he owed her anything, much less an explanation.

But Bull Martin did. Stroud felt a heavy hand on his shoulder that spun him around.

"I don't know what you want, Stroud," Martin grated. "But whatever it is, you ain't gettin' it."

"I want you to get outta my way," Stroud said.

"And I want you to stay outta my tent. You better not let me catch you inside again."

"It's a free country," Stroud said. "I paid my entry fee."

"And here's your exit fee," Martin said, punctuating the sentence by slugging Stroud in the gut.

Stroud doubled over. Shit, that hurt! The strong abdominal muscles he'd built up shoveling all those years ago were long gone, and he felt like he was about to vomit.

Slowly he straightened and tried to turn the movement into an uppercut. His meaty fist took Martin on the jaw, but the strongman's head merely bounced back, and then he was on Stroud, pounding and pummeling. Stroud could barely keep the blows from turning his face to mush, and at last, he collapsed to the ground, Martin standing over him, fists clenched.

Stroud was barely conscious, but he was aware of three things. The first was Martin saying, "Keep outta my tent, and keep away from Seraphina." The second was the crowd of faces, some townies, some carnies, ringed around him. The townies looked curious, but some of the carnies looked contemptuous. And the third thing was Sara. She was in the crowd, a part of it but standing out like a sore thumb. Her expression was neither curious nor contemptuous. It was sad. Then she was gone and the crowd was dispersing as McGuire helped Stroud to his feet.

McGuire half-carried Stroud to his trailer, and Stroud practically fell inside. He kicked the door shut, and staggered through the small space. Sara wasn't there.

"Fuck it," he mumbled through broken lips. "She'll be back."

He took a hefty slug of whiskey from a bottle on the kitchenette's meager counter, and the liquor seared his cuts. Then he swayed past the closet-sized bathroom and into the bedroom, which was the size of two closets, and collapsed on the bed.

But Sara didn't come back. Not that night. Once he woke, Stroud decided not to work the ball toss today. His jaw ached, his lips were swollen, and he could barely see straight through puffy black eyes. He was in no condition to lure the rubes. Sara would just have to do it by herself for once. Where the hell was she?

At last she showed up, just a couple of hours before opening. Stroud was sitting in the kitchenette, feeling like shit.

"You'll need to work the booth by yourself today," he said after she'd come into the trailer.

"No, John."

"What do you mean, no? I'm in no condition…."

"And whose fault is that?"

"Bull Martin is an asshole…."

"You don't think I know what's going on? You think this carnival is like some big city where you can hide your indiscretions across town?"

"What indiscretions?"

"Everyone knows you have the hots for Seraphina. It's goddamn embarrassing."

"I never did anything with her."

She snorted a laugh.

"I guess that's why Bull beat the crap out of you."

"You gotta believe me, Sara...."

"No, I don't. I did once, but that's over. I'm leaving."

"Leaving? Sure. Whose going to take you on? Every show in the carnival is...."

"I'm leaving entirely," she said. "I'm getting out."

"Where the hell are you going to go?"

"Dunnison," she said. "They offered me a permanent job at the diner there. I'm sick of all this traveling around and not feeling like a real person."

"So," he said, contempt in his voice. "You're going to be a townie."

"Better than being here with you," she said. "Now, I'd like you to leave while I gather my things."

For a second, Stroud almost balked, almost grabbed and brutalized her. But he held back. Making a play for Seraphina and getting beaten for it would be okay with the rest of the carnies. That was life. But beating a woman who was trying to leave him because he didn't want her wasn't going to get him anywhere but ostracized. He couldn't afford that. Finally, he just turned and exited the trailer, grabbing the bottle of whiskey off the counter as he went.

He sat on one of the chairs outside, drinking from the bottle and staring at the other carnies and the trees surrounding the field where they'd set up, not really seeing anything but the redness blanking out his mind.

At last, she came out, dragging a suitcase and a duffel bag—the same ones Stroud had left home with.

"You can have those," he said, "but you're not taking the truck."

She looked at him, pity in her eyes.

"I pray to God you find success, John" she said, "because if you continue on the path you're on, you won't find any peace."

Then she was gone around the corner of the trailer, and a few minutes later, he saw her friend, Carol, driving her away.

"You fucking bitch," he muttered. "Fuck you. I don't need you."

But he did need her. Now, he had to set up the ball toss and break it down alone. And on top of that, there was cooking and housekeeping. Though the trailer was small and required little cleaning, it quickly became a mess. He took to eating in diners and cafes, though he was careful to avoid places where Bull Martin and Seraphina might be. Since the beating, Seraphina had ignored his surreptitious glances, but Bull openly sneered at him or made snide comments. It reminded Stroud of Wally Leavon, and Stroud would have killed Bull if he could.

Alone with his bitterness, Stroud slogged through the remainder of the season. When the carnival retreated to Dunnison for the winter, Stroud went along only long enough to store his game booth. Then he turned his pickup around and headed straight for Houston. There was no way he was going to spend the whole winter in the same small town as Sara. Not this soon, at least. Not when he was this down-and-out. There was no way he was going to give her the slightest edge....

It was night when he hit Houston's outskirts. He'd been in the city only a couple of times since his days of driving a truck for Richmond Lumber, but he'd always like it. Liked its size and its bustle. Houston was a city on the go, and Stroud was a man with a destination. If he could just see it. Maybe one of Houston's many signs would help point the way.

6: GIMMICK

THROUGH DECEMBER AND early January, Stroud lived in a shabby tan brick motor court that consisted of twenty or so tiny, one-bedroom duplex units spread across a two-acre plot close to where Old Galveston Road intersected Broadway Boulevard. The place was older than he was, and he stayed there as little as possible. Instead, he spent a lot of time a couple of miles toward downtown, consoling himself with cheap booze and the cheaper company that came with it in the low-rent bars along Harrisburg and Navigation Streets, down in Houston's waterfront district.

Stroud was now thirty-one, and despite all his efforts to better himself, it had all come to naught. He saw himself as he saw all the old, drunken failures at the bars and the old carnies who'd never made it but had to keep working the circuit until they dropped dead or couldn't work and ended up in some run-down trailer court sipping rotgut and whining about the past.

He wasn't going to end up like that, he thought. He couldn't. Besides, he was burning to possess Seraphina, and all he could think about was how she and Bull Martin were together in their cozy winter cottage in Florida, playing with the python.

Then he met Joe Wheeler. And the doll.

Fetish?

Promise and power.

But all that was later. Right now, he was spending the evening in Rudy's Bar and Grill, the cheap, limited menu and tap beer as good an excuse as any not to leave until last call. He was sitting in a

113

booth near the back, nursing his half-empty mug and trying to keep some distance between himself and the losers at the bar while he pondered his plight and wracked his brain for a gimmick or some other solution to his life. At last, he got up to go to the john. That's when he first saw the old man in a booth near the restroom doors. He didn't pay much attention on his way toward the men's room, but as he returned, he noticed how the old man hunched over his beer, trying to remain in the shadow cast by the booth's tall back.

Stroud's years with the carnival had taught him something about human nature—at least the natures of others—and he knew how to read body language. The old man's body spoke eloquently that he had something to hide as he shrank into the booth, trying to counter any attention he might receive from the folks bellied up to the bar or sitting among the tables scattered around a tiny cleared area in front of an aged jukebox.

As Stroud went by on his way back to his own booth, he slowed a bit to get a better look at the old man. Well, maybe not as old as Stroud's first impression. He wasn't decrepit yet, but he looked used up, worn, and beaten down. It wouldn't be long before decrepitude set in. Maybe it was because Stroud slowed to look at him that made the old man reach out and clutch at his sleeve.

"Say, mister, can you tell me how to get to Westheimer near Kirby? I ain't been around here for a while. It all looks so different."

Directions are free, Stroud thought. He might need someone to guide him sometime. He started to tell the old man, but one of the barflies dropped money into the jukebox, and the music caused the noisy chatter from the bar to increase increased in volume, and the old man couldn't hear Stroud's explanation.

"Come on." Stroud tugged on the old man's arm and gestured with his head toward the door. The old man rose and dragged a duffel bag out from beneath the table. As Stroud urged him through the small crowd, he noticed that it took a lot of straining for the old man to lift the bag. He practically had to drag it out the door.

Outside, it was chilly, and tatters of clouds were running across the moonlit sky—the wake of the cold front that had moved across the city the day before. Stroud realized that it felt a lot better out here than it had in the smoky, overheated interior of the bar. He'd just meant to tell the old man how to get to where he wanted to go, but he felt restless. "Oh, hell," he said to the old man. "Come on. I'll take you."

It surprised him that the old man pulled back.

"No, no. That's okay. Just tell me."

Now that they were outside, Stroud could hear that the man had an odd accent. Something like Midwestern overlaid with a sort of trill, as if he'd been speaking a foreign language for years.

But the way really was a little complicated and hard to explain. And it was too late for busses and too far for an old man on foot, and Stroud told him so.

"I've got a pickup," Stroud said hopefully. "I can have you there in fifteen or twenty minutes."

"Why would you do that?"

"Why not?" Stroud shrugged. "I'm sick of those rubes in there. Might as well get out and drive around some. I don't have anywhere particular to go. Besides, that duffel looks too heavy to carry far."

The old man cast a glance at the big, olive-drab bag and hesitated. Stroud could see he was considering the offer.

"I brung it a long way," the old man said. "I can tote it a little farther."

"Fifteen miles?" Stroud asked.

There was another pause while the old man considered Stroud's offer. "Okay," he said at last.

Stroud led him to the car and lowered the tailgate so the old man could put his duffel in the back. He noticed that the old man didn't just toss the bag into the bed but hoisted it carefully and laid it down like something inside might break. Whatever it was, it was heavy, and the old man grunted as he lifted it.

"You must be a sailor," Stroud said as he pulled out of his parking spot and steered toward downtown.

"What makes you say that?"

"The duffel. And meeting you in a dive bar on Navigation. Not many people in there who aren't sailors."

"You?"

"No. I'm not a sailor."

"I was. U.S. Navy then the Merchant Marines. Not no more. Not for twenty years."

"My name's John Stroud. You?"

"Joe Wheeler."

"Well, Joe, you may not be a sailor any more, but I can tell you came here from somewhere else. Somewhere south."

Wheeler wore a sweatshirt with a hood, but no real jacket or coat, and he was shivering. Stroud turned up the heater.

"South America. Been down there for a long time."

"What brings you back to the States?"

"My daughter. Iris. I ain't seen her since 1922, when she graduated from high school."

Stroud wondered at that. Joe looked to be in his mid to late sixties, which was certainly not old enough to have a daughter the same age.

"Is that where we're going?"

It was. Wheeler had an address about three blocks from the intersection he'd named, and as Stroud promised, they were there in short order.

"Thanks for the ride," the old man said when they pulled up in front of the house. "Just lemme get my duffel."

"You can leave it there," Stroud said. "Until you make sure you're daughter is still there. Fifty years is a long time."

"That's okay. I'm gonna take it with me."

Stroud got out with the old man and went to the back of the pickup to lower the tailgate. He was going to help the old man drag the duffel out of the bed, but Wheeler shouldered him aside and did the dragging himself. He might be old, Stroud thought, but he's still pretty solid.

"Want me to wait?" Stroud asked as Joe hefted the duffel's strap over his shoulder.

"Naw. Thanks for the ride."

Stroud got in the truck, but he didn't leave. Instead, he watched the old man shuffle down the front walk, bowed beneath the duffel's weight. He let the duffel down on the front porch then knocked. The door opened a few moments later, and Stroud could see another, much older man silhouetted in the light from the entry hall.

The two spoke for a few minutes, then the man in the house shut the door, and Wheeler, shoulders even more stooped than before, turned and stared into the night. Then he saw Stroud waiting, and he hoisted the bag and trudged to the truck.

"Get in," Stroud said.

Joe stowed the duffel in the back and got in the cab.

"What happened?"

"She ain't here. She ain't been here for a long time. She got married and moved up to Minneapolis."

"Who was that at the door?"

"The man my ex-wife married. He said she died about ten years ago of the cancer. Too bad. She was a good woman. Too good for me."

"What now?"

"I got to go to Minneapolis. See if I can find Iris. He give me an address. Ain't nothing else I can do."

"Where do you want to go?"

"I don't know," the old man said. "I'm tired. I can't think."

"You want to come to my place?" Stroud asked. "You can rest, get something to eat."

Joe eyed Stroud warily.

"Look," Stroud said. "I haven't done anything to you, and I've had plenty of chances. I'm just trying to help you out. If you don't want it, I'll just drop you off somewhere."

"Okay," the old man said, weariness overcoming his wariness.

Stroud pulled off and drove back to his small unit. There, he fed the old man, who afterward lay down on the sofa and fell asleep, clutching the handle of the duffel bag.

As the old man slept the sleep of the dead, Stroud couldn't help but stare at the duffel and think of how protective Joe had been with it. It was heavy. Heavy like it contained a lot more than an old sailor's meager possessions. Stroud knew about the ancient civilizations down there in Mexico and South America. Mayan and Incan pyramids. Lost Aztec gold. Maybe the old man had found some of that gold down there.

Stroud approached the sofa and looked down at Wheeler. Then he bent forward, gently pried the sailor's stiff fingers from around the strap, and half carried the bag across the room.

It was heavy as shit. Nearly a hundred pounds. Stroud was amazed that the old sailor had managed to drag it around much less all the way from South America. The guy was stronger than he looked. Stroud grunted as he carefully propped the bag upright against his easy chair. If there was Aztec gold in there, he didn't want it to rattle, or whatever sound gold made knocking together. Stroud had no idea. He'd never owned anything made of gold—at least not since he'd dropped the ring he'd wanted Claire to wear. But he sure didn't want to wake the old man at this stage of the game.

The bag wasn't locked, just closed with a hasp. He thumbed it open, folded the canvas flaps back from the duffel's mouth, and peered inside.

The odor of unwashed human immediately assailed his nostrils. He drew back instinctively, wrinkling his nose. Then he peered closer. A wad of dirty clothes plugged the opening. He pulled them out, and piled them on the table. Next were more clothes, these relatively clean, followed by more personal possessions. Then there was a bundle about the size of a book, wrapped in some kind of animal skin with short, light-brown fur. He unwrapped the bundle, only to find that it was a book: a volume on maritime law. He put the book and skin next to the growing pile of items he'd already removed from the duffel. Next was another cloth-wrapped bundle. He tried to pull it out, but it resisted his efforts. A little patting down the sides of the duffel told him why. This bundle completely filled the bottom two-thirds of the bag. That made it about three feet long and more than a foot in diameter.

The Aztec gold.

Stroud peeled back the duffel from the top of the bundle, which also was wrapped in animal skins, laid the duffel on its side, and pulled the bundle free. Cradling the bundle, he lifted it to the table-top. Whatever the skins hid was what made the bag so heavy, but Stroud was having doubts about it being gold. It seemed like there was only a single object wrapped up in the skins. If that single object had been gold, Stroud doubted that he and the old man combined could lift it. For a moment, he studied the bundle and its wrappings.

Not gold, he thought, but something valuable enough to drag its weight here from another continent. Stroud paused. Did he want to go further? If he did, if he unwrapped the bundle, there was no way he'd be able to rewrap it the same, and the old man would know for sure that Stroud had gone through his things. Or Stroud could stuff everything back into the duffel right now and put the bag back beside the sofa, and the old sailor would be none the wiser.

But Stroud hadn't come this far to let his curiosity remain unsated. He had to see what was inside. He set his big, clumsy hands to teasing open the bundle. He didn't know what he expected to find, but by the time he'd reached the final layers, he knew it was some sort of human figurine or statue. He could feel its shape beneath the last of the skins. He located the end where the head should be and pulled back the final skin.

And stepped back with a gasp. Then he caught hold of himself and bent forward for a closer look.

It wasn't gold, but it was something that might be more valuable. A means to obtain gold—to obtain anything he wanted.

Fate had dropped his gimmick right in his lap.

But first he had to get the thing out of the old sailor's possession and into his.

Stroud couldn't sleep. After he'd wrestled the figure from the duffel and unwrapped it, he was too excited. And there was too much to think about. Besides, he didn't want the old man to wake up while Stroud still slept, repack the duffel, and make for the highway, taking Stroud's future with him.

It wasn't the weight that made the figurine so impressive. It was the way the thing looked. It was shaped like a person, only it's head was somewhat oversized for the body, which was compact, nearly hairless, and very realistically proportioned. The bestial yet too-human face held an expression hovering somewhere between a fiendish leer and a grimace of pain, and the mouth was filled with sharp teeth, doglike canines protruding over the bottom lip. Shuttered by half-opened lids, the eyes were black and glittering and so artistically wrought that they seemed to shine with a baleful malevolence. The limbs were powerful looking, and the fingers on each hand ended in yellowish and very sharp talons, while the toenails were short, flat, horny spikes. The scalp was covered with some kind of black hair that was stiff and spiky.

Unlike similar bogus creatures—called gaffs—that Stroud had seen in the past, it was not clumsily covered in a pelt, nor did glued

119

or sewn seams betray its construction. Instead, each hair seemed to be individually implanted. Maybe the body had simply been fashioned from some animal. That seemed likely, since the "skin," which was a dark reddish-brown, felt like it could be fine-grained leather. Whatever frame it was stretched over was as solid as it was heavy. Some kind of wood carved to shape? Had to be. Mahogany, maybe.

God, he thought. What a hell of a lot of work. It was so realistically wrought that the total effect was creepy and frightening. And the more Stroud looked, the more realistic the thing was. The level of detail was stunning. Little clumps of stiff hair "grew" out of the gristle around the canal of each slightly pointed ear, and the fingers revealed wrinkles over each knuckle and perfectly sculpted cuticles at the base of each talon. The thing even had male genitals, though much shriveled and darkened beneath a skimpy patch of black hair. The skin of the face was dark-hued and similar to the shrunken heads he'd once seen on exhibit, except this one didn't have its eyelids and mouth sewn shut.

Exhibit.

Once he'd finished removing the animal skins, he found half a dozen leather pouches hidden in the space between the legs. He opened one to find that it was filled with a gray-brown, musty-smelling powder. He cinched the bag shut and put it and the other bags next to the book.

Then he moved to the kitchen counter and reached for the half-full bottle of bourbon that sat there, nearly knocking it over because he couldn't tear his eyes from the doll. He sat in his easy chair, drank from the bottle, and stared. And drank. And stared. And when the bottle was empty, he wasn't drunk, but he was still staring. And planning.

When the old man woke the next morning, Stroud was ready. He had the doll propped on a chair, and old man, bleary-eyed when he groaned and sat up on the sofa, came fully awake when he saw it. He swung his feet to the floor, and with more speed and energy than Stroud would have imagined he had, he darted to the chair, wrapped his arms around it, and started to lift it.

Stroud moved toward him, trying to halt the old man's frantic haste to get the doll back into the duffel, but the old man quickly laid the doll on the duffel and whirled on Stroud, a long, wicked-looking knife in his hand.

"Get back, you bastard," he hissed.

Stroud backed off a couple of steps, hands raised.

"Hold it, Joe," he said. "I didn't mean any harm. I just wanted to look at it."

"You got no right."

"That's true. But I wasn't trying to harm it. Or you. Do you know what you've got there?"

"I know a lot better than you."

"That thing there is everything we need," Stroud said, ignoring the old man's sarcastic tone.

Joe snorted a laugh. "You dumb shit," he said. "I. It's everything I need." He stretched the duffel on the floor, opened its mouth, and began trying to slide the doll inside while still holding the knife on Stroud.

"Careful," Stroud warned. "You're going to break it."

That just brought another derisive snort, but the old man stopped struggling with the doll after a moment, realizing the futility of trying to put it back in the bag and hold Stroud at bay all at the same time.

"Just hear me out," Stroud said. "If you don't like what I'm saying when I'm done, I'll go out and let you pack up that thing and leave in peace. But listen first."

The knife didn't waver in the old man's hand, nor did his defensive posture relax, but a weary acquisition crept in behind the hostility in his eyes.

"It won't do no good," he said, straightening. "But talk."

"I don't know what that thing is," Stroud said, gesturing to the doll on the floor, "but I can tell you one thing for sure—I can make us a lot of money with it. We can share it, fifty-fifty."

"I don't need nothing from you."

"Sure you do. Look at you. You haven't got anything. You're lugging around a hundred pounds of duffel bag, you got no car, you got no money, you got no family, and you got nowhere to go. That's why you spent last night sleeping on a stranger's sofa."

"I can go to the sailors' home on Harrisburg."

"Okay. Say you do go over there. For how long? You told me last

121

night that you wanted to go up to Minneapolis to find your daughter, but how are you going to get there with no cash or transportation? Walk with all that weight on your back? Maybe you could get a job on a ship? Sure. Like they're gonna hire a broken down old swabbie like you when you haven't even worked as a sailor in twenty years."

"I can get by."

"Bullshit. You came here to find your daughter, but she isn't here. You're all used up, and you got nothing. Minnesota's colder than shit in winter, and you can't even afford to buy a coat. You got nothing but that doll. And me. You go in with me, and I'll finance your trip up to Minneapolis and throw in a few hundred bucks in traveling money."

"Why the hell would you do that?" Stroud could see that the knife was wavering in Joe's hand. "What do you get out of it?"

"I get to use that doll while you're gone. I work for a carnival, and I can exhibit your little friend and make some real money. When you get back from visiting your daughter, I'll split it with you, fifty-fifty."

Joe looked thoughtful for a few moments.

"Fifty-fifty, you say?" A shrewd look gleamed in the old man's eyes. "Suppose I ask for sixty?"

"Nothin' doin'," Stroud said. "It's my caravan, I'm the one with connections, and I'm the one who can make it work. And that's fifty-fifty after expenses."

"How do I know I can trust you?"

"If you couldn't, we wouldn't be having this conversation. You'd still be lying on that sofa, but you'd never be getting up."

"I gotta think about it," Wheeler said.

"Sure. You think about it. Like I said, I'm going out. I'll be gone one hour. There's the kitchen," he pointed. "You eat, you think. If you don't like my proposition, pack up and leave before I get back."

Without another word, Stroud left the unit. It was a terrible gamble, he knew. The old man might go and take that fantastic thing with him, and there would go Stroud's greatest possibility for a gimmick, right out the door. But what else could he do? He couldn't just beat Wheeler senseless and take the thing. And despite what he'd said about the old man not waking up, Stroud was no killer.

No, he had to have Joe Wheeler on his side. Once the money started rolling in, he'd see that Stroud was right, and then things would go smoothly. But right now, Stroud had to take a chance and let the old man know he was safe to deal with. But not too much of a chance. Stroud got into his car and drove out of the motor court, but he only went about a hundred yards before he turned around and parked on the shoulder. If Wheeler decided to leave, he'd come out this way, and if he did…. Well, Stroud would just have to deal with that if it happened.

But it didn't happen. The hour passed with no sign of Wheeler. Even so, Stroud returned to the apartment, heart thudding in his chest, hand clammy on the knob. The old man could have sneaked out the back way….

Relief flood through Stroud when he opened the door and saw Wheeler on the sofa, eating from a plate, and the doll propped once again in the chair.

"He probably don't like to be stuffed in that bag, anyway," Joe mumbled around a mouthful of food.

Stroud waited patiently for the old man to finish eating.

"Okay, Joe," he said when the sailor was done. "You gotta tell me what that thing is and where you got it. I need to know everything."

7: JOE

"ME AND MY wife was married for only a year before Iris was born. We lived up in Chicago, and I was working for the Atchison, Topeka and Santa Fe Railroad as an apprentice mechanic in the engine repair shop. By the time the Great War broke out, I'd worked my way up to journeyman mechanic. The Army said I was too old for the trenches, but the Navy liked my experience with diesel engines. They was going from coal-burners to diesels, and I served in the engine room of one of the new ships: the Pennsylvania. It was the flagship for Admiral Mayo, and we even had President Wilson on board once, but we didn't see much action." He chuckled. "Wasn't enough fuel oil to go 'round, even for an admiral."

After the war, Joe gravitated to the Merchant Marines. The shipping line he worked for was based out of the now-bustling port in Houston, so he moved his small family to the burgeoning city. During the next few years, he sailed all of the Seven Seas and made every major port of call. But the one port he failed to visit often or long enough was his home port.

"My wife left me in '22, right after Iris graduated from high school." Joe chuckled again. "She always was a smart woman."

Iris went off to college to become a teacher, and the next year, his wife remarried. With no reason to come back to Houston, there wasn't much for Joe to do but keep on shipping out. Nor was there much to do but drink to kill the boredom and loneliness.

"Things kept on like that until after World War Two. Funny, during the first war, I was in the Navy, protecting Merchant Marine ships, but in the second, I was the one being protected." He shook his head sadly. "I guess the war protected me in a lot of ways. By then, my drinking was out of control. I was drunk half the time I was on duty and all the time I was off. My shipmates knew I had a problem, and the officers did, too. Only one who didn't was me. But with the war on, the country needed every available man. And I knew my way around an engine. No doubt about that. I was good at my job. But then, I screwed up big-time."

It was right at the end of the war. Everybody knew the conflict was just about over, but everybody still had to go through the motions until the armistice paperwork was signed. The freighter Joe worked on was carrying a full load of fruit from Central America to the port in Mobile. It was a comfortable run, and out in the middle of the Gulf of Mexico, in relatively calm water far from marauding U-boats, Joe felt safe enough to stay drunk on duty. And there, in the middle of that safety zone, while Joe was soused, the engines caught fire, crippling the ship. Although no lives were lost, the ship was stranded for nearly two weeks until repairs could be made, and by then, the entire cargo of fruit had spoiled.

The inquiry board wound up blaming Joe. Although he argued that the fire had been caused by substandard engine parts, the powers were arrayed against him.

"Got me a book on maritime law," Joe said, "but it didn't do no good. They knew the law better than me."

One broadside from that ship of state was sufficient to blackball him from most merchant vessels for life, and no reputable shipping line would have him. Desperate, he hung around the docks along the Houston Ship Channel, watching his funds dwindle. He needed work, but he was in his mid sixties, and all he knew was ship engines. At last, down to the dregs of his money, he found a berth aboard a South American freighter registered out of Chile.

It was an independent, owned by her captain, and he didn't seem to care about the blackballing as long as Joe could keep his engines running at minimal cost. Joe served aboard the ship for three years as she hauled produce, timber, ore, or whatever the captain found that would pay. Mostly the ship plied the waters of Latin America, but occasionally they made port in the U.S.generally at one or more of the ports along the Gulf Coast, but on two rare occasions the West Coast.

In 1949, the captain sold the ship, and the new owners, looking to cut costs, fired many of the crew, Joe among them. The bad news came while the ship was docked in Belem, Brazil. With little choice, Joe took a job tending the engine of a small, shallow-draught steamer that made regular runs up the Amazon and its tributaries. The boat's owner and captain, Javier Estrada, was pleasant enough and fair enough, and Joe's Spanish, picked up during a lifetime of visiting Latin American ports, was good enough to make the switch to Estrada's Portuguese. The two men got along well, and Estrada didn't even seem to mind Joe's drinking as long as Joe wasn't plastered.

But Joe was used to the wide sky of open waters, and the gloom beneath the massive foliage that arched over long sections of the rivers, constantly blocking the sky and masking the horizon, burdened him like a great weight. And the bugs! Having lived in Houston, Joe knew all about mosquitoes, roaches, and other insect pests, but it seemed that for every bug Houston had, the Amazon had ten thousand. Even worse was the forest's constant chatter, especially at night. It was downright unsettling. But at least the air wasn't oppressively hot. Humid, yes, but not hot, which surprised him. The temperature rarely rose above eighty-five degrees, and the nights were cool.

Fate seemed to be leading him into the jungle. The steamer broke down just about as far up river as they could go, in Caballococha, just across the border into Peru.

"Only the Nile is longer than the Amazon," Estrada said when Joe gave him the bad news that the broken part couldn't be fixed here in the forest. The boat would remain where it was until somebody fetched a replacement.

"I didn't know that," Joe said.

"Yes. The Amazon is about six thousand, eight hundred kilometers long, and we are only four hundred from the end."

"You're saying it's a long way back to Belem."

"Much closer to go upstream as far as you can go then hike over the mountains to Guayaquil, Ecuador. There is a large enough port there for you to find what you need."

"You're saying you want me to hike through hell-hole jungle, over the Andes Mountains, and another couple of hundred miles more to find the part? Alone?"

"Who else knows what is needed?" Estrada shrugged. "And I must stay behind to guard my boat. I will give you enough money to buy the part and to pay for food and a guide. You will be back in two months. It would take that long just to get to Belem, and twice that to get back."

Joe was a seafarer, not a landlubber. His greatest familiarity with land was with the ports of call he'd made for more than thirty years. He looked at the jungle he would have to trek through and felt fear rise in him like a living thing. But there was no help for it. To get back on the water, he had to have the part, and the part was six hundred miles away across jungle and mountains. He'd have to trust his guide just as he'd learned to trust the compass, winds, currents, and stars. So he packed up his duffel and followed his guide, who carried a machete to help clear the trail.

The journey started well enough, first by canoe. Eventually, though, as the land rose toward the foothills of the Andes, the river became impassible, even for the small craft. The paddlers were happy enough about that. Muttering about Jívaros and wanting to keep their heads, the paddlers returned downstream, leaving Joe and his guide to trek through the rain forest toward the still-distant mountains.

His guide was a degredado—a criminal sentenced to go into the jungle to learn tribal languages. Joe would have preferred someone more reliable, but this far up the Amazon, nobody was reliable. The guide told Joe that the local tribes were Jívaros, the headhunting people of the Upper Amazon Basin. Collectively, they were more properly called the Shuar, though there were a dozen or more individual tribes, each with a different name. The guide was known among them, and he had a smattering of their tribal tongue. He told Joe that the headhunters wouldn't bother them.

"Besides, José," he laughed. "They want the heads of strong warriors, not somebody as old and gray as you."

Turned out that the guide was as black hearted as the jungle was oppressive. As soon as he discovered that Joe carried a substantial sum to pay for the engine parts, he led him, unknowing, into a practically unpopulated area. As they entered the area, they were warned by people in a village they passed through not to go farther. It was haunted, they said, by some legendary tribe called the Huambisa, and certain death awaited them there.

Joe, unfamiliar with the Shuar language, didn't understand the exchange, and his guide didn't care. He had no intention of going farther into Huambisa territory than necessary. Just a few miles farther into the empty forest, he attacked Joe, slashing him twice across the chest with his machete before stealing the money and abandoning the sailor to his fate.

That fate promised to be short-lived. Severely injured and without bearings or food, Joe wandered for two days before collapsing in delirium on the edge of a tiny stream.

He didn't expect to wake, but he did, though the total darkness made him think he was dead. He jerked upright, but burning pain across his chest caused him to cry out and fall back onto the pallet from which he'd risen.

The pain and the echo of the cry in his own ears made him realize he wasn't dead, and a moment later, he heard a rustling from the darkness. Suddenly, some of the darkness folded back, admitting a smoky torch held in the hand of an Indian man. As far as Joe was concerned, the adult Indians of the Amazon looked like they were either in their twenties or as old as Joe. They seemed to age rapidly, maybe because of lifestyle, maybe because of the environment. Whatever the reason, few seemed to be of virile middle age, as this man was. A pair of women came behind the man, and while one held the torch, the man bent over Joe and said something to him in a language he couldn't understand.

But if Joe couldn't understand, he could comprehend what the man meant. Joe had been found by some Indians, he was in some hut, and he was being tended. He still expected to die from his wounds, which sent searing pain across his chest and torso every time he moved, but at least someone in this godforsaken jungle gave a crap. As the man peeled back an ugly looking poultice from the wounds, Joe gasped and passed out.

There ensued a period of intense suffering and delirium. The man and the women did things to him. He didn't know what.

Once, he woke to find his body completely covered in a light gray paste that stank. Another time, the man forced him to drink something that tasted foul while the two women propped him up and held his feebly protesting limbs. Things got worse after that, but mostly, he was mercifully unconscious.

Eventually, he woke feeling lucid, and over the course of a week, he came to realize that he was healing, thanks to the ministrations of his benefactors. Joe didn't comprehend their language, but as he healed, he learned that the man's name was Tuchaua, and the two women were his older and younger wives, Entash and Ukunchkit.

"That was a mouthful to say," Joe mused, a faint smile twitching the corners of his mouth. "Ukunchkit. Meant hummingbird in their language. I learnt it quick enough. Their language was pretty simple. They can't even count past ten. But they have a million names for all the plants and animals. I never did get all that, but pretty soon, I could converse with 'em pretty well for most purposes."

As he lay there, he couldn't help but wonder why Tuchaua had saved him. The tribesmen this far back in the forest were not known for humanitarian deeds. The Jívaro were killers of invaders to their territory and known for taking the heads of the vanquished and shrinking them down to the size of a baseball. Some of the tribes sold them, and those made their way down the river and across the oceans to museums and the homes of collectors of the bizarre and morbid. Joe had seen enough of them up and down the river in the three years he'd worked on the riverboat. And he was wondering why his head wasn't being shrunken right now.

It seemed that Tuchaua had plans for Joe, and for those plans to work out, he had to be able to communicate with the white man. As soon as Joe's pain had diminished enough for him to take instruction, Tuchaua started teaching Joe the Shuar language. Or, at least, the Huambisa version of Shuar. And in the course of the instruction, Joe learned about Tuchaua and the Huambisa, as well as why Tuchaua had saved his life.

The two men who'd found Joe were hunters seeking game. They hadn't killed him because he was a white man. That made him more than a curiosity. The Huambisa bore a significant amount of European blood, bequeathed by the Spanish women taken captive after the Huambisa had slaughtered their menfolk at Sevilla del Oro in 1599. The European genes gave the Huambisa inches in stature over their enemies among the neighboring tribes, and size was an advantage in battle and the taking of tsantsa—the severed heads of enemies taken in battle. If Joe had been an Achuar or Jevero or of any other nearby tribe, the men who'd rescued him would have left him to die. But being an inki, he represented breeding stock.

But only if he lived.

The two hunters carried Joe to Tuchaua's home, which must have been quite a task since that was more than ten miles and Joe easily outweighed either of the two men. They took Joe there because Tuchaua was the Huambisi's most powerful shaman—not just a wawek, or bewitching shaman, capable of sending out lethal magic darts, but a pener uwisin, or a curing shaman, without peer. Tuchaua would know how to heal Joe and what to do with him afterward.

Tuchaua shared with the two hunters the desire to add Joe's blood to the blood of the Huambisa, but he also was extremely curious about Joe and the world from which he came. After all, if Tuchaua, like all the Huambisa, bore the blood of white men, then Tuchaua had ancestors among Joe's people as surely as he did among his own. He wanted to know how they lived so that he could more properly honor them, and also, more important, how to protect Huambisi territory should the white men invade.

Also, being a shaman of great power, Tuchaua was impressed by the many tattoos etched on Joe's body. All Shuar, including the Huambisa, painted magical and otherwise meaningful symbols on their skin, but these marks on the man he'd helped were indelible and undoubtedly magical. Even more remarkable was the magical talisman of many strange white leaves bound together and marked with more magical symbols. Tuchaua wanted to know the secrets hidden in those symbols. The talisman had been found by the two men who'd found Joe. After they'd taken him to Tuchaua, they'd backtracked Joe to the site of his ambush. They gathered his scattered things, including the book on maritime law, and brought them to Tuchaua.

Joe was able to emerge from the hut after two weeks, but there was no way he could leave its environs. He was too weak, and he

131

didn't know where he was or which way to go. He wasn't about to start wandering around in the jungle all by himself. Few in these parts would be as friendly as Tuchaua. Beside, things rapidly grew quite comfortable for the old sailor. He healed remarkably well and remarkably fast, though he bore two horrendous scars slashed across his chest and abdomen.

In fact, Joe felt better than he had in fifteen or twenty years. It was as if Tuchaua's ministrations had rejuvenated him as well as healed him. He didn't have a mirror, but he could see himself reflected in still pools and pots of water. He even looked younger.

Joe wasn't a hunter and warrior. Not like Tuchaua and his people. He later learned, but at first, he just did what little he could around Tuchaua's hut to earn his keep. He gathered firewood, repaired the hut, and tried to keep the area clean. That didn't help much, at least by his standards. The Indians were pretty grubby people. They just threw their trash where it was convenient, and damn the nasty odors. After a few years, when things got too bad, they simply moved off a mile or so, rebuilt the huts, and went on as before. Gradually, over the course of several years, he not only learned to speak their language, he went on hunts, butchered the kill, learned to make the dart poison from the sweat of tiny red and black and extremely deadly frogs, and became a fair shot with a blowgun, which was the Huambisa's preferred weapon.

And there was Ukunchkit. She was an Achuar whose husband had come to Tuchaua's home to kill Tuchaua and take his tsantsa. But his tsantsa had been taken instead, and afterward, in a brazen show of personal power, Tuchaua boldly walked to Ukunchkit's husband's hut, took Ukunchkit, and brought her back to his own camp. That had been two years ago, and the husband's tsantsa hung inside Tuchaua's hut, along with several others, to ensure Ukunchkit's obedience and loyalty.

Although she was technically Tuchaua's second wife, bound by her ex-husband's tsantsa, Ukunchkit seemed to take to the sailor more than she did to the shaman. Joe was pretty worried about that at first, especially after she sneaked into his hut one night with more on her mind than medical ministrations. It scared the hell out of Joe.

"Not the idea of, you know…." He laughed. "I was a sailor, after all.

Naw. I was more worried that Tuchaua would find out and use some of that dart poison on me. Or one of his secret magical darts that a shaman can cast into the soul of an enemy to weaken or kill him."

He told Ukunchkit that since she was Tuchaua's wife, she had to leave, but it turned out that Joe needn't have worried. Half the reason he was alive was to add his stature and strength to the Huambisi gene pool. Tuchaua knew Ukunchkit was in Joe's hut because he'd sent her there himself. Ukunchkit returned to Tuchaua empty handed, so to speak, and told him the reason Joe had turned her out.

Tuchaua was impressed with Joe's loyalty, but he still wanted Joe's genes. The next morning, soon after Joe emerged from his hut, sat on a log, and began poking the fire with a stick, Tuchaua approached, Ukunchkit following close behind. The shaman held something dark and round in his hand.

A rock, Joe thought. He's going to brain me because he thinks I'm fooling around with her.

But the thing in Tuchaua's hand was not a rock. As Joe rose from the log and faced him, he held out the object and said, "For you."

It was a shrunken head of Ukunchkit's ex-husband.

"Now Ukunchkit is your wife. Her loyalty is to you, Joe."

Ukunchkit stepped from behind the shaman and walked over to Joe. She wasn't much taller than his chest, but the light in her eyes and the smile on her face as she looked up at him weren't those of a child.

"But what about you, Tuchaua?"

"We will go seeking tsantsa soon," the shaman said, and he smiled. "Perhaps I will gain another new wife, too."

Joe gradually became acculturated in the ways of the Huambisa, and he learned not only to live their simple lifestyle but to appreciate its unhurried pace. Tuchaua taught him how to hunt the tapir, python, birds, big cats, and other prey for their flesh and skins and plumage. The hunting was easy, too. They rarely had to walk more than a few miles to bring back enough meat to last out the week.

Tuchaua showed the erstwhile engineer how to use everything from their prey, including the skins. Even the teeth and bones were used for handicrafts and sorcery. Before long, Joe was stripped to a loincloth and a brilliantly feathered headdress of his own fashioning, squatting over fire, and roasting a dart poison frog alive to force it to secrete its toxic sweat. Unlike many of the Jívaro and even other Huambisa, Tuchaua's people favored the frog's toxin over curare, which was more difficult to prepare and less instantly lethal.

And there was always Ukunchkit. Ukunchkit carrying her tarpo, a sharpened stick used for agriculture, or bearing an armload of fruit or a coconut bowl filled with honey. And in the night, there was her own fruit, her own honey. And her ex-husband's tsantsa hung over their pallet to ensure that all things marital remained blissful. By the next year, they had a son, and the year after that, a daughter.

* * *

Together with Tuchaua, Joe went seeking tsantsa, though he understood that the shrunken heads weren't the real point. Tuchaua had explained that a man had three spirits. His *wakani* was his own, and survived his death. But he also had *arutam*. To Joe, this seemed something like a cross between visionary insight and some kind of spirit power. Whatever it was, it supposedly protected a man from violent death. A man could gain arutam by going on a soul journey in which he communicated with plants and animals and learned to live in harmony among them. A man also could steal another man's arutam by killing him in battle.

The problem with that was the defeated foe's third spirit: his *muisak*. This was a vengeful spirit created when a warrior imbued with arutam was killed. The muisak not only would spiritually assault his killer and family, it would travel to the underworld to do harm to the killer's ancestors. The only way to control a defeated foe's muisak was to cut off his head. Tuchaua didn't know how long ago his ancestors started shrinking the heads, but he said there were two reasons. Neither involved any kind of ritual. The first was to keep the heads, the tsantsa, as a souvenir of a successful battle and as a reminder to captured women of who was boss. The second was tied to the first in a practical way: Full-sized, untreated decapitated heads had a way of rotting quickly in the jungle, making them problematic and unpleasant keepsakes. Somewhere along the line, the Jívaro began to cure and shrink the heads to keep their homes a little more tidy, and in the process, they created one of the few Jívaro knickknacks.

134

Joe went with Tuchaua, but not to take his own tsantsa, which he was reluctant to do. He might have begun to acclimate to his environment and the behavior of his companions, but he wasn't yet ready to murder in cold blood and then cut off the head of his victim. Nor had he built up sufficient animosity against the man of the household they raided. Animosity, apparently, was the key to who a Jívaro man attacked. They built up hatred for each other over a long period, frequently as part of some sort of family feud, but just as often over some obscure wrong or slight. Finally the animosity would erupt in murder, and with the Jívaro, there was plenty of that.

Instead, he went along to watch Tuchaua's back. It seemed to Joe like it was some sort of test of his strength and will. He was determined not to fail. He didn't want to disappoint his savior, who was, Joe recognized, a special sort of man. A man of deep knowledge and wisdom. Never mind that an engine would baffle him. Joe knew engines, but that was nothing. An engine was just a dead thing given artificial life when it was running.

Tuchaua knew the jungle like no other, and he had the names of hundreds and hundreds of kinds of birds and an equally deep grasp of the other animals and of the incredibly diverse plants. At any time, you could look in any direction and see thirty types of plants. Then you could take a hundred steps and see thirty different ones. And Tuchaua knew them all, especially those with medicinal or magical properties.

He'd also saved Joe and made him feel better than he had in thirty years. And somewhere along the line, the craving for alcohol dropped away almost unnoticed.

So Joe was determined not only to protect Tuchaua, but remain steadfast, no matter what happened. The raid tested that resolve. It ended in a violent and bloody fight between Tuchaua and his opponent, a semi-distant neighbor named Isawant. The feud between Isawant and Tuchaua was of long standing, and the latest insult had been when Isawant crept into Tuchaua's environs and stole some special plants that were growing about a mile from Tuchaua's hut.

Joe had no idea how Tuchaua knew the plants were gone much less that Isawant was the one who'd taken them. It probably didn't matter. The Jívaro, he'd learned, were a pretty volatile people, quick to take deadly offense at the least slight, real or imagined.

The neighbor had protected himself well, and his arutam was powerful, but eventually, Tuchaua managed to pierce him with a magic spirit dart. The tsentsak weakened the neighbor's hold on life, and Tuchaua had to strike before Isawant could employ a pener uwisin to heal the spirit wound.

Tuchaua found Isawant at home, shouted his intentions, and bearing a short, metal-bladed spear, flung himself at his opponent. Isawant was surprised by the attack, but a Jívaro man always has weapons within reach. Tuchaua already had told Joe that no poisons would be involved in the fight. This was a battle for supremacy, not just victory. Joe watched, his whole body electrified, as the fighters jabbed at each other, each drawing blood from gaping wounds. And finally, both men, gripping knives, fell to the ground and grappled, looking for an opening. Tuchaua found one first, and his knife slid between Isawant's ribs. Isawant gasped and tried to slash Tuchaua's face, but the strike was weak and slow. Before it could land, Tuchaua withdrew his blade and rammed it again into Isawant's chest.

Isawant gasped, dropped his knife, and fell back, blood pumping slower and slower from the wounds. But even if Isawant was dead, or nearly so, Tuchaua wasn't finished. His people frequently mutilated the bodies of their defeated foes, and he picked up his fallen spear and went to work. When he was done, there was just a bloody tatter of a body where a man had once been. Tuchaua smeared his body with his victim's blood then used his knife and spear blade to cut off the head, which he held aloft, fearsome glee distorting his features.

Joe thought he was going to vomit. But he didn't. There was something too primeval about it. If he'd seen a civilized man do what Tuchaua had done, he'd have run far and fast, but here in the forest, it seemed almost inevitable. There were no laws here except survival. If something or someone threatened that survival, it or he should die in a manner that would send a clear warning to others inclined to encroach on one's livelihood and well-being.

Joe might have been the only person to accompany Tuchaua, but somehow all of Tuchaua's immediate tribe knew of the feat before Joe and Tuchaua even got back to Tuchaua's hut with Isawant's former wife. The taking of tsantsa called for a celebration called *numpenk*, which Joe understood to mean something like "his very blood."

Numpenk was, Tuchaua told Joe, the first of three feasts that marked a successful raid. Each feast was about a year apart. The reason for the separation was to give the killer time to gather a new harvest since it was he who provided all the food and libation. By custom, all the people of the tribe were invited, and numpenk usually lasted several days.

"It is well that the taker of tsantsa gains his enemy's arutam," Tuchaua said smiling, "since he is usually impoverished by the celebration afterward."

The celebration was something Joe would never forget. There were more than a hundred people, some who came from as far as twenty miles. Until now, he had no idea there were so many people in Tuchaua's immediate tribal group. The Huambisa did not live in villages. Their huts were scattered throughout their range, and because of their volatile nature, they tended to come together only for feasts. There was food and music and revelry, but it was all pretty weird, Joe thought, since the Jívaro men, who were naturally aggressive and easily affronted, tended to avoid eye contact. They also covered their mouths when they talked to avoid spreading their saliva, which they considered precious.

The center of the celebration was a big iron pot of manioc beer, and almost everybody imbibed, which ramped up the aggression factor, and it was not uncommon for scuffles to break out. Joe kept his distance from the pot. At the time, he hadn't had a drink in more than two years, and he thought that was pretty good for a dedicated rummy. He felt cleaner and better than he had in decades, and it might not entirely have been because he was sober, but that probably contributed. The other reason he kept back was that the women all spit into the pot to aid the fermentation of the manioc mash. Apparently female saliva wasn't as precious as male saliva. Even so, Joe didn't think he was desperate enough to get drunk to start drinking stuff that fifty women had spit in.

But there was that concoction Tuchaua made from the leaves of a bush growing near the door of his hut and two other herbs he kept dried in leather pouches. It was no accident that the plant grew there. Tuchaua cultivated it and several other nearby plants with great care. That concoction was something else.

"You do not drink the beer?"

Joe still felt like an outsider, and somewhat abashed by the sheer number of tribesmen all around. He hadn't seen this many people together in one place in a long time.

"No. It's not for me."

Tuchaua nodded. He, too, was sober, and Joe had never seen him drink alcohol.

"Perhaps you are ready for an arutam encounter. Come with me."

The shaman took Joe to the bush beside the hut door, pointed out how to tell choice leaves from those of lesser quality, and indicated how many to pick. Then he showed the sailor how to crush and steep the leaves and mix in the herbs from the pouches to make the drink. An arutam encounter, Joe learned, was when the soul took a journey into some sort of netherworld where it could communicate with the souls of all the plants and animals.

"It will allow you to live in harmony among them," Tuchaua promised.

It had to be the nastiest drink Joe had ever voluntarily swallowed, but he drank it all down. Tuchaua downed his own cup of the brew. Then he took Joe over to a small alcove cut in the forest wall. At the back was the bole of a towering tree, and it was a spot where Joe could sit and be comfortable and also be out of the way.

"You will journey soon," Tuchaua said. "Do not be afraid. When the journey is finished, you will return here."

He left Joe there and went back into his hut. Joe felt like he was in some sort of box seat at the theater, watching a complex and ancient drama unfold before him. He saw people eating and drinking and talking and fighting. He saw people dancing and chanting, and even some coupling.

Then something changed. It wasn't that the scene before Joe was any different. It was he who was different. He felt like he was swelling inside, and then the swelling burst through his skin. The people in front of him took on the forms of caricatures as the swelling sensation merged with the forest around him. He looked around at the embracing foliage, up at the twisted branches above. They rustled in response to his attention. The foliage beckoned.

The people didn't matter. It was the jungle that was the all. Almost without volition, Joe crawled around the trunk of the tree and a little way through the low growth. At last, the revelry around Tuchaua's hut receded into a muffled mutter, and Joe lay back on the forest floor, staring up at the branches of the towering canopy. Sparks of sunlight fell like dazzling rain between the leaves. The jungle embraced him. Animals came to him and spoke their names and welcomed him. A vine told him to consume three of its leaves if he was constipated. Other plants spoke. There were so many, that he could remember only a few of their names.

And he understood in the marrow of his bones that the jungle was a huge, living organism with the Amazon River pulsing in annual diastole and systole through its heart. Every plant, every animal, and every rock was alive. Everything had its place and function. One only had to open up to it all and take it in, like food for the soul, to live in harmony with it.

The forest spoke to him for an uncountable time, then something remarkable happened to refocus him. Joe saw a stealthy movement in the branches overhead. It was the head of a huge python creeping along a branch almost directly above Joe. Normally, a python would not dare approach a full-grown human much less attack. But an incapacitated human was easy prey.

"I am going to crush and eat you," the python told Joe. "It is the way of the jungle."

"Yes," Joe thought. "It is the way." He didn't want to die, and he especially didn't want to be crushed to death, but his arms and legs wouldn't work right. There was no way he could escape the snake.

That's when the ocelot came. As Joe saw it edge through the foliage just five feet away, the rational part of his mind, which was still operational even if it was sequestered, knew he should be as afraid of the cat as he was of the snake. But the ocelot ignored Joe as it leapt forward and swiped its paw at the python's head. The python evaded the blow and drew up, beyond the cat's reach.

"He's mine," the ocelot told the snake. "Go back into your tree."

"He's yours," the python agreed, and it pulled back and disappeared into the foliage.

So, Joe thought abstractly. Instead of being crushed and eaten, I'm going to be clawed and eaten.

The ocelot padded over to Joe and sniffed at his face. Its breath smelled of carrion, but Joe was too mesmerized by the cat's eyes to do more than notice. The eyes bore into Joe's own, and they were filled with a savage intelligence that was totally alien to the sailor.

Suddenly, the big cat lay down beside Joe, snuggling its rough fur against Joe's naked chest and belly. And so they lay for some time, and as they did, it felt to Joe as if the cat's spirit merged with his own. He felt its implacable ferocity and savage instincts as it taught him how to hunt the tapir. But he also felt its tenderness toward it young. And he knew that the cat sensed his humanness and the worldliness of his experiences and learned from them.

The two of them were still like that when Tuchaua appeared from the bushes. Joe barely recognized him. He was dressed in an elaborate headdress of colorful plumage, and his body was almost completely covered with thick and cracking gray paint that was, in turn, almost completely smeared with blood. In one hand, he clutched the new tsantsa, in the other his short spear. Expressions of wild exuberance animated his features with frightening contortions, but when he saw the ocelot laying next to Joe, his expression became one of savage delight.

The ocelot did not move except to raise its head and glance at Tuchaua.

"Brother Wampurush," the shaman said.

"Ancient among men," the ocelot said.

"Brother Wampurush saved me from Brother Pagki," Joe said. He didn't know how he knew the names. The jungle told him.

"Brother Wampurush," Tuchaua repeated with a nod to the ocelot. Then he faded back into the foliage and was lost to sight.

The ocelot got up soon after, rubbed Joe's cheek affectionately with its own, and then, too, was gone into the brush.

Joe lay there for a little while longer, but then an uproar from the celebration roused him. He managed to rise on tottering legs and stagger back to Tuchaua's hut. There, in the clearing, was Tuchaua, clutching the tsantsa and his spear and reenacting his victorious battle, his bloody painted body contorting as he fought and slew his enemy and took his head.

Then the shaman spotted Joe, darted to him, and dragged him out into the clearing.

"Joe is no longer inki!" he shouted. "Brother Wampurush has given him such arutam that he has defeated Brother Pagki with only a thought!"

Excitement thrilled through the revelers. New blood, and now, powerful arutam. The white man not only was a boon to the Huambisa, he had become one of them and made them more powerful. And suddenly, Joe was in the crowd, dancing and chanting, though he barely knew what he did or said. Eventually, the night faded into an obscure mist, then darkness.

Joe woke in his hut, feeling weak, sore, and sick to his stomach, but somehow more whole than he'd ever felt. He was no longer inki, he was Huambisa. Wasn't that what Tuchaua said? And Joe knew it was true, but not by the words or even by the way the other people in the tribe treated him as one of their own. He felt it deep inside as an overwhelming sense of inner acceptance of himself and by a calm knowing that this place where life had tossed him like some indefinable jetsam was the right place to find himself.

And so, more than fifteen years passed. He hunted and fished and battled rivals. He learned about the ways of the jungle and the plants it sheltered. The five children Ukunchkit bore him grew strong and inherited the large stature and lighter-colored hair of their father.

About half-way through this time, a small band of rubber tappers came through the area. Most were Pálta from over the mountains in Ecuador who had given up their traditional way of life to seek wealth for Europeans. They were led by a degredado, and Joe dredged up enough memory of Spanish to learn that the Pacific Coast was only a month's hike away. The degredado even drew a rude map of the way to Guayaquil. Joe kept the map even though he had no intention of returning to civilization. He liked it too much in the village. He could think of no place better to grow old.

Even though he didn't seem to be doing that. Nor were Tuchaua, his two wives, or Ukunchkit. Joe might have chalked his own feelings of vitality to giving up alcohol and living a robust outdoor life, but he didn't think those factors would have erased his wrinkles, healed lungs deadened by years of smoking, or eliminated the chronic pain he'd suffered since he'd broken his leg in 1936. Or made his hair go from the gray it had been turning for fifteen years back to light brown. Joe didn't know what was going on, but he knew it was real because even though Tuchaua's household didn't seem to age, the rest of the tribe did.

He soon learned why. Apparently, by resisting the temptation provided by the rubber tappers to return to civilization, Joe cemented Tuchaua's trust in him, and the shaman began to initiate him into two secrets of which the rest of the tribe was unaware.

"I have no apprentices among my own people," he told Joe. "I can't trust them. If I show these powers to them, they will turn them against me to steal my arutam. You will have to do."

The first secret involved a complex herbal concoction. That didn't surprise Joe. By now, he'd imbibed the drug potion that sent him on arutam journeys many times, and he knew that some of the jungle plants had truly magical properties. In fact, he often thought that it was the drugs, not the ritual acts, that were important. The rituals just seemed to be a way to order the actions required to properly focus the drug's effects.

Tuchaua spent nearly a week showing Joe how to gather and pick the correct plants, then they sat down outside Tuchaua's hut to grind, mix, and steep the herbs. In the end, there was a small iron pot filled with murky green-brown liquid. Tuchaua ladled the liquid into five cups and passed out the cups to his family group. He said a few words then tossed off his own cup, and the others followed. The stuff tasted pretty nasty to Joe, but no worse than the arutam journey potion.

Within an hour, Joe and the others—Tuchaua included—were sick as hell. It started with vomiting, and Joe quickly became too weak to do anything but lie on his pallet next to Ukunchkit, who was groaning and clutching at her belly. Both of them oozed a viscous yellow sweat. Fever, near delirium, aches, and diarrhea followed. And more vomiting.

Two days later, Joe staggered from his hut. Ukunchkit still lay on their pallet, too weak to move, but they both needed water. Joe fetched a gourd of water from the nearby stream, and on his way back to the hut, he ran into Tuchaua. The shaman looked tired and worn, but somehow, better than he had before the ordeal.

"The sickness will pass quickly," he told Joe, then he went on to the stream.

And it did. Even by the time Joe had returned to his hut and helped Ukunchkit drink, he felt stronger. And by the day's end, stronger still. Stronger than he could ever remember feeling. When he next went to the stream, he found a still nook in the bank where he could see his reflection. Did he look younger?

He did, and Tuchaua told him why. The concoction they'd made and consumed was a rejuvenating potion that Tuchaua had learned to make from his own teacher, the most powerful shaman the Huambisa had ever known. It would, Tuchaua said, reverse the effects of aging up to a point and would extend youthfulness by about ten years. He'd administered the potion to Joe when he'd first arrived, wounded and nearly dead. By then, nothing else could have saved the dying man's life. And that was why none of them seemed to grow older. They weren't aging. And they wouldn't as long as they consumed the potion about every ten years.

And then Tuchaua showed Joe the manin-pasuk.

* * *

Tuchaua woke Joe in the middle of the night while the women and children slept. Curious why the shaman was being so secretive, Joe gathered his weapons, took the unlit torch that Tuchaua handed him, and followed the shaman into the forest. He wondered about the torch. The Jívaro never went into the jungle with torches. But even if the torch remained unlit, the night did not frighten Joe, though he knew it hid predators powerful enough and brave enough to attack a human. Brother Wampurush protected him, and the others—even the jaguar—would sense that and steer clear.

Although the darkness beneath the canopy was nearly absolute, Tuchaua moved with sure feet. He took many twists and turns, but Joe, having hunted this area now for many years, kept his bearings. They didn't travel far—maybe only two miles—before Tuchaua stopped at the base of the worn stub of a mountain that protruded above the rest of the rugged terrain. Joe had been here many times, and he'd even climbed to the low summit to absorb the breathtaking view above the forest canopy.

The forest around the base of the mountain was less dense than where it spread out across the relatively flat lands below, and the gibbous moon lit their way as they went about a third of the way around the mountain to the left. Suddenly, Tuchaua ducked behind a bush and was lost to sight. Joe hurried forward and around the bush only to find the concealed mouth of a seldom-used path that led up the slope along the edges of granite abutments. They climbed about two hundred yards, and Tuchaua stopped. As Joe caught up, the shaman faced him, a serious look on his face.

"You have had many chances to leave and return to your home, Joe," he said. "Why haven't you?"

Joe was nonplussed. He hadn't thought of home in a long time. Then he knew why.

"As soon as we leave this place," he said, "we will go back to our home and to our wives and children."

A twinkle of satisfaction glimmered briefly in Tuchaua's eyes, though his expression remained grave.

"Let us sit." He gestured to some rocks beside the path. "I want to tell you of my master, Yawáa." Yawáa, Joe knew, was the word for jaguar. "That was not his birth name, which he guarded so well that even I never knew it. But like you, his spirit protector was a big cat. Yawáa was a very powerful sorcerer. I learned both wawek and pener uwisin powers from him, and it was he who bequeathed me the longevity formula and the tsentsak that others in our tribe so fear."

Joe knew the Huambisa believed completely in the deadly power of the magic darts, but he wasn't sure he did. He might have been adopted into the tribe, but that couldn't erase his upbringing in a culture based on science and technology. But he understood that Tuchaua was an uncanny man who possessed secrets unknown to Joe's former people.

"I am teaching you what I know for two reasons. First, my people will need a new protector if my arutam is taken and my muisak harnessed by an enemy."

Joe almost laughed. Tuchaua was the most vital and powerful person he'd ever known. The thought of him going down in a defeat of any sort was absurd. But the shaman was obviously deadly serious.

"The second reason is that, of all my people, you are the one who does not covet my power."

144

*　*　*

Yawáa, Tuchaua told Joe, lived at a very special location—near a spring inhabited by a magical presence who taught the shaman two important secrets. The first was the formula for the longevity potion. But the idea of living extremely long lives was useless, the magical presence said, if the inki incursion into Huambisa territory continued. The livelihood of the tribe was endangered, disease had decimated several villages, and the Christian missionaries seemed hellbent on destroying the tribe's social and familial structure. It was time, the magical presence told Yawáa, to kill as many of the inki as possible and drive out the rest.

"All this happened a very long time ago," Tuchaua said. "Long before I was born, at a place called Sevilla del Oro."

The inkis had two main and fairly populous settlements. Huambisi didn't have any numbers over ten, but Joe took Tuchaua to mean that there were many, many thousands. Too many, the spirit presence told Yawáa, for the Huambisa to kill them all without taking crippling losses. So it taught Yawáa the second secret: how to create and control a manin-pasuk. A demon warrior.

The slaughter was great, and when it was over, the vultures feasted for weeks on the remains of the inkis who hadn't escaped. Huambisa land once again belonged only to the Huambisa.

"When I was born, Yawáa was already ancient," Tuchaua said. "So old that the longevity potion barely worked. He knew that his powers had weakened and death was near when he took me under his wing and taught me everything he knew."

Tuchaua was silent for a moment as his eyes gazed into the dark air. Maybe he was remembering Yawáa.

"I have showed you many things since you came to me," Tuchaua continued at last. "Now I'm going to show you the most dangerous secret of all. But first...."

He gestured toward the torch, and Joe handed it to him. It took the shaman only a few moments to light the torch with flint and steel. He rose then and beckoned for Joe to follow him farther along the trail, but they went only about fifty feet before Tuchaua halted in front of a cleft in the rock face that was choked with dead brush.

He bent forward and pulled the brush aside, revealing a narrow, four-foot high hole that opened into the mountain. A cave. In a second, he'd ducked inside, and Joe followed.

The cave didn't seem especially large, though Joe couldn't discern all of its boundaries by the torches' flickering light. It also was remarkably dry. He might have worried that some dangerous creature made the cave its home, but the sight of the altar set up along one wall dispelled any such thought. The altar was constructed of a nearly flat slab of rock about four feet long and two wide. On the stone wall above it hung arrays of colorful feathers, jaguar teeth, and dried plants, and arcing over it all was the articulated skeleton of a python. On top of the slab lay an elongated bundle wrapped in jaguar skins.

Tuchaua approached the altar, beckoning for Joe to follow. They knelt before it on a pad made from more jaguar skins.

"Wrapped in these skins is the manin-pasuk," Tuchaua said. "A manin-pasuk can live for many centuries, but this is not the same one that Yawáa created to kill the inkis. That one was so badly burned in a raid on an Achuar village that it could no longer hunt effectively, so Yawáa destroyed it and made a new one while I assisted and learned."

"Why do you keep it here? So far from the huts?"

"The manin-pasuk can be a terrible weapon to wield against one's enemies, but it can be even more dangerous to its masters. It is dangerous—soul corrupting—to live close to it. I keep it far from me, where few will venture and none will stay, and I go to it when I need it."

Tuchaua jammed the butt of the torch into a crack and peered at Joe in the flickering light.

"I helped create this manin-pasuk under the guidance of Yawáa, bit I am not going to tell you how to create a manin-pasuk," he said. "Perhaps later, when we have more time. I will only say that it was a terrible act to turn a living man into that," Tuchaua gestured to the bundle. "I have told you about the three spirits possessed by men. When we kill an enemy warrior, normally his own spirit, his wakani, departs to the underworld, but his arutam, his spirit power is absorbed by the victor. And we then take his tsantsa to prevent his vengeful muisak from haunting us and our families.

"When a man is transformed into a manin-pasuk, all three of his spirits remain imprisoned within the flesh, but the muisak becomes the most powerful of all." Yawáa shook his head sadly. "It is a terrible thing to do to a man and terrible to behold."

Yawáa had chosen as his victim a man named Tulamayo, who often had threatened to kill Yawáa and steal his arutam. That might have been a possibility. Tulamayo was a powerful warrior with potent arutam, and he posed a definite threat. And his strong arutam guaranteed an equally vindictive muisak. Yawáa and Tuchaua sneaked to Tulamayo's hut, and Yawáa shot him with a blow gun dart bearing just enough of the poison to incapacitate Tulamayo. Then they took their victim back to the magical spring.

There, Yawáa had Tuchaua bind Tulamayo's limbs.

"At first, the manin-pasuk will be very dangerous," Yawáa explained. "It has very great strength and cannot be killed by poisons or piercing, though it can be hacked apart or burned up."

It was night when Tulamayo finally woke. His eyes took in Yawáa and Tuchaua and they filled with murder. And the murder never left them, even after, beneath Yawáa's ministrations, terrible and painful things happened to him. By the time the pain subsided and his body was no longer his own, the murderous rage had coalesced deep in his heart, ensnaring his arutam and trapping his wakani in the grip of his muisak's bloodlust.

Yawáa was right about the strength. Once the deed was done and Tuchaua watched the thing wrench at its bonds and throw itself futilely at the two men, he knew that he was seeing the incarnation of pure destructiveness. It was nearly dawn before the manin-pasuk's struggles ceased, and it simply lay back on the ground and became rigid.

"It is safe now," Yawáa told Tuchaua.

He went over to the inert form and picked it up like a cradled infant, though obviously it weighed considerably more than that. He set it on the stone slab already sheeted with jaguar skins and beckoned Tuchaua to come closer.

"Have no fear. It can't move now unless we command it."

As Tuchaua approached the slab where the manin-pasuk lay, Yawáa began loosening its bonds.

"You would kill us if you could, wouldn't you?" he said to it. "But you can't move, so listen to me very carefully. I am Yawáa and this is Tuchaua. Only we two can give you the power to move. We give you life with our own blood, so that when we release you, you will smell our blood and do our bidding. Remember, if we ever release you and you kill us, you will soon become rigid and never be able to move again. And when we do release you, you will kill for us. You may freely feast on the blood of those you slay, but be certain to return to us while you still can or you will spend an eternity lying on the jungle floor, staring at the branches above or the earth below. And then you will be swallowed by the earth, but you will still know yourself, and you will lie in the damp earth, feeling yourself for many lifetimes, rotting and wishing you had followed my instructions."

"It can hear us?" Tuchaua asked, incredulous.

"It is as fully alive as you or I. But it is locked inside a body that only you or I can animate."

"I? I don't know…."

"You do. The longevity potion. I have shown you how to use it to increase life by mixing it with water. But a pinch mixed with blood will reanimate the manin-pasuk. But be certain that it is your own blood, or it might turn on you. One dollop placed between its lips will revive it for a quarter of a day. Two, half a day. To send the manin-pasuk against an enemy, you only have to tell the manin-pasuk the enemy's name, feed it the elixir, and stand back and let it do its work. I will show you now."

Yawáa pulled a leather pouch from his bag and small bowl from a niche in the cave wall. The bowl was carved from mahogany and darkly stained. He then drew his knife, cut a shallow gash across his forearm, and collected a small amount of blood in the bowl. To this, he added two pinches of powder from the pouch, and stirred it with his finger. Then, he turned back to the manin-pasuk. "You have heard what I have said. I send you now to kill Tatuyo and anybody else of his tribe that you encounter during the day. You will return here by nightfall."

Holding the finger he'd used to stir the mixture to the manin-pasuk's mouth, he smeared a bit between the thing's lips. Then he stepped back, watchful. Tuchaua grew terrified as he saw the thing's fingers then limbs twitch to life. In just a few minutes, its body was supple enough to sit up. The look it gave Yawáa and Tuchaua was filled with hatred and murderous rage. Tuchaua cringed inside, and he didn't foul himself only because he feared to lose Yawáa's respect more than he feared death at the hands of the manin-pasuk.

But the monstrous little thing did not attack. Instead, it made for the cave entrance and was gone into the rising dawn. Soon after, Yawáa and Tuchaua returned to Yawáa's hut near the sacred spring. The next morning, they went back to the cave. The manin-pasuk lay on its back inside the entrance, eyes glaring malevolently but body rigid as a log. It was covered with blood.

Yawáa had Tuchaua pick it up and clean off the blood. Then he laid it on its jaguar-skin pallet. Maybe he sensed his pupil's reluctance to touch the hideous thing and was simply forcing Tuchaua into greater familiarity with their creation. If so, the ploy wasn't immediately successful, but over the course of a decade, Tuchaua grew used to the little monster. After Yawáa was killed by a tsentsak that wracked him with pain, caused a huge lump to grow inside his belly, and wasted his flesh, Tuchaua had no hesitation in sending the manin-pasuk to kill the rival shaman who had shot the dart into Yawáa's soul.

After the manin-pasuk returned from this task and Tuchaua washed it and laid its stiff form on its pallet, he stared at the diminutive humanoid for some time. He was remembering the warrior and how he'd died without releasing his spirits. How they remained trapped inside that rigid flesh. What a horror that was, even for a Jívaro steeped in a culture of violence and bloodshed. And he felt, not for the first time, an uncharacteristic sense of regret.

"One day, Tulamayo" he promised the manin-pasuk as he leaned over it. "One day, I will set you free. But not yet. The inkis come in great numbers, and soon there will be much work for you to do."

Tuchaua could have sworn that the manin-pasuk's eyes glittered with understanding, and he felt an aura of delight and bloodlust wash over him.

"Now," Tuchaua told Joe, "our people are in danger once more. The inkis have learned that there is gold to the east of us, and they have moved in to dig it from the ground. The Aragurana who live there are being driven out, and even as we speak, they send a raiding party to kill me to remove my protection over the tribe so they can take our land."

"We can't let that happen," Joe said, amazed at the power of the feeling of protectiveness that surged within him. These were his people, and he would do whatever it took to safeguard them.

"We will not," Tuchaua assured him. "But this time, we will let the manin-pasuk do our work for us."

The shaman turned to the skin-covered slab and reached out to unwrap the bundle. Joe could tell that whatever was concealed was stiff. There were two layers of skins, and as Tuchaua peeled back the second, Joe recoiled at the sight of the thing the shaman had revealed. But then he moved closer. He could show no fear, and anyway, the thing was inert.

It was like a tsantsa, but one made from an entire body, not just the head. It was about three feet long and covered with dark skin. The body was stocky, with powerful limbs, and the head was somewhat oversized, the scalp bristling with stiff, black hair. The bestial face had basic human proportions but there was nothing human about the ragged fangs protruding from beneath the lips or the yellow talons at the ends of its blunt fingers. The nails on the toes were thick and horny and ended in points sharp enough to rip flesh. The black eyes were partially open and seemed to stare right into Joe's own.

Joe had been a lot of places during his life and he had seen many things, but nothing like this. Then he nearly recoiled again as he realized that the thing was alive. He knew it was alive. He could feel it's power, contained to the bursting point, just waiting to be set free. But it was a power that could only bring death. He found himself thanking the spirits that the manin-pasuk was inert.

Tuchaua stepped up beside Joe and bent over the demon warrior.

"This is Joe," he said to it. "You will obey him as you obey me."

The manin-pasuk did not move, but Joe could tell that it under-stood. Grudgingly.

"We have a task for you," Tuchaua went on. "An Aragurana raid-ing party led by a warrior named Pataxó comes from the east to slay me and steal my arutam. You will slay them instead. All but one. Let that one see you kill the others, then let him return to his tribe to tell the tale. After that, return here."

The manin-pasuk did not react. Visibly. Tuchaua turned to look at Joe, death in his eyes.

"Are you ready?"

Joe could only nod. But he cringed inside when Tuchaua cut his own arm, adding one more slice to the half-dozen scars already there. Joe had always wondered about those scars. Tuchaua collected the blood in a small wooden bowl then produced a leather pouch, opened it, and put four pinches of the powder inside into the blood. After he cinched the bag and set it aside, he used his finger to mix the powder into the blood.

"In this is the longevity formula," he told Joe. "Mixed with blood instead of water, it will give the manin-pasuk life. Each smear in his mouth will give him one-quarter of a day of life. One day for this task should be sufficient."

After smearing four portions into the manin-pasuk's mouth, the shaman stepped back. Joe watched in amazement as the thing began to twitch, then it flexed it limbs with a creaking sound and struggled to sit up. Obviously it was stiff, but it grew more limber by the moment. In just a couple of minutes, it stood up, wavering slightly, looking between Tuchaua and Joe, who felt like he ought to run, even though he knew flight would be futile.

But Tuchaua and Joe were the only ones who could grant the manin-pasuk life, and without them, it would be doomed to live in its frozen but fully conscious state until it rotted or was destroyed by some outside agency. The diminutive demon understood that clearly enough to cut through its bloodlust.

"Go." Tuchaua pointed toward the cave entrance.

With a supple power reminiscent of a big cat, the thing stalked to the entrance and disappeared into the night.

Joe let out the breath he'd been holding and looked at the

shaman. But his next breath gave him no words. There were no words for what he'd seen.

"Let us go home," Tuchaua said. "Our work is done for now, and we will soon hear of the manin-pasuk's victory."

They went back to their huts, and once there, Joe asked Tuchaua if they should prepare to defend themselves against the Aragurana raiders.

"There is no need. Let us sit here and listen to the forest."

They did, and in mid-afternoon, they heard distant yells, cries, and screams. Then silence.

Tuchaua nudged Joe, and they rose and went off in the direction the screams had come from.

They found eight bodies, seven strewn around a half-acre area and the other about half a mile to the west. Or what was left of bodies. The remains were eviscerated, torn, and dismembered—barely recognizable as human. Of the manin-pasuk, there was no sign.

* * *

The Aragurana did not again approach Huambisa territory, but other people did. Degredados, bandeirantes, and other inki began filtering through the forest in greater numbers. Some were explorers, some were rubber tappers, and some were prospectors looking for gold or oil. The Huambisa killed some but many tribesmen were killed also by the inkis' new weapon of choice amid the dense foliage: the sawed-off shotgun.

In the end, the Huambisa simply tried to defend their territory against those who encroached, though some had to flee from the southwestern quadrant of the tribal lands. There, a mining outfit dug a huge, open-pit mine and enslaved local villagers—the men to labor in the pits and the women to labor on their backs.

"It is as Yawáa said," Tuchaua mused one evening as he and Joe swung in hammocks strung near the fire, where a tapir was roasting on a spit. "The inkis come in great numbers. Soon they will try again to overrun our land. Perhaps we should revive the manin-pasuk."

"You're right about the inkis invading," Joe said. "But Yawáa was wrong about one thing: The manin-pasuk is not enough to destroy them all. There are more inkis than there are stars in the sky, and they will keep coming until they have taken everything they want, leaving the Huambisa with nothing."

"No," Tuchaua said sadly. "Their wakani is ill-shaped."

"But their arutam is powerful, and their muisak deadly, and we cannot take tsantsa from all of them." Joe waved around the clearing in which the hut stood. "If we did, we would not have room for ourselves."

The incursion of inkis troubled Joe's mind as much as it endangered the tribe. He'd lived among the Huambisa for nearly twenty years, and he'd become so enwrapped in the tribal culture that Joe Wheeler, the sailor, had nearly vanished from his mind. But not quite. Now, more and more, thoughts about his past life rose. It was almost as if seeing the inki's greed made Joe remember his own. And with that came another feeling he hadn't had in a long, long time: guilt.

The guilt wasn't over the several men he'd killed in battle and whose tsantsa he'd taken. That was normal here—accepted and acceptable. The guilt came every time he greeted his children and their children and saw, with his mind's eye, a fresh-faced girl rush up to him, throw her arms around him, and tell him she loved her daddy.

Iris.

What had become of her? Did she remember her father? And if so, how did she remember him? As the man who had abandoned her?

The guilt was like the shoot of a fast-growing jungle vine that soon had twisted itself inextricably through the branchings of his thoughts. And before long, the groping vine touched and awakened the scheming part of his mind. Did he really belong here in the Amazon forest? Tuchaua had taken him in, and his tribe had accepted him, but inside, Joe was still inki. He remembered living somewhere besides a dirty hut in a lonely, out-of-the-way place. Somewhere clean, with beds and sheets and movies and restaurants. Somewhere that he truly belonged.

The scheming part of his mind also told him something else. If he could take the manin-pasuk back to civilization along with the longevity powder, he could become very rich and powerful for a very long time. He could live in luxury, not in filth with a bunch of savages. And he could exact revenge. His first target would be the members of the inquiry board who cashiered him, the owners of the

153

line, and the people responsible for the faulty parts that had caused the fire. Those who still lived.

Joe laid his plans and memorized the map that the inki had given him so long ago. He also spent many months collecting the ingredients for the longevity potion and making enough of the powder to last a very long time. Finally, when Tuchaua was away from home, attending a person afflicted with a tsentsak, Joe acted. He hurried to the cave, put the manin-pasuk, powder, and the book on maritime law into his old duffel bag, and headed west.

He no longer had any trepidation about making his way through the forest and over the Andes alone. He now knew how to survive in the wild. It took several weeks, and the duffel containing the heavy manin-pasuk was a struggle to drag over the mountains, but he finally arrived in Guayaquil. His appearance, dress, and weapons caused a stir, but the thing that amazed him most was just how rusty his native tongue had gotten, like some old engine exposed too long to salt water.

He had no money, and he may have been old in terms of total years, but the longevity formula made him younger, and the forest life had made him strong. He found work on the docks, and though it took a year, he finally accumulated enough cash to buy passage back to the States. Back to Houston to find Iris.

And to meet Stroud.

8: POSSESSION

JOE WHEELER DIDN'T tell Stroud all of that. In particular, he left out that the powder could be used to increase longevity. But he told him enough, including the fact that the manin-pasuk could be activated, though not how. Not that Stroud believed much of it. The timeline of the story just didn't add up. If Wheeler was already into his late twenties by the time World War I broke out, he ought to be ninety, at least, not the sixty something he appeared to be.

But Stroud didn't care about the details as long as he got his hands on that doll.

"You gotta believe me, John," Wheeler said in conclusion. "It wasn't no picnic up in that jungle."

"You sure tell a good story," he told Wheeler.

"Didn't figure you'd believe me," Wheeler replied.

"The truth doesn't matter where that thing is concerned," Stroud said, gesturing toward the doll. "The way it looks speaks loud enough."

The old sailor seemed to relax a little.

"Okay," he said. "You say you're gonna finance my trip to Minneapolis. How much did you have in mind?"

Stroud took a moment to rapidly calculate his available funds. He didn't want to drive Wheeler off by lowballing it, but he didn't want to go overboard, either.

"I could go you a grand," he said. "And I'll buy your bus ticket to Minneapolis."

"How about plane fare? I never been on a plane."

"All right. When do you want to leave?"

"I'd leave right now if I was sure you'd still be here when I get back."

"Does it look like I'm going anywhere?" Stroud asked, waving around the shabby room. "I couldn't afford to if I wanted."

"You can afford to give me a grand," the sailor pointed out.

"Which leaves me with just about nothing," Stroud lied. He had nearly forty grand stashed in various banks along the carnival's circuit—money he'd scraped to save and kept hidden from Sara.

Wheeler thought about it long and hard. This Stroud fellow was right. He could have killed Joe while he was sleeping and taken everything. But here he was, offering to help. Wheeler didn't really trust Stroud. He didn't trust anybody except Tuchaua and Ukunchkit, even though he'd betrayed them. But he really didn't have a choice. Stroud was right. He couldn't lug the manin-pasuk all over the country. And Minneapolis was a big city. Iris might have moved from the address her stepfather had given him, and it might take a while to find her.

"Okay," said at last. "Gimme the money."

"I don't have that kind of cash lying around," Stroud said with a short laugh. "I'll get it out of the bank tomorrow and then take you to the airport."

"I gotta have a suitcase," Wheeler said. "You can keep the manin-pasuk in the duffel. He fits pretty good in there."

The next morning, with Wheeler riding along, Stroud went to the bank and withdrew $1,500. He gave Wheeler a thousand and kept the rest to pay for the suitcase and air fare. The old man fumbled through the cash like it was a foreign object.

"Don't lose that," Stroud warned. "There's no more where that came from."

"This is my Iris," Wheeler said, waving the wad. "I ain't gonna lose her again."

That night, Stroud took Wheeler out for a good meal at a nearby Piccadilly Cafeteria.

"Gotta fuel up for your trip," he told the old man.

"Long as you're buyin'."

When they were done, Stroud drove them back to the apartment. He didn't know what else to do. He really didn't want to spend the evening with the old man, but he was afraid that Wheeler might have second thoughts and take off with the doll if Stroud didn't watch him.

He needn't have worried. As soon as they got back, he switched on the little black-and-white TV that sat on his dresser, and as the picture and sound faded in, Wheeler stared.

"Is that one of them TVs?" he asked, peering at the set.

"It is," Stroud said, puzzled until he realized that Wheeler had been out of touch during the time that TV had taken over the airwaves.

"I heard about 'em. Like having movies in your own home. How come there ain't no color?"

"There are color sets," Stroud explained, "but they're too expensive."

Wheeler was fascinated with the TV, and the evening passed with him glued to the set while Stroud sipped whiskey and stared with equal fascination at the doll.

In the morning, Wheeler packed his few belongings, leaving only the doll wrapped in its jaguar skins and encased in the duffel. Stroud drove him to Hobby Airport, bought him a round-trip ticket to Minneapolis, and walked the old man to the gate.

"I'm kinda scared," Wheeler said as they watched through the concourse's wide windows as planes landed, debarked and embarked passengers, and took off, roaring, into the sky.

"Nothing to it," Stroud assured him. "Just like a bus only faster and higher off the ground." Stroud had never been on a plane in his life, but he figured that's how it would be.

And then it was time for Wheeler to board the plane.

"You sure you're going to be here when I get back?"

"We're partners in this thing," Stroud said. "You find Iris then come back, and we'll make a bundle. After that, you can take care of her for the rest of your life."

Then Wheeler was gone through the boarding gate. Stroud watched long enough to see the plane surge into the sky before leaving the airport.

Back at the apartment, he was tempted to take the doll out of the duffel and look at it once more, but that could wait. Instead, he quickly packed, gassed up his car, and left Houston, heading for Dunnison.

The carnival's wintering grounds were just the same as when

Stroud had left for Houston: dismal and surrounded by pine trees. No wonder he'd left. But he was back now, with something in his possession to keep him preoccupied.

No one said much to him the first few days. Stroud wasn't the best liked among the carnies, and some of them thought he'd driven Sara away. Fuck 'em, he thought. She left because she wanted to, not because he had anything to do with it. The one operator he did look for and missed was Seraphina. She and Bull Martin were in Florida, and it made his blood boil just thinking about it.

It was just as well that she wasn't around and that the other carnies left him alone. He had a lot to do as he pondered the future and worked up the rudiments of his shtick concerning the doll. He used Wheeler's tale as the backstory for the spiel, playing up the headhunting and mayhem.

Finally, he thought he was ready to approach Dixon. He slid the doll into the duffel and carried the bag to the truck. It was a quarter of a mile to Dixon's house, and Stroud wasn't about to carry the doll's seventy pounds there and back. He drove down the dirt drive, parked in front of the house, dragged the duffel off the seat, and toted it up the porch steps to the front door.

Dixon answered on the third knock.

"Stroud," he said as soon as he saw who his visitor was. "Heard you were back. Sara still gone?"

"Her choice," Stroud said.

"They come and they go," Dixon shrugged. "What you want?" His eyes rested on the duffel sagging from Stroud's shoulder.

"Half an hour of your time."

"Time's cheap this time of year. Come on in."

Stroud had never been in the house, but there was nothing special about it. It was just an old two-story frame farm house. Dixon led him through the front hall to a living room sparsely furnished with a shabby sofa fronted by a coffee table and a couple of armchairs with side tables. Faded wallpaper lined the walls. Wallpaper with vines and leaves. Stroud tried to ignore it, noticing the one new amenity in the room: a color console TV against the wall opposite the sofa. It was on, showing a baseball game. Dixon went over, shut off the TV, then turned to Stroud.

"I want to start my own act," Stroud said, feeling lame.

"Okay," Dixon said, nodding toward the duffel. "Show me what you got."

"Don't you want to hear about it first?"

"Ain't no use in hearin' if the seein' don't pan out," Dixon said.

Stroud lowered the duffel and laid it on the coffee table, wondering if it would collapse under the doll's weight. Carefully, he pulled out the doll, tossed the duffel aside, and unwrapped the jaguar skins.

"Holy fuck," Dixon breathed. "Where the hell did you get that thing?"

He came closer, bent, and peered at the doll.

"Came across it in Houston. Bought it off an old sailor who said he stole it from a tribe of headhunters down in the Amazon. I've been working on a spiel based on his story."

"Well, it better be a good one to go with that, otherwise it would be like putting a diamond into a tin-foil ring. This is the best damn gaff I've ever seen, and I've seen plenty." Dixon straightened and looked at Stroud. "You wouldn't consider selling it, would you?"

"Not a chance. I've been waiting for something like this for a long time."

"You and the rest of us." Dixon stared at the doll for a few moments longer. "All right," he said. "You got your chance. Make the best of it. You'll need a tent. Tell you what. I think you've got something special here. I'll trade you a tent for your ball-toss game, even-steven."

That night, Stroud sat in his trailer, drinking whiskey and working on his spiel. He only had about a month to develop and memorize it so that every detail would pop into his head at the right moment. And the more lurid, the better. At first, Stroud set the doll on the narrow kitchenette table so he could see it and take inspiration. But the drunker he got, the freakier the thing was. He could have sworn that it was watching his every move and was just itching to get at him.

That was ridiculous, of course, but as he rewrapped it in its skins to hide its face, he realized that that was the way to play it. The doll —the manin-pasuk—was alive, like Wheeler had said, but frozen, and it was just waiting to flex its body into a killing frenzy.

Yes, Stroud thought. There was a killing to be made, and the doll was the key.

During the next few weeks, in addition to working on his act, Stroud found a local cabinet maker who constructed a sturdy wooden case with a glass lid that could be fastened down or removed entirely. The doll fit perfectly in its little coffin.

Most of the carnies who'd been wintering elsewhere returned by late February to spruce up their trailers, repair their games and act venues, and otherwise get ready for the long season ahead. Seraphina and Bull came in toward the end, looking happy, tan, and wealthy by carny standards. Seraphina and the Serpent was a winning act. But Stroud had too much to do to keep a steady eye on them. They weren't going anywhere that Stroud wasn't, at least not until November.

At last, the carnival pulled out of the wintering grounds and headed for the first town on its circuit. When they arrived, roustabouts under Hick's direction set up Stroud's tent and spread sawdust across the grass inside and out. The top line of the lurid lettering on the sign outside the tent proclaimed: "Do you dare face evil incarnate?" Below that, in large red and yellow letters blazing like fire, read: "The Terrifying Devil Child from the Amazon." And below that was a disclaimer: "Management not responsible for deaths from fear."

"Wasn't so long ago it was you bringing the sawdust," Hicks said to Stroud as the roustabouts went about their work.

"That was another lifetime ago," Stroud replied.

"Yup. Guess it was. So what's this Devil Child? Dixon says it's a pretty good gaff. Maybe the best he's ever seen."

"It's special, all right," Stroud said. "Come on in sometime and you can see it. No charge for you, Hicks. You got me going here."

"I appreciate that. Right now, I got too much to do. But good luck with your act. Dixon says you got a winner."

Maybe, but Stroud's first show was a miserable failure. It was a lot harder to keep an audience's attention than it was to draw a gullible teenager with the lure of a big plush teddy bear. His carefully memorized story disintegrated beneath the stares of two dozen eyes, and his delivery was stilted and stumbling. By the end of the night, ten shows later, he was completely drained.

He knew he'd have to improve both the story and its delivery, and he'd have to get used to the gazes of his audience members, which ranged from the skeptical to the moronic. But he knew something else just as important. His story and its delivery didn't really matter. Once he whipped the cloth off the glass-fronted case and the rubes saw the doll, they were hooked. He could say nothing at all and still have a hit.

Even so, he vowed to improve his act. And his props. The doll was good by itself, but it could be better. It was one thing to claim the doll might come alive and attack the audience, but they had to believe it might actually happen. He began constructing a spring-loaded pad set into the case beneath the doll. When it was perfected, he could step on a pedal to release the catch, and the pad would jerk the doll forward a little. Not too much—he didn't want it to topple out onto the sawdust—but just enough to give the audience a thrilling surge of fear. The first time he tried it in the tent alone, he had to admit it was a pretty freaky effect, though he could hear the sound of the spring uncoiling. He hoped his audience would be so focused on the doll to notice.

He implemented the new effect about a month into his act. By then, he'd grown used to the eyes of the audience on him, and his patter had smoothed out. He even added a few lurid details—some garnered from the story Wheeler had told him, some invented. He thought that the story was now good enough, but he still had to work on its delivery to make the biggest impact when he finally revealed the doll.

The night he tried the new effect for the first time, he was so intent on watching for the audience reaction that he almost fumbled it. It was the first show of the night, and the case with the doll was propped up on the table he used to hold it. After a few minutes of letting the rubes look at the doll through the glass lid, he opened the lid so the doll wouldn't crack the glass when it popped up.

"I've opened the case, folks, so that you can see the Devil Child's eyes. Look closely, folks. Those aren't glass eyes like you see in taxidermy. Those are the real thing, and at this very moment, the Devil Child is looking right at you with only one thing on its mind." He paused a beat for dramatic effect. "Blood," he intoned at last. "If this little thing could come alive right now, it would lay waste to everyone in this tent. But don't worry, folks. It's safe for now. Only the Jívaro witchdoctor who created it can make it come alive, and thankfully, he's still down there in the Amazon jungle."

The audience chuckled, which was Stroud's intent. Loosen them up, he thought, right before jerking their chains.

"So come on up, now, folks. This might be the only chance you have to see this little monster up close."

The twenty or so people in the tent edged toward the table, some craning forward to get a better look. When they'd gotten close enough, Stroud felt with his foot for the pedal to release the spring, but his foot only found sawdust.

Fuck! he thought. He'd buried the pedal in the sawdust to hide it, and he'd lost it somehow. He couldn't get down and grope around for the damn thing or he'd give it all away. Then, just as a ten-year-old boy was reaching out to touch the Devil Child's face, Stroud's toe snicked against something hard. He lifted his toes and levered his foot down on the pedal.

The effect was even better than he thought it would be, thanks to the kid trying to touch the doll. The spring sprang, jolting the Devil Child forward, causing its forehead to bump the kid's outreached fingers. The kid screamed and grabbed his father, but the sound was almost lost in the cries of the other people in the tent as they all jumped back about three feet.

"Careful, now, folks," Stroud improvised, stepping forward and closing the case's glass front. "I think that was just a freak twitch. Don't worry. This case is specially constructed with bullet-proof glass. Even if the Devil Child came fully alive right now, it couldn't get out of there. But we better play it safe for now. The exit is right this way." He ushered them toward the tent flap. "Don't panic, now, and be sure to tell your friends and neighbors to come in to witness the Devil Child for themselves."

When the tent was empty, he went back to the case and looked at the doll. Fucking eyes really did look like they were staring into him with malevolent intent.

"You and me are going places," Stroud told the doll as he reloaded the spring mechanism.

The rest of the shows that night were sold out. And so it went as the season progressed. The first audience in a new town would be only adequate, but word quickly spread that the Devil Child was something to see. And Stroud frequently noticed repeat customers. He was pretty amused by that. Seemed to him that they'd get some inkling that things weren't on the up-and-up since he was delivering the same shtick every show, and the doll would faithfully pop out at the end. Then he realized that, just like his patter, it wasn't the effect that mattered but the Devil Child itself. Stroud didn't believe that the thing really was alive, but he had to admit that it held a strange sway over those who gazed upon it.

By the time the end of the second month rolled around, Stroud had his spiel down pat, and his tent was packed every show, every night. They were in Dry Creek, Louisiana, and he was in the middle of his fourth show, when he saw a familiar face in the audience. Most of the carnies had come in to see the show at least once, so seeing another wasn't surprising. But this was a carny he hadn't expected to see: Seraphina. And Stroud noticed that Bull wasn't with her.

The last two months had been hectic for Stroud, what with working up his act, fixing up his tent, and perfecting the spring mechanism, and all that time, he thought of practically nothing but the doll. Practically, because Seraphina was never far from his thoughts, especially during the long nights alone inside his trailer. Sometimes, he even wished Sara was still around to provide physical release, but he knew that he was sugar-coating the memories and forgetting the consequences of ignoring their diverging needs.

When he spotted Seraphina standing at the back, he nearly dropped his lines, but he recovered and ignored her as he went through his spiel. But he kept a surreptitious eye on her when he tripped the spring mechanism, and was gratified to see her jump along with the rest of the audience. Then, as the rubes shuffled cautiously forward for a better look at the Devil Child, she slipped out of the tent, into the early evening.

Well, he thought. I guess she's as curious as the rest about my little prize.

He tried to put her out of his mind, but her face and lush body kept popping into his imagination all through the rest of the evening. When he finally shut down at midnight, he went back to his trailer hauling the Devil Child's case on the dolly he'd bought. No way he was going to leave the doll unattended for some unscrupulous carny to walk in and walk out with it, and he sure wasn't about to carry the thing back and forth to the tent every day.

He stowed the case in the trailer, retrieved the bottle of bourbon from the kitchenette, and went outside into the relative cool to drink and contemplate Seraphina's visit.

Could be she was just curious like the rest of the carnies, but Stroud hoped it was something more. In less than half a season, his act was out-grossing all the others except for Seraphina and the Serpent. Stroud guessed that sex would always outsell horror, but maybe even that would change. As an act, Seraphina and the Serpent was pretty much limited to adult men, though women occasionally attended the performances. But the Devil Child attracted everyone Seraphina and the Serpent did, and more. In any case, Stroud's act was now definitely up in Seraphina's league. She had to be interested in that. Later, as he lay in his bunk satisfying himself with little satisfaction, he cursed the roughness of his palm even while dreaming of Seraphina's soft flesh.

Stroud emerged from his camper late the next morning feeling pretty good, and at first, the day got even better. He was sitting around the commissary tent, drinking coffee, when Hicks came up.

"Dixon wants to talk to you," he told Stroud. "He's in his trailer."

What the hell does that old bastard want? Stroud wondered as he strode down the midway toward Dixon's trailer.

"Come on in," Dixon said pleasantly enough when he opened the door to Stroud's knock. "Have a seat." He waved toward a fold-out chair facing the carnival owner's desk.

"How long you been with the outfit?" Dixon asked as he sat across from Stroud.

"I don't know." Stroud thought back. "Ten, twelve years."

"And in two months you went from the middle to the top."

"I guess so," Stroud said warily. What did Dixon want? A higher percentage?

"I been thinking," Dixon went on. "'Bout your act and the current layout of the midway. When you started, I wasn't sure you'd make a go of it, even if you do have that damn good gaff. So I stuck you down at the end of the midway. But you done good, and I'm thinking of moving you up to the middle where you'll be more prominent."

"What's it going to cost me?"

Dixon laughed and waved off the question.

"I ain't gonna charge you any more than I already do. You're raking it in every night, and that means more business for me and everybody. I might be happy with that, 'cept I think you can do even better with a better position and a bigger tent. I don't need to raise my percentage if you keep drawing in the rubes. We all profit, and that's the name of the game."

"I can't afford a bigger tent," Stroud said.

"I can. I'll sell it to you at cost. You can pay it out over the season."

"You're not talking about a partnership, are you, because…."

"Nothing like that," Dixon said, leaning forward, his elbows on the desk. "I just see higher profits by helping you out. Anyway, I know you got yourself something good with that Devil Child, and I don't expect you'll ever sell even a small share of it."

"You're right about that," Stroud said. "So where are you thinking of placing my new tent?"

"Right across the midway from Seraphina and the Serpent. You both got acts connected to the jungle, and I was thinking of getting a few fake palm trees to set up in front, between you and Seraphina. Kinda make a jungle theme in that area. At my expense, of course. I'm hoping that'll attract the rubes even more."

Not that I need it, Stroud thought. I'm drawing them in like flies to honey. But the idea of a bigger tent and better positioning appealed to him. Dixon could spend all the money he wanted on props, as long as Stroud was the one to profit.

"You talk to Seraphina and Bull about that?" he asked Dixon.

"Thought I'd broach the subject to you first. You leave them to me."

"You can count me in. How long until the new tent arrives?"

"Not long at all. Fact is, I got one stored in the barn back in Dunnison. I'll tell Hicks to send a few of the boys for it tomorrow, and they should be back in time to meet us in Sugartown."

"Okay, it's a deal."

Maybe it was a deal, but it wasn't one Bull Martin liked. After Stroud finished his conference with Dixon, he went back to the commissary tent to grab some lunch and another cup of coffee. He got his food and sat down, and a few moments later, he was joined by Hicks, who sat on the bench opposite him.

"Dixon told me what he wanted to talk to you about," Hicks said, an appreciative smile on his face. "Looks like you finally hiked it up to the top."

"Just got there," Stroud said. "Can't brag too much."

"Don't matter. You got that Devil Child and a good pitch. You'll make it big."

Stroud shrugged, but inside he was feeling pretty good. He already figured he had his ticket, but for a long-time carny like Hicks to say it really meant something. He was just about to lift a forkful of scrambled eggs to his mouth when Hicks looked up at something behind Stroud, brow darkening.

Hicks quickly stood, but not before a heavy hand fell on Stroud's shoulder and twisted him around so fast he barely had time to swing his feet high enough to clear the bench. The heavy hand hauled him to his feet, and he found himself facing Bull, whose countenance was fuming.

"What the fuck you think you're pulling, Stroud?" Martin grated.

"Settle down, Bull," Hicks said.

"Fuck you, Hicks. This ain't got nothin' to do with you. This is between me and this cheap piece of shit here."

By now, all the carnies at the commissary were looking on, and Stroud heard camper doors opening in the background as other carnies emerged to see what the ruckus was about.

"So, you cheap piece of shit," Martin said to Stroud. "What the fuck do you think you're doing setting up right across from me and Seraphina?"

"It was Dixon's idea, not mine," Stroud said.

"Well, fuck that. I don't want you anywhere near me, my tent, or Seraphina."

"You ain't got that say," Hicks said.

"I told you to shut the fuck up, Hicks. I don't give a shit what Dixon wants."

"Then you go say that to his face," Hicks said. "And last I heard, it was Seraphina, not you, who's drawing them in. Dixon needs you like he needs another hole in his ass. Maybe he'll just get rid of you, or maybe he'll put you and Seraphina down in the shadows at the end of the midway, where your little porno show belongs."

"What porno?" Bull raged. "We got a dramatic act."

"That's right, and in half a season, Stroud's even with you in bringing in the rubes. By November, he'll be taking in twice what you and Seraphina make put together. You think Dixon's gonna ignore that? You'll be lucky if you get some of his overflow business."

Martin turned from Hicks to Stroud.

"Okay, you cheap piece of shit. Maybe I can't do nothin' about where you set up, but if I catch you looking at Seraphina one time...."

He shook a fist in Stroud's face, then stormed off, shoulders hunched and fists balled.

"Thanks," Stroud told Hicks, though he didn't really feel thankful. Hicks had stepped in for Stroud, who should have taken care of his own problem. Even if he'd been beaten up, he'd still be respected, but letting Hicks do his work for him had made him lose face.

"Don't know what that guy has against you, Stroud. You know him before, or something?"

"Never saw him until I came here, and I never did anything to him. And I never touched Seraphina."

"Well, you let me know if he threatens you again. Dixon don't want no violence on the lot."

"Yeah, I will," Stroud replied, thinking that he was going to have to find a way to eliminate Bull on his own without getting beaten up in the process. Right now, about all that he could do was out earn the striptease act to force Bull's hand economically and attract Seraphina to him. Hell, he figured he might be able to earn enough to let her quit.

The new setup on the midway took three weeks and three towns to accomplish, but when it was done, Stroud had to admit it looked pretty good. His new, larger tent was right across from Seraphina and the Serpent, and five fake palm trees decorated the space between them. Jungle monsters on both sides, he mused appreciatively, thinking of Bull, not the serpent.

But the proximity didn't make Seraphina any more present in Stroud's world. Bull must have threatened her, because Stroud barely saw her, even at the commissary tent. And when he did see her, Bull was always there. Stroud thought about going into town to see if she was eating locally like she used to do before her association with Bull, but he resisted. Even if she was in some restaurant, the strongman would be with her since he never let her out of his sight. And if Stroud was going to get beaten by Bull, he wanted it to be in full sight of the other carnies, not a bunch of townie rubes. That way, Dixon would have to get involved, and Bull wouldn't dare get physical with the carnival owner. If he did, he'd never work another carnival again.

So instead of bedding Seraphina as he dreamed, Stroud contented himself with the lot lizards who thought that some of the Devil Child's magic might have rubbed off on him and that some of it might rub off on them, too. And later, as he sat alone in his camper with the doll, he plotted his future and tried to figure out a way to remove the impediment of Bull Martin from his life.

9: THE FUTURE

"AND THIS, LADIES and gentlemen," Stroud said, holding aloft a stoppered amber vial filled with a colorless liquid. "This is the potion that restores life to the Devil Child."

He paused. All eyes were on the vial, though some nervously shifted back and forth between it and the doll. And that was a lot of eyes. It was Stroud's second season showing the doll, and he'd not only perfected his act, but he'd also learned a lot about manipulating his audience. And the audience was always large—here in Oakdale and everywhere else. The tent was packed full, just as it was every show, every night. People who'd seen the doll the season before were back for another look. Hell, people who'd seen the doll last night were back.

He pulled the stopper from the vial, and was pleased to hear a couple of subdued gasps from women in the audience.

"Don't worry, folks," he said amiably. "My deadly little friend here would need to drink all of this to acquire the vitality to go on a killing spree. But let me show you what just one drop will do."

"No...," murmured someone, but Stroud paid him no mind. He leaned over the doll and carefully dripped a single drop between the doll's dark lips. The liquid was distilled water. Stroud figured a few drops of that nightly wouldn't hurt the doll, and it gave a reason for the doll to jerk "awake" every night on command.

"Watch closely, folks," he said as he straightened. "It takes a few moments to take effect. You'll hear him take a hissing breath when he does."

169

As anticipated, most of the audience leaned closer to see the doll come alive. Stroud waited until most seemed certain that nothing was going to happen and had started to relax when he stepped on his hidden pedal. He'd exchanged the old spring-loaded mechanism for a pneumatic device that made the doll sit forward much more convincingly. The only problem was that the motion was accompanied by a hiss of air, which Stroud had cleverly disguised by claiming the doll was making the sound.

The doll sat forward, the audience jumped back, and Stroud felt, not for the first time, a surge of pride.

I could sell these yokels the dirt out of my pocket, he thought.

Stroud had to admit, though, as he ushered the audience out, that it wasn't his cheap pneumatic pump trick that kept the rubes coming back. It was the doll itself, as if it possessed some sort of inner presence of evil beneath its frozen exterior. And though he now owned the most successful act Hanley Brothers Carnival had ever seen, he had discovered that he wasn't any happier than he'd been the day before he met Joe Wheeler and acquired the doll. And as he stood there, holding the flap for the departing audience, he stared across the midway and knew the reason why.

Seraphina. No. Seraphina with Bull.

The exotic dancer remained attached to the strongman, and Stroud rarely saw her despite the proximity of their tents. But when he did, he was sure she was looking at him with greater curiosity and admiration now that he alone was topping her act. She had to be wondering about him.

But wonder was all either of them could do as long as Bull was in the picture. Give it another season, Stroud reasoned. Another season of big bucks and greater influence. Another season for her to realize that Stroud was her ticket, not Bull.

Another season of waiting, Stroud groused to himself as he closed the tent flap and went back inside to reset the pneumatic lift and tidy up before the next crowd came in. Shit, was that all life was: waiting for this then waiting for that, with nothing ever quite making all that waiting worthwhile?

That night, he closed early, forgoing the last show. Instead, he made a wide circuit of the carnival grounds and came up on

Seraphina and Bull's tent from behind. He wasn't worried about Bull catching him. He and Seraphina had just begun their final show of the night—the one where she disrobed entirely before embracing Bull as the lights went down.

Stroud wasn't sure what he was doing here. Maybe he was just pressing his luck. But he had to get a look at her. The longer he was kept away, the more his desire for her grew. Visions of her riding him endowed his nights with a restlessness that only whiskey in sufficient quantities could quell. He wanted to wake up and see her there, with him. It wasn't love, he realized, but to hell with that. When had he ever been shown love? Fuck love. Call it lust or call it possession, but he wanted her just the same.

Stroud eased in through the flap at the back of the tent, but he didn't go far. He didn't need to. From here in the shadows behind the stage, he could see the act plenty good. He had to admit that Seraphina did a good job. There probably wasn't a limp dick in the house by the time she rubbed her bared breasts against Bull's chest and her crotch against his thigh while the snake pretended to be something else.

Then the lights went out, and Stroud quickly eased back out into the night. With nothing left to do, he went back to his trailer, found the bottle of whiskey he kept in the kitchen, and poured himself a stiff one. Instead of helping erase his despondency, the liquor only brought up memories of Woodville and all the rest of the crap he'd had to deal with in his life. It didn't matter that his mother was an old woman living in obscurity, that Andrew Buchman still owned the town, or that Claire was long gone—where he didn't know, and he couldn't have cared less. Time might have exacted its toll on some of those who'd wronged him, but it hadn't given him the satisfaction of doing the damage himself.

Not that he really cared, anymore. Fuck 'em, he thought. What mattered was the future, but despite his success with the doll, that didn't seem all that bright. Was he doomed to hawk a freakish gaff to stupid rubes for a dollar a pop for the rest of his life, and then return to a cold and empty trailer each night?

The knock came while he was just pouring his fourth drink. It was so faint, he wasn't sure he heard it, but it came a second time.

Who the fuck is that? he wondered. Nobody ever came to his trailer. Nobody liked him that much, and he wasn't the sociable sort. He set the bottle on the counter next to the glass, went to the door, and opened it.

Seraphina was standing there at the bottom of the steps, gazing up at him. She was wrapped in a blanket, although the night was warm.

"You going to invite me in?" she asked.

Stroud suppressed an urge to glance around for Bull, who rarely let Seraphina out of his sight. For a moment, Stroud wondered if this was a set-up. But Seraphina didn't seem particularly nervous and was staring up at him with an open countenance.

"Don't worry," she said. "I sent Bull into town for ice cream. He won't be back for an hour."

Stroud stepped back and ushered her inside. Her odor as she brushed by him was more intoxicating than the liquor he'd consumed. She glanced around, then sat on the bench seat at the table.

"Nice trailer," she said.

"It's new," he said. "Better be nice." He'd bought the Airstream with the profits from his first season showing the doll.

She gave a small chuckle.

"You've been doing pretty well," she said. "You and that hideous little shrunken man of yours."

"Well enough."

"Where'd you get that little bastard?"

"Like I say in my spiel: I got it from a sailor who acquired it in the Amazon jungle."

She chuckled again.

"Sure."

"It's the truth."

She gave him a piercing look that relaxed after a moment.

"I saw you tonight. At the last show. Bull didn't see you, but I did."

"Yeah," he admitted. "I was there."

"You like what you saw?"

Stroud didn't know what her game was or what to do about it.

"You know I do," he said, standing over her, looking down at her upturned face.

She stood and let the blanket fall open. She was naked underneath.

"You gonna do something about it?"

Stroud clutched her to him and ran his big hands down over her hips and buttocks as her mouth hungrily sought his. Her fingers fumbled at his belt and zipper then slipped inside to stroke his scrotum and growing erection.

"Got a bedroom?"

But they were barely there when the door burst open, and an enraged Bull barged in.

"You fucking bastard!" Bull bellowed as he slammed down the short hallway to the bedroom.

Panic wracked Seraphina's features, but Stroud barely had time to react before Bull was on top of him, pounding with merciless fists powered by more muscle than Stroud could muster. All Stroud could do was try to flail away the strongman's punches and protect his face. But Bull quickly wore him down, and the beating only stopped because Seraphina fled the trailer and came back with Hicks and three roustabouts before Stroud was completely senseless. Or dead.

The carnies hauled Bull off Stroud, dragged him out of the Airstream, and dumped him on the ground twenty feet away.

"Don't go back in there, Bull," Hicks warned. "You do, and you're finished around here."

"He was fucking Seraphina!" Bull yelled. "He was fucking my woman!"

"Go back to your trailer," Hicks ordered.

"This is a free country," Bull said, rubbing his fists and wincing. "I ain't gotta do what you say."

"That's right, Bull," said a new voice. "You ain't gotta do what Hicks says, but you better obey me." It was Dixon. "Go back to your trailer, and cool off."

"Fuck you all," Bull snarled, then he looked at Seraphina. "Come on."

"Forget it, Bull," Dixon said. "She's staying with Dottie tonight. And if you harm one hair on her head, you'll never work another carnival as long as you live. You already lost me enough revenue tonight, so don't say another word. Just git!"

Bull gave Dixon one last rage-filled look, then he turned and stalked off into the darkness. Dixon gestured to Hicks to follow him into Stroud's trailer.

"Let's see what the damage is," he said.

Stroud was still conscious when the two men entered the bedroom, but just barely.

"I know you can hear me, Stroud," Dixon said. "I understand what happened here tonight. I don't like it, but I understand. But I'm going to tell you this one time only. You mess around with Seraphina again while she's still with Bull, and I'm going to fire the lot of you. I don't care how much it costs me. I can't have the local law coming down on me for murder and mayhem among my own people. You keep it straight, or you're out." He turned to Hicks. "Get him taken care of. See if he needs a doctor."

With that, Dixon was gone, leaving Hicks staring down at Stroud, sadly shaking his head.

"You gone and done it now, John," he said. Then he bent over the bed. "Here, let me look at you."

*   *   *

If anything good came of the beating, it was the clamor from the rubes that the Devil Child show was put on hold for the rest of the carnival's time in Jonesboro. Stiff, sore, and face swollen and bruised, Stroud was in no condition to stand before an audience five hours a day and act happy about it. But now he knew he had a winner—and how important he'd become to the carnival. During the long days in the trailer, he began to hatch a plan to take over Hanley Brothers. Dixon was a forceful man, but he was old now, and his days of traveling the circuit were numbered. If Stroud could get the cash together to buy him out, he was certain Dixon would agree. Hicks, who probably wanted ownership for himself, might not like it, but Stroud would keep him on. Hicks was a good manager, and his even hand in most matters of dispute made the show run smoothly.

And if Stroud owned the carnival, he could dump Bull at the first crossroads.

By the time the carnival moved on to Leesville, Stroud's body had recovered enough for him to resume the show. But while he

174

could cover the bruises on his body, he couldn't erase the marks from his face. He didn't want to have to cancel his act until his face completely healed, which could take weeks longer. That meant a lot of lost revenue. So he did the next best thing, and it worked out so well that he thought about learning how to use make-up to appear injured, like they did in the movies.

"Sorry about the way I look, folks," he told the audiences in Leesville. "You might think I've had a tiff down at the local road-house, but that just wouldn't be true. No, folks, I'm going to tell you the truth. I was doing a show at our last stop, when I accidentally dropped too much of this life-giving elixir into our little friend's mouth. I managed to get the audience out without harm, but I had to wrestle the Devil Child into submission. As you can see from my appearance, that was no small feat. Thank the Lord above that I didn't give him more, or I wouldn't be standing here now. So rest assured, folks, that I'm going to be extra careful not to make that mistake again."

He said the last with real feeling. No, he wasn't going to make the mistake again of confronting Bull head-on. But Bull better watch his back.

* * *

Nearly a month later, Stroud had healed completely, and he contemplated the make-up shtick but finally nixed the plan. Too much trouble. He'd not only have to learn to apply the make-up convincingly, he'd have to refresh it several times during the night. And that would be wasted effort. The tent was packed full every show, and make-up couldn't make the tent larger. Besides, he didn't want the rubes to think he was constantly so clumsy that he had to do battle with the Devil Child every night. He smiled, thinking that some of they probably would like to see that happen. But of course, it never would.

By then, the carnival was in Crossett, marking the beginning of its sweep through Arkansas. And then, during the last show of the last night in Crossett, there he was, standing at the back of the audience, staring at Stroud. Staring at the doll.

Joe Wheeler.

175

Stroud nearly dropped his lines when he spotted him, and when he activated the pneumatic pump to activate the doll, he felt embarrassed at the sarcastic gleam he caught in the old sailor's eyes.

He was washed out when the final customer left. Or the next to the last one, for there was still Wheeler. There he stood, looking older than before. More defeated. Somehow, it reminded Stroud of the way Charlie Folger at the sawmill had looked in his final months as night watchman.

God, Stroud hoped he'd never look like that. Like the life was oozing out in slow motion through Joe's pores and evaporating, leaving a miasma lingering in the air.

"I see you found me," he said.

"Weren't hard, seeing as how you travel all over the region, advertising yourself." Wheeler's tone gave voice to the same sarcasm his eyes held.

"You ever find your daughter?"

"Yeah, I did. Wish I hadn't. For Christ sake, she looked older than me. I mean, Tuchaua give the potion to me twice…." He suddenly stopped then went on hurriedly. "I mean, I guess I look pretty good for my age. Not like the age I really am."

"I suppose you want your cut of what I've taken in over the last couple of years."

"I do," Wheeler said. "I need a grubstake."

"A grubstake? For what?" Would the old man be content to take the money and go off somewhere else?

"I'm going back to Tuchaua and his people. They're the only ones I have left. I stole our entire future—mine and them—when I took the manin-pasuk, so I'm taking it back to them. They can kill me if they want, but it's the least I can do."

"Sorry, old man. You're not taking that thing anywhere. It's my meal ticket, my future, and a damn good one. Tell me what you want for it. I'll pay you good money."

"Money!" Wheeler looked incredulous. "You already owe me money. You'll pay me what you owe me, and then you'll give back the manin-pasuk."

"Forget it, Joe. You're going to sell me the doll without a fuss, then you go your way, a little bit richer, and I'll go mine."

"You know I can't do that," Wheeler said. "The Huambisa were the only important thing ever happened to me. I gotta take the manin-pasuk back to them, and I ain't gonna go without a fight."

"You called it, old man," Stroud said, and he stepped in.

It wasn't much of a fight. Stroud was a big man with big hands. Long-fingered, rawboned knuckles, knotty with tendons and veins, all dusted with dark hair. It was as if they'd been grafted onto the rest of him. They were manly hands, but they were clumsy hands. Hands meant for a shovel. He could eat and hold a glass and brush his teeth as well as anyone, but when it came to anything else, the tender touch eluded him. Eluded his hands. Clumsy hands. Clumsy with delicate things, clumsy with women.

He hammered a fist into the side of Joe's head, and the old man fell to the ground. Wheeler tried to rise, but he got no higher than his knees before he collapsed to all fours and vomited.

Then Stroud went to work with his big, clumsy hands. Wheeler moaned and pleaded, but Stroud's hands didn't seem to care, because they went on bruising and breaking. And through the red haze that clouded Stroud's vision, he didn't see Joe. Instead, he saw Bull caving beneath his blows, and he liked it. Finally, the sailor just lay there, groaning and twitching.

"I just want to live," he moaned, fingers scrabbling in the sawdust. "I just want what's mine...."

But his words were cut short as Stroud's foot came down on his neck. A crack sounded in the still air, and the old sailor convulsed once then was still.

Stroud straightened, panting, the red haze dissipating. He saw Wheeler lying there, the puddle of vomit nearby. Stroud kicked sawdust over it. Sweeping it under the carpet, he thought sarcastically.

But he couldn't so conveniently get rid of Joe's body. At first, he wasn't going to bury the corpse, just drive out on some country lane, stop at some remote spot, drag the body into the woods, and leave it. But the countryside wasn't as empty as it used to be. Sure enough, somebody might just smell the stink from the road. Or some farm dog would drag home a rotted forearm for its master to see.

So in the end, he still drove toward a remote spot, but he brought

177

along a shovel. The area he chose was half an hour east of Crossett, right along the edges of the Mississippi River basin, though the river itself was another hour farther on. The darkness out here was profound, and he had a hard time spotting side roads, but he finally found a promising dirt track that led into the woods. He drove cautiously down the track, hoping like hell it wasn't somebody's driveway. But the track began to peter out after a mile, so he figured he was safe enough. He parked, hauled the body out of the bed of the pick-up, where he'd hidden it beneath a tarp, and dragged it a hundred yards into the woods. He went back to the truck, retrieved the shovel and a lantern, returned to the body, and set to work.

The sandy soil liberally mulched with rotting pine needles, was denser than the sawdust he'd shoveled in his youth, but his body remembered the rhythm. And his hands were calloused from helping the roustabouts set up and strike his tent every week. He could close his eyes, fall into the familiar movements, and imagine another kind of life. Somewhere else.

But he was still here when he finished the grave: a trench about four feet deep and barely as long as the body. Not the requisite six feet, but it would have to do. Dawn was fast approaching, and he had to be back at his tent by sunup to prepare for the move to Warren. On no sleep. On digging a grave.

On murder.

He bent to dump the body into the hole and hesitated. Then he leaned closer and ripped open Joe's shirt.

"Fucker was telling the truth," he muttered, staring down at two horrendous scars slashed across the dead man's torso. At least about the machete attack.

Without bothering to close the gaping shirt, Stroud levered the body over, and it toppled into the grave. He hastily shoveled the pile of dirt onto it then spread pine needles over the raw mound of earth. In a few months, it would be invisible.

When he got back to his tent, he noticed for the first time that Joe's suitcase sat next to the wall just inside the entrance flap.

Fucker left me everything he had, Stroud thought as he hefted the suitcase and toted it to his trailer. He wondered what was inside, but there wasn't time now to go through it. The roustabouts were already moving about, striking rides and tents and loading trailers. He just tossed the suitcase inside the Airstream, cleaned up a little, then went back to his tent to help.

He was physically exhausted when the caravan headed out for Warren, and he was afraid that he might fall asleep behind the wheel. But a strange excitement buzzed in his brain. It took him a while to realize that it was a sense of total freedom to do as he pleased. He hadn't realized how much he'd dreaded Joe's return these last two years, dreaded having to deal with the old sailor. But all that was taken care of. Now, all that was left was Bull.

That would come in good time, but right now, he felt great, if tired. Luckily, when they arrived in Warren, he didn't have a hell of a lot to do. The carnival wouldn't open for business until the weekend, which gave him plenty of time to plan his next move. He paid the roustabouts extra to set up his tent without his help then went to his trailer, fell onto the bed, and slept the best sleep he'd had all year.

*   *   *

He woke at dawn the next day, having slept nearly eighteen hours. After a quick breakfast at the commissary tent, he went back to his trailer where Joe's suitcase waited.

The suitcase didn't hold anything Stroud hadn't seen before. There were clothes, which Stroud piled in a corner, figuring he'd get rid of them later. There was the book of maritime law, and there were those leather bags. Four of them, each with it's mouth tied by a leather thong. Stroud opened each of the bags and peered at the dried powder inside. It was gray-brown and musty smelling.

Normally, Stroud would have ignored the book of maritime law. Joe had said he bought it to fight his conviction. But a piece of paper poking out from beneath the dirty, worn green cover prompted Stroud to open the book. The paper was a crudely drawn map—obviously the one that Wheeler had used to escape the jungle and make his way to Guayaquil, which was the only feature that was labeled. He set the map aside and thumbed through the book's pages, expecting to see nothing but obscure legal phrases concerning a seafaring world that Stroud didn't give a shit about.

All that was there, and more. The flyleaf and margins of the book were filled with handwritten notes made by some sort of crude pencil. Stroud rubbed a finger across a couple of the words, which smeared. Some sort of charcoal, he thought, visualizing Joe, wearing only a loincloth, squatting beside a fire, writing the notes with the sharpened and burned tip of a small stick.

Joe's writing wasn't neat, and a lot of the words were nearly illegible from smudging, but it didn't take long for Stroud to realize that the notes were a spare diary of Joe's sojourn among the Huambisa.

Might be something here to add to my spiel, he thought, so he doggedly worked his way through the volume. The notes spoke of the attack by Wheeler's guide, the sailor's recovery under the care of Tuchaua, and many other things. Most of the notes seemed to be aids to help Joe remember things about plants, animals, and other aspects of Huambisa life. About half way through, Joe related his otherworldly experiences under the influence of some kind of drug that Tuchaua gave him, and it even included the formula for the drug potion.

Then Stroud came to a long passage about what Joe called a "long life formula." The notes claimed that consumption of this formula, which apparently was contained in the leather pouches, endowed one with ten additional years of life. Wheeler hadn't mentioned that to Stroud.

And then there came the doll. The manin-pasuk. Wheeler detailed everything he knew about the doll, including the story Tuchaua had told him about its origins. The same powder in the leather pouches, mixed with human blood and fed to the doll, would supposedly bring it to life.

Stroud wasn't sure what to make of Joe's diary. The old sailor clearly believed what he'd written, but Stroud wasn't some rube who'd accept any wild story as true. He shook his head. The old sailor must have been mad. He'd spent too much time isolated in the jungle, living like an animal. He was better off being in the ground.

But Stroud kept going back to the book, opening it up, taking in its story and the procedures it laid out. At first he told himself he was just looking for additional elements that would lend credibility to his spiel, but after extracting a few, he found he was rereading

Wheeler's notes for a different reason. Maybe it was the tone of conviction discernible behind the words, or maybe it was the high level of internal consistency in the details. Maybe it was just wishful thinking. Whatever the reason, Stroud found himself being sucked into Wheeler's story, and if he still didn't believe, he was growing more curious. Especially about the part where Tuchaua had sent the doll to kill his enemies.

It's all a crock of shit, Stroud told himself. But during the next week, every time he took the doll out of its case, he found himself wondering. He already knew that there was something special about the thing. Something that made it more than a gaff concocted in some demented taxidermist's workshop. Something that even his yokel audiences felt. Could Joe actually be telling the truth about the manin-pasuk and the powder that could confer longer life?

Well, Stroud sure wasn't going to mix up and drink a batch of potentially fatal poison just to test Joe's veracity. But he was intrigued by the idea that the powder could activate the manin-pasuk so it could deal with one's enemies. Stroud definitely had an enemy. He could mix up that potion and feed it to the doll, per Joe's instructions, and it would work or it wouldn't. Either way, Stroud would be no worse off.

But he couldn't bring himself to do it. Not yet. It was too crazy. It was almost as if accepting Wheeler's story enough to even give it a try would prove to Stroud the one thing he most feared: that he was just another credulous small-town yokel, no better than those he conned every night in his garish tent.

*   *   *

Three weeks of brooding only made matters worse. By then, the carnival was in Nashville, its last stop in Arkansas before heading back to the Lone Star State via Texarkana. Most of the caravan had arrived by Tuesday night, and the roustabouts were well on their way to having everything set up by Thursday. Stroud was in the commissary tent that morning, sipping black coffee and trying to ease through his mental haze and fight back a pounding headache. He was drinking himself into a stupor every night. Wasn't fuck else to do and no other way to ease the mental pain that kept him awake without the alcohol. Or without Seraphina. And now he saw Hicks coming his way. What the fuck did he want?

"Mornin', John."

"I guess it is."

"Dixon wants to see you. He's in his trailer."

"What about?"

"That's for him to say."

"Okay."

Stroud didn't want to talk to Dixon any more than he wanted to talk to anybody else right now, but business was business. He took another swig of his coffee, tossed the remainder into the sawdust, and took the cup to the tub of dirty dishes. In another three minutes, he was knocking on Dixon's door.

"Come in!" Dixon called out.

Stroud opened the door, mounted the steps, and entered the dim interior.

"Shut that fucking door before all the cool leaks out," Dixon snapped.

When Stroud had, Dixon gestured toward the folding chair in front of his desk.

"What's this about?"

"I gotta tell you, John, I ain't very happy right now."

"Something wrong?"

"We've been doing pretty good with our jungle theme," Dixon said. "You as well as me and Seraphina and Bull. But it looks like you gone and screwed that up."

"If you're talking about what happened with Seraphina and Bull, you know as well as I that Seraphina came to me. I didn't go to her. I took the beating and lost money, not anyone else, and I didn't do a damn thing."

"You can say that all you want, but that don't make it so. I lost money, too. Problem is, you can't keep your eyes off that woman. You can't expect her not to respond to that, 'specially since you're making more than her and Bull put together. You might not 'a called her, but she came anyway, you let her into your trailer, and she was stark naked when Bull found you."

"So, what's happened now? Must be something for you to call me in here and chew me out."

"Ain't chewing you out, Stroud. I'm informing you. Seraphina and Bull are leaving at the end of the season, and they won't be coming back. They're taking a job with Peabody Attractions out in the Midwest."

"You're saying they're leaving because of me?" Stroud snorted. "If they do, they're fools. They make more as part of our jungle than they can separately."

"Tried to tell them. I think Seraphina might listen, but Bull says he won't work anywhere around you." Dixon stared at Stroud for a long, uncomfortable moment. "Aside from this, you ain't been any trouble since you came here, and these last couple of years, you turned into our best earner. I ain't gonna throw that away, but I gotta have your word that you'll stick to the straight and narrow from now on. Seraphina and Bull are good earners, too, and I'm gonna be poorer when they leave. Don't want nobody else to leave on account of trouble that didn't have to happen."

"If there's trouble, it won't be coming from me," Stroud assured Dixon in a level voice, but inside, his guts were boiling. That fucking Bull....

Back in his trailer, Stroud nearly lost control. But instead of tearing the place up, he grabbed his whiskey bottle and tossed back a couple of slugs. The liquor didn't make him any less angry, but it helped him regain his focus. The end of the season, Dixon had said. A couple of months. Plenty of time to do something before Seraphina slipped through his fingers. Plenty of time to do something about Bull.

But what? He couldn't whip Bull in a fair fight, which made doing to the strongman what Stroud had done to Joe an impossibility. Besides, nobody knew about Joe except Stroud and the hole the sailor was buried in. Bull would be different. Stroud couldn't just kill him somehow on the sly and bury his body out in the woods. The sailor wouldn't be missed, but Bull would be. And suspicion would fall directly on Stroud. He might be able to kill Bull and get away with it, but the stigma would drive him from the carny crowd. They would tolerate a lot, but not murder of one of their own.

No, Stroud had to find a way to kill or otherwise dispose of Bull that left him totally in the clear. Like a car wreck or some kind of freak accident. But that would be hard to engineer, and he didn't want to hurt Seraphina in the process.

Try as he might, he couldn't figure out what would work. And the drink didn't help. In the end, all it did was fuzz his thoughts and enflame his rage. No, it focused his rage, turned it into something implacable. When he'd killed Wheeler, he'd felt the same sort of cold rationality knifing through the red haze. The same sense of inevitability. Joe had to die, and now it was Bull's turn. And, by God, the same thing would happen to anybody who got in Stroud's way. He was tired of being the one who was pushed around. Now it was time for him to do the pushing.

But how? Stroud slugged back another swallow, and he was so hot inside that it didn't even burn going down. It was easy enough to push those who were weaker or less powerful than Stroud, but what about the Bulls of the world? What about the Dixons and all the others Stroud would have to deal with if he was going to rise?

He lifted the bottle for another drink, discovered it was empty, and set it down. He wasn't drunk. At least, not drunk enough. But the bottle had been his last. Surely there was a liquor store in town. He found his truck keys and went outside.

He was a little shocked to see that the sun was going down and that he'd brooded away the whole day. The carny encampment was settling into its evening routine, and nobody seemed to notice Stroud as he got into his truck and pulled out of the field and onto the two-lane blacktop that led into Nashville. He found a liquor store on the outskirts of town, bought three bottles, and went back to the carnival. Night had fully settled when he drove to the encampment and circled it to his trailer.

He made it inside without breaking any of the bottles. He set two on the counter but opened the third and carried it to his chair. And he sat there and drank. He drank for hours, and he drank to erase the frustration and rage. But the more he drank, the more something else began to impinge on his consciousness. Something from outside him. Something, he finally realized, that was under the bench seat in the trailer.

The manin-pasuk.

*   *   *

"Why you got to be so goddamn heavy?" Stroud complained as he dragged the doll's case out from beneath the bench seat and propped it against the counter opposite his chair. The doll just looked back through the glass front with those beady black eyes that could see nothing but seemed to see it all.

This is crazy, he thought, but the next words that ran through his head were: Joe believed. Joe saw it come alive with his own eyes. Stroud thought it probably all was a load of crap. But then, Joe had come back for the doll. He'd died for it. That had to mean something....

"The fuck it does," Stroud sneered at the doll. "I ain't no rube. You're just a fake."

The doll stared implacably back with those glittery black eyes, as if to cast doubt on who was the fake. What the fuck was it thinking?

"Fuck you," Stroud said, but the hideous little monstrosity just stared unblinkingly at him.

The trailer suddenly became claustrophobic. Stroud got up, grabbed the bottle by its neck, and stumbled out the door, down the two steps to the ground, and over to the chair and table set up under his Airstream's awning. The night air was still warm, but a cooling breeze wafted through the trees surrounding the carnival grounds.

Fucking pines.

Stroud sucked on the bottle and watched the few carnies who were still up and about finally drift back to their respective trailers and campers.

What if the doll *could* come alive? he wondered. That would be the easy part. The hard part would be to assure his own alibi since everyone knew of the enmity between him and Bull. Maybe even harder would be to separate Bull from Seraphina. He didn't want her to get hurt. Or to see what put the hurt on Bull. But since the Stroud's beating at Bull's hands, the strongman rarely let Seraphina out of his sight.

There was one time each day, though, that he did. After the carnival shut down at midnight, as with most of the carnies, he and Seraphina would retreat to their trailer to eat. A couple of hours later,

185

he typically came back outside to work out for an hour with barbells and a medicine ball in the area behind the trailer. Seraphina never joined him but stayed inside doing whatever it was she did at night.

The carnival wouldn't open for business until tomorrow, but most carnies kept a night-owl schedule, and if Bull was keeping to his, he'd be outside in an hour or so.

Stroud had to down half the bottle to drown the feeling of idiocy that echoed in his brain when he thought about going back into the trailer. Or was it fear? What if the powder worked and the doll actually came alive? What if it attacked Stroud instead of Bull?

But that's not what Joe's notes said would happen. Somewhere in there was the statement that the manin-pasuk was bound to obey the person who supplied the blood in the mixture that was fed to the doll. If Stroud supplied the blood, what could go wrong?

Plenty, Stroud thought with one of the last shreds of reason that were tattering beneath the storm of his alcohol-fueled rage. Hell, the damn little thing was from the Amazon, for Christ sake. It probably only understood whatever gibberish Joe'd learned while he was living down there. Certainly not English. But maybe not. It had been around these parts for two years, hearing lots of people talk. Maybe it had picked up a little English. Maybe he could teach it to understand him.

Fuck! Stroud thought. What the fuck was he thinking?

He drank three more stiff slugs. His head was reeling. Most of that was alcohol haze, but then he realized that he'd somehow staggered to his feet and was turning toward the trailer door. He made it up the steps and inside. Without putting the bottle down, he shuffled over to the doll's case lying in front of the bench seat and stood there, swaying over it, staring through the glass.

The manin-pasuk stared back. Fuck, was that sarcasm gleaming in its eyes?

"You little bastard," Stroud grated, setting the bottle on the table.

He bent, opened the glass lid, lifted the doll out, and laid it on the bench seat. Then he moved around the trailer, searching for three items. One was a bag of the powder, one was the book of maritime law, and the last was a flyer for the circus. Just three acts were depicted: Stroud's, the mentalist, and Seraphina and the Serpent. Stroud clumsily folded the flyer so that only Bull's picture showed.

186

When the items were arrayed on the table next to the doll, Stroud pulled a coffee mug from a cabinet and a spoon from a drawer. Now, he needed a knife.

No. Not a knife. If he was going to have a cut, it had to seem natural. He wrapped a hand around the neck of the nearly empty whiskey bottle and smashed the bottle against the edge of the table. When the last shards had tinkled to the floor, Stroud looked at what was left: a ragged rim of edges glittering in the light from the lamp. He stepped forward and shook the ragged rim in the doll's face.

"You better work, you little fucker," he snarled. "Or I'll make you wish you had."

At first he was going to cut his arm, but considering what he was about to do—or what he hoped the doll was about to do—he changed his mind. He loosened his belt, dropped his trousers, and stared down at his long, white legs. Funny how he never much thought about his legs, and now he was about to mutilate one. Fuck it, he thought, and before he could change his mind, he sliced the ragged rim of glass against the side of his thigh.

"Fuck!" he gasped, looking down at the damage. Blood was flowing from several shallow cuts and two deeper ones. He dropped the broken bottle neck, snatched up the mug and pressed its lip into the flesh beneath the wound. Blood ooze over the rim. The pressure of the mug so near to the traumatized flesh hurt like a mother, but Stroud held it tight until the mug had a tablespoon of blood pooled in the bottom.

Feeling slightly nauseous and somewhat more sober, he set the mug on the table, then he grabbed the dish towel from the kitchen counter, wadded it up, and pressed it against the wound. After a minute, he pulled the towel away. Blood still oozed. Stroud opened another bottle of whiskey and splashed some on the wound, hissing and cursing in response. Then he quickly tore a strip from the dish towel and improvised a bandage with it and duct tape. The fucking cuts hurt like hell, and they would probably hurt worse tomorrow. He'd be lucky if he hadn't left some glass in his leg, though he hoped the whiskey would help fight off any infection.

He pulled his trousers up, grabbed the whiskey bottle, and drank, staring at the doll. Finally, he had to do something other than drink and stare. He set the bottle aside, opened the book, and read how to mix the blood and powder in correct proportions. Then he picked up the pouch of powder, took a pinch, and stirred it into the blood. A pungent but not unpleasant odor filled the air. Stroud glanced at the doll, and for once, he could have sworn it wasn't staring at him but at the bowl in his hands.

Stroud snatched up the picture of Bull and held it in front of the Devil Child's face.

"Bull," he said, jabbing a finger at Bull's picture. "Bull. He's the one." He pointed to his left. "Over there," he said, feeling stupid but having to say the words anyway, even if the doll couldn't understand. "Two hundred feet over that way. Bull."

He dropped the folded paper to the floor and leaned over the doll, holding up the bowl.

"My blood." He poked his forefinger at himself. "You understand? My blood. You do what I say, or you never move again. Kill Bull, come back here, and get back in your box." He gestured toward the case.

If the doll understood, it gave no indication, though its eyes seemed to glitter more brightly than usual.

Taking a deep breath, Stroud spooned enough of the bloody paste between the doll's lips to give it several hours of life. Then he stepped back.

Nothing happened. The doll just lay there.

"I knew it!" Stroud raged. "A fucking con! That's all that fucker was: a fucking c...."

What the fuck? Stroud stepped back farther.

The fucking thing's fingers and toes were twitching. Then it flexed its arms and legs with an audible creaking. Then it sat up. Sat the fuck up! A sharp odor suffused the trailer's small space.

Stroud cowered back against the cabinets as the manin-pasuk swung its legs off the bench and stood up, staring right at Stroud. Its eyes blinked, and it smiled a horrible grin as it raised its hands in front of its face and flexed its talon-tipped fingers. Then it looked back at Stroud and licked the residue of the bloody paste from its lips.

"You have to do what I say," Stroud stammered. "You can't hurt me. It's my blood."

The Devil Child just stood there.

One of the hardest things Stroud had ever done was to grab the whiskey bottle, turn his back on that little monster, and walk out the door. He nearly fell down the steps, but he was careful to leave the trailer door ajar since the thing might not know how door knobs worked.

In two minutes, he'd staggered into the commissary tent. A few carnies were there, chatting over late snacks and drinks, and they all noted Stroud's entry. Stroud collapsed into a chair and drank heavily from the bottle to calm his nerves. The thought of that hideous little monster alive in his trailer…. Alive!

He drank more. And again. But not heavy swigs like before. He had to make the bottle last until the deed was done. The whiskey was nearly half gone when bellows shattered the air. The bellows quickly turned to panicked screams that cut off to abrupt silence.

Stroud came to his feet with the other carnies in the commissary tent, and he followed them out into the night. Despite the amount of liquor he'd consumed during the day and evening, he suddenly was completely sober. Everyone rushed toward Seraphina and Bull's trailer, and about half the carnies were already there when Stroud arrived. But none of them went too close to the pile of gore crumpled beside Bull's barbell bench. Seraphina stood slumped against the corner of the trailer, looking pale and weak.

Hicks came up right after Stroud did.

"Dottie," he ordered. "Get Seraphina, and take her to your trailer."

Dottie complied, urging Seraphina away from the scene, leaving Hicks to push through the ring of carnies and cautiously approach the body. Dixon arrived as Hicks bent over Bull, reached out a tentative hand, and touched fingers to Bull's neck. The part of the neck that remained. He straightened as Dixon came up, and he looked at the carnival boss and shook his head.

"What the fuck could have done that?" Dixon asked, staring down at Bull.

"Couldn't say," Hicks replied. "Looks like some wild animal."

"Sure," chimed in one of the roustabouts. "What kind of wild animals they got around here that could do something like that?"

This set up a murmur from the crowd that Dixon patted down.

"Look, we don't know what happened here, but we all know I

gotta call the cops. Probably would be best if everybody went home right now. I'm sure the cops will want to talk to everybody."

As the carnies began to disperse, Stroud noticed that Hicks gave each one a careful look—a look that lingered on Stroud a moment longer than on anyone else.

Searching for blood, Stroud thought. And signs of a struggle. Well, let him look. He wouldn't find any, and neither would the cops. Stroud hadn't done the deed—at least, not with his own hands —and he had a perfect alibi. But he went back to his trailer anyway, not so much to acquiesce to Hick or to remain in the background, but to check on the manin-pasuk.

The door to his trailer was ajar, and smears of blood marred the step and door frame. Feeling more frightened than he'd ever been, Stroud pushed the door open and peered inside.

The manin-pasuk, still animated, sat on the bench cushion. It was licking the blood off its arms and hands. As the door swung inward, it looked up, piercing Stroud with a steady gaze. Then, horribly, it grinned.

Stroud nearly fled into the night. But he couldn't do that. Everything had to seem normal. He had to act normally. But how could he do that with what he'd seen, with what he knew? With that thing sitting there in his trailer, grinning at him?

The manin-pasuk went back to licking the blood off itself, and Stroud forced himself up the steps and into the trailer. He shut the door. He was alone with the manin-pasuk. And he was afraid.

But the little beast ignored him as it preened, so he just stood there for a long time, watching it. He'd had the doll for two years, and he thought he knew it well, but seeing it move like any other living thing made it something completely different from the doll he was familiar with. No, it wasn't a doll. It was a creature—a manin-pasuk. Maybe it used to be a man, and maybe it used to be Stroud's meal ticket, but now it was something else.

Stroud knew its secret, and it was Stroud's future.

After half an hour, the manin-pasuk sighed, lay back onto the cushion, and went rigid. And not a moment too soon. Sirens were sounding in the distance.

Cautiously, Stroud approached the manin-pasuk, half expecting it to sit up again. But it just lay inert, though its eyes shone more fiercely than Stroud remembered. He reached out an poked its leg, which again felt like wood beneath his fingertip.

The thing had managed to lick off only a small amount of the blood that covered it. Feeling like he was picking up something dead, Stroud lifted it, carried it to the head, and propped it up inside the shower stall. He turned on the water and positioned the manin-pasuk beneath the stingy spray then went back to the kitchenette to clean up. There was blood, but not as much as he expected considering the damage the manin-pasuk had done to Bull. He could easily clean everything up in half an hour. Except for the bench cushion. It bore a small butt print in blood where the manin-pasuk had sat, cleaning itself, and a full body impression where it had lain down to stiffen.

Stroud cleaned up the blood smears. As for the cushion, well, there wasn't much help for that. He'd have to replace it, but for now, he just blotted up as much of the blood as he could then flipped the cushion over.

He went back to the shower and finished cleaning off the manin-pasuk. He had to leave it leaning up inside the shower stall to dry since he didn't want to lay its wet body back on the silk lining inside its case.

Then he went outside, locking the door behind him.

By now, the police had cordoned off the area behind Seraphina and Bull's trailer. Hicks had some of the roustabouts set up klieg lights around the area, and the rest of the carnies flocked to their glow like moths then stood milling in a loose ring outside the police lines. Bull's body still lay on the ground next to the barbell bench, though now it was covered with a sheet already soaked red.

The murmur from the carny crowd was filled with speculation, innuendo, suspicion, and fear. Anything that could do that to Bull…. And what the hell *could* have done that? In under a minute, Stroud caught a couple of the carnies giving him wary looks. Everybody knew Stroud had motive.

Dixon was off to the side, talking to an older man dressed in a police uniform with lots of doodads on it. The police chief, no doubt. Hell, not only were all the carnies here, so was all of Nashville's police force. All five of them.

191

I ought to go into town and rob the bank, Stroud thought. But, no. Now that he knew the secret of the manin-pasuk, he'd never target some podunk bank. If he was going to use the doll to steal, he was going to steal power as well as wealth.

But for now, he simply had to evade suspicion from the police. Hicks was off to the side, standing alone near one of the kliegs, and Stroud made his way over to him.

"The cops know anything?" Stroud asked.

"Bull's dead," Hicks said, staring at Stroud. "And he's pretty torn up. That's about all anybody knows right now."

"I've seen some people giving me nasty looks," Stroud said. "I hope you don't think I had anything to do with this."

"Can't say it didn't cross my mind," Hicks said, then he gave a faint smile. "First thing, in fact. But I checked around and found out you were in the commissary tent when the screaming started. And I saw you when we all came around here to find Bull, and you didn't have no blood on you. Whoever or whatever did that," he nodded toward the sheet-covered body, "would have a lot of blood on 'em."

"Bull and I had our differences," Stroud admitted. "But Dixon told me he and Seraphina were leaving at the end of the season. Even if I thought about killing him, there'd be no point since he was leaving, anyway."

"I guess so." Hicks looked back at the body. "Anyway, whatever did that to Bull couldn't have been human. I saw him close up, and he looked like he was bit and clawed to death."

"I hear there are still a few cougars roaming around these parts."

"Could be. Maybe there'll be tracks. If it's a cougar, they can trail it with bloodhounds."

Shit, Stroud thought.

"Well, I'm not going to stand around here all night, looking at a bloody sheet. I'm going back to my trailer."

"Fine. Just don't go to sleep yet. The police are gonna want to talk to everybody before the night's over."

Stroud returned to his trailer and locked the door behind him. The manin-pasuk was nearly dry, and Stroud finished the job with a towel. Then he lay the thing in its case and slid the case under the bench seat. Only then did he go outside to his chair beneath the trailer's awning, sit, and try to relax. His first instinct was to reach for the bottle of whiskey, but he dampened the reflex. He'd had enough of that for now. Now what he needed was sober thought.

He began to plot to use the manin-pasuk to take over the carnival, but another thought soon pushed that aside. Joe's crazy story that the manin-pasuk was really alive wasn't so crazy after all. So what did that mean about using the powder to increase longevity? If Stroud followed Joe's instructions and used the formula on himself, would he grow younger or gain more life?

He went back inside and was reading through Joe's notes when a knock came on his door. It was Hicks.

"Cops are interviewing everybody in the commissary tent. Time for you to go over there."

"I don't see why," Stroud said. "You know I was in the commissary tent with the others."

"Well," Hicks said. "I guess you all gotta be each other's alibis."

"What about tomorrow night? We still going to open."

"Don't see much of an alternative. We gotta eat. Let's just hope what happened here tonight don't drive away the rubes."

The police interview went smoothly enough and was mercifully short. The cops had already spoken to some of the others who'd seen Stroud in the commissary tent when Bull was killed. After it was over, Stroud went back to his trailer, but he didn't pick up the book of maritime law. Instead, he undressed, climbed into bed, and slept.

The carnies still felt a lot of anxiety the next afternoon when the carnival opened for business, but if Hicks had thought the murder would keep the townies away, he'd been very mistaken. Even before official opening, people were flocking to the carnival grounds, a lot of them caring less about the carnival than about the murder. Bull's remains had been moved to the morgue, but the spot where he'd been killed, still soaked with blood, became the carnival's biggest attraction.

"Well, Bull, I guess you finally got to be the headliner," Stroud muttered sarcastically to himself as he moved the manin-pasuk to his tent and set up the pneumatic effect. "For one day." Maybe Dixon should set up a tent over the barbell bench and charge admission.

Of Seraphina, there was no sign. Stroud heard she was staying in Dottie's trailer, still too shaken up to face anybody. Her act remained closed for the duration of the carnival's stint in Nashville. Stroud ached to see her, but he contented himself with studying the details of the brewing of the longevity potion. But as impatient as he was to brew the potion and try it out, he waited. Joe wrote that it would make him sick as hell for several days at least, and Stroud wasn't about to lose that much time during the peak of the carnival's season.

So he waited. And performed. But now, there was something different about his act. It wasn't that he'd changed the wording of his spiel or the timing of its delivery, but that he, himself, had changed. Before, he'd been delivering a spiel, a story, but now, he was telling the truth, and his belief somehow came across to even the dumbest yokel. So, as he waited, he raked in the cash.

About three weeks later, Seraphina resumed her act. Or rather, resumed the act she'd had before she'd teamed with Bull. Can't eat grief, Stroud thought. But he still kept away from her. By now, none of the carnies thought Stroud had anything to do with Bull's death, but the enmity of the two and the subsequent mauling aroused wariness in some of the more superstitious among the them. Most, though, remained friendly enough, and Stroud didn't want to push things by making a blatant play for Seraphina too soon.

*   *   *

The season finally over, and the carnival retreated to the wintering grounds outside Dunnison. For the past two seasons, Stroud had hightailed it for Houston, but this year, he had other business: growing younger.

He lived in his trailer and waited another week for things to settle down. He noticed immediately that Seraphina didn't leave for other places as she and Bull had done for the past couple of years but stayed in her trailer at the wintering grounds. Stroud was happy enough about that, but he ignored her, too.

His first order of business was to hire a local welder to fasten a large, waterproof metal box to the bed of his truck, just behind the cab. There was no way he was going to keep the manin-pasuk in his Airstream. Not now. It was too creepy. It would be safe enough in the metal box and far enough away from where Stroud slept that it didn't keep him awake at night. No wonder Tuchaua had kept the thing in a distant cave instead of in his hut.

He also parsed out the powder. It took more of the powder to confer longevity than it did to animate the doll. There was enough powder, he calculated, to animate the doll a few dozen times or make the longevity potion eight times. It all depended on how he used it, but even if he used half to animate the Devil Child, he'd still have enough to give him a much longer life—plenty of time to accomplish what he wanted.

Next, he readied himself for testing the longevity potion. If he was going to be sick as hell, he had to prepare for that. Food, water, whatever he might need. Then, on the morning of the tenth day, he opened Joe's book, followed the instructions, and brewed up a cup of the potion. He eyed it for a long time after, pooling there in its innocuous cup. Potion, or poison?

"Fuck it," he said finally.

He picked up the cup, and tossed it off, nearly choking at the foul taste. The more bitter the medicine, the better. Isn't that what Gladys, his mother's black maid used to say when she dosed him with some nasty tasting concoction during his childhood illnesses? If so, this ought to be the best medicine yet.

The sickness that followed made him doubt that. Weakness, sweats, nausea and vomiting, cramping, the shakes—it was like the worst case of flu combined with food poisoning, with a migraine thrown in for good measure. By evening, he couldn't even rise from his bed. Nor the next day, but he didn't remember much of that, and the night brought delirium and fever. The day after was a complete blank.

He woke on the morning of the fourth day, feeling something cool pressing on his brow. He tried to reach up to touch it, but his hand was too heavy. So were his eyelids, but he managed to open them though their lids were half stuck together with gummy residue.

"He's awake," came a woman's voice.

"You there, John?" asked a man.

Two amorphous shapes hovered over Stroud, and gradually they came into focus. Seraphina was sitting on the edge of the bed, and Hicks was standing just behind her.

"You've been sick," Seraphina said.

"Sorry we barged in," Hicks said, leaning down. "Nobody saw you come out for a couple of days, and we got worried."

"Water," Stroud croaked, and Hicks fetched a glass and handed it to Seraphina, who helped Stroud take a few sips.

The water almost made Stroud vomit, but he managed to choke back the bile that rose. He looked up at Seraphina, and she smiled.

"Don't worry, John," she said. "I'll take care of you."

10: DEADFALL

"THANKS, MR. STROUD" the kid said. "You won't regret taking me on."

"We'll see. Go to the commissary tent over there. You look like you could use something to eat, and you can't do this kind of work on an empty stomach. Tell them I sent you. Then find Hicks, here, and he'll show you what to do."

"Thanks, Mr. Stroud." The boy hurried off toward the commissary with a stride that said he was hungry.

"Don't tell me he reminds you of somebody," Stroud said to Hicks as they watched the boy's retreating back.

"You?" Hicks snorted a laugh. "Don't nobody remind me of you, John. You're one of a kind. Don't know nobody else who looks like they keep getting younger all the time. 'Specially in this business."

"I'll take that as a compliment. So, where do we stand with renting Billups' land in Homer?"

"He says it's a go this year, but he's getting too old to farm, and he's selling out before next year. No telling if the new owners will rent it to us after that."

"We'll cross that bridge next year," Stroud said. "Everybody paid up on their rents?"

"Everybody except Fred Catterall. You know he was down with the flu real bad, and…."

"Yeah, yeah. Fred's always got some excuse. You tell him I'll accept half of what he owes me for now, and he can pay off the rest next month. But he better get his ass in gear, or he's going to be hauling his ring toss outta here."

"He's been with us a long time."

"Then he can pay his rent on time."

"I'll tell him," Hicks said. "Anything else right now?"

"I guess not. Make sure the new kid stays busy. We don't need any freeloaders."

Hicks nodded, turned, and walked toward the commissary tent. Stroud watched him for a moment, noting the set of his shoulders. Hicks wasn't happy about coming down on Catterall, but damn it, somebody had to crack the whip around here.

The six years since Stroud had activated the manin-pasuk had been profitable. In just two, he'd managed to buy out Dixon, who'd seemed to have lost hope following Bull's.... Was it murder, or slaughter? Whatever it was, Dixon was only too happy to sell the carnival, and Stroud beat Hicks to the punch by ten thousand dollars. Stroud had sweetened the deal by allowing Dixon to live out his life in the farmhouse on the carnival wintering grounds, which Stroud acquired as part of the bargain.

"Don't worry, Hicks," Stroud assured the carnival manager at the time. "I'm not getting rid of you. In fact, you'd better keep saving. I have bigger plans than this, and I'll probably want to sell this place before too much longer."

And it was the truth. Once he acquired the carnival, Stroud discovered that he pretty much hated being the owner. There were too many details and too much responsibility. People knocked on his door at all hours, and he had to deal with kids like the one he'd just sent to the commissary: wanna-be carnies with no brighter prospects than a life of constantly pounding in stakes and pulling them out again. He often longed for the days when he could sit beneath his trailer awning, polish off a bottle, and not have to speak to a soul while he was doing it.

But those days were past. He'd quit drinking after he dosed himself with the longevity potion. The sickness that followed had mostly been swallowed by delirium, but when he finally came to, he could smell the sour stench of alcohol permeating his bedding and the air of the room. As he lay recuperating under Seraphina's tender ministrations—and they'd once been tender instead of whiny and conditional—he realized that at least part of the way the potion worked was to purge the body of toxins. A lot of that for him had been the whiskey he'd regularly consumed by the bottle. He could only feel grateful that he hadn't been a smoker, too. He might not have survived the ordeal.

Now, all he had to do was figure out how to survive the ordeal of living with Seraphina.

With a sigh, he headed for his office trailer instead of the trailer he called home. Seraphina was in there watching soap operas, and if he went in, he'd have to watch them with her or watch her eat and grow fat. She'd quit the Seraphina and the Serpent act soon after Stroud acquired the carnival.

"I'm the owner's wife," she said. "I can't be doing coochie shows. It's not dignified."

Maybe not, but being a fat, lazy bum wasn't dignified, either. And the "wife" bit was mere supposition on her part.

Besides, he was sick of that fucking snake. She insisted on keeping the damn thing even after she dropped her act. It wouldn't be so bad if she stored its cage in the back of the truck, but she kept it inside the trailer, instead.

"Slinky and I have been together a long time," she said. "A lot longer than me and you."

"You mean, Stinky, don't you?" he asked as he stepped out the door.

It had gotten so that Stroud couldn't stand the smell of the thing, which permeated the Airstream, and more and more, he found himself dossing out in his office trailer. It wasn't as comfortable, but at least he could think without smelling that damn snake.

After the weekend, when the carnival finished its stint in Farmerville, everybody packed up and moved on to Springhill, and that's where things changed. That's where he met Ira Simmons.

It wasn't the first time Stroud had seen him. Or the second. Show after show this season, town after town, he'd noticed the slender, ginger-haired, bespectacled young man hovering at the edges of the crowd. He seemed more intent than the rest of the rubes. Smarter. Smart enough not to be taken in by Stroud's spiel about the doll, even though, as Stroud knew only too well now, the spiel was just about one hundred percent true.

The shows in Springhill were no different. There the young man was, keeping back but watching the doll intently the entire time. Funny thing was, he never tried to come up to Stroud afterward, and Stroud never saw him hanging around. But there he was, every show, almost every night. He must have some bucks and free time to keep that up for months, Stroud thought.

Stroud put the young man out of his mind and concentrated on the business of running the carnival. As usual, the midway and rides were set up by Thursday, and things quieted down that afternoon as the carnies prepared themselves for the weekend and long hours ahead. Stroud took the opportunity to get the hell away from it all —Seraphina's cooking, especially—and he hopped into his truck and steered toward town. If he remembered correctly, there was a pretty good diner on the south side.

He found the building, went inside, sat, and perused the menu. A scrawny, fifty-something waitress with nicotine-stained fingers came over with a glass of water. He ordered the blue plate special, which today was fried chicken, mashed potatoes, and string beans. The waitress left. Was that what Sara looked like now? he wondered. Did she still wait tables in that diner in Dunnison?

To keep his mind off that unfortunate memory, Stroud glanced around at the other tables. Not much happening at most of them at this mid-afternoon hour, but someone at the counter arrested his eyes. Perched on a stool near the end was the young man who kept coming to the shows. And he was staring right at Stroud.

A small but twisted smile twitched Stroud's lips. Kind of ironic, he thought, running into the guy here since his admission during any single night was paying for Stroud's meal. He looked away then and stared out the window and saw a few pedestrians and meager traffic. Just another podunk town in a podunk state. Just one more stop in the life of a carny.

Stroud was getting tired of it. There had to be something more. After a time, the waitress brought his food: fried chicken, mashed potatoes, and peas. The blue plate special.

She left, but then, suddenly, he was aware of someone standing next to him. He glanced up, thinking the waitress had forgotten something, but it was the young man, instead.

"I've seen your Devil Child."

"You've seen it a lot," Stroud said. "I recognize you. You want a discount or something?"

"I just want to know about it."

"You've heard my story often enough you could probably recite it for me."

"Is it true? The story?"

"It is," Stroud said, amazed that, for once, he could be honest about the doll.

"What happened to the sailor? The one you got it from?"

"He's long in the ground."

Stroud dropped a pat of butter on top of the mound of mashed potatoes and mixed it in.

"I know it's real," the young man said at last. "The Devil Child."

"'Course it's real." Stroud picked up a chicken thigh. "You've seen it almost as much as I have this season."

"Alive, I mean."

"Yeah, sure it is. You keep coming back, then, and watch it pop up out of its box right on time, every show."

"I'm not talking about that bicycle pump trick, or whatever it is you use to make it move. I've seen you pushing that foot pedal in the sawdust."

"There you have it. A phony doll and a cheap pneumatic trick." Stroud didn't know why he didn't just tell the guy to get lost. There was that intensity.... He forced a laugh. "I've been hawking that thing for nearly nine years, and you think you know more about it than I do?"

"Maybe not, but I know it's alive. Really alive."

"And just why do you think that?" Stroud took a bite of the chicken thigh.

"Because you're afraid of it."

Stroud swallowed the mouthful before it was completely chewed, and unmasticated chicken crust clawed its way down his throat. He stared into the other man's eyes. The intensity remained undiminished behind the glasses.

"Yeah, sure, fella," Stroud said when he could speak. "The Devil Child is really alive. And it's one dangerous little fucker. That's why I keep it frozen all the time." He said it lightly, as if he was bullshitting, but deep down, he felt good about admitting the truth to somebody. Even a stranger. Maybe especially a stranger.

"Is that what happened to that strongman? Bull Martin?"

Stroud nearly choked.

"You must be nuts," he said.

"Am I? Bull gets killed by some unidentified wild animal that shouldn't exist in these parts, and right after, you get his girl and then buy the carnival."

Stroud put down his silverware and stared into the other man's eyes.

"You're talking a lot of shit. You'd be laughed right out of court with accusations like that."

"This isn't a court," the man pointed out. "And I'm not trying to cause you any trouble. I just want to know."

"Why? What the fuck is it to you?"

"I'm not sure. I just can't keep away. It's like it's calling to me."

Fuck, Stroud thought. He felt the same thing. Did this guy really feel it, too? And understand?

"Yeah," he said. "Well, you just keep on feeling like that and coming to every show. I appreciate it. In fact, I'm eating on your gullibility right now. So, if you'll just move on and let me finish in peace, I'd be grateful."

The young man nodded and paused as if he was going to say something else, but then he went back to the counter. Stroud wolfed the rest of his meal, paid up, and hurriedly drove back to the carnival.

Maybe his act was too convincing, Stroud thought. Maybe he ought to glue something to the doll to make it seem fake. But he knew that wouldn't work. It wasn't how the thing looked, though that was fearsome and believable enough. It was that it radiated its vile vitality so strongly that anyone nearby could sense it if they cared to. Maybe even if they didn't. Sometimes Stroud could feel it even when he didn't have it out. That's why he'd quit keeping it the trailer, but in the heavy-gauge steel toolbox bolted to the bed of his pickup, right behind the cab. Not only did he feel safer with the manin-pasuk locked up, he knew it was always with him wherever he went. Nobody was going to steal it while he was away.

It was late afternoon when he got back to his office trailer. He and Hicks spent an hour going over logistics for the next stop, then he went to his own trailer to shower and get ready for his evening shows.

"I don't see why you have to keep shilling that damn doll," Seraphina complained as he donned his performing costume, which was a simple, narrow-lapeled black suit, a bolo tie sporting a clasp with a large turquoise stone, and a straw boater. "You're the owner. You shouldn't have to work."

"The owner works harder than anybody," he said, wishing she'd just shut up. "Besides, if you want to winter in Florida, I have to come up with the scratch. It isn't cheap staying down there."

"We're doing okay, Johnny," she whined. "Maybe if you just did two or three shows every night instead of five we could have more quality time together."

Sure, he thought. Real quality time. Right in the middle of nightly operations.

"I'll think about it," he said, but only to placate her. He had absolutely no intention of spending more time with her than necessary. "I have to get to work."

He left the trailer and went to his truck. He kept a pair of wooden steps handy so that he didn't have to clamber into the bed of the truck every day, and he moved them beneath the tailgate. After climbing them, he unlocked the tool box, hauled out the case, carried it to tailgate, and set it down. He descended the steps, lifted the case, and set it on a dolly to trundle it to the tent.

I wonder if that ginger-haired yokel is going to show up tonight, he thought as he pushed through the back flap, but the thought dissipated as he turned his attention to setting the case on its stand and attaching the pneumatic mechanism. By then, the carnival was open for business, and he went outside to hustle the rubes with his come-on spiel. It didn't take long for them to line up. The Devil Child was a perennial favorite.

Inside, during the first show, Stroud finally thought of the young man again and glanced around to see if he was there. Stroud didn't see him, and oddly, a sense of disappointment surged through him. Nor was he at any of the other shows, and by the end of the evening, Stroud figured he'd actually driven him off.

Good riddance, he thought as he began to pack up the doll. But he still felt a pang of…something. What was it?

He didn't want to know, but he did, suddenly. Some of it was that the young man really felt the manin-pasuk's living presence, but even more, he'd recognized that Stroud's fear of it proved that it was alive. Stroud had lived with that recognition for six years, and it had been nice, if unsettling, to share the fear.

Pushing the thoughts aside, Stroud set the doll's case on the dolly and wheeled it to the door flap and into the night.

And there he was.

"You," Stroud said with more surprise—and relief—than he cared to convey.

"I wanted to stay away," the other said. "But I couldn't."

"What do you want?"

"To talk. That's all."

"It's late. Come back another time."

"When you're gone? When I have to chase you to another town?"

"You don't have to chase me at all. You can go home."

"That's just it," the man said. "I don't want to go home. Not the way it is there."

Stroud could sympathize with that. What better did he have to do right now? Go back to that home *he* hated?

"All right. We can talk. Follow me."

Stroud rolled the dolly to his truck and stored the case in the steel box. Then he led the young man to his office trailer. Inside, he gestured to the single guest chair then settled himself behind the desk.

"Okay, you want to talk. Talk."

The young man's name was Ira Simmons. He was twenty-six and married with an infant son. The year before, he'd had graduated from Tulane with a masters degree in business management.

"Don't tell me you want to become my business manager," Stroud snorted.

"Not exactly. More like a partnership."

"I don't partner with anybody," Stroud said.

"Okay. But I still think we can work together."

"I already own this outfit," Stroud said. "What more do I need?"

"There's always more," Simmons said, an odd look in his eyes.

"Like what?"

"You own a carnival, but what is that, exactly? Some tents, some rolling stock, and a name."

And a bunch of headaches, Stroud thought.

"What's your point?"

"Maybe there's more out there. Something more permanent and valuable. Something we can get for ourselves if we work together."

"Such as?"

"How about a town?" Simmons said. "Or more. A parish. Maybe have influence in the state legislature."

"I'm already as famous as I want to be," Stroud said with a short laugh.

"I'm not talking about fame," Simmons said, staring intently into Stroud's eyes. "I'm talking about money and power."

"And how do you think we can swing that?" Stroud asked, trying to keep his voice nonchalant despite the sudden churn in his gut. He remembered Andrew Buchman all too well and knew what owning a town and having parish-wide influence meant. It meant telling people to shovel sawdust while you raked in the dough. Without traveling all the time like you were always on the run.

"I told you I went to business school," Simmons said. "It wasn't what I really wanted, but my father forced me to. He's owns one of the banks in Oakdale, and the bastard wants me to follow in his footsteps."

"Sounds like you have a problem with him."

"To the community, he's a model citizen. But he regularly beat the crap out of me and my mom. I went to business school because that's the only college he'd pay for."

"And now you want revenge."

"That," Simmons nodded. "But I also want everything he has, and if you help me, I'll share it with you fifty-fifty."

"So, now you've told me what you're going to do for me. What do I have to do?"

"Kill him."

"Your father?"

Stroud couldn't help but snort a laugh.

"You think this is funny?" Simmons asked, angry but also a little nonplussed.

"I think it's funny that you think I'm some kind of assassin for hire."

"I didn't think that," Simmons said quickly. "But even if you don't do it yourself, I think you can make it happen. Like you did to Bull Martin."

"You don't know anything about Bull…."

"I know you fought with him and he beat you up. I was there."

That had happened in Oakdale, the town Simmons said he was from. He could have seen it—there were enough of the townies still hanging around, especially teenagers.

"And then," Simmons went on, "Bull was killed."

"That was much later," Stroud said. "And I was in the commissary with others when it happened."

"That's right. I checked up on the case. Bull was killed by some kind of wild animal that was never seen, heard, or identified. The kind of wild animal that doesn't exist in these parts. Except maybe the Devil Child."

"I already told you that thing is just a prop."

"And I know that's not true. I don't know what it is, but I know it's not just a fake. It's alive, and you somehow got it to kill Bull. I want you to use it to kill my father. While I'm far away and can't be tied to his death. After that, when the estate is settled, I'll set you up as a member of the bank's board of directors. You become respectable, I get rid of my bastard father, and we both get rich and powerful." He paused, staring into Stroud's eyes. "Look, you're boss around here," he said at last, "but you—and I—could have so much more. What do you say?"

"I say I ought to throw you out of here right now."

"But you're not."

"Let's say I could do what you suggest—and I'm not: What's to prevent you from welshing on the deal and taking it all?"

"Well, I certainly can't turn you in. I'd implicate myself. Besides, nobody would believe you sent some carnival prop to murder my father. And anyway, you could use it on me anytime, too. I read about what happened to Bull. How torn up he was. I don't want that to happen to me."

"But to your father?"

Simmons shrugged.

"I have scars, and so does Mom. Call it karma for all of those. After that, there's plenty to go around."

"I want to think about it," Stroud said. "We're going down to

Ringgold next week. Stay away from me and my show until then, then come see me, and I'll give you my answer."

"Okay," Simmons said. "I'll see you in Ringgold."

Then Simmons was gone, leaving Stroud to ponder his next move, which was whether he actually was going to do what Simmons wanted. There were a lot of reasons not to. Stroud was making good money and he was boss of his own outfit, and that counted for a lot, even if some of the details, like his relationship with Seraphina, weren't ideal. But he could always get rid of Seraphina and replace her with someone younger. He'd have to eventually, anyway, since she'd only grow older while he stayed young. But for that same reason, he'd eventually have to abandon the carnival, anyway.

And the truth was, Stroud was sick of the carny life and its transience. He saw himself eventually growing old and fearful like Dixon had. He wasn't sure what he wanted, but he knew it was more than a life filled with marginal people and an inevitable end in solitary retirement at some decrepit farmhouse in the woods.

Plus, it wasn't like he hadn't killed before to get what he wanted, both with his bare hands and with the manin-pasuk. And there was no reason to believe that anyone might even remotely suspect that he had anything to do with the elder Simmons' death. The carnival would be far away, and the manin-pasuk would ensure that no one believed that anything other than a wild animal had done the deed. As Ira had pointed out, he couldn't point the finger at Stroud without incriminating and endangering himself, too. And certainly nobody would believe a wild tale about the manin-pasuk coming alive at Stroud's command. If Stroud killed Simmons' father and then Simmons grew too problematic, well, Stroud could kill him, too, without the least bit of suspicion falling on his head, almost from the comfort of his own trailer.

By the time the carnival was packing up to leave for Ringgold, Stroud had made up his mind.

* * *

When Simmons showed up in the tent for the last performance in Ringgold, Stroud signaled for him to stay until the rubes had cleared out.

"Let's talk here. I don't want anybody around here to see us together."

"Does that mean you're going to do it?"

"It means you'd better hold up your end of the deal."

"Fifty-fifty," Simmons said. "At first."

"What's that mean?"

"Later, we're going to make enough together that you'll think the deal was a worth a whole lot more."

"Then let me tell you this, Ira. I joined this carnival nearly twenty years ago as a roustabout, and now I own it, lock-stock-and-barrel. If I'm going to move on, I won't stand for less."

"Then you're the kind of partner I need."

Simmons extended his hand. It was slender and weak as Stroud took it in his own meaty grip.

"So," Simmons said. "When are we going to do it? When the carnival goes to Oakdale?"

"Not then," Stroud said. "You said you don't want to be around when it happens, and I don't want anyone to notice that the carnival was in town at the same time that your father meets his end. You remember what happened to Bull, and others might, too. Give me your phone number and go back home to your wife and son. I'll figure out something and be in touch."

"Maybe this'll help," Simmons said as he wrote down the number. "My father's a hunter. He and his buddies go out almost every weekend during the deer season, which is coming up. Might be best to have the Devil Child kill him out there in the woods. Makes the idea of a wild animal more believable than one stalking around in town."

"When's deer hunting season start?"

"The middle of October. Even better, for the first couple of months, they don't allow them to hunt with dogs."

That was good. Stroud didn't want dogs tearing up the manin-pasuk, though he suspected that a smart dog would keep away and a dumb one would get more torn up than the manin-pasuk.

"The carnival will be wintering in Texas by then. I can be where I need to almost any time. You find out when and where your father's going to be hunting during the first couple of weeks of November, and I'll call you on November first. Until then, stay home or go work at the bank, or do whatever it is you do, and keep away from the carnival. We don't want anybody to connect us, at least not yet."

* * *

September and October crept as slowly as molasses. Stroud tried to keep his mind off November and everything that could go wrong, but there was no use in crying over milk that hadn't yet spilled. Oddly, his nightly performances were most affected, becoming, somehow, more sublime. Maybe it was just that he was going to miss them in some strange way. He'd learned to enjoy freaking out the rubes almost as much as he liked taking their money. Whatever it was, he got a real kick out of watching them jump when his foot stroked the pneumatic pedal. It was almost as good as sex.

Seraphina was another matter, and almost none of it sex. If she sensed that anything was different, she didn't show it, but then it was kind of hard to appreciate that life might change suddenly when your whole world is the inside of an Airstream, the screen of a TV, and the glacial feeding schedule of a python. Stroud made every effort not to reveal that soon things would be much different. He had enough trouble coming home at night and playing nice until it was time to go to bed.

And then, at last, the final week of October rolled around. The carnival had been making its gradual and circuitous sweep southward through East Texas, toward its last stop in Diboll. Stroud found a pay phone in town and called Simmons.

"John," he said when he realized who was on the line. "I wasn't sure you'd call."

"I wasn't, either. You'd better play this straight with me, Ira."

"There's plenty to go around for the two of us," Simmons replied. "We can make much more together than either of us can separately."

"Maybe. Do you have the information I need?"

"I do. He and a couple of buddies are going to be at a deer lease not far outside of town the second weekend in November. They usually go out there on Friday afternoon so they can get up early on

Saturday and catch the deer grazing." He gave Stroud the exact location, but couldn't provide much of an address. "You go north on state highway out of town for twelve and a half miles, and there'll be a dirt road on the left with an aluminum gate across it painted white. Or at least it used to be. It's pretty faded now. The deer lease is about five miles down the dirt road."

"Is the gate locked?"

"Yes. With a chain and combination padlock."

"All right. I need a few things from you: the combination, a photo of your father, the bank address, and his address."

"How am I going to get them to you?"

"Take them out to the gate and leave them under a rock near the...."

"No rocks out there," Simmons interrupted. "But there's a big oak about ten feet from the gatepost where the hinges are. It lost a lower branch a couple of years ago, and it's lying on the ground behind the tree. I'll put the photo and other information behind that."

"Do it today or tomorrow," Stroud said.

"Anything else?"

"Take your family to New Orleans for the weekend. Have a nice vacation."

"Should I just come back after that?"

"Somebody will probably call you to come back," Stroud said. "There's going to be a family tragedy, remember?"

Stroud waited two days, then told Hicks to hold down the fort while he went away on business. Hicks obviously thought that was odd since Stroud had never done that sort of thing before.

"What about your shows?" the manager asked.

"I'll be back by then," Stroud assured him.

Hicks just nodded, but Seraphina was a little harder to deal with.

"But what am I going to do while you're gone?" she whined.

"Whatever the hell you do while I'm here," Stroud said. "It's just for two or three days."

"Why do you have to be so mean, Johnny?"

Stroud didn't answer. Anything he said would just antagonize her.

He relaxed some as soon as he pulled out of the carnival grounds and headed east, toward Louisiana. Many of the roads he drove were familiar, but for some reason, they now looked fresh. Even the pines, the fucking pines, seemed less oppressive.

I'm going somewhere different, he thought. Out of the same old circuit. The same ruts. The future is wide open.

It took several hours to get to Oakdale, and when he arrived, he checked into a motel on the outskirts of town. He figured that was safe enough. He was just another person passing through. Then, with Simmons' instructions in hand, he drove out toward the deer lease.

He located the dirt road with the white gate easily enough. He pulled off the side of the road and found the deadfall branch near the gate. Tucked beneath its rear side and dusted with leaves was a small, shallow Tupperware box. Inside was a photograph and a slip of paper with the gate combination and addresses written on it. The photo showed a man with close-trimmed hair graying at the temples. He looked a lot like Ira Simmons but bulkier. Meaner. On the back was written, "James Simmons." Stroud slipped the photo into his pocket then went over to the gate to try the combination.

The lock popped open, and Stroud swung the gate wide, stepped through, and stared down the road. Five miles to the hunting cabin, Ira had said. Ten miles round trip. Too far to walk. He hated to drive down the dirt road since he wasn't supposed to be here, but it would take hours to walk what he could drive in a few minutes. Anyway, he figured that nobody would be here in late afternoon on a weekday.

The road wound through the forest. The air was quiet and still. Stroud didn't know what to expect, but when he finally pulled into the camp, he found that it consisted of a plank cabin flanked on one side by a shed and on the other by an outhouse. No plumbing out here, nor did an electric line snake to the cabin from the road. But despite the cabin's simplicity and outdoor plumbing, there was nothing shabby about it. It was well maintained and sported a relatively new coat of green paint, the windows were covered with wooden shutters, and the door looked solid enough and was fastened with another combination padlock.

Stroud wished he could have gotten a look inside, but no matter. He didn't need to know the layout of the interior. The manin-pasuk could wait outside until the elder Simmons stepped out to take his morning shit.

Stroud climbed out of the truck, went to the rear, and opened the tailgate. A few moments later, he'd opened the doll's case and propped the little monstrosity so that it could see the clearing and the cabin. Then he held the photo of James Simmons in front of its face.

"Him," Stroud said, pointing at the photo and then at the cabin. He'd kept up his English lessons with the diminutive demon, and sometimes he even let it watch TV. He hoped it understood at least a little by now.

He repeated the action a couple of more times, then returned the manin-pasuk to the case and the case to the metal box. He'd done everything he could for the moment, so he got back into his truck and drove to the two-lane. There, he opened the gate, pulled through, and relocked the gate.

It was dark by the time he arrived in Oakdale. He grabbed a bite to eat at a diner near the motel, then returned to his room. Early the next morning, he found the elder Simmons' house. Luckily, Simmons kept banker's hours, and his car—a brown Cadillac Eldorado—was still in the driveway. Stroud parked down the block and waited until Simmons left home and drove to the bank. Stroud followed, watched the man park, lock the Cadillac, and enter the bank. Then Stroud left Oakland and drove back to the carnival, dreaming of driving his own Eldorado instead of a pickup.

*　*　*

The carnival's stay in Diboll went as usual, but Stroud was constantly on edge and found it difficult to concentrate on his patter. Not that it mattered. He could have just stood the manin-pasuk up in front of the rubes and not made a dime less. But at least the shows were better than the scanty time he spent in the trailer with Seraphina.

"What's wrong, Johnny?" she asked in that perpetual whine she'd adopted. "Are you mad at me?"

"No," he said. And it was the truth. He wasn't mad at her, even if he was sick of her. "I just have a lot on my mind right now. I have a new deal going on, and there's a lot to think about."

"You never told me about a new deal," she said. "What is it?"

"It's big," he said. "I'll tell you when the time's ripe."

That seemed to placate her, though he frequently caught her giving him glances that ranged from bewilderment to suspicion.

"It isn't another woman, is it, Johnny?" she asked once. "Don't you like me anymore?"

"No, it's not another woman," he assured her. "Like I said, I'm just preoccupied with business."

After Diboll, the carnival moved on to its wintering grounds. Most of the carnies were ready for it after the long season. A lot of the more transient roustabouts left to find work elsewhere, and Stroud let Hicks take care of hiring the ones who would work in the shop. Stroud just didn't have time to deal with any of that. He was too busy preparing for what would happen over the next week. And worrying.

On Wednesday, Stroud called Hicks into his office trailer.

"I'm going to be out for most of the rest of the week," he said. "I'm leaving you in charge until I get back."

"We just got here," Hicks said.

"No help for it. I have business in Houston."

"Houston?" Hicks was a little taken aback. The carnival never went to Houston. "You going to try to get us gig there?"

"Personal business," Stroud amplified. "I'm leaving in the morning, and I should be back by Saturday night."

On Thursday, Stroud woke early and drove toward Oakdale. When he arrived, he checked into another motel on the other side of town. No sense in making himself too obvious by staying at the same place two weekends in a row.

He restlessly spent the next few hours before bedtime wishing he still drank. But, no. He didn't, really. He'd been plastered when he'd sent the doll to kill Bull, but now the stakes were much higher, and he wanted a clear head. So he sat in front of the TV, barely watching it, and waited.

The next morning, he cruised by Simmons' house but didn't spot his car, so he drove to the bank. The Caddy was there, in its reserved spot right in front. And there it stayed until three in the afternoon, when Simmons emerged, got into the car, and drove home.

Apparently, Stroud wasn't the only one who'd prepared for the weekend in advance. Simmons was inside for only a short time before he came out dressed in hunting clothes and carrying a rifle case. He put the case into the car, went back into the house and brought out a box that he set in the trunk.

Supplies, Stroud thought. Supplies he won't need. What, he wondered, would people do differently on their last day if they knew they wouldn't see another?

Stroud followed the Cadillac as far as the edge of town to make certain it was going toward the deer lease before he turned around and went back to his motel to wait until the time was ripe.

It was ripe at 2 AM. Stroud got up and dressed. Leaving his room key on the dresser, he went out to his pickup and drove toward the deer lease. The gate across the dirt road was shut and locked, but Stroud unlocked it easily enough, drove through, and shut the gate behind him. He didn't lock it. Back in his truck, he drove about half-way to the cabin. That should be far enough, he thought, that his headlights couldn't be seen from either the road or the cabin. He got out, unlocked the steel box, and lifted the case onto the truck bed.

Stroud opened the lid, leaned over, and used a small flashlight to illuminate the photo of Simmons he held in front of the Devil Child's face. He pointed to the photo, then down the dirt road. If the message wasn't clear enough, Stroud didn't know what else to do. He wished he could have mixed up the animating potion ahead of time, back in the motel, where he could clean and bandage the cut he had to make to get the blood, but he figured that the blood might coagulate before he could feed the mixture to the manin-pasuk and mess things up. So he cut himself in the glow of the flashlight, again making the slice on his leg. Once he'd collected enough blood in a cup, he staunched the flow and pressed on the bandage he'd prepared in advance. Then he stirred in the powder with a teaspoon.

Stroud bent over the manin-pasuk and spooned the potion between its lips.

Stroud had been drunk the first time he'd animated the doll, but he remembered well enough the creaking from the creature's limbs as it flexed them to life and the rasping suck of air through its

214

mouth. Much worse was the twisted grin it showed as it sat up and stared at Stroud. A pungent odor permeated the still air.

"My blood," Stroud said, pointing to himself and the bloody paste still in the cup. He held up the photo again and pointed down the road. The manin-pasuk's gaze followed his gesture, then the hideous little thing stood, stepped out of the case, and hopped off the tailgate. In another second, it was trotting down the dim dirt track in the direction Stroud pointed. It was quickly lost in the gloom.

With nothing else to do, Stroud returned to his truck and sat in the darkness of the cab, watching the dark dirt road and waiting. He knew that this might take some time. But surely, sometime around dawn, Simmons would emerge from the cabin to go to the outhouse. And when he did....

Before long, Stroud's eyes adjusted to the dim moonlight filtering through the trees, and he listened intently through the open windows for any kind of sound that wasn't natural, like a scream or a gunshot. But nothing came except the hiss of a light breeze in the treetops. For hours. At last, Stroud began to think that something had gone wrong. It was too long. Maybe he hadn't given the manin-pasuk enough of the animating potion. Maybe it was frozen up and lying around in the woods near the cabin. Shit! Maybe Simmons or one of his hunting buddies had found it. Stroud would lose everything.

His anxiety reached near panic levels by the time dawn began to tinge the sky. He was almost ready to start the truck and either drive away from here or approach the cabin, when he saw a diminutive figure shambling down the road. Relief flooding through him, he burst out of his truck and ran over to the manin-pasuk. It was barely mobile, its limbs already stiffening, and as soon as it saw him, it fell to the dirt.

Stroud was reluctant to pick it up while it still had any semblance of life, but he had to. He could see blood clotting its skin and hair. But he had to pack it up and get the hell out of here. He retrieved the towels he'd brought along, and went back to wrap up the doll. No sense in getting blood all over himself or the case.

"You should like me," Stroud told the Devil Child as he wrapped it up. "I have a lot for you to do."

As he lifted it, its body still had some give, and Stroud could feel its muscles flexing stiffly in his grip. In just a few minutes, he had the thing back in its case, the case back in the metal box, and the truck turned around and headed back toward the two-lane.

When he reached the gate, he forced himself to act calmly. He opened the gate, drove through, then closed and relocked the gate behind him. Then he was on the road, but he didn't head back to Oakdale. Instead, he steered west, toward the Texas border, hoping like hell that the blood on the doll belonged to James Simmons.

The drive back to the carnival was uneventful, which was just as well since Stroud felt like a nervous wreck on top of a lot of driving and not much sleep. He pulled up behind his office trailer in early afternoon. He didn't go in but went to find Hicks.

"Everything going okay?" he asked the manager.

"Just the normal."

Stroud went to his office trailer, got two hundred dollars in cash out of the safe, then locked up and went to the trailer he shared with Seraphina.

"You're back," she said as he came in through the door. She tried to give him a hug and a kiss, but he brushed her off.

"I'm too tired," he said. "I need to get some sleep. Why don't you get Dottie to drive you into town and get something to eat and do some shopping. You've been complaining you need new clothes. Here." He handed her the two hundred. "And get some new towels."

"What's wrong with the old ones?"

"I messed them up."

"Why can't I just drive myself?"

"I might need the truck before you get back."

The truth was, Stroud needed sleep badly, but he wanted Seraphina out of the trailer for a more important reason. He couldn't clean all the blood off the manin-pasuk with her watching. If he was lucky, he'd be napping when she got back.

After Seraphina drove off with Dottie, Stroud pulled the manin-pasuk's case from the truck and carried it into the trailer. There, he propped the doll in the shower stall and washed it down several times with shampoo. When the water running down the drain was no longer tinged with red, he toweled the doll then propped it up in front of a fan to finish drying it. He lay down on the bed to wait, and the next thing he knew, someone was banging on the trailer door.

"Baby!" It was Seraphina. "I'm back, but the door's locked."

Groggily, he stumbled across the trailer to the bathroom. The manin-pasuk was clean and dry, so he laid it in its case and shut the lid.

"Baby!" Seraphina called again, louder this time. "Johnny?"

"Maybe he's in his office," Stroud heard Dottie suggest.

"Yeah," Seraphina said. "He probably locked me out on purpose."

Her voice faded.

The bloody towels—the ones he wrapped the doll in after the deed had been done and the one he'd used to wash it—lay heaped in the shower stall. He stuffed them into a plastic trash bag, and after cracking the door to make sure that Seraphina and Dottie had left, he carried the bag to his truck and put it on the floor of the passenger seat. He could get rid of it later.

He went back into the trailer, and Seraphina showed up in a minute or two.

"Where were you, Johnny?" she whined. "I knocked and called."

"I was in the bathroom," he said. "I couldn't just get up and answer the door." He glanced at his watch. "I'm going over to my office for a few hours."

"Business, I suppose."

"That's right."

That night, he brushed her off again before he collapsed on the bed and slept.

The next day, after taking care of carnival business in the early hours, Stroud drove into town to find a pay phone. On the way, he disposed of the plastic bag of bloody towels in a dumpster behind a convenience store. Even if it was found, there was no way anybody was going to connect the blood with a murder two hundred miles away in a different state. Then he found a pay phone.

"You did it," Simmons said softly but excitedly when he answered and realized it was Stroud on the line.

"I didn't do anything," Stroud reminded him.

"Well, it's done, and it was done quickly. We barely finished breakfast on Saturday when I got the call to rush home. Like you said: a tragedy. Some wild animal."

217

"No sense in wasting time," Stroud said pointedly, and apparently Simmons not only got the point but sharpened it.

"Don't worry, John. There's no way I'd renege on our deal. We've only just started. When do you want to move to Oakland?"

Move? The word took Stroud by surprise, though he realized it shouldn't. Wasn't that what was necessary? But until this moment, it had been nothing but an abstract concept.

"As soon as possible."

"Great. Look, the reading of the will is tomorrow, and after that, I'll be in control of the bank. I already have a nice house scouted out for you—a two-story in a good neighborhood. I have enough cash on hand to front you the purchase. I'll make the arrangements, and you can sign the papers when you get here. When do you think that'll be?"

"A few days. Maybe a week."

"You bringing that woman—Seraphina—with you?"

"I'll be coming alone."

"She looks older than you, but I though you and she were together."

"You could say that," Stroud said, thinking, yeah, I'm ten years older than she is and look ten years younger.

"You don't sound happy about it."

"These days," Stroud said, "I measure my sexual prowess by how many hot flashes I give her."

"All right," Simmons chuckled. "Come see me when you get here. I'll be in the president's office at the bank."

* * *

The next week was busy for Stroud. He spent much of it surreptitiously packing and making preparations for his departure. He didn't want Seraphina to know before he was ready to walk out the door. She was enough trouble as it was. But she must have sensed that something was different.

"What's the matter, Johnny?" she asked one afternoon. "Didn't that business deal you went away for work out?"

"It worked out fine," he replied.

"Then what's wrong?"

"Nothing is wrong." He nearly snapped the words but managed

to blunt the cutting edge of his tone. "I just have a lot on my mind."

"Are we going to Florida this year?"

"Not this year."

"You know I prefer Florida to Texas."

"Then go to Florida," he said bluntly, staring at her. "I have other matters to attend to."

"I don't know what you're planning, Johnny, but I don't like the way you're acting."

"Fine," he said. "I'll remove myself so you don't have to see the way I'm acting."

Leaving her in a huff, he went to his office trailer. Just as well, he thought. He had a lot of paperwork to do before he departed for Oakdale. And plans to make.

The notes Joe had left in the margins of the maritime law book said that the longevity mixture needed to be ingested about every decade. It had been only six since Stroud first tried it, but he was about to embark on an endeavor that would require the performance of a lifetime and all the energy and personal power he could muster. He decided to dose himself one more time before he went to Oakdale.

But not here. Not at the carnival, where he'd be tended by Seraphina. He was beyond that, now. He didn't need her, or anybody else who was here.

But he still had some business with them. He called Hicks into his office trailer.

"Sit down, Hicks. We need to talk."

A worried look on his face, Hicks sat. Stroud was a dour man, but he didn't usually look this serious.

"When I bought Hanley Brothers, I told you it probably was going to be temporary."

"You're not saying you're getting out, are you?"

"That's exactly what I'm saying. Carnivals used to be the hit entertainment of the year. Carnivals all spring and summer, and in the fall we'd work the state fairs. A good act could rake in the dough and winter in someplace warm. Now it's all TV and movies and theme parks. No telling what's coming next to distract everybody. But whatever it is, you can be sure it doesn't have 'Live Carnies' on the marquee. We're a dying breed."

"But what will you do? Far as I can tell, you ain't done much but carny. You got carny blood."

"Maybe, but I know there's no future in the business, and there's something more for me out there in that big, wide world. I'm tired of traveling from town to town but never getting anywhere."

"You ain't talking about putting down roots, are you?" The older man looked astounded.

"Not the kind you're talking about. We travel from place to place, skimming the cream. But if you put your mind to it, you can own the cow. And that brings me to our own cash cow. I know I snatched it out from under you when I bought it from Dixon, so I'm offering to sell it to you for the same amount I paid for it."

"That's pretty generous, John."

"You're the one who vouched for me in the beginning and got me on here," Stroud said. "You were decent to me all those years, and you've been a loyal manager. And you know this outfit better than anybody, even me. There's only one stipulation. When I bought from Dixon, I told him he could live out his life in the farmhouse at the wintering grounds, and you have to live up to that agreement."

"That won't be much of an effort," Hicks said. "Dixon done for me like I done for you. I'd never turn him out."

"All right." Stroud extended his hand, and Hicks shook it.

"When do you want to do the actual deal?" Hicks asked.

"We can go into town and find a bank with a notary. They can transfer the funds and notarize the paperwork."

"All right. As a matter of fact, I keep my savings in the Dunnison State Bank."

"There's one more thing," Stroud said.

"Name it."

"I'm not taking Seraphina with me."

"That's cold, John."

"Maybe, but that's the way it is. We're not getting along, but that doesn't mean I bear her any ill will. I'd appreciate it if you let her set up her Seraphina and the Serpent act again. She can have my tent and trailer. You get the office trailer for yourself."

"I'll do it, but it ain't going to go as well as it used to. She ain't the woman she was then."

"Maybe not, but she'll get back into it if that's all she has."

"All right, John," Hicks said a little sadly.

"Don't go all mopey, Hicks. You're now sole owner of Hanley Brothers."

The next day, Stroud and Hicks went into town to make final arrangements, and afterwards, he went back to his—Seraphina's—trailer to do his final packing and to tell Seraphina the news.

She didn't take it well and flew at him in rage. He flung her back onto the bed and loomed over her, stance threatening.

"Stay there," he ordered. "You get up and interfere with me, and I'll hurt you."

"Why, Johnny?" she sobbed. "I been good to you."

"You've been good to yourself," he snorted. "It's time for me to move on."

"But how am I going to make it without you?"

"Hicks promised to keep you on. You can have the trailer and my tent. Go back to doing Seraphina and the Serpent."

"Slinky's too old."

"Here." He tossed an envelope onto the bed next to her. "That's ten grand. Enough to buy yourself another snake and stake you until your act gets going."

"You're a cruel man," she said, picking up the envelope and glancing inside.

You have no idea, he thought as he picked up his suitcase and headed out the door. Everything else that he needed was in the pickup, and in five minutes, he was out on the blacktop, heading toward Oakdale.

When he arrived, he didn't immediately call Ira Simmons. Instead, he checked into a hotel—a good one, this time—and retreated to his room where he hung the do-not-disturb sign on the door. Then he mixed a batch of the longevity formula and drank the nasty shit down.

Three days of violent illness ensued, but even while it went on, he realized that it wasn't as bad as the first time. Obviously the formula rapidly cleaned toxins from the body, and since the first time he'd taken the formula, he'd been careful about his diet. And he'd cut out alcohol entirely.

Afterward, when he could do things without shaking with

weakness, he checked the bags containing the powder. Plenty more doses, he figured, to give himself extra years and to use the maninpasuk to his advantage.

But eventually the bags would be empty. What then?

Joe's notes didn't cover that. Maybe the old shaman—Tuchaua —never told him. Maybe even Tuchaua didn't know. He'd used the stuff for a couple of centuries, it sounded like, and he was still feisty enough to need two wives.

Two centuries, and still feisty. It made living a long time appealing.

But running out of the powder was decades away, and he'd deal with that problem then. Right now, it was time for other matters.

He picked up the phone and called Ira Simmons.

11: SYNDICATE

1978

THE RUMOR AROUND town was that Bigfoot killed James Simmons. Couldn't have been anything else around these parts, folks said. Must have come out of the forest. Probably a whole family of them living back in there.

Ridiculous as it was, the talk made the police want to close the case as quickly as possible. The official story was that it was a bear mauling. Or maybe it was a cougar. Big cat like that could do some real damage. It had to be something like that. What else could have attacked Simmons so silently and chewed the heart right out of his chest?

Where either a bear or a cougar had come from in southwestern Louisiana remained a mystery. Some folks thought that the creature had strayed up from the swamps to the southeast, where there were remnant populations of both. A few even thought it might have escaped from a circus or carnival, but the one carnival that came through town regularly didn't have a bear or any animals and never had. And anyway, it hadn't been around for a month or two and was over in Texas somewhere when the attack occurred.

Stroud had been amused by the rumors, some of which even made the local headlines considering how important James Simmons had been to Oakdale. But it looked like his son, Ira, was stepping into his shoes quite nicely, and the bank and other investments didn't suffer so much as a blip in their pulses. Must have been because the younger Simmons had gone to college and learned business administration, people thought. That sounded pretty good to the merchants in town who did business with the bank, and to homeowners whose ability to have a roof over their heads depended on loans.

Not long after James Simmons' death, one of the other prominent board members dropped off the board, citing a desire to spend more time with his family. Ira didn't have to ask Stroud to use the manin-pasuk to accomplish this. He already had enough dirt on the man—dirt formerly used by his father to assert control over him. But Ira didn't want to control the man, he just wanted to get rid of him. He might have been an asset once, but now he was opposed to Ira and was a liability. And Ira needed that empty board seat to make room for Stroud.

Stroud's first board meeting was held in the conference room at Simmons' offices. Simmons introduced Stroud as a venture capitalist looking to invest in Oakdale.

"Why Oakdale?" asked Thomas Fitzsimmons. "This is a nice town, a prosperous town, but still relatively small compared to Baton Rouge or New Orleans. What could you possibly invest in here that would make your investment worthwhile?"

"I might ask the same thing of you, Thomas," Stroud said. "You're one of the scions of Oakdale and a wealthy man in your own right. Why are you still here in Oakdale?"

"I was born here, for one thing," Fitzsimmons answered. "My family has roots here."

"That's no answer," Stroud said. Fitzsimmons started to bristle, but Stroud saw it coming and damped him down. "It's a reason, and maybe a good one, but it doesn't address the actual issue, which is: Why invest in a small town like Oakdale? The answer is simple. Oakdale is a wonderful town that is ready to grow, and grow in a big way. Everybody in this room knows that. That's why we're all here. I want to help make that happen."

"Just to be clear," put in Jeff Goins. "Do you intend to do that at our expense?"

All the board members were concerned about the hasty departure of one of their own so soon after James Simmons' death and the intrusion of this stranger.

"I assume you mean your personal expense," Stroud said. "But I'll include the town, as well. Absolutely not. The way toward growth isn't a matter of taking control of Oakdale, but in taking control of the rest of the parish and making Oakdale its economic hub."

"Mighty big plans for a new board member," Fitzsimmons said, his tone bearing a slight undercurrent of hostility.

"You're right," Stroud said. "I do have big plans."

"Perhaps you'll enlighten us as time progresses."

"The board will be the first to know," Stroud promised.

Talk then moved on to other board business, most of which Stroud tuned out. None of it really mattered—or wouldn't as time progressed. At last, the meeting was over, and the rest of the board members departed, leaving Stroud and Simmons alone.

"What you said about not wanting to take control of the town," Ira said. "I thought that's exactly what we want to do."

"We do," Stroud assured him. "And we are. But it's a mistake to go after the head until you've dealt with the body. We'll play them out like the rubes they are, and when we reel them in, they won't even realize that they bit the hook voluntarily and offered themselves up for dinner. Anyway, we need them—or most of them—for the time being to make things happen smoothly."

"Fitzsimmons looks like he might be a problem."

"If we need to, we can oust him from the board. Any dirt on him?"

"Not anything that would stick."

"We'll find a way if necessary. In the meantime, we need to begin our own venture."

"I was thinking of calling it S&S Holding Company," Simmons said. "We can incorporate, which will shield us from personal scrutiny as well as from legal liability."

"I like that," Stroud said.

Simmons nodded.

"I'll have the articles of incorporation drawn up right away."

"As soon as you do, I've targeted our first investment."

"Already?"

"Already." Stroud didn't tell him that he'd planned on this purchase for decades. "It's an outfit up in Woodville called the Richmond Lumber Company. I want you to buy it lock-stock-and-barrel and cheat the owners as much as you can."

"Sounds personal," Simmons said, smiling.

"Very."

Very personal, maybe, but not very simple. Andrew Buchman, now in his late sixties, was willing enough to sell Richmond Lumber, but he was asking top dollar. The nearby cities—and even the larger towns—were booming, and Buchman told the buyer Simmons sent to open inquiries into the company that Richmond Lumber always operated at full capacity. In fact, he could double the size of the operation and still keep everybody busy. To make matters worse, he was already in negotiations with a national company that produced plywood and wood chips for paper pulp as well as lumber.

"Have your representative tell Buchman that I want to speak with him personally."

"I can do that. Any particular time?"

"Yes. And place. His mill, but it has to be after closing time. Tell him I'm out of town and am just flying in and can't make it earlier. I don't care what day it is, as long as it's a weekday. Oh, and Ira: Don't mention my name."

"A weekday at night?" Simmons frowned. "No one else around. You're not going...."

"Nothing that drastic. Not yet. Just a little demonstration to convince him to sell to us at the lowest possible figure."

"You're going to show him the manin-pasuk?"

"Let's say I'm going to introduced them."

Stroud saw a look that combined jealousy with disappointment creep into Ira's eyes.

"Ah, yes," he said, understanding. "You're right to be upset. One of our enemies is going to meet our little protector before even you have seen him in action." Stroud gave a short laugh. "Ira. You told me were partners, right?"

Simmons nodded, his eyes now blank. Was that from fear? Or relief?

"Fifty-fifty," Stroud went on. "I wouldn't dream of leaving you out. Why don't you join me and Mr. Buchman? Then you can meet the manin-pasuk, too. I promise that he will come to recognize you as my partner. In any case, the presence of the president of a bank should sweeten the lure to make sure we get Buchman alone."

It did. The appointment was set for Thursday night at eight. By then, everybody would be gone except for the night watchman, assuming they'd bothered to hire a new one after Charlie Folger died. If they had, it probably was another cancer-ridden mill worker on his way to the great pine plantation in the sky.

* * *

"It's spooky out here in the woods with no one around," Simmons said as he stopped his Cadillac where Stroud indicated. Dusk had not yet fully settled, and the dirt track they'd turned down five minutes earlier was a pale lane between shadowy forest buttresses. The meeting with Buchman was less than an hour from now.

"It's about the get a lot spookier."

They got out and went to the rear of the car, where Simmons opened the trunk. Inside lay the manin-pasuk, securely wrapped in a pair of blankets. Stroud lifted it out, laid it on the ground, and unwrapped the blankets. Simmons hissed when it's features were revealed.

"I haven't seen it lately," he said. "I forgot how...how vital it is."

"You haven't seen anything yet."

Stroud retrieved a small paper sack from the trunk and opened it. Inside were the things he needed to animate the doll. There remained enough light to do what he needed to do. He'd premeasured the powder and brought it folded up in a small piece of paper. He was going to have to let Ira see how the manin-pasuk was animated, but there was no sense in giving him more information than he needed.

The blood part, well, Ira would have to see that. Stroud quickly dropped his trousers, carved a shallow cut beside the scars from the previous cuts, and caught the blood in the demitasse he'd bought just for this purpose. He slapped a bandage on his leg, refastened his pants and, without any explanation, opened the packet and dumped the powder into the blood. Before, he'd used a teaspoon to mix up the potion, but this time he used his finger. He felt gross doing it, but the showman in him made him go on. The freakier and more intimate it was for Ira, the more control Stroud would be able to exert over him later.

Harder was using that finger to smear the paste into the damn thing's mouth. As his finger, bearing a dollop of the potion, neared the manin-pasuk's lips, Stroud fleetingly wondered if this was going to be the last time he saw that finger. The doll's lips were hard beneath his touch as he smeared the paste between them. He kept his finger, but the corners of the thing's mouth were already twitching as he pulled back.

"Don't move," he cautioned Simmons, who looked more frozen than the manin-pasuk, whose limbs popped and creaked as they flexed.

Then the thing took a deep breath, sat up, and stiffly got to its feet. It stood there for a moment, swaying slightly, gazing between the two men.

"You know us," Stroud said to it. "I am your master, and this is my partner. I've told you what you are to do. I am ready for you to do it." He looked up at Simmons. "Ira, get the blankets and put them back in the trunk."

Simmons remained rooted to the spot, simply staring at the manin-pasuk.

"Ira! Put the blankets in the trunk."

Woodenly, and shying back from the manin-pasuk, Simmons complied.

"Get back in the car."

Simmons obeyed, and Stroud opened the back passenger door and gestured for the manin-pasuk to get in. Then he got in the front seat and shut the door.

"Drive up until you can turn around, then drive to the mill."

"I don't know if I can," Simmons said, his face pale in the gathering dusk. "I didn't realize...."

"Drive, Ira. You can do it."

Simmons did, though he had to fumble the car into gear and his fingers trembled on the steering wheel. He could feel that horrible Devil Child back there radiating pent-up rage, madness, and ravenous hunger just waiting....

Eventually the short road to the mill came into view, and Simmons couldn't have been more glad to be out of the confines of the car. But then Stroud opened the back door and let the thing out with them.

"Follow behind," Stroud told it. "Do not let yourself be seen until I call you." He turned to Simmons. "It's time to go strike our first deal, Ira."

Stroud went into the mill, Simmons close behind. Simmons glanced back to see if the manin-pasuk was following, but within moments, it faded into the shadows cast by the silent machinery, and he lost track of it. Stroud seemed to pay it no mind as he strode purposefully forward.

"You seem like you know where you're going," Simmons said, staring around at the confusion of machinery, piles of lumber, and shadows.

"I do."

They met no one as they made their way through the darkened mill. At last, Simmons could see a light from an open door shining up ahead. The room beyond was an outer office with a desk and other office furnishings. Simmons saw Stroud give the desk a look that was unreadable, then he approached a door set in the far wall and knocked.

"Come in," came a voice from beyond.

"Don't close the door behind you," Stroud told Simmons as he reached for the knob. "Stand to one side after you go in."

Stroud turned the knob, opened the door, and went inside. Simmons followed and immediately stepped to his right, away from the door, as Stroud approached the desk. The man behind it stood, came around, and extended his hand.

"Andrew Buchman," he said to Stroud. "You must be Ira Simmons."

"No," Stroud said, waving at Simmons and ignoring Buchman's hand. "That's Ira."

A bit nonplussed, Buchman lowered his hand.

"Then you must be the investor." Buchman peered at Stroud. "Do I know you from somewhere."

"You do. I'm John Stroud."

Buchman recoiled.

"My god. John. We didn't know what happened to you. Your mother thought you were dead."

"I was."

"She died last year. Did you hear?"

"I heard but do not care," Stroud said, then he waved toward Buchman's chair. "Shall we get started?"

"What do you want?" Buchman asked as he took his seat. Even though he seemed to gain some sense of protection behind his big mahogany desk, Stroud could see that his hands were trembling. Stroud and Simmons took the guest chairs.

"Richmond Lumber Company. For starters."

"I've told your representative my price."

"Your price. Maybe your price for others, but not for me."

"What does that mean?"

"It means that the money you and my mother used to buy out Old Man Richmond was rightfully mine. The way I look at it, the mill is half mine already. So here's my offer: I'll pay you exactly half your asking price."

Buchman laughed, and for the first time since he'd learned who Stroud was, he began to relax.

"You stole my daughter's virginity—not to mention my car and a lot of money—and now you want to steal my company?"

"Stole her virginity? She gave that to me, not that it mattered. She did worse to me. She stole my heart. So let's just say the car and cash were payment for that."

"So that's what this is about. Claire."

"No. Maybe once, but not now. I don't even know where she is, nor do I care. I'm glad she turned me down."

"Doesn't matter one way or another," Buchman said. "I'll sell you the mill, John, but you'll pay what I'm asking. You're not the only interested party."

"I'm the only one who should interest you," Stroud said. "I'm at a turning point in my life, Buchman, and which way I go depends a lot on your personal ethics."

"Mine? And what about yours?"

"We'll see about those after we discover yours."

Buchman leaned back in his chair, perusing Stroud.

"You're different, John," he said. "I can't put my finger on it, but you're not like I thought you'd turn out."

"I'm here for your company, not a philosophical discussion. I'll want the deal done now, before we leave."

"Is that right?" Buchman said. "Sounds like there might be a threat in there somewhere." He turned to Simmons, who sat rigidly in his chair. The smaller man was clearly nervous about something, Buchman realized. "How about you, Simmons? You okay with that? I did a little checking on you before this meeting, and I know you're who you say you are: a fine, upstanding citizen of your community. What are you doing associating with a low-life like John Stroud?"

"Look at me, Buchman," Stroud commanded before Simmons could answer. "I'm the one you're dealing with. Ira is just here as a witness."

"Well, I'm glad somebody is here besides me and you," Buchman said, standing and coming around the end of his desk. "Now he can witness me ordering you out of my mill. No deal for you, Stroud. Not even at double the price."

"That's not what he's here to witness," Stroud said, remaining in his chair. "Manin-pasuk."

Buchman saw Simmons shrink into his chair as if cowering inside, and then he saw something else come through the door.

"Fuck!" he gasped, taking a step backward and raising his hands. "What the fuck is that?"

"Meet my personal protector, Buchman." Stroud didn't bother to look at the manin-pasuk, though the eyes of both other men were riveted on it. He simply remained relaxed in his chair as he waved it into the room. "I am its master, and it will do anything I tell it to do. Anything." Finally he twisted enough in his chair to see the manin-pasuk, and he urged it closer to Buchman.

"I want him to get a good sniff of your scent," he told Buchman. "That shouldn't be hard right now. I can smell your fear, myself. It might help him when he hunts you down and rips you to shreds. You and anybody else around. By the way, he likes to eat the heart right out of his victim's chest. I think he does it while they're still alive."

By now, Buchman had retreated to the far side of his desk, and the manin-pasuk had him backed into a corner. Stroud rose and approached them, stopping about six feet from Buchman, the little monstrosity between them, staring up at Buchman with a sarcastic and vicious leer. Buchman had urinated on himself.

"What do you say, Andrew?" Stroud asked pleasantly. "Shall we make it a deal? Ira has the papers with him, ready for you to sign, and I have a cashier's check for the amount I've already mentioned. Or shall we deal with your heirs? That would be Claire, right?"

"Yes," Buchman managed to get through a mouth drawn tight with terror. "We can deal."

Stroud touched the manin-pasuk's shoulder.

"Wait beside the car. Don't let yourself be seen."

The little horror turned and walked out of the office.

"Maybe you ought to sit down," Stroud said, leading Buchman over to his desk, where he collapsed into his chair. "The papers, Ira."

Simmons pulled the documents from his briefcase and passed them with a shaking hand to Stroud, who placed them in front of Buchman along with a pen and the cashier's check.

"No need to read them, Andrew. We've just discussed the terms of the agreement." He pressed the pen into Buchman's hand. "Don't hesitate. You understand what failure to sign means."

Buchman signed. Stroud gathered up the papers, handed them back to Ira, who notarized them. When he was done, Stroud looked at Buchman.

"Our new manager will arrive on Monday," he said. "I trust you'll have your office cleared out by the end of the weekend." He straightened and walked to the door. There, he turned and gave Buchman one last look. "I wouldn't tell anyone about what transpired here this evening." He laughed. "Remember what will happen if you do. Besides, who would believe you, anyway?" He nodded at Simmons. "Let's go, Ira."

They walked back through the darkened mill to their car. The manin-pasuk was waiting there for them, and Stroud made it climb into the trunk, into its nest of blankets.

"I'll bet they didn't teach you advanced negotiations like that in business school, did they, Ira?" Stroud asked as he closed the trunk lid.

Simmons bent over and vomited on the pavement.

That night, Stroud left his hotel room and drove to a familiar location: Buchman's house. Or rather, the back of the house. There, he sneaked into the shed where he and Claire had made love all those years ago. He snorted. Made love.

In the beam of the flashlight he'd brought, the interior was even shabbier than he remembered. The pallet where he and Claire had lain was gone, replaced by two rusty power mowers on top of which lay a careless pile of equally rusty gardening implements. Thick dust lay over everything. Nobody had been out here in a long time.

He turned and shone the flashlight beam toward his left, took a couple of steps in that direction, and knelt down. The ill-fitting juncture of the wall and warped and cracked floorboards looked washed out beneath the light. He bent closer and changed the angle of the beam.

Could it really be? he thought, seeing a vague curve of something wedged down in the crack. He used his pocket knife to pry the object out, but even before he had, he knew. The ring. It lay there in his hand, dirty and unused. He blew and brushed off the dust and saw the golden sheen beneath.

With a small smile and a slight shake of his head, he dropped the ring into his pocket and left the shed.

1984

Ira Simmons might have been completely terrified during his first encounter with the animated manin-pasuk, but that didn't mean he wasn't eager to repeat the experience.

"I'm telling you, John, we have to get rid of Garrett."

He and Stroud were in his office, discussing strategy.

"And I'll say it again," Stroud said. "We can't have the thing slaughtering willy-nilly around town."

"Well, can't we just use it to scare him? Like you did to Buchman?"

"The fewer people who see the manin-pasuk the better. A lot of folks around these parts saw it when I was hawking it at the carnival, and I don't want anybody to recognize it. Or me. Haven't you found any dirt on him like you did that defunct board member?"

"Not the kind of dirt we need. I hired a detective agency out of Baton Rouge, and they tell me Garrett has some sort of connection to the mob in New Orleans. In fact, it looks like it's the mob who's financing him, but there's nothing we can substantiate. At least for blackmail purposes. As far as Oakdale is concerned, Garrett is a solid citizen. Can't even find any significant indiscretions from when he went to college." Simmons paused then went on. "Look, John, we can get along without this guy's support, but we can't face his opposition. He's got a lot of connections, and he has his sights set on being our next mayor. And he doesn't need us to get there. Either we bring him on board with this deal, or we eliminate him. And I can tell you right now, he's not going to be convinced by a buy-out offer. Not with mob money behind him."

"We'll see," Stroud said. "We haven't begun negotiations yet, and I think that Garrett's aspirations might be all the leverage we need. After all, he can't be happy being under the mob's thumb."

The deal Simmons referred to concerned a shopping mall that S&S Holding wanted to build on the edge of town. Over the span of four years, S&S had bought up thousands of acres through various shell companies to avoid giving notice of its plans. Most of the property lay in the parish outside of the city limits, but there was some overlap, so the project had to be approved by the city council. The mall was critical for S&S's financial future. It was the anchor for several housing developments the company was planning to erect surrounding the mall, which in turn would provide housing for workers for the four manufacturing companies that S&S was in the process of convincing to come to Oakdale. Under S&S auspices, of course.

Longtime city council member William Garrett might not have known about all those other negotiations and deals. He was against the project for his own reasons, foremost among them was that he was secretly investing in a company proposing a similar mall across town. And the fact was, Oakdale just wasn't big enough for two malls. Not yet, at least. But if Garrett was ignorant of S&S's larger plans, Simmons, being president of Oakdale's most prominent bank, was quite aware of his.

"All right, Ira," Stroud said at last. "I can see you're convinced we need to employ our special bargaining tool. But frankly, I think you just want to see it in action again."

Simmons stared, then laughed.

"Maybe you're right," he said. "I promise I won't throw up again."

"At least you did it before you got in the car," Stroud said. "How do you propose to get Garrett alone?"

That, it turned out, was simple. Garrett, unaware that Ira Simmons was one of his economic rivals, had applied to the bank for a loan to help cover his share of the competing shopping mall. The amount was substantial, and in a small town, negotiations like that could easily be conducted outside of normal business hours and not raise suspicion. Simmons simply invited Garrett to his home to discuss the loan over dinner.

There was to be no dinner. Simmons told his wife, Elizabeth, that he was having a business meeting at the house and asked her to take their children, Patrick and Mindy, to the movies.

Garrett arrived on time, almost to the minute. Simmons answered the ring of the doorbell, ushered Garrett inside, and led him to the living room. Stroud was already there.

"I'm not sure I understand, Ira," Garrett said as Stroud stood. "I thought we were going to discuss my financing."

"We are," Simmons said.

"With a third party present?"

"For the moment, consider John to be a consultant."

Garrett's eyes narrowed as they gazed at Stroud, then he stepped forward, hand extended.

"All right. Bill Garrett."

"John Stroud," Stroud said, shaking briefly.

"Do I know you?"

"I don't recall ever meeting," Stroud said.

"No matter," Garrett shrugged. "You just look familiar. I must have seen you around town."

He and Stroud sank into armchairs, and Simmons took the sofa. "You have something to say, say it," Garrett said easily enough. "But know this right up front: I'm not particularly interested in sharing my project."

"That's a mouthful to say to a consultant," Stroud laughed.

"Cut the shit, John. I can smell a deal-maker a mile off."

"All right, Bill, I'll get right to it. You're right that I'm here about your deal. And ours. You have to know that a company called S&S Holdings is trying to do the same thing as you on the other side of town."

"S&S Holdings," Garrett mused, his eyes lighting. "Simmons and Stroud. Or is that Stroud and Simmons?"

"It's both," Stroud said.

Garrett shook his head.

"Your mall isn't going to happen without the approval of the city council. You need to take it up with them."

"We are, and we want you to throw your influence our way."

"And cut my own financial throat?"

"You wouldn't walk away empty handed," Simmons said.

"That mall is my future," Garrett said. "No way I'm just handing things over to the opposition."

"I'd like to convince you that if you do not do as we suggest, you will not have a future."

"Are you threatening me?" Garrett stood, shoulders tense. "If you know about my deal, maybe you also know about my backers. They're not the kind of people who back off."

"No, they're not," Stroud said. "But Ira and I have a secret weapon that can nullify any opposition."

"The New Orleans mob?" Garrett snorted a laugh.

"Don't laugh until you meet the manin-pasuk." Stroud pointed.

Garrett's eyes turned in the direction indicated by Stroud's finger then widened and a gasping inhale sucked between his teeth as the manin-pasuk stepped in through the dining room door.

"Holy shit!" he said on the exhale. "That's the Devil Child!" Garrett tore his eyes away from the manin-pasuk and stared at Stroud. "The barker. Now I recognize you. You shaved the mustache and sideburns." His eyes went back to the demonic little figure. "It's really alive. You weren't shitting everybody."

"So you recognize us," Stroud said. "Maybe that makes things easier."

"Not for me," Garrett said, eyes still riveted on the manin-pasuk. "I'm caught between a mob execution and being torn apart by that thing." His voice was surprisingly steady.

"The choice doesn't have to come to that."

"What, then? I have nothing to offer if you can just have that thing rip it all away."

"That's not true. If I eliminate your mob problem, you can then freely offer your loyalty."

"And if I give it, what makes you think I won't turn on you later?"

"If protection isn't enough, how about greed?" Stroud smiled. "I think that you'll quickly learn that you can make a hell of a lot more money and gain even greater power by joining us."

"By dropping my mall project."

"By doing that, then turning around to invest your money in our venture."

"I own thirty percent of my mall. What's my cut of yours?"

"Ten percent, but we'll throw in some of the profits from the housing developments."

"Housing developments?" Garrett's eyes widened a little.

"Your ten percent will exceed the thirty percent you forsake. And now for the sweetener."

Garrett cocked his head, eyes narrowing.

"We're prepared to back your political career, all the way to the state legislature."

"In return for influence?"

"Of course." Stroud laughed. "But since you'll own a piece of the company that's benefitting, let's just say that it will be influence well spent."

"It would be illegal…."

"Don't worry about the legalities," Simmons put in. "We can bury your involvement behind a string of blind companies. But the power will be real, and so will the money."

"And the alternative is…that?" Garrett waved at the manin-pasuk.

"Or the mob. You know they'll turn on you eventually. But do we really need the Devil Child to convince you to share millions of dollars with us and have us help you get elected to the state legislature?" Stroud asked. "Maybe even a higher office than that. I just want you to meet my little friend to know what potent allies you have in Ira and me. We'll take care of any mob entanglements you might have. Who knows how far we can go with a friend like the Devil Child. I assure you that Ira and I plan to go very far. It would be wise to invest in us."

"I must have seen that Devil Child a dozen times over the years," Garrett said. "I always thought there was something strange about it." He rubbed his jaw and stared at Simmons. "Wasn't your father torn apart by some sort of wild animal?"

"My father met a tragic end," Simmons said. "Others might, too. We can either be the ones meeting that end or the ones profiting from it."

"By the way, Ira," Stroud said, seeming to change the subject. "I hear that you and some of the other town fathers are opening a private academy for gifted students from our parish."

"We are. It will be one of the first facilities built to serve the new subdivisions. My own son, Patrick, is already enrolled. Why?"

"Bill has a son, doesn't he? Howard? Isn't he the same age as your son? I'm pretty sure that he'd like to see Howard admitted."

"Sure," Simmons nodded. "Howard should be going there. I'll see to it."

"Anything else?" Stroud asked, staring at Garrett.

"I guess I have no choice," Garrett shrugged. "But I want you to know this: I'm more interested in the benefits than I am afraid of your little friend. Death awaits us all in some form or other, but fortune and power are for the very few. I'll gladly join you if I get to be one of those."

"I like your fortitude, Bill," Stroud said. "I'm glad we had this chat. We'll go a long way together."

*   *   *

"Face it, John. This is small-town Louisiana. Folks notice things and are going to talk. You know the score. You need to get a woman, and I don't mean the whores at the Cozy Inn. Somebody regular."

"You aren't talking marriage, are you?" Stroud frowned. "I'm not having that."

"Okay, then. No marriage. But you need to put up a front. Find someone and have her move in with you."

"Won't they talk more about me shacking up unmarried?"

"They'll admire your balls. Trust me on this one, John. Better they think that you're indiscreet than that you're queer or banging hookers."

"I don't know." Stroud shook his head. "I tried that a couple of times before, and it didn't work out well."

"Fine, so maybe this time won't either. That's not the point. If you have trouble, you can drop her and get another."

238

"I don't even know how to go about finding a woman, any more," Stroud said. As if he ever had, he thought disgruntledly.

"Joanne and I can help out."

"Set me up with a blind date?" Stroud laughed. "That's ridiculous."

"I was thinking more about a party. Plenty of guests to defuse the situation, and I'll make sure Elizabeth invites several of her most eligible friends. That way, you can look them over and maybe talk to them informally. You're damn good looking for your age, and one of them will stand out. You can take it from there if you want."

And that's how Stroud met Carol Mignon. She wasn't the only woman there interested in Stroud, but there was something about her vivacious personality that Stroud liked. She was so completely different from the other women in his life that he thought, maybe, things might not play out the way they had before.

Carol was a thirty-three-year-old divorcee who'd grown up in a small nearby town and moved to Oakdale when she married right after college. He husband had been a philanderer, and Carol dumped him after the third time she'd caught him with a mistress. She worked as a secretary for a local furniture company.

She and Stroud had their first date—not a blind one, thank goodness—two weeks after the party, and two dates later, she invited him into her house when he brought her home. She was good in bed—a hell of a lot more responsive than the whores he'd resorted to over the past few years.

And she didn't ask many questions, though she obviously wanted to know more about the man she'd let into her house and into her body. Stroud told her he was from Woodville, had saved enough to invest, and had invested wisely. Now he was in the business of business. Not much to tell, really. It was all planning and a bunch of boring negotiations, followed by more planning.

Carol understood that and was content enough, for the moment. This new man in her life was mysterious, and she'd crack him eventually, but until then, he was interesting and well off and displayed a decent mixture of masculinity, tenderness, and inventiveness when he had his way with her.

The mob in New Orleans—the Baldovino crime family, to be specific—was not happy when Garrett flipped on them and threw his support behind the S&S project instead of theirs. They sent two men to Oakland to let him know that his association with them was to be terminated. Permanently.

"Take your wife and son on an unscheduled road trip," Stroud suggested to him when they learned that two tough looking men had just checked into a motel on the south side of town. "Go up to the Ozarks or Hot Springs. We'll take care of matters while you're gone. Drive your wife's car, and give me the keys to yours."

After Garrett left with his wife and son, Stroud made plans. He was reluctant to use the doll around Oakdale. One mysterious wild animal attack was a phenomenon, but more than one a decade would arouse suspicions. The two mob enforcers weren't locals, though, and their deaths wouldn't be noticed if they died elsewhere. And the method of their death might be disguised.

The enforcers were good at their job and, thanks to information planted by Stroud and Simmons, soon discovered that Garrett and his family had fled. They were hiding, the enforcers learned, in a small hunting cabin half an hour north of town.

It was the cabin where the manin-pasuk had killed James Simmons. It was still in the Simmons family, but no one ever went out there. Not since Simmons' terrible death. Stroud was waiting for them. He'd driven out in Garrett's car and left the gate to the dirt road unlocked. He parked in front of the cabin. It was looking pretty shabby these days, and its formerly crisp coat of paint was cracked and peeling. He unlocked the door and carried the manin-pasuk inside. There, he brought the doll to life with the bloody concoction.

"Two men," he said. "Wait here for them, but kill them outside. I will wait for you in the woods."

He left the cabin and shut the door but did not lock it. In thirty seconds, he was hidden behind the bole of a large pine. He noticed that, oddly, he wasn't at all nervous. But then, it wasn't him who should be nervous.

The enforcers showed up right on cue. They didn't drive their car all the way to the cabin, but in the still air, Stroud heard it approach and stop about a quarter of a mile off. Ten minutes later, he could see the first of the men cautiously edge around the last bend in the dirt road and peer at the cabin. It must have looked safe enough because he signaled to the man behind him, and both came toward the cabin, moving quickly, guns drawn.

At the cabin door, they didn't bother to knock. The bigger of the two kicked in the door, and the smaller one started to rush in, but he almost instantly fell beneath the weight and ferocity of the Devil Child. The bigger man bellowed in fear and shot at the little demon. There was no apparent effect, and the man turned and ran for the dirt road. He made it half way across the clearing before the manin-pasuk, moving with pure speed and energy, streaked toward him and pounced on his back. In seconds, it had shredded the enforcer's neck with vicious swipes of its taloned fingers.

Blood fountaining into the air, the man fell onto his back, pawing at the remains of his throat. The manin-pasuk climbed onto his chest, chewed through the clothing and flesh, reached into the gaping wound, and wrenched the heart free. It raised the heart to its mouth, took a large bite from it, then cast it aside as it went back to where the smaller man lay, twitching. The man's weak screams ended wetly.

The manin-pasuk stood over him, dripping gore, and eating the heart he'd ripped from the smaller enforcer. By now, Stroud had walked into the clearing. He stared down at the dead men—at the gaping holes in their chests—then he looked at his demon warrior. Its glittering black eyes held nothing but the desire to kill again.

"Soon," Stroud promised. "Very soon."

Ignoring the blood that smeared his hands and clothes, Stroud fished in the dead enforcers' pockets until he found a set of car keys. He went down the road until he located the car and drove it back to the clearing. He opened the trunk and with effort, levered the larger man into the trunk. Then he did the same for the smaller man.

Stroud waited until dark, then he drove their car to a dilapidated and abandoned service station about three miles from the entrance to the road that led to the cabin. There, he dragged the bodies out of the trunk and put them in the front seat. Gas from the two five-gal-

241

lon cans he'd brought with him completed the preparations, and it only took the touch of a lighter to the trail of gas to ignite the car. Stroud had opened the car's gas cap, but he wasn't prepared for the explosion, which nearly knocked him to the ground.

After that, he hurried off. It would take him nearly an hour to get back to the relative safety of the dirt road. He'd gone only about a quarter of the distance when he had to duck into the roadside brush to avoid being seen by the occupants of a pair of cop cars driving full-tilt toward the fire, rooftop lights blazing. Finally, he reached the cabin. The manin-pasuk was lying beside Garrett's car, rigid.

Stroud doused it with water from a five-gallon gas can to clean off the worst of the blood, then he wrapped the doll in a blanket and put the bundle into the trunk. He changed his own clothes, stuffing the bloody garments into a plastic bag, then he drove without lights down the dirt road. He stopped just around the last bend before the gate, got out, and walked to the gate to stare up and down the road.

Nobody was coming. All the excitement had already drawn law enforcement and the curious. Stroud unlocked the gate, pulled through, relocked it, and drove back to Oakdale.

But that wasn't the end of the matter. Once the two enforcers failed to return, the Baldovino family would send others. If there remained a Baldovino family to do that. Stroud intended to make that event unlikely.

*   *   *

The Baldovinos lived on a ten-acre estate just outside of New Orleans. It was modeled on the design of an old Southern plantation, with the exception being that the quarters where slaves might have lived were upgraded to house Baldovino muscle, two of whom would never be coming home. The property backed up to a marsh and the rest of the perimeter was surrounded by an eight-foot hurricane fence topped with razor wire.

The Baldovino's must have believed that their compound was a virtual fortress, Stroud thought as he cruised by in his new Lincoln Towncar the day after he'd taken care of the enforcers. Maybe it would be safe from human interlopers, but not from the manin-pasuk.

242

That night, he drove back and parked a hundred feet down a dirt road he'd spotted during his scouting trip. The road led up to the mound of a levee about a quarter of a mile from the Baldovino fence line, but Stroud only went far enough that his car couldn't be spotted from the blacktop. He got out and stared toward the house. He could easily see it despite the dark and distance of nearly a mile since it was almost totally exposed above the wetlands and lit up like a rocket gantry.

Stroud opened the trunk, lifted out the blanket-wrapped manin-pasuk, and laid it on the ground. In short order, he'd unwrapped it, carved a new slice on his leg beside the growing number of scars and the cut from yesterday, mixed in the powder, and smeared it between the manin-pasuk's lips. It was an extra-strong dose. There were a lot of people in the house, and taking care of them might require some time. He didn't want the doll freezing part way through or somewhere out on the marsh.

"There," Stroud pointed at the lit-up house as soon as the manin-pasuk was on its feet. He'd already given his instructions to the demon warrior, but he reiterated. "Kill everybody. Do whatever you want. Take all night. I'll be waiting here for you at dawn."

The manin-pasuk disappeared into the scrubby marsh brush, heading in the direction of the house. As Stroud watched it go, he wondered what would happen if an alligator out there tried to attack the doll. Stroud had no doubt that the manin-pasuk would win, but a gator might tear it up pretty badly. He listened intently, but he heard nothing. Maybe gators would be smart enough to stay away.

Stroud had intended to leave the vicinity then return an hour or so before dawn, but he couldn't tear his eyes away from the lit-up house. Without turning on his headlights, he drove farther along the road and ascended the levee. There, he parked so he could have a clear vista of the house. For a long time, it just sat there, shining and glowing and throwing glitters off pools in the intervening marsh.

Stroud glanced at his watch. Half an hour had passed, and still the house just sat there. Ten minutes later, Stroud thought he saw a flash of light from one of the downstairs windows. He stared harder, wishing he'd brought binoculars. Yes. There were more flashes, and he could discern faint popping sounds carried on the marsh breeze.

The flashes came from more and more rooms in sequence, moving through the downstairs then upstairs, ending at the rear of the second floor. Soon after, two figures burst from the front door and raced toward the cars parked on the circular drive in front of the mansion. A third, smaller figure followed them, moving faster. It caught them near the cars, and while it pounced on one man, the other fired at it. The bullets had no effect, and in a moment the shooter was down, too. Stroud could see a gush of crimson in the glare of the floodlights illuminating the front yard. Then the smaller figure left the two inert men and went back into the house.

After that, there were no more flashes of light or popping noises. The house just sat there as before, the only difference being the dead men near the cars. Stroud glanced at his watch. Only half an hour had passed since the first flash. He wondered if he should drive back down to where he'd dispatched the manin-pasuk, but he couldn't stop staring at the house. It looked so normal from this distance. What was it like inside? What was the manin-pasuk doing in there?

Stroud shook off the thought. It was doing what he'd sent it to do. That was all. No need to think about it. The Baldovinos were mobsters and murderers, and they had to know they'd die violently. How that violence occurred made no difference.

Finally, at four, he drove down the levee, parked where he'd sent the manin-pasuk into the marsh, and waited. An hour and a half later, with dawn just tingeing the sky, the manin-pasuk emerged from the brush at the side of the road and staggered toward the car. Stroud got out and hurried toward it.

Its trip back through the marsh had washed off much the blood and gore that had stained it, but Stroud was horrified to see that it had sustained serious damage from gunshot wounds. A chunk was missing from its upper left arm and another from the side just below. Two rounds had completely penetrated its torso, leaving gaping holes that were larger on its back. And it's right hand was missing two fingers.

"Fuck," Stroud snarled as he helped it lie down on the blankets. "I didn't mean for you to get hurt."

It just stared up at him, eyes glittering and mouth stretched in a fiendish grin. Despite the damage, the damn thing actually looked happy. Stroud didn't know how many bodies there were in the house across the marsh, but he figured that the manin-pasuk probably never had taken down so many at one time. No wonder it was happy.

"You did well," Stroud told it. "I'll try to fix you as best as I can."

With what? he wondered. Superglue and caulk?

Stroud bundled the manin-pasuk into the trunk and drove back to Oakdale. But by the time he got there several hours later, took the manin-pasuk into the house, and unwrapped it to get a better look at the damage, he was amazed to see that he might not need to do anything to fix it. The wounds were already healing. If that's what it could be called. The edges of the holes weren't as ragged, and they'd begun to fill in. Even the ends of the severed fingers had covered over and begun to regrow.

"I guess you really are alive," Stroud mused, staring down at the little demon. Then he smiled. "Hope you enjoyed yourself."

The manin-pasuk's grin didn't change, but its eyes brightened.

The news the next day was filled with reports of a horrendous gangland massacre at the Baldovino compound. There were no survivors, and if any of the opposition had been killed or wounded, the attackers had carried them away.

The medical examiner and the crime scene team wished the attackers had carried off the Baldovinos and their henchmen, too. Although plenty of gunfire had been expended—evidenced by the bullet holes in nearly every wall, ceiling, and floor—none of the victims had been shot. The bodies were gashed, limbs were broken or half severed, throats were torn out, and the hearts of four of the victims had been ripped right out of their chests and couldn't be found. None of the forensics team had ever seen such carnage, and even seasoned veterans of horrendous traffic accidents felt their stomachs churn.

"It has to be the Mexican cartels," the lead investigator confided to a reporter. "They've been getting more violent, and they're trying to muscle their way into New Orleans. They're the only ones crazy enough to kill like that."

1990

Stroud and Simmons had drawn a coterie of other individuals into their inner circle. These were the people who'd seen the manin-pasuk come alive under Stroud's hand. He showed them the living proof of his power to make certain they understood the hierarchy of the organization. Stroud, with his control of the doll, was at the top, but Ira Simmons was right up there with him. Then came William Garrett, who by now was safely ensconced in the Louisiana legislature, and Wallace Medford, well known as the best attorney in the parish—and maybe the whole state. Even better, he had a city councilman, a councilwoman, and two judges in his pocket, making him critical to S&S Holding Company's plans.

Stroud let Simmons, who'd known Medford his entire life, make the overtures, but it eventually came down to a display of the manin-pasuk. This was accomplished in the garage of Medford's palatial home, which sat a good way back on the fifty-acre parcel that surrounded it. Medford was married, but his children had long since fled the coop. Simmons kept Elaine Medford occupied in the kitchen while Stroud spent a few minutes convincing Medford that joining S&S was the wise course of action.

"I'll tell you, Wallace," Stroud concluded. "We're going to own this state in another ten or fifteen years. Wouldn't you like a piece of that sort of action? Who knows what benefits you might accrue."

"Just get that damn thing out of my house," Medford said, his voice shaking. "And keep it away from my wife."

"We're having a meeting at my house on Wednesday night," Stroud said. "Eight o'clock. You probably ought to be there."

Signaling for the manin-pasuk to follow, Stroud walked through the garage door and into the night.

Carol Mignon wasn't happy when Stroud told her that he was having a business meeting at the house on Wednesday and that she would have to go somewhere until it was over. In fact, Carol wasn't happy for many reasons. She'd been with John Stroud for six years now and had lived with him in his house for the last three, and he was still so closed-mouthed about his activities that she had no idea exactly what he did.

That reticence had made her grow suspicious—and wary—of him. She knew he was in cahoots with the Ira Simmons and some other town bigwigs, like that state representative…what was his name? But despite the upstanding nature of the company John kept, Carol had long ago figured that something underhanded was going on. Their meetings were just too secretive. Hell, John didn't even allow her to go into his office, which he kept locked when he wasn't in it.

Carol wasn't sure she was ready to believe that John was some kind of criminal, but she knew that business and politics could be nasty battlegrounds. And she knew enough about S&S's activities to realize that those were what John was deeply immersed in. But certainly, after six years, he could confide *something* to her. He hadn't, though, and in the end, his lack of trust in her had eroded her trust in him.

So, on Wednesday, when he asked her to go out for the night, she was already on edge.

"I don't see why I have to leave the house every time you want to have a meeting," she snapped. "I can stay upstairs. Or, why don't you meet at Ira's office? Doesn't he have a conference room there?"

"We meet here because I want us to meet here," Stroud said. "And we discuss matters that shouldn't be overheard by anybody."

"Even your…." She almost said, "wife." But that was a completely different bone of contention. Really, after six years together, couldn't he ask her to make it legal so that she didn't have to suffer the stares and whispered innuendo?

"Even you," Stroud finished for her. "They'll start arriving at seven thirty. I'll need you to be gone by then."

"Sure," she said. "I'll go out for the night. But if I do, I won't be coming back."

"Suit yourself," Stroud said flatly as he turned away, hoping to spur her to leave. It was about time, anyway. She was growing older and probably noticing that he wasn't.

Stroud, not wanting to have to deal with Carol's anger, left the house to grab some lunch, and when he returned a couple of hours later, she was gone. And so were her toiletries and some of her clothes. During the rest of the week, more and more of her belongings disappeared every day when he wasn't home, and at last, there was nothing left of her. Ira learned through his wife that Carol had moved to Houston.

247

No matter, Stroud thought. He could find another woman. Right now, he had to prepare for the meeting. He and Ira had long discussed the need to have a reliable—which meant criminal—accountant on the S&S board. Over the last couple of years, matters had grown too complex for Ira to handle all the number crunching by himself, and he already had his eye on someone. Her name was Bonnie Cullen, and she worked as the chief accountant at Ira's bank. But recently, Ira had learned that she'd embezzled more than $165,000 over a three-year period.

"You want to hire somebody who stole from you?" Bill Garrett asked when Simmons broached the subject at the meeting that night. "That doesn't seem very smart."

"On the contrary," Simmons said. "It's very smart. We need a sharp accountant, and she managed to hide her theft of a considerable sum through three tax cycles, which makes her an excellent bookkeeper from our perspective."

"She's also a thief," Stroud said. "She knows it, and now we know it. But nobody else does. That makes her vulnerable to us."

"And the fact that she's a thief," Simmons went on, "means she'll have no qualms in assisting our thievery if she gets to profit more handsomely than her embezzlement would have allowed, especially if I send her to prison."

"Have you spoken to her about any of this?" Stroud asked.

"Not yet. She doesn't even know that I know about the embezzlement. I thought we might talk to her together. Along with our little friend. If she's going to be the accountant for S&S, she needs to understand that the consequences of stealing from us won't be an appointment to a better position in a more powerful organization."

"You're going to show her that thing?" Wallace Medford asked. So far, he'd been quiet through the meeting, though he seemed to take some comfort from Garrett's presence, as if that somehow legitimized what was going on.

"I think we'll have to," Stroud said. "And I think we're going to have to bring her into the inner circle if she's going to be privy to our financial situation."

"But we don't know anything about her," Garrett protested. "She could turn on us."

"Would you turn on us, Bill?" Stroud asked. "Or you, Wallace? Even if I took the manin-pasuk out of the equation? Think of what you stand to gain with us. My Devil Child is just an excellent bargaining chip. Something to tilt the negotiations in our favor." He paused a moment, staring among them. "Do any of you doubt that we're going to succeed?"

The chorus of "No" sounded solid, even from Medford.

"Then, I doubt that Mrs. Cullen will, either, once she sees matters for what they are." He glanced at them again then said, "Are we agreed, then? We'll invite her to our next meeting."

Simmons told Bonnie that he wanted her to bring a packet of legal documents to a meeting he was having with an important client. It was after hours and at a private residence, and all that was a little irregular, but the client insisted on the arrangements. If she would be so kind, Simmons would make it up to her later....

*   *   *

Bonnie Cullen was brunette, thirty-two, and good looking. She arrived with the packet of legal documents on time, and she expected to hand them to Ira and then be on her way. But Ira, who opened the door despite the fact that it wasn't his house, ushered her inside and led her to the living room. Three other men sat in chairs and on the sofa. She recognized all of them.

"Have a seat, Bonnie," Simmons said, taking the documents from her and gesturing to an empty chair. "We were just discussing a matter that concerns you."

"Me?" she asked.

They know, she thought, her heart sinking faster than she as she sat. Now her one chance to get out of this town and away from Ray was gone. Shit, she should have killed that abusing bastard when she had the chance. Then she'd have gone to prison for something worthwhile instead of for stealing.

"We asked you here for a couple of reasons," Simmons said. "First, I know that you've been taking funds from the bank."

Bonnie almost collapsed inside, and she barely registered Simmons' next words much less understood them.

249

"I'd like to congratulate you on a well-executed scheme."

She blinked at him. Did he just praise her for stealing from him?

"You're plan was exquisite," Simmons went on. "So exquisite, in fact, that I and the other gentlemen in this room are the only ones who know about it. I discovered it quite by accident while I was cooking a few a books myself."

What did he just say? Did he implicate himself...?

"I could, of course, have you arrested and sent to prison."

"I know that," she murmured.

"My friends and I have a better idea."

Jeezus, she wondered. Do they want to gang-bang me?

"I'm John Stroud," one of the men said.

"I know who you are, Mr. Stroud." She'd seen him often enough when he visited the bank for meetings with Ira.

"Not mister," he said. "Call me John." His stare made her uncomfortable, not because it was sexual but because it was intently appraising. "After Ira discovered you were embezzling, he also found that you weren't spending the money but saving it up in several different banks around the state. That's not like most embezzlers who go right out and buy new cars and clothes."

"I was going to buy...."

"Spare us fabricated details of what you intend to do with the money," Stroud laughed. "We know quite well that you're trying to escape from your husband, Ray. And we intend to help you do just that."

"How?"

"You'll see momentarily."

"Okay. Why, then? Do you want the money I took for yourselves?"

"Not really," Stroud said. "We have plenty of money. We're going to let you keep that as part of your hiring bonus."

"My what?"

"This isn't an interrogation," Simmons clarified. "It's a job interview."

"You want me to be your secretary or something?"

"No, we want you to join our little group," Stroud said. "Be on our board. Be our accountant. Help us take anything we want."

She stared at them. The most powerful banker and the most prominent attorney in the parish, a state legislator, and John Stroud. Something of a mystery there. They wanted her to join them?

"Is there a salary or something?"

Stroud laughed again and waved around.

"One fifth of everything," he said.

She couldn't believe it. It was impossible. But what if it was true? Maybe she could use her new-found wealth to extricate herself from Ray. And if she couldn't buy him off, maybe she could hire somebody to bump him off.

"You haven't asked about the other part of your hiring bonus."

As if $168,267.93 wasn't bonus enough for an accountant who wouldn't make that in four years of regular employment.

"What is it?" she asked.

"Freedom from Ray."

"You said that. But how?"

"I'd like you to meet my enforcer. Manin-pasuk."

All eyes turned to stare to Bonnie's left, so she did, too, and she nearly fell out of her chair screaming. But no one else moved except for Stroud, who stood, strode casually to the horrible little monster who'd walked into the room, and laid his hand on its head.

"This is the Devil Child," Stroud said.

"Yes," she gasped, shrinking back. "Yes. I know. I remember it, and you, too, now. The carnival. What is it?"

"If you remember us, you remember the story," Stroud said. "The story was true, even if nobody believed it."

"Keep it away. Please."

"Have no fear," Stroud said. "He's not here to hurt you, but to help." Stroud crouched beside the manin-pasuk. "Remember what we talked about?" The thing nodded, its eyes lighting. "Ray Cullen. I showed you his picture and where he lives. Go now."

The horrible little demon child turned and left the room. A moment later, they all heard the back door open then close.

"Now," Stroud said, returning to his chair. "While we wait, let's fill Bonnie in on S&S Holding Company."

Wait for what? Bonnie wondered, but that question was soon lost in the welter—and literal wealth—of information she was bombarded with for the next hour and a half. Then, right in the middle of an explanation of Garrett's current maneuvers in the statehouse, there came the sound of the back door opening and closing again.

The manin-pasuk came into the room. It had managed to lick some of the blood from its body, but enough remained to fill the room with its iron scent.

"Go upstairs to the bathroom, get into the tub, and wait for me," Stroud ordered, and the Devil Child obeyed.

"That blood?" Bonnie said. "Is...it...."

"Look at me, Bonnie," Stroud said. "Ray isn't going to be a problem for you any more."

"We'll need to wait for a little while before you go home," Simmons said. "Maybe I should drive you. We'll say that your car wouldn't start. That way you'll have an alibi for your entire evening."

"An alibi." It was all she could say.

The meeting concluded an hour later, and before Ira drove her home, he turned on the headlights in her car to make the battery run down to add plausibility to Bonnie's alibi.

As Ira's Cadillac turned onto Bonnie's street, she could see police lights three blocks down, right in front of her house. Ira parked and walked her to the police barricade. Her husband, she learned, had been killed by some kind of wild animal. Neighbors had been alerted by his screams, but they hadn't seen the animal that attacked him. It wouldn't be a good idea for her to see the body, they told her.

They took her statement and Ira's. Yes, Bonnie had been with him and several other board members of a local corporation all evening. He told them their names, leaving out Stroud's. Was there, the police asked, someplace she could stay? The house was a crime scene and might be sealed for weeks to come.

"Let me take you to a hotel," Ira told her. "Tomorrow, you can buy whatever you need, and I'll have a real estate agent I know find you a place to live."

Stunned, Bonnie let him lead her back to his car. He drove her to the best hotel in town, booked her a room, and left. After she'd gone into her room and locked every lock the door had, she fell onto the bed and wept. Not for Ray, but with relief.

At last, she slept.

* * *

Four weeks later, at the conclusion of the Wednesday meeting, Stroud asked Bonnie to stay afterwards to discuss something. Simmons, Garrett, and Medford said goodnight, and as the door closed behind them, Bonnie turned to Stroud.

"So, what is it you want to talk to me about?"

"Let's go upstairs," he replied.

She wasn't surprised at his attention. She'd felt his eyes on her since she'd joined S&S. She knew that she was a pretty good looking woman, and she'd often suffered stares of sexual interest, but Stroud's eyes held more than rutting desire, though that was there, too. She'd learned that he was the only unmarried member of the group. Apparently he'd had a long-time girlfriend, but she'd left him a month ago, so by now he must be pretty horny.

"If I say no, what does that do to my new employment?"

"You stay employed, as we've discussed."

"What about the others?" she asked. "What will they think?"

"What they think doesn't matter."

Bonnie wasn't sure she wanted to get involved with Stroud—at least on an intimate level. But Ray also had been dead for a month, and she was pretty horny, too. Besides, in addition to being rich and powerful, Stroud was pretty handsome in a raw sort of way. He had an aura of…. She wasn't sure what it was, but it was palpable on her skin whenever he looked at her.

"Let's go upstairs," she agreed.

Stroud fucked her just about as thoroughly as she'd ever been fucked. Three times. His big, strong hands roamed her body with a command and gentleness that Ray would never have understood. Bonnie didn't know how old Stroud was, but he made love like a man with experience, patience, and control. Ray would have failed to make her cum and then beaten her for it.

Stroud was, Bonnie realized, a complete mystery, and one she intended to unravel. She wondered about the women who'd come before. Wondered if there would be any after her. When she'd met him, she had no idea how powerful he was in Oakdale. In the whole state. He just looked like a tall, relatively handsome man in his late thirties who was well-off. In the beginning, after that first meeting—her "job interview"—when she began to realize just how powerful and wealthy he was, she'd tried to learn the source of his wealth. Had he been born into it? Earned it?

Later, when she delved into his financial paper trail, she could glean almost nothing from it. John Stroud had come into public existence only twelve years earlier. He'd invested some money, though not a huge sum, in S&S Holdings, and now, he and Ira owned a whole lot more of the state than anyone but the S&S board members realized. The only thing she did know about him was that he'd once worked in a carnival, displaying that hideous Devil Child. She knew that because it had freaked her out every time she'd ever gone to see it when she was a teenager.

She hadn't known why at the time, but she did now.

"How did you go from being a carnival barker to all this?" she asked him after he'd ravished her a second time, brushing sweaty strands of hair away from her eyes.

"The question is why did I have to be a carnival barker, at all?"

He saw her frown. Damn she was good looking, he thought.

"All right," he said. "I was a carnival barker until I learned the truth about what I'd been hawking. After that, things were different."

"I remember seeing you when I was a teenager," she mused. "You don't look much older now than you did then."

"I joined the carnival right out of high school," he said. "The mustache and sideburns probably made me look older." He failed to tell her that he'd been with the carnival for almost twenty years by the time she'd visited the Devil Child show and that his true age was fifty-one. Maybe he was over fifty, but his vitality was fifteen years more youthful. To prove it, he reached for her again.

"Do you want me to come back?" she asked him the next morning. "For this, I mean."

"No," he said, but before the disappointment that shot through her could really register, he finished, "I want you to move in."

Bonnie wasn't sure she was ready for that, but really, was she ready for any of this? Besides, she'd been living in an apartment since she'd moved out of the house she'd shared with Ray, and she longed to have a house again. She could easily afford to buy one on her own now, but John's proposition was much more interesting.

"All right," she said, hoping she wasn't making a mistake. "When?"

"Today."

"I'll go pack my clothes and toiletries," she said, fluffing her hair in the dresser mirror. Then she turned to face him. "I hope you aren't just taking advantage of me," she said.

"I plan to take advantage of you at every opportunity," Stroud promised.

After she'd left to get her things, Stroud went into his office, opened a safe bolted to the floor of the closet where he kept the the Devil Child and a trunk filled with carnival memorabilia. From it, he pulled out the single pouch that lay inside. He loosened the drawstrings and peered inside. There wasn't much powder left. There'd been more enemies than he'd counted on, and he'd carelessly squandered some of the powder on demonstrations of his power over the manin-pasuk to solidify his will over his minions. That's how he thought of them, now. His new word to replace yokels and rubes, but it all amounted to the same thing: the people who would pay him for the privilege of doing his bidding.

He needed more of the powder. A lot more if he expected to expand his empire and live for a very long time to enjoy it.

He cinched the pouch shut and put it back inside the safe. He'd find a solution. Somehow.

12: DEPARTURE

STROUD PARKED HIS Lincoln Town Car in the large but sparsely occupied lot and got out. Thank goodness the summer was past, he thought as he reached in and snagged his suit jacket from where it lay on the passenger seat. He put on the jacket, shut the door, and walked toward the building. It was a contemporary structure, tasteful gray panels alternating with glass, four stories tall, and sprawling over half of a five-acre tract.

Most of the remainder of the space was taken up by a man-made lake, surrounded by a grassy swath and sporting a twenty-foot fountain in its center. It's surface was ruffled by the slight breeze, and the bright sun threw sharp glitters of harsh light off the diminutive wave tops. Three small pavilions sheltering picnic tables lay scattered along the grassy margin between the building and the water.

An eight-foot-tall pylon just outside the doors read, "Gerthen Laboratories, Inc." The lab, located in Houston, was reputed to have the best chemical analysts in Texas, and its clients included industry, law enforcement, and the huge Texas Medical Center just a couple of miles to the north. Its expertise was why Stroud was here.

As he pushed through the doors, he felt as nervous as if he'd come for a report on a potentially failing heart or a growing tumor. In a sense, he was. Could Gerthen help him?

"If you'll wait just a moment, Mr. Stroud," the receptionist said after he'd introduced himself and the purpose of his visit, "I'll have someone escort you to Dr. Baker's lab."

The escort, a young man in a white lab coat, emerged from a side door inside of three minutes.

"Hello, Mr. Stroud. I'm Tim Ehlers, one of Dr. Baker's lab assistants. If you'll follow me, I'll take you to his lab."

They went up an elevator and down a couple of halls before Ehlers ushered Stroud into a large room filled with gleaming equipment. Stroud suppressed a wry smile. It took a lot of spotless high-tech to analyze a little bit of dirt.

Across the room, a middle-aged man, also wearing a white lab coat, was bent over a centrifuge.

"Dr. Baker," Ehlers said as he led Stroud over. "Mr. Stroud is here."

"Fine," Baker said, standing and turning. He stuck out his hand and Stroud shook it. "Nice to see you again, Mr. Stroud."

"You, too, Dr. Baker."

"That's all for now," Baker said to Ehlers. "I'll speak with Mr. Stroud."

If Ehlers was disappointed that his boss had dismissed him, he didn't show it. He left, closing the door behind him. Baker busied himself for a minute or so, pulling a file folder and a small glass vial from a desk drawer. He set both on the top of the desk, but he didn't open the folder. Instead, he picked up the vial, held it up at eye level, and stared at it. It was half-filled with a gray-brown powder.

"This is quite a complex substance you have, here," Baker said, looking at Stroud. "You said it came from the Amazon?"

"That's right. From a shaman."

Baker shook his head as he set the vial next to the folder.

"There are a lot of plants in those jungles down there that are little known and even less understood. I ran a full analytical panel on it with an eye, as you suggested, to being able to synthesize it, but I'm afraid that its molecules are so complex and diverse that only part of it can be synthesized. A lot of the drugs available to modern medicine are like that. We still must rely on Mother Nature to supply many of our needs, and about eighty percent of pharmaceuticals contain compounds from plants in the Amazon. The chemist looked at him quizzically. "I don't believe you've told me what it's for."

"I'm not sure myself," Stroud lied. "As I told you when I brought it in, it was given to me by a friend, now deceased, who only told me that it has significant healing properties."

"Perhaps," Baker mused, opening the file folder and scanning the top page. "But if so, it's nothing overt or already known to science. Were there any instructions for its use?"

"Not specifically, but I know it reacts with blood."

"Reacts? How?"

"I was hoping you could tell me."

"I would, but we don't have any blood to test it with."

As Baker looked on with curiosity, Stroud removed his suit jacket and hiked up his sleeve.

"Do you have a scalpel?" he asked.

"You can't be serious," the chemist said, pulling back a little.

Instead of answering, Stroud reached into his pocket, pulled out a pocket knife, and to the chemist's horror, cut himself on his forearm.

"Better get a petri dish," he told Baker.

"This is highly irregular...."

"I'm already cut. Let's not waste this opportunity."

The chemist walked to a cabinet as if in a daze and returned with a small glass dish. Stroud took it, dropped some of his blood into it, then stirred in a pinch of the powder.

"Is that enough?" he asked, indicating the mix.

"This will take some time."

"How much time?"

"An hour. Maybe a little longer."

"I'll wait." Stroud sat at the desk and blotted his arm with his handkerchief.

Baker went to work, and his absorption in the task seemed to calm his nerves. At last he came back over to Stroud.

"Look, I can't really say what's going on," he said. "Not in so short a time and without running a battery of other tests. But it appears that the presence of iron and oxygen in the hemoglobin is acting as a catalyst with the chemicals present in the powder, but I can't tell what's happening or why. Maybe I could tell more if I had more time, more of the powder to work with, and some specifics about its intended treatment."

"I don't have more of the powder," Stroud said. Or more time. And I'm not telling you it endows the user with a longer life and animates the Devil Child. "But if I can get more, I'll be in touch. Until then, thank you, Dr. Baker." He gestured toward the folder containing the analysis. "Is that for me?"

"Certainly."

Grimly disappointed, Stroud left the building. It was now 1993, and he'd last used the formula about five years ago. In another five years, he'd have to use it again, and then it would be nearly gone. And he'd just potentially wasted years of life by sacrificing some of his dwindling supply on a futile chemical analysis.

What a waste, he thought as he pulled out of the parking lot and headed toward the freeway. The organization that he and Ira had built over the past fifteen years had grown powerful and extended tentacles into every aspect of Louisiana state government and business. But in a few years time, barely extended by the last dose of the longevity formula, it all would be meaningless. Everything he'd worked for would crumble with his aging body.

And just as bad, he would no longer be able to reanimate the manin-pasuk. He'd had to revivify the doll on too many occasions since the slaughter of the Baldovinos. Some of those had been to convince individuals who were reluctant to sell some needed property, others had been to eliminate threats. Fortunately, those occurrences had been either years or miles apart, and nobody had linked the fatal and particularly savage wild animal attacks that had taken the owner of an oil drilling company in Baton Rouge, a banker in Monroe, and a developer in Shreveport. In many cases, Stroud had simply disposed of the bodies in the Louisiana swamps, leaving only a missing person report.

Only the S&S board knew any details about the manin-pasuk, but the many people Stroud had intimidated with it—some of them recruited for upper-level management position in the darker side of S&S Holdings—also knew, though they didn't speak of it. And the rest, having seen the organization's enemies fall to a similar gruesome fate, recognized that whatever power had caused the deaths was under Stroud's control. Stroud appreciated that fact. Each of them knew that they might be next if they crossed Stroud or Simmons, and that knowledge kept them in line. But Stroud couldn't afford to squander any more of the powder on underlings. He had only enough of it for one more rejuvenation and one or two more reanimations. After that, the manin-pasuk would be frozen forever. And so would Stroud.

Well, he still had some time to figure out something. He might be in his mid-fifties, but he looked and felt like he was in his mid-thirties. Almost. He had spent so many years at his current arrested age that even the slightest decline in his vitality was noticeable. Especially when he was with his mistress. Bonnie had been living with him ever since they'd first coupled. It just wasn't fair that his physical powers were waning at a time when his temporal powers were peaking. He didn't want any of it to decline, much less end. Hell, if he could have the formula synthesized, he might even give doses to select other individuals.

If the threat of the unknown kept Stroud and Simmons' minions at bay, certain knowledge kept the board in line. Although they'd been present on several of the occasions when Stroud had animated the manin-pasuk and sent it to eliminate their enemies, most of them didn't know about the powder and blood mixture. He wanted them to believe he could animate it at will, instead of with a dwindling supply of a vital ingredient.

The board members had been terrified each time—even Ira. But Stroud had lived with the thing so long and had used his own blood often enough to give it temporary life that he'd come to think of it as his reliable friend.

Bonnie was the only person who knew where Stroud kept the manin-pasuk. There was no way he could keep it a secret from her since she was living in the house with him, and Stroud quit trying to hide it from her. He frequently brought it out of the closet and propped it up so it could see out of the window. She'd even caught him talking to it like it was an old friend.

It *was* Stroud's old friend. Maybe his only real friend. Over time, the need to commune with it grew steadily. It was his confidant as well as his enforcer, and he knew it would never tell his secrets, though maybe it would have if it could speak. The more he talked to it, the more he realized that it understood what he was saying. The damn thing had learned English! In fact, the last two dozen times he'd used it, he'd just shown it a photo of the intended victim then verbally directed it to its target instead of sketching the route. Maybe Joe Wheeler's notes were right when they reported that the Devil Child had once been a man who'd been shrunken whole.

"Does it bother you?" he's asked Bonnie once, when she came in while he was going over some documents as, across the room, the Devil Child stared out the window.

"It's creepy," she admitted. "But not really. It's important to us."

"He's my advisor," Stroud said with a small smile. "I can talk to it, and it doesn't talk back."

"You think I talk back, John?"

"I want you to talk back, Bonnie. That's what a good accountant does. But don't ask too many questions."

"Well," she said with a smile. "Maybe I shouldn't ask what you want for dinner."

Bonnie seemed nonchalant about the Devil Child, but Stroud frequently suspected she opened the secret closet when he was out of the house and did her own communing with the manin-pasuk. No matter. She was the only one besides Ira who knew how Stroud re-animated the doll, but he kept the remaining pouch of powder in the safe where she couldn't get at it.

An old steamer trunk filled the space not taken up by the safe and the Devil Child's case. The trunk was a relic of Stroud's days with the carnival and was filled with memorabilia, such as posters, newspaper clippings, and his barker's costume, complete with straw boater and bolo tie. For the life of him, he couldn't seem to work up the desire to get rid of the stuff. Or maybe it was lack of nerve. He'd lived that life for so long and with such conviction and tenacity that it was hard to let go. Shit, he had more love for that life, despite its occasional hardships and beatings at the hands of Bull Martin, than he'd had for any woman.

And Stroud hoped he'd have many more of those during the decades—or centuries—to come. But unfortunately, the manin-pasuk would become just a creepy artifact as soon as he ran out of the animation powder. And eventually he, too, would become another artifact that also lost its power of animation. In the end, he knew that there was only one thing to do.

* * *

The morning after his visit to Gerthen Laboratories, Stroud told Bonnie he had some business to attend to at the bank. Thankfully, she was fairly complacent about what he did, maybe because she was an important part of S&S Holdings. Business was a daily matter. Anyway, she wasn't as demanding of his emotional loyalty as Sara had been, and she wasn't as insistent on holding his attention as Seraphina was. And whatever she knew about Stroud, she kept to herself.

No one hindered Stroud as he walked through the bank's lobby toward Ira Simmons' office. He was well known at the bank as Simmons' principal business partner and a board member for the bank, and all he got were smiles and nods and a "Nice to see you, Mr. Stroud," from Madge, Ira's secretary.

"John," Simmons said, rising from behind his desk as Stroud entered. "I wasn't expecting you."

"We need to talk, Ira," Stroud said, closing the door behind him.

"Must be serious." Simmons waved to a guest chair in front of the desk, and Stroud sat. "What's on your mind?"

Stroud looked at Simmons, wondering how to begin. Simmons was still slender and fit, but at forty-one, he was beginning to show his age. Maybe that was where to begin.

"Don't you have a question for me, Ira?"

"Many, John. Which one are you referring to?"

"How old do I look?"

"Yes. That question. I've always wondered about that. Why you're so much older than me but don't look it. I have to admit I've always been a little jealous of that. Does it have something to do with the manin-pasuk?"

"Not directly, but I'm going to tell you so you'll understand why I have to do what I'm going to do. The powder that animates the manin-pasuk also has another purpose."

"To make you younger."

"Something like that, but it's more like a severe detox coupled with retarded aging. It can't turn back the clock—at least not by much. But it can arrest the inevitable for a long, long time."

"You never shared that with me." Simmons looked hurt though he tried to mask it.

Stroud snorted a laugh.

"Wasn't that much to go around since we used up a lot bringing our little friend to life."

"Why are you telling me this now?"

"I'm running out. I had only a limited supply."

"So now, we not only can't animate the Devil Child, you're going to age like the rest of us."

Stroud shook his head.

"I have no plans to do that."

"What then, if you're out of the powder?"

"I'm going to go get more."

"Going? Where?" Then Simmons' eyes lit. "To the Amazon?"

"It's the only way. I need to locate that old shaman, Tuchaua, and force him to give up the formula. If I can secure more of the powder, it will give us both decades more life. Maybe I can bring back the plants used to make it so we'll never run out."

"Why don't you just have it analyzed and have more of the formula synthesized?"

"I tried that. The chemist said that the molecules are too complex to create in the lab. At least, not without more of the powder to work with. Besides, I might have to tell them what it's for, and I can't do that."

"No, I suppose you can't." Simmons leaned back, looking thoughtful. "I don't know, John. This sounds like some kind of crazy treasure hunt. People go into that jungle looking for lost cities and gold and what not, and they never come out."

"I'll come out, Ira. And I'll come out with a treasure that will make us virtually immortal. What's the use in spending a lifetime gaining what we have if we can't continue to enjoy it? Think of it: lifetime after lifetime."

"But what makes you think this Tuchaua is even still alive. Or that you can find him?"

"I know there are no guarantees, Ira, except one. If I don't get more of that powder, we're both going to be dust in fifty years. I'm willing to go down there and look considering what's at stake."

"I wish I could talk you out of it, but I know you too well. What about our businesses?"

"You're the administrator. Keep on administrating. But there is one thing. I want to sign over my house and some of the dividends from my end of the businesses to Bonnie. There's no telling how long this will take, and I don't want to leave her in the lurch."

"Why? She can easily afford her own house."

Ira's sharp tone reminded Stroud that his partner had grown jealous of his relationship with Bonnie. It was an enmity she's come to reciprocate. But it was because of that very relationship that Stroud now trusted his mistress more than he did his business partner.

"Maybe, but all my belongings are in that house, and I want to make sure they're there when I get back."

"Including the manin-pasuk?"

"Yes, and that's another good reason to get more of the powder. We can't do without our little friend, especially if we intend to move into New Orleans. The mob there has brought in some vicious enforcers since we wiped out the Baldovinos, and we'll need the Devil Child."

"I can't argue with that," Simmons said. "All right, I'll have Madge do the paperwork on the house and income. They'll be ready for you to sign tomorrow. Say about ten?"

"I'll be here."

Stroud left the bank, strangely dreading the next item on his agenda. Now that the moment approached for him to tell Bonnie that he was leaving, he was a little surprised to discover that he dreaded it. Had he actually developed feelings for her?

He found her in the upstairs bedroom she used as an office, going over the books of a trucking company that S&S wanted to buy to transport contraband in addition to legitimate cargo.

"I have something to tell you," he said, sinking into a chair.

"What is it, John?" Worry creased her features. "You're not telling me it's over, are you?"

"No. Not exactly."

"What, then? Exactly."

"I have to go away. Business. But I might be gone some time."

"What's 'some time' mean?"

"I don't know. Maybe a year."

"A year? What kind of business takes a year?"

"I have to find someone, and I'm not sure exactly where he is."

"Can't you hire a private detective?"

"Not where this man is." He took a breath. "He's somewhere in the Amazon jungle."

"The Amazon!" Then sudden understanding lit her eyes. "It has something to do with the manin-pasuk, doesn't it."

"Yes. I need to find the man who made it."

"That's crazy, John. What do you need to do that for? To make another? Isn't one of those things enough. Besides, all you do with it anymore is keep in a closet."

"The reason I keep it in the closet is that I'm running out of the powder I need to reanimate it. I need to get more."

"Do we really need that thing, now?" she asked. "The company is strong and well diversified. We're rich beyond our wildest dreams. We don't need it, or Ira or any of the rest of them. We can break away and do whatever we want."

"I don't know what I want," he admitted. "But whatever it is, I intend to get it, and I still need the Devil Child's help."

She rose from her chair, anger and frustration conflicting with apprehension on her face.

"You can't leave, now. I haven't told you yet because I was waiting for the right time. But you're always so busy."

"Waiting for what?"

"I'm pregnant," she said. "Three months."

Oh, fuck, he thought. He stood, too, wanting to rage that he didn't want or need a child. That he planned to still be young when any child he might sire was long moldering in the grave. But he kept calm. He couldn't afford to drive her away. Not now. He needed her to stay in the house and keep the manin-pasuk safe.

"I wish you'd told me this sooner," he said, keeping his voice level. "But it really wouldn't have mattered. I have to find that shaman. Everything depends on it. And don't worry about yourself or the child. I'm signing the house over to you along with enough stocks to keep you well off until I get back. I only ask one thing: Keep the Devil Child safe."

The promise of financial security and a speedy return seemed to mollify her. A bit.

"A year, you say?"

He reached out and grasped her by the shoulders.

"It will pass quickly," he said. "Then we can resume our lives. You like our lives, don't you?"

She nodded, some of the stiffness going out of her shoulders.

"All right, then. We'll go to the bank tomorrow morning to sign over the deed and the stocks."

"You're going that soon?"

"The sooner I leave, the sooner I'll return." Soon was good, he thought. He had to get out of this damn house before that damn child was born. What the hell use were children, anyway? "I just have do take care of a few things before I leave."

He didn't tell her that one of those things was to be sick as hell for four days. Late one night, while Bonnie was asleep, he mixed a batch of the longevity potion and drank it. That left enough of the powder for one or two animations of the manin-pasuk.

The sickness—the purge—took hold almost immediately, and by morning, he was almost delirious. Bonnie wanted to take him to the doctor, but he resisted, telling her it was just the flu and that he'd be fine in a few days. She nursed him, worried that the illness was more severe than he claimed, but after two days he began to recover. The next day, he could get out of bed, and two days later, he announced that he was leaving the next day.

"But you just got over that flu," Bonnie protested. "You're still weak. Can't it wait?"

"I'll be fine."

And she had to admit that he did look fine. Not only was he recovering fast, the illness seemed to have rejuvenated him. On Friday, Stroud had one of Ira Simmons' assistants at the bank drive him to the airport in New Orleans, where he began the first leg of his journey.

* * *

Bonnie wasn't happy about his absence. At least in the beginning. Even now, after three years of intimate relations, John Stroud was an enigma to her, but he had treated her well and given her everything she wanted, including a more lucrative career than she ever could have hoped for. He hadn't given her love, but he obviously had affection for her, and he always seemed to appreciate her contributions to S&S and to their domestic situation. And the sex was good enough that, as he labored over her in the darkness, she could pretend he felt something for her.

She'd looked at the manin-pasuk many times over the past three years. In fact, she probably talked to it almost as much as John did. She was shocked that it was alive, but not actually surprised. Bonnie might have been a middle-class girl from a large town, but that town was in Louisiana, where the air was rife with voodoo, and superstition often ruled the day. She might not have believed half of what she'd heard about spells and such, but she knew one thing for sure: The Devil Child wasn't a prop manufactured in somebody's workshop. Not only had she seen it move, she'd opened its case, touched it, peered closely at its hair, each strand of which was clearly protruding through the skin. And she'd looked into its eyes and seen the light of demented life flickering in their depths. Felt the insane violence pent up inside the thing's hardened flesh.

Now, with John gone, she was left to guard it. John had been specific about that. "Keep the Devil Child safe," he'd told her, and she intended to do just that. And with a shock, she realized that it wasn't because John frightened her, though he had an intensity that was frequently intimidating, but because, even if he didn't love her, she'd come to love him. And she was bearing his child.

It was going to be a girl. She knew it. And she made a vow to herself. She would never let anything come between them like she'd let come between her and her own parents, now long dead, assuring that their conflict would never be resolved. Better not to cause the need to arise in the first place.

Months passed, and with no word at all from John, it was a bleak period. But as her pregnancy progressed, it occupied more and more of her time, energy, and thoughts. She was bringing a new life into the world, and she had a lot to prepare for. And that was made easier by the only light in her life: her new neighbor, Abby Kinnon. A slender and energetic middle-aged woman, Abby moved in next door with her husband, Elliot, two months after John left.

As soon as she met Bonnie and saw that she was alone and pregnant, Abby took Bonnie under her wing. In the beginning, when she asked about the baby's father, Bonnie told her that John was off on business in another part of the world and let it lie at that. Abby seemed to understand her reticence on the subject of Mr. Cullen, which is what she at first believed was Bonnie's husband's last name. After all, what sort of man would up and leave his pregnant wife for a whole year? But if Bonnie was reluctant to talk about John, Abby was happy enough to tell Bonnie about her own husband.

"Ever since Elliot became regional manager for Ace Hardware, all he ever does is travel. Not that I'm complaining. He's a fine husband. Fact is, I met him because he was traveling. That was when I was living in Lafayette."

Abby often brought over food, refusing to listen to Bonnie's protests.

"It's pretty hard to cook for one, so I might as well share. And you're far enough gone that you don't need to be standing around in the kitchen when I can help out. Gives me something to do while Elliot's on the road."

"Do you have any children?" Bonnie asked.

"Nope," Abby said, not appearing upset by the fact. "We met too late." She shrugged. "But that's okay. I have Elliot."

The friendship between the two women had solidified by the time Bonnie entered her third trimester, and Bonnie was thankful. She needed the emotional support. John had said he'd be gone a year, but now, four months later, she'd heard nothing at all from him. Not a letter or telegram or phone call. That worried her. She had no illusions about his feelings for her, and she'd read the consternation in his eyes when she told him she was with child, even though he'd tried to mask it. But she didn't think he was going to abandon her. If so, why had he set her up in this large house with an assured income for life when he could have just tossed her out?

And there was the Devil Child. His one precious possession. He'd left that in her care, hadn't he? Surely he'd come back for it.

If he was still alive.

That thought haunted her. She'd visited the library the week after he left, read about the Amazon, and grew more frightened. It was a dangerous place, with headhunters, criminals, unscrupulous governments and businesses, and trackless jungles filled with dangerous animals and disease. She wished he hadn't gone. She wished he was here with her as she carried their child to term. She wished....

But no amount of wishing could change the fact that he'd gone down to the Amazon for some ungodly reason. She knew it had to have something to do with the Devil Child. Wasn't that where it came from? All she could hope for was that he'd find what he was looking for and come back soon.

* * *

But Stroud didn't come back soon. The months passed quickly enough, what with the preparations for the baby and all. But as her due date approached, her thoughts turned more and more frequently to her missing paramour. Where was he? What was he doing? Was he all right? Why wasn't he here with her?

During those months, she often went into his office to sit in his chair and soak up the ambience of his fading presence. And to commune with the Devil Child. Until her growing belly kept her from lifting up such a heavy weight, she sometimes took it out of its case and leaned it up against the door while she sat in the chair, facing it. Talking to it, and half wishing it could talk back because it had been with John for such a long time. It had to know something about him.

Then one night, her water broke, and she thanked her lucky stars that she had Abby for a friend. Abby came quickly at her call, and she and Elliot bundled Bonnie into their car and drove her to the hospital. The labor was intense. More intense than she expected, though she knew that first-time mothers usually had the most trouble birthing. But then it was over, and the nurse passed her the bundle-wrapped child. A girl.

"Don't worry," Bonnie whispered in her ear. "Your daddy will be home soon." She didn't know if the words were for the child or for herself, but she wanted to believe them with all her heart.

And then Abby was there, giving her support and saying what a beautiful child Bonnie had. Not long after, the nurse came in with a form to fill out for the birth certificate.

"I just need the names of the parents, your birthdates, and the name for your new daughter."

"I'm Bonnie May Cullen. I was born on March 8, 1965. I don't know who the father is." She looked down at the baby and stroked her cheek. "I want to name her Ellen Louise Cullen."

"Ellen Louise Cullen it is," the nurse said, writing on the form. A moment later, she was gone.

"Why did you tell them you didn't know who the father is?" Abby asked. "Isn't it that man you were living with? John Stroud?"

"Yes, but…." Bonnie shook her head, a strange look in her eyes. "I don't know," she said sadly. "I just have a feeling I shouldn't connect him to us right now."

Abby had never known about S&S Holdings or that Bonnie had been its accountant, so there was no point in mentioning any of that now. There was no way she was going to tell Abby that she'd helped run one of the state's largest criminal organizations until about the time that Abby had moved in next door.

"Does that make a difference between us?" she asked the older woman, glancing up at her.

"Not a bit, my dear," Abby said. She smiled, reached out, and brushed a strand of hair off Bonnie's forehead, then touched Ellen's blanket. "May I hold her?"

"Yes, please," Bonnie said, carefully passing the bundle to Abby. "I'm thinking of naming you her godmother. If you don't mind."

"That would be lovely," Abby said as she bent over the infant and lightly stroked her head with her fingertips.

For the moment, with Abby cooing over the infant, everything seemed fine. But it wasn't fine because John was still absent. And he stayed that way throughout her daughter's infancy. And as the months dragged into two years, she despaired of ever seeing him again. The only lights in her life were her child and Abby, who seemed to take almost as much delight in the toddler's antics as Bonnie did.

And so time passed in an idyllic state as the baby grew through the seasons to a toddler, and the two women grew close. Then, one afternoon, while Ellen was napping in her bed upstairs, Bonnie heard an uncharacteristic knock on the front door. Heavy. She knew it wasn't Abby. Abby always came to the back door.

John, she thought excitedly. He's back!

She rushed to the door and flung it open, only to have disappointment flood through her. It was Ira Simmons.

"Ira."

She was a little surprised to see him. Her worry over John's absence and the pregnancy had worn her down to the point that she had difficulty concentrating on the S&S bookkeeping. Three months after John's departure, she'd handed in her resignation.

"I just can't keep doing this," she told the other board members. They were upset to lose their inside accountant, and she suspected they might worry about her and what she knew about them and S&S Holdings. But surely they knew that anything she said to the authorities or anyone else would only implicate her, as well. And she wasn't about to risk anything now. Not with a child on the way.

But now, here Ira was, and she realized that there was something unpleasant about him. Something shifty. Something untrustworthy and dangerous. She'd always wondered why John, who she thought of as a strong man, would need a man like Ira. She knew he owned the bank and was wealthy and powerful in his own right, but she also saw how he deferred to John. And she sensed in him an underlying fear of John. She didn't know the reason. Maybe John knew something about Ira's past. Whatever the reason for their association was, it didn't mean she had to like him.

"Hello, Bonnie. May I come in?"

She was reluctant. She hadn't seen Ira at all since she'd resigned. What could he want with her? But there wasn't a legitimate reason to deny him a few minutes. She led him into the living room, where he sat on the sofa while she took John's easy chair.

"How's your daughter?" Ira asked.

"What do you want to talk to me about?" she asked. She didn't want to engage in small talk about anything with Ira, especially about her child. Besides, small talk wouldn't get him out of the house, which is where she wanted him to be.

"John's been gone a long time," Ira said.

"He said he'd be gone a while."

"He said he'd be gone a year, and it's been three. In all that time, have you heard from him?" He nodded at her silence. "I thought not. Nor have I."

"Did you expect to?"

"I expected some word. But there's been nothing."

"He's in a jungle. He can't just pick up a phone or mail a letter."

"The Amazon has plenty of towns and settlements. He could have sent some sort of word if he wanted."

"What do *you* want, Ira?"

"Something simple. I'll get right to the point. I want to buy the Devil Child from you."

"What makes you think I have it?"

"John told me he was leaving it with you, which means it's still here in the house."

"Yes," she admitted. "It is. But I can't sell it."

"Can't, or won't?"

"It's John's," she told him. "If he wanted you to have it, he would have left it with you in the first place. It's staying here until he comes back."

"You fool," Simmons said. "That old bastard is dead in the jungle."

"You're wrong," she said, wondering briefly why Ira called John old. He wasn't more than forty. "He'll be back. I know it."

"Maybe," Simmons said. "But if he does come back, I'll have the doll." He stood up, stepped forward, and loomed over her. "You're going to sell it to me or there's going to be trouble. The board wasn't very pleased when you resigned. They're worried about you, Bonnie. Worried that you'll say something…."

"Get out," she said, standing.

"Not without what I came for." Ira rose, too.

"You're not going to hurt me. Not now. Not with your car parked outside. And my next door neighbor probably saw you come in."

"There will be plenty of opportunities," he said with a smirk. "And as John's business partner, I have power of attorney over his holdings."

"The house and stocks are mine. You can't take them from me."

"Perhaps not," Ira said, standing and staring down at her. "But there are things that can be taken that are more precious than houses or money."

"Let me tell you something, Ira," Bonnie said, leaning close in to his face. "I've lived with the Devil Child for a long time, and I talk to it frequently. I know just as much about it as you, and probably more. John left enough of the powder to bring it alive a few more times. Enough for you and all the rest of the board. You tell them that the next time any of them threaten me or my daughter. You know what will happen."

It was a bluff. She knew about the powder, but if John had left any of it, she didn't know where it was. But the bluff worked. Simmons blanched and took an involuntary half-step back.

"In fact," she said, seeing Simmons pale and pressing her advantage, "I might even do something tonight. Or any night. And you have a family, too, don't you Ira. A nice wife and a son and daughter."

"You'll regret this," Ira snarled, backing away from her.

"Not as much as you will if I ever see you or anybody connected to you around here again. This is my only warning. Stay away from me and my daughter."

Simmons spun and stalked toward the front door, body stiff. And then he was gone, and she heard his car start up and drive away.

The tension suddenly drained from her body, and she collapsed into John's chair, shaking. At first, she almost burst into tears, but then a short laugh escaped her lips. Ira Simmons was one of the most powerful men in the state, and she'd backed him down with a bluff.

She hoped.

A knock sounded at the back door, then, sending a shiver of fear up her spine. Was Ira back so soon? She went to the kitchen, intending to get a carving knife from the drawer, but then she saw Abby standing there.

"Come in," Bonnie said, opening the door.

Abby did, carrying a plate of cookies.

"Thought you and the little one might need a snack," she said, then she got a look at Bonnie's face. "What's wrong, dear? Is everything all right?"

"I don't know."

"Was it that man who was just here? He didn't hurt you, did he?"

"No, nothing like that."

"What did he want?"

"Something he can't have."

Abby's presence helped calm Bonnie's nerves, and then her daughter woke and she had to put Ira's visit behind her. But that night, after the child was asleep, Bonnie's thoughts returned to Ira and the bluff she'd used to keep him at bay.

Bonnie went into John's office, opened the closet, and looked down at the Devil Child through the glass front of its case. It stared back, not looking any different than it ever had. Not looking truly inert. Next to it were the trunk and safe. She always thought that the safe held John's more important papers, such as the deed to the house and maybe some cash, but no. Now she had the deed, and he would have taken any cash with him. So what was still in there?

She did something that would have been unthinkable even this morning. Before now, she'd frequently gone into the office to commune with the doll, but this time, she began going through John's desk. The upper drawers held only items she expected, such as papers and pens and paper clips, but no combination to the safe.

She searched through every folder in the drawers of the filing cabinet, looking at every piece of paper. After four hours, when her eyes were bleary with scanning and reading, she found an envelope labeled, "Ames Safe & Lock." Inside was a receipt for the purchase of the safe, and on the receipt was the lock's combination. She took the receipt into the closet, knelt, twirled the dial with shaking fingers, and opened the door. Inside was a book and one almost-flat leather pouch. That was all.

She took the book and pouch to the desk and sat. First she opened the pouch and peered inside. She'd seen John animate the doll on numerous occasions, and she immediately recognized the musty-smelling graying powder, though there was precious little of it.

So, she *could* bring the Devil Child to life. Once, at least.

She dropped the bag onto the desk, picked up the book, and turned it over in her hands. It was old, tattered, worn, and water stained. The title on the spine said it was a book of maritime law.

Why would John need to know about that? Then she opened the book and saw the cramped, smudged writing filling the margins and every blank space on the pages. It wasn't in John's hand. And she read. And when dawn broke and she heard her child cry from her room down the hall, Bonnie carefully replaced the book and pouch in the safe, shut the door, and twirled the lock's knob.

Now she understood why John had gone to the Amazon. And why Ira had called him old when he looked young. Before reading the book, she's known almost nothing about John's past beyond the little he'd reluctantly told her and the story related by the memorabilia in the steamer trunk. But even if none of this gave her solid information on his past, it did open greater depth into the man she'd been living with and whose child she was bearing.

She stared down at the Devil Child and gathered herself, vowing not to reveal anything about John to anybody. She had to be strong, for herself and her daughter until he returned, and the manin-pasuk was the key to keeping Ira Simmons at bay.

Then her daughter cried out again, and Bonnie shut the closet door and hurried down the hall.

* * *

The next week, she hired a handyman out of the want ads in the free shoppers weekly distributed out of a wire rack at the grocery store. She made sure he was old, poor, and single.

Over the next few weeks, he built a second closet over the original one in John's office, hiding the original behind a secret door. She'd managed to move the trunk and case holding the Devil Child to another room before the handyman started, but he saw the safe, which she couldn't unbolt from the floor.

"You musta got some kinda treasure in that safe, Mizz Cullen," he commented. "What with coverin' it up even more."

"Actually, Mr. Cheney, the safe is empty, and I'd like you to remove it."

When Cheney finished, she had him pose in front of the new closet door.

"I want a photo of you with your fine work, Mr. Cheney," she explained, and he smilingly obliged as she snapped a couple of photos with a Polaroid camera.

Then she paid him and sent him on his way.

Late that night, long after she'd put Ellen to bed, she dragged the Devil Child's case from the closet in her own office, opened the lid, and stared down at the diminutive demon.

"Tonight you're going to do my bidding," she told it.

She got the materials necessary to animate the Devil Child, cut herself on the leg as she'd seen John do, collected the blood in a large measuring spoon, and mixed in the powder. It took all that remained in the pouch. Then she smeared the paste between the Devil Child's lips.

"Follow me," she ordered when it was mobile and standing before her.

She led it down to the car and let it into the back seat. Then she drove toward the outskirts of town. Toward the address where Mr. Cheney lived. She cruised by his house and pointed it out to her passenger.

"That's the house," she said, then she drove on for half a mile and through several turns. She stopped the car, switched off the headlights, and leaned over the back seat, one of the photos of Cheney in her hand. "This is the man. Do it quickly, then come back here and get into the trunk."

The manin-pasuk let itself out of the car and quickly disappeared in the direction of Cheney's house. As soon as it had, Bonnie got out, popped the trunk, and spread spread several old blankets over the trunk floor. Then she waited.

She half expected to hear shouts or screaming, but Cheney, who often smelled of alcohol, was probably in a drunken sleep. Whatever the reason, nothing broke the stillness of the night. And then there it was, striding purposefully toward her. As she expected, it was covered with blood. It got into the trunk, and she flipped the edges of the blankets over its body then closed the trunk and drove home.

There, she cleaned the Devil Child, which had once again grown rigid, beneath the shower and restored it to its case. It had been a long night, and now it was nearly dawn and she was tired. There was still one more thing to do, but that could wait until later. Gratefully, she sank into her bed for a couple of hours of sleep before Ellen woke her, wanting breakfast.

"You're looking peeked this morning," Abby commented when she came over for morning coffee.

"I didn't sleep too well last night. But I have to go out to run a couple of errands this morning. Would you mind watching Ellen?"

"You take your time," Abby said. "But when you get back here, I expect you to take a nice nap."

Bonnie promised she would, then she left the house and drove a few miles away until she found a pay phone. There, she dialed Ira Simmons' office number. Madge answered, but after all these years, she didn't recognize Bonnie's voice.

"I'd like to speak to Mr. Simmons," she said.

"May I ask who's calling?"

"Jane Adams," Bonnie said. "He and I spoke about a business arrangement, and I'm calling him with my answer."

Madge was obviously puzzled that she didn't know about it, but she put through Bonnie's call.

"Ira Simmons here."

"It's Bonnie."

"Bonnie. Have you thought about my offer to buy the Devil Child?"

"I have. My answer will be in the morning newspaper. Remember, it can happen to you and your family at any time. Do you understand me?"

It was a bluff, but Ira and the rest of the board didn't know that, and apparently he believed she could animate the Devil Child any time.

"I understand," he told her, and she hung up on him without another word.

She then called the police to report the crime. After she hung up, she returned to her car, drove home, and slept while Abby tended Ellen.

13: THE AMAZON

WHEN STROUD ARRIVED in Guayaquil, Ecuador, and began his trek in search of Tuchaua, he knew that the location marked on Joe Wheeler's map probably wasn't where the shaman now lived. It had been more than twenty years since Joe had left, and from what Stroud learned in his research on the tribe, the Huambisa tended to move periodically. But certainly they'd still be in the general area. In any case, it was the only place he could start.

Recalling how Joe's guide had hacked him with a machete and left him to die in the jungle for what he carried, Stroud vowed not to make the same mistake. He'd brought along a .357 and plenty of ammunition, choosing a chrome model to help resist the rust that would be inevitable in an extremely humid environment. The revolver and ammo added several pounds of weight to his pack, but Stroud had no intention of dying in the jungle due to lack of self-defense.

He was equally cautious in hiring a guide. He spent nearly a week in Guayaquil, talking to people about weather, the state of the tribes, and most importantly, a reliable guide. The most helpful was a man named Diego Sandoval, who ran a tourist service, but even he wasn't encouraging.

"This will be difficult," Sandoval nodded, looking at Joe's map. "What you are asking is beyond my services. Right now, there is much tension between between Ecuador and Peru. We have fought before, and some say war is again inevitable. The armies on either side might suspect you are an agent of the enemy and kill you on sight. And the

Indians are drunken, violent, unfriendly louts. I urge you to return to America, or, if you must go where you desire, perhaps you should go to the Atlantic side and travel up river to your goal."

"Too far," Stroud said. "That could take most of a year, not weeks."

"Life, not death."

But Stroud was adamant, and Sandoval finally relented.

"I cannot hire the guide myself," he said with an apologetic shrug. "I might lose my license. But go see Carlos Menendez. He might guide you for the right price. Best of all, he speaks Shuar." Stroud knew that that was the language spoken, with slight variations, by all the Jívaro tribes. "He can talk to most of the people down in the basin."

The address Sandoval gave Stroud was in one of the poorest districts of Guayaquil, which was, as far as Stroud was concerned, just one big slum. The cab driver was reluctant to enter the district, but Stroud waved a large denomination bill in front of his face, so he simply shrugged, set his jaw, and drove.

The traffic was maddening. There were no controls, like traffic lights and stop signs, and none of the drivers, the cabbie included, seemed to understand the function of the brake, though they were well versed in the use of the horn. Miraculously, the cab made it to the address without collision or major confrontation, stopping in front of a tan three-story brick and stucco building that had seen better days. Laundry hung out of some of the windows, and a few curious faces showed themselves as Stroud emerged from the cab. He tore the bill in half and gave one piece to the cabbie.

"To ensure you're still here when I come out," he told the obviously disappointed driver. "You'll get the other half after you take me back to my hotel."

The look on the driver's face said he thought Stroud might not come out with the other half.

The apartment Stroud wanted was on the third floor at the rear. He kept his hand on the butt of his gun, hidden beneath his sweat-stained shirt as he went through the front door and up the stairs, but no one confronted him.

"What do you want?" came a bleary voice from the other side of the door when he knocked.

"I'm looking for Carlos Menendez," Stroud said. "Diego Sandoval sent me. I need a guide."

The door cracked far enough to show a surly face hovering over shabby, disheveled clothes. Alcohol fumes leaked through the crack.

"Why did he send you here?" the face demanded. "Why did he not hire me himself?"

"I want to go where he doesn't usually send people."

"Where?"

"Over the mountains. Into Peru."

"You crazy," Menendez said and started to shut the door.

"I'll pay you well."

The door stopped moving.

"How much you pay?"

Stroud quoted the price that Sandoval had suggested, and he saw greed flicker in the depths of Menendez's eyes.

"Not enough," Menendez said, but he didn't close the door.

"Sandoval says it's enough."

"How I know you pay me?"

"How do I know you won't abandon me in the jungle?"

Menendez gave a short laugh.

"I'll tell you what," Stroud said. "I'll leave the money with Sandoval and give him a secret word. When you get me where I want to go, I'll give you the word, and you can come back, tell the word to Sandoval, and he'll give you the money."

Menendez hesitated for a moment, then he chuckled again and opened the door.

"Sí," he said. "Is a good plan. Safe for us both. Come in. Show me where you want to go."

Stroud spent the remainder of the day and all of the next with Menendez. First, they went back to Sandoval's, where, under Menendez's watchful eyes, Stroud handed over the money and whispered the secret word in Sandoval's ear. They then traveled around the city, gathering supplies. The day after that, they were off.

Apparently, things had changed a lot in this region since Joe had left the jungle. For one thing, there were more roads, and Menendez had Stroud hire a car to take them to a small town named Puyo, which lay just over the eastern rim of the Andes. From there, they

281

had to walk. Stroud had heard that walking downhill, which was mostly what they did, was just as hard as walking up, and within a few hours, his knees and the muscles in the backs of his thighs agreed. But he wasn't about to complain to Menendez, whose rolling gate seemed to take any incline without effort.

Menendez carried two guns: a sawed-off double-barreled 12 gauge shotgun and a long-barreled .38 revolver. Both looked well worn but also well maintained. The shotgun, he told Stroud, was for protection, and the pistol was to procure game.

"Wouldn't a rifle be better?"

"A rifle is good for shooting at long range," the guide said. "But one cannot see far in the forest."

Stroud didn't mention that he carried his own weapon.

Stroud was surprised at how many people were here. And they weren't just along the paved roads back the way he and Menendez had come. Even as they hiked the seasonal trails that led down the mountainsides, they found settlements and villages scattered throughout the foothills.

"We're going down into the Amazon basin before the rains," Menendez said as they descended the long slope. "It is very good the wet season has not yet started, or these trails would be fast-running streams. All of them feed the Amazon." He peered at Stroud. "You been up the Amazon?"

"No," Stroud said. "Maybe I'll go down that way when my business is finished."

"Maybe a good thing you do," Menendez shrugged. "Find a boat, slide down the river, smooth as silk." He waved his hand across in front of him, palm down. "What you going into that green hell for, American? You look for lost cities?" He laughed.

"A lost man."

"Oh. He lost looking for lost cities?"

"No, he's just lost in time."

The drive up to the crest of the Andes had taken a whole day, but the descent took five. At first, the view was spectacular. Almost every bend they rounded revealed a vista of the huge bowl of the Amazon basin, with the mountains stretching like a gargantuan, raggedly sloped wall to both sides. Below, the bottom of the bowl was filled with interminable rolling green lushness overlaid by haze that limited the view, even from their great height, visually melting into the forest canopy.

The first night, they found shelter in an empty hut, but after that, they had to camp. Each night, Stroud was bone weary from the arduous trek, but sleeping was difficult. It wasn't just the hard ground or the thousands of insects that, even if they didn't bite, buzzed annoyingly around his head and crawled over his face and arms and into his clothes.

He found he was too keyed up to fall asleep quickly, anyway. Around the meager fire Menendez stoked up each night to cook their simple meals, just to pass the time and stop the buzzing in his brain, Stroud had the guide teach him a few rudiments of Shuar. By the time they emerged from the foothills and immersed themselves in the vast, forest carpeting the undulating landscape, he could ask for food and water and directions.

"Do not call the Indians Jívaros," Menendez warned. "That means 'dirty peasant.' It is best to call them by their tribal name, but you also can call them Shuar."

The Amazon forest wasn't what Stroud had imagined it would be. Instead of sweltering temperatures, the air was usually balmy, if humid as hell. And before they reached the basin floor, the terrain was like the rugged foothills of any mountain range, except it was almost completely choked with vegetation. Menendez proved to be an excellent guide, though, and he found passable trails where Stroud's eyes saw only walls of foliage.

When they reached the edge of the basin, Menendez told Stroud that it would take two or three weeks to travel to the location where Tuchaua once lived. As they made their way through the forest, Stroud began to wish he knew Spanish or Portuguese. It seemed that the villages held as many speakers of those as of the native language.

"Many are here to seek their fortune," Menendez laughed when Stroud remarked on the number of people they ran across. "Rubber tappers, banderiantes, people seeking biological samples or oil, and garimpieros." He noticed Stroud's blank look. "Wildcat gold miners. There are even cattle ranches, but none of those have come this far upstream yet. All who come here take riches from the Shuar and pay in misery and strife. Some people who come here worry about the dangers of the jaguar, the dart-poison frog, or poisonous plants, but the most dangerous thing you can meet is another man."

There was a lot of time to spare as they sat around the modest campfires that Menendez stoked each evening to cook their food, and Stroud took the opportunity to learn as much as he could about the area they were traveling through and the people there. Spanish, it seemed, was the main language spoken in this region, aside from Shuar, though Portuguese dominated not much farther to the east. Stroud didn't plan on spending enough time in the Amazon to make learning Spanish or Portuguese necessary, but the smattering of Shuar Menendez taught him helped pass the time.

For his part, Menendez wanted to know about the United States. He'd guided a lot of people through the Amazon during the past fifteen years, and he always was curious about the civilization that existed beyond the borders of the jungle. Stroud, who's whole life before this journey had been spent in Louisiana, southern Arkansas, and East Texas, couldn't speak from experience about most the U.S., but he drew on a wealth of memories from movies and TV to paint a glowing portrait of his home country. After all, his years as a carnival barker had thoroughly taught him the art of bullshit.

*   *   *

They were still a day or more away from the general locale of Tuchaua's hut when they came across a village that lay in ruins. Half a dozen corpses, now mostly tattered skin stretched over disjointed bone and surrounded by greasy patches crawling with vermin, lay scattered between collapsing and burned huts. More were inside the ruins. Most were children and old people, but there were a handful of adults. The bodies had lain long enough that the sense of decay in the air was stronger than the odor of rotting flesh. There was no way to determine exactly what had killed the people, but Stroud could guess from the shell casings that lay strewn about.

"This is no good," Menendez muttered, unlimbering his shotgun and scanning the surrounding brush.

"Somebody slaughtered them," Stroud said, drawing his own gun. Menendez gave it a quick glance as if he already knew Stroud carried it. "But who?"

"We must be cautious," Menendez said. "I have seen much of this before. We have run into a mining operation. You see there are few adults among the bodies?"

Stroud nodded.

"The men are enslaved to work a mine," Menendez went on, "and the women to serve the men who operate the mine."

"But surely they wouldn't do anything to us," Stroud said.

"You think no?" Menendez gave a sardonic chuckle. "You're a big, strong man, John Stroud. Just the sort to make a good miner. Come. We will rest for the night and move on in the morning."

Thankfully, Menendez led them several miles away from the dead village before he stopped.

"No fire tonight," he said. "And make as little sound as you can. There might be patrols."

They took turns keeping guard during the night, though truthfully, Stroud could barely sleep when it was his time to rest. Now that he was this close, his mind churned with possibilities—chiefly the possibility that he might never find Tuchaua, no matter how close the shaman now seemed. In the morning, he told Menendez that he wanted to talk to the manager of the mine to find out what he knew about the shaman. Menendez was leery.

"These people are very dangerous," he told Stroud. "You see what they did at that village back there."

"I have no choice," Stroud said. "I have to find the man I'm looking for, and he once lived around here. The mine manager might be the only one who can tell me."

"I do not like this. The mine will be guarded by mercenaries, and this sort of work draws the worst of the worst. If we just come in out of the forest, we will probably be shot on sight."

"What can we do, then?"

"There will be a road," Menendez said. "Leading to the river. It would be safest if we found it and approached that way." He laughed without humor. "Like civilized men."

They circled the area, and by noon, they'd found the road—if a worn and potholed set of muddy tire tracks winding between the trees, dipping through mucky depressions, and climbing over mas-

285

sive clumps of roots could be called a road. Two hours later, they came across their first guard. The man was sitting on a makeshift stool leaned up against the bole of a large tree. A sawed-off shotgun lay across his lap, and an empty whiskey bottle was on the ground beside the stool. The man was asleep and snoring, and he didn't wake until Stroud and Menendez were standing over him.

As the guard started to consciousness, his hand groped for the shotgun, but Menendez tapped him on the arm with the barrel of his own sawed-off.

"We're not looking for trouble," Menendez said in Spanish. "Comprende?"

The man nodded dumbly, staring between the two of them.

"This man," Menendez indicated Stroud, "Wants to talk to the manager of the mine. You will take us there. Get up. You may keep your shotgun, but if you raise it, I will shoot you. Then I will tell your manager about that." He indicated the empty bottle.

The guard nodded again and rose unsteadily from his stool.

The mine was another hour away, but they began seeing other guards within fifteen minutes. The first, also armed with a shotgun, bristled when they came in sight, but a quick palaver with Menendez convinced him to let them pass. He joined their little train, falling in behind Menendez and Stroud. After that, there were no delays, but as they continued along the road, Stroud couldn't help but feel hostility radiating from the man behind him. He wondered how long it would be before he also felt a shotgun blast slice through him.

They were still half an hour away when the sound of the mining operation began to rise in the background. Eventually, the mine came into view. More than ten acres of trees had been felled and burned away to expose a huge, irregularly shaped open pit that could have swallowed a city block. A handful of wooden shacks sat at the far right side of the pit, and to the left was a fenced compound, topped with razor wire, enclosing a cluster of rude huts.

A couple of dozen men carrying assault rifles or shotguns stood at intervals around the edges of the pit. On the far side of the pit, workers wielding chain saws were hacking down and chopping up trees half a millennium old, while shackled Indians hauled the remains to one of several huge bonfires. A hose from one of two large, gas-powered water pumps snaked off into the jungle while the other dropped down into the pit. A single hose from the second pump led out of the pit and over to a sluice, where more shackled Indians labored under armed guard.

At first, Stroud couldn't see what was going on inside the pit. But as the the guards led them around the edge, he could glimpse inside. One man was water blasting soil from the earthen walls, while standing around him in the knee-deep muddy water, a dozen Indians used makeshift paddles to sweep the muck toward the intake hose of the second pump, where it was siphoned to the sluice above. The noise wasn't deafening, but it was loud enough to make talking difficult.

Another two hundred feet took them to the wooden shacks, where a large gasoline generator stood nearby. The two guards led Stroud and Menendez up the steps of the most substantial of the shacks, and the one who'd fallen in behind them now stepped forward and knocked on the door.

"Entra," a voice called out, and the guard opened the door and ushered them inside.

They found themselves in a small, plain room furnished with a desk and a couple of chairs. Maps were tacked to the walls, and a closed door behind the desk led to the back of the structure. The man behind the desk looked up, the incuriosity on his face turning to a scowl when he saw strangers standing before him.

"Who the fuck are you?" he demanded in Spanish.

"This man is an American," Menendez said. "I am his guide. He seeks knowledge of the people who once lived in this area."

"Who the fuck gives a rat's ass about those scum?"

"I do," Stroud said after Menendez had translated. "One of them. A man named Tuchaua."

The mine manager might not have understood English, but he recognized the name Tuchaua, and his brutal demeanor hardened even further.

"And what does the American want with Tuchaua?"

"I don't know," Menendez shrugged. "Perhaps Tuchaua has something the American desires."

"Well, tell him this: That bastard led a revolt that slaughtered half my men when we first opened this mine. I'd kill that tricky bastard on sight, and if the American is smart, he'll do the same."

"He simply wishes to find Tuchaua and ask him some questions," Menendez said, translating Stroud's reply. "If you can point the right direction, we will leave you to your operations."

"All right," the manager said, a calculating look in his eyes. "But what's in it for me?"

"Tell him that I have nothing to give right now," Stroud said. "But after I speak with Tuchaua, who knows?"

"Then you will have nothing to offer," the manager said. "But I don't need you around here, so I might as well show you which way to leave. Wait outside while I speak with my men," he indicated the two guards, "about where to take you."

Stroud and Menendez left the cabin and walked down the steps and into the harsh sunlight to wait for the guards.

"Do you think he's really going to point us in the right direction?" Stroud asked.

"I think he will have his men lead us into our own pit." Menendez waved toward the mine. "Or maybe not even that."

"They're going to kill us?"

"Most likely," Menendez nodded.

"Why?" Stroud asked.

"You seek one of the tribe that lived here, and what have you found?"

"A mine."

"A mine with members of that tribe shacked and doing slave labor. And others are lying dead all around this district. Do you think the manager can permit us to leave and tell others what we have seen?"

"I don't give a shit about the slaves or dead Indians," Stroud said truthfully. "I just need to talk to Tuchaua."

"Do you think the manager can afford to believe that? It will be much simpler and more certain to kill us."

"What can we do?"

"Kill them first."

Stroud was a little taken aback. He'd murdered Joe Wheeler, but that had been in the heat of the moment. And the people he'd sent the manin-pasuk after…well, the manin-pasuk had been the one who killed them, hadn't it? A gunfight, though, was too personally dangerous.

The two guards emerged from the cabin, jogged down the steps, and came over to Stroud and Menendez. The one in charge said something to Menendez.

"He says they will guide us for the first few miles then point the way to go."

"I don't like this."

"I don't, either, but at least we get out out of the camp, where there are a couple of dozen guards. We'll just have two to deal with."

"It sounds like you've done this before."

"The Amazon is a dangerous place," Menendez said without looking at Stroud.

"Do you think they suspect we know what they plan to do?"

"It is safe to believe so."

The two guards waved toward the muddy track that led to the mine. Once out of sight of the mine, the one in charge indicated that Stroud and Menendez should go ahead.

"I never heard of a guide letting the guided lead," Stroud commented under his breath.

"We will be safe enough as long as we're on the road. They won't want to leave our bodies in plain sight. They'll want us to go off into the forest a mile or so before they act, so they don't have to drag our bodies or smell us afterwards."

"How long?"

They said a few miles. I think they'll have us turn off in a couple of miles. That's when we should act." Menendez peered sideways at Stroud. "Be ready to use your gun."

After another hour, the guard in charge called out.

"He says we're going to take the next trail to the right," Menendez said tightly. "It's time. As soon as we come to the trail, I will say, 'Now,' and we must act. I will take the leader, you will take the other."

Menendez didn't ask if Stroud was ready.

Stroud slipped his hand beneath his shirt tail and gripped the revolver. Just ahead, the trail opened to their right, and as he and Menendez approached it abreast, Menendez muttered, "Now."

Stroud jerked the gun from its holster, whirled, and spotted his target, who was lifting his shotgun. His victim's sudden movement sent a wash of fear and desperation across his face, but Stroud was too fast for him. A round from the .357 tore through his shoulder, sending him spinning to the ground. In almost the same instant, Menendez emptied both barrels of his shotgun at the other guard, whose chest and neck erupted in a spray of blood. The man went down beside his companion, but as he fell, his finger convulsed on the trigger of his own shotgun, and the blast shattered Menendez's left side. The guide fell to the ground, clutching futilely at the massive wound.

The man Stroud had shot was writhing in the mud, but despite his pain, he was groping for his gun.

"Finish him," Menendez gasped. "Quickly."

Without thinking, Stroud stepped up and put a bullet through the man's skull. Then he hurried to Menendez and crouched over him, reaching out to check the wound. But Menendez weakly pushed him away.

"Don't bother," he said. "I am finished."

"I'll get you out of here," Stroud said.

"You'll be lucky to get yourself out of here," Menendez said with a choking chuckle, then he waved toward the now half-headless man Stroud had shot. "Get his shotgun and shells. Check his pockets for other weapons or tools."

Stroud, feeling a lot less numb than he thought he would, did as he was told.

"Now the other," Menendez said, more faintly than before.

When Stroud had stripped the guards of anything useful, which included pocket knives and a cigarette lighter as well as weapons and ammunition.

"You must go, now," Menendez said.

"What about you?" Stroud asked. "I can't just leave you here."

"But I'm about to leave you," Menendez said. "There's nothing you can do except go as quickly as possible. The men from the mine will find the three of us, and you must be gone before they get here. Just leave me my shotgun in case I live long enough to take one or two more."

"But I don't know which way Tuchaua went," Stroud said.

"It doesn't matter," Menendez said. "They think you'll continue on, but you need to double back and return to Guayaquil."

"No, I can't," Stroud said. "I need Tuchaua."

"If you're smart, you'll do as I say. Otherwise, you will die."

Stroud shook his head.

"You don't understand. Tuchaua means life to me."

"Then go find him, if you must. But quickly. Time runs short. But first, I have done what I contracted to do, and now you must pay me."

"You're dying, and you want your payment?"

"It is the way of the world," Menendez groaned. "Quickly, now: the word. The secret word you told Sandoval."

"Your name," Stroud said. "The secret word is Menendez."

"Menendez," the guide said, a smile playing across his face. Then he died.

Stroud quickly gathered up the bandoleer of shells and other items that he'd stripped from the dead guards and hurried back to the road.

Two hours, he thought, before the mine manager realizes that his men weren't coming back. Another two hours for his men to find the bodies. Four hours. Four hours for Stroud to make himself scarce.

He looked up the road, but couldn't see far before it wound out of sight in the dense forest. He could take that, but the manager would have a vehicle that could travel along the track far faster then Stroud. Besides, he'd leave obvious footprints in the muck. The trail the guards had directed them to wouldn't be much better. Instead, Stroud set off along the road, but he kept to the foliage along the side so he wouldn't leave an obvious track. Surely there would be another path he could follow.

He found one half a mile farther along, on the other side. He crossed the road, trying not to leave obvious footprints, then hurried down the path as fast as he could.

*　*　*

Nightfall caught up with him several hours later, and he was forced to stop and make camp. He chose a hollow beneath a large bush that backed up to a huge tree that was about ten feet off the path. It was only then, as he unshouldered his pack and tossed it into the den, that his true situation became apparent. During their trek down the slopes of the Andes and across the forest to Tuchaua's home grounds, Menendez had done most of the work of acquiring game and edible plants, making a fire, and cooking their meals.

Now, Stroud was forced to fend for himself. He'd grabbed the stuff he'd taken from the guards, but in his nervousness to leave the area, he'd neglected to go through Menendez's pack and pockets. Somewhere on the body was the compass Menendez used to ascertain direction is this directionless place. Also in the pack were the remnants of the smoked meat from the last kill. But Stroud figured that he could shoot something and use the lighter he'd taken from one of the guards to start a fire to cook it, so at least he wouldn't starve.

But not now. He couldn't risk the sound of a gunshot in this area right now. He could go hungry for one night, and at least he'd found a cozy hole to nestle in for the night. The trouble was, he didn't feel all that cozy after night fell and the forest came alive with chattering and squawking. Stroud hadn't worried about all that with Menendez around, but now, he realized that the pandemonium could easily mask the padding approach of a jaguar or the slither of a large constrictor. He sat with his back to the bole of the tree, shotgun across his lap and .357 in its holster on his belt, as he grew hungrier and more tired. But sleep eluded him, and he started at every nearby sound.

He must have slept at last, for he woke suddenly to some sound. Light was beginning to filter through the canopy of leaves, and birds were twittering their morning songs. Then the sound that wakened him came again, and he froze. It was the sound of muffled voices. He stood as silently as he could and peered around the trunk of the tree in the direction of the path. At first, he saw nothing but forest, but a few moments later, two men came cautiously down the trail. Both carried shotguns at the ready, and Stroud recognized one as another mine guard.

If there were two, surely more were not far behind. Apparently, the mine manager wasn't about to let Stroud leave the area alive.

He expected the two trackers to see where he'd veered off the trail and into the brush, but they passed without noticing. He thanked his lucky stars that he hadn't made a fire, for the telltale odor of smoke would have led them right to him. But it wouldn't be long before they realized they'd overshot their mark and doubled back, and then Stroud would be caught between them and any more still coming up the trail.

He did the only thing he could do. As soon as the men passed by, he eased around the other side of the tree and raised his shotgun. He sent one blast at the closer of the two men, catching him along his upper back and neck. As the man fell onto the path, the other whirled, but Stroud's second barrel tore off half his face, and he went down beside his companion.

Shouts came from the direction the men had come, and Stroud heard the sound of footsteps pounding down the path. A man carrying an AK-47 burst into view, and he saw his companions lying dead, then Stroud, and he sent a chatter of bullets in his direction, ripping nearby foliage.

Stroud had no chance to grab his pack, only duck and blunder through the underbrush as fast as he could. More shouts came, and more shotgun blasts shredded plants near him. He didn't stop to think or plan. There was only time to keep moving. Surely there was a limit to how far they would chase him if only he could stay ahead.

His pursuers right behind him, he raced—blundered, really—through the undergrowth. Branches tore at his face and arms, and his clothing sagged with sweat. More bullets ripped nearby leaves and fronds. They were going to catch him, he realized. In minutes if not seconds. There was no telling what they'd do to him when they did, but it would be bad.

A shotgun blast shattered the air all to close. He had to put something between him and his pursuers, if only for a short while. He couldn't afford to be shot. Then he saw, just ahead a fallen giant of the forest, its huge root ball ripped from the forest floor and huge trunk rotting into the ground. If he could get on the other side of that, it would put a barrier between him and the men shouting and running after him. He raced through a dense covering of knee-high ferns toward the root ball end and cut close around it, intending to disappear into the forest beyond, but abruptly, the ground disappeared beneath his feet, and he tumbled painfully into a ragged, five-foot-deep hole in the ground.

The hole was the cavity left when the root ball had been torn out of the ground, and its depth had grown over the years as the remains of the taproots rotted beneath. Stroud didn't see it beneath the masking fronds of the surrounding ferns until he stepped into it, and then it was too late.

The instant he hit bottom, Stroud realized that this hole would be either his salvation or his grave as he heard the men who'd been tracking him come up and gather near the end of the fallen tree. Luckily, none of them came close to the hole, or it *would* have been Stroud's grave. It sounded like there about ten, and they were arguing. He didn't understand what they were saying—they were speaking either Spanish or Portuguese, Stroud couldn't tell which—but he presumed it was about which way he'd gone.

So far, they hadn't seen his almost invisible hole. All he had to do was stay still and silent until they passed, but his breath hissed all too loudly in his own ears. He slowly lifted the barrel of his shotgun, trying to keep his hands from shaking with exertion and adrenaline. If they found him, he intended to take one or two of them with him.

The almost immediate tickle on his forehead said he might have trouble making no further movement or sound. It was some insect crawling from his hair onto his face. And then there were more insects crawling, now all over him. Only they weren't insects but spiders. There were hundreds of them. Stroud held himself frozen as the one on his forehead crawled lower, over his open right eye. An eye he dared not close. Lower, it began to explore his right nostril.

Others crawled around his open, sweat-stained collar, his sleeve openings, and the openings of his trouser legs. His ear canals.

He'd never been more afraid or revolted in his life, and he couldn't lift a finger to stop it or move to get out of the pit and its arachnoid populous. Not with the men above still arguing, still seeking him. Frozen, he waited for the men to find him and haul him out or the spiders to attack or his own bated breath to suffocate him.

After many long minutes, the men split into two groups and vanished into the forest, and at last, mercifully, the sounds of pursuit faded in the aural gloom. Screaming inside but keeping his lips sealed, Stroud surged up and scrambled out of the pit, hands furiously brushing at his head and clothes, not knowing if the spiders were poisonous or if any of them had bitten him. He ripped off his clothing, brushed off any arachnids still on his skin, then shook out his clothes. He examined himself—as much as he could see and touch—but found no obvious bite marks. Apparently his stillness had saved him.

He re-dressed then looked and spotted a trail—some faint animal track. It led off in a direction away from both parties pursuing him, so he turned onto it. After a short time, he again heard sounds of pursuit, though far away. Taking a chance, he darted into the brush again, hoping anybody still following him would continue along the trail. It must have worked, because the sounds of pursuit faded entirely. But Stroud kept moving as fast as he could. Eventually his trackers would discover he'd tricked them, and they'd be on his ass again. His only chance was to stay ahead of them. Eventually they'd tire of the chase and go back to the mine.

Half an hour later, he came on another game trail, this one larger than the other, and he went along it in a direction he judged was opposite that of his trackers, though he really had no way to tell. He could be blundering right into their arms. At last, he had to stop, rest, and ease his panting breath. Adrenaline and panic had wiped out his hunger, but now he was thirstier than ever, and he'd left his canteen behind with his pack and everything else, including the cigarette lighter. Menendez had taught him that some large-leafed plants could hold enough rainwater to drink, but nothing like that was in sight.

As soon as his breathing subsided, he rose and continued along the path, ears pricked for the sound of pursuit, eyes sharp for the sight of a pursuer. But nothing came except the sounds and sights of the forest, monotonous and close.

Eventually he came across a small stream. The water looked fairly clear, and anyway, he didn't have any choice. He knelt and drank. It tasted rank, but after he'd rested, he drank some more.

He didn't have food, but the stream meant he'd have water as long as he traveled along its course. And streams flowed to larger streams, and those to rivers. And that meant people. Eventually.

As he went down the streambed, following a riparian game trail, he managed to spot one of the same plants Menendez had collected to complete their meals. It was a tuber, and the cluster held six, all of which Stroud uprooted and washed in the stream. He couldn't cook them as Menendez had done, so he ate half of them raw while he walked. Without cooking, they were tough and bitter, but they filled his stomach, though he'd have preferred meat. But even if he killed an animal, he couldn't start a fire, and he wasn't sure he could stomach raw flesh.

* * *

Four days later, he would gladly have eaten even a rotting carcass, if he could find one. He was staggering now with hunger and exertion, and he knew that he wouldn't last much longer. But he couldn't just lie down beside the stream and die, so he kept his feet moving despite the increasing difficulty of doing that. He spent his nights huddled beneath bushes, barely sleeping and jerking awake at the slightest sound. By now, he knew he'd lost his pursuers, but he was, himself, irrevocably lost. Beneath the dense canopy, he couldn't even tell where the sun rose and set, leaving him completely without direction.

By the morning of the fifth day, Stroud's clothes were hanging limply around his wasting flesh. He'd found more of the tubers, and some berries that he cautiously consumed, but he'd had no protein since his last meal with Menendez. As dawn filtered through the canopy, he rose from the rude nest he'd made to spend the night and simply staggered on downstream. The stream had doubled in size since he first started following it, but he still hadn't run across any sign of humanity in this green hell.

Mid afternoon saw him on the verge of collapse, but he forced his feet onward, cursing every obstruction and every bend the stream took. And then, as the atmosphere beneath the canopy took on that sullen light that said dusk was not far off, he saw a camp.

The presence of the small tent informed him instantly that it did not belong to an Indian. Stroud wasn't sure if that was a good thing or a bad. But there was one good thing: Whoever owned the camp was not present. Even better, he could see a cloth sack suspended six or seven feet off the ground by a rope looped over a tree branch. The only reason to do that would be to keep scavengers away from food inside the sack.

He held himself back, despite the sudden and massive salivation that drenched his mouth at the thought of food. But five minutes of creeping and peering around the camp was all he could stand. Finally, desperate, he burst into the little clearing, rushed over to the suspended sack, and cut it free with his knife. As it fell to the ground, he dropped his shotgun and nearly collapsed beside the sack. He tore it open and wolfed the first morsel he could get his hands on: a palm-sized slab of dried meat.

It was tough but it filled his mouth with pleasure.

He peered into the sack again to see what else it contained, when he heard a rustle behind him. His hand groped for the shotgun he'd dropped beside the sack, but a voice halted him.

"No!" the voice said.

Stroud couldn't tell if the command was in English, Spanish, or some other language, but the meaning was clear.

"Stand up and turn around." English.

Stroud cautiously obeyed. A dark-haired, medium-sized Anglo man in sweat-stained khakis was looking at him over the barrel of a sawed-off shotgun. He also wore a holstered pistol.

"Quel es su nombre?" he asked, then at Stroud's blank look, he said, "Your name. What is your name?"

His accent placed him as an American, though not from the Midwest, Northeast, or South.

"Stroud. John Stroud."

"Well, John, some places, doing what you're doing will get a man shot, and this is one of them. Out here, a person might just think you're trying to steal something. But seein' as how I don't have anything to steal, I'd have to say what you're doing must be pure malice."

Stroud felt himself flinching under the man's words, and hating himself for it.

"I'm hungry," he said. "I haven't eaten for days. I just wanted food."

"You're an American," the man said. "I'd ask you what the hell you're doing way the hell in the middle of nowhere's hell, but first I think you'd better relieve yourself of that gun on your hip and the bandolier of shells. At least until we get to know each other a little better. Be careful, now. I couldn't miss an ant's ass at this distance."

Stroud unsnapped his holster, gingerly removed the .357, and laid it on the ground. The bandoleer followed.

"Go over to that tree and sit with your back to it." The man indicated a large tree about ten feet from the tent.

Stroud obeyed, and the man kept him covered with the shotgun as he picked up the pack and tossed it to Stroud.

"Have at it, John."

Stroud did, while the man watched, keeping him covered with the shotgun. When Stroud was done, chasing the food with water from a fired clay jug the man carried over to him, the man tossed him a coil of rope.

"Tie one end around your ankles," he ordered. Stroud started to object, but then he obeyed. If the man intended him harm, he would have shot Stroud before wasting food on him.

"Now give yourself four feet, and tie one of your wrists." Stroud did, and the man said, "Good. Now sling the other end around that tree." He pointed with the shotgun. When Stroud had, the man said. "Tie your other leg."

After that, the man approached, his shotgun trained on Stroud's face. With his free hand, he looped the rope around Stroud's other wrist and tied it off. Then he backed off a few feet and lowered the shotgun, leaving Stroud effectively but loosely and comfortably bound to the tree.

"I realize that you probably can get out of that rope easily enough," the man said. "Don't."

He stuck his sawed-off through a thick leather loop at his left hip, then collected Stroud's shotgun and revolver. The latter he turned over in his hands, then he glanced at Stroud and nodded.

"Stainless. Good choice for these parts, even if it is heavy. And a .357. Will shoot .38s, too." He peered at Stroud. "You have ammo for it?"

"About thirty rounds. In my pockets."

The man took the two guns and bandoleer of shotgun shells to the tent and put them inside, but he didn't ask Stroud to empty his pockets. Then he came back with a rude stool, sat, and stared at his captive.

"Two guns but no pack, canteen, or supplies. Do you even have any idea where you are?"

Stroud shook his head.

"My guide had a compass."

"What happened to him?"

"Mine guards killed him. They tried to kill me, too, but I got away."

"Obviously you haven't been in these parts for long, or you'd know better than to go near any mines. What were you doing around there, anyway?"

"That's my business."

"When you tried to steal my food, you made it my business, too," the man said. "Especially with garampieros on your trail. How long ago did they kill your guide?"

"Five or six days. I lost track."

The man laughed.

"You lost it, all right." Then he sobered. "Now tell me what you're doing out here."

"I'm looking for someone," Stroud said, but plainly the man wasn't going to let it stand at that. "A man. His name is Tuchaua. I was told he used to live around where the mine is."

"Tuchaua." The man repeated, saying the name like a statement, not a question.

"You know him?"

"I've heard of him, but I never met him. I've been in the forest off and on for ten years, but he was gone before I arrived. He wasn't just any man, though. He was a powerful shaman. The tribes around here remember him with great fear. They say he commanded some sort of spirit called the manin-pasuk. That means something like 'demon warrior' in Shuar." He paused, calculation in his eyes. "What would you want with a man like that?"

"I don't know anything about that," Stroud said, knowing that elements of truth always bolstered a lie. "I had a friend back in the States who got waylaid out here, and this Tuchaua saved his life. My friend felt he never really got to thank Tuchaua, and when he died recently, he asked me to find Tuchaua and do that for him."

"You must have owed your friend big time to undertake something like this."

"I owe him everything. So I guess I owe Tuchaua everything, too."

The man nodded.

"In my experience, most of the non-indigenous people out here usually owe big debts to someone. The thing is, most of them are out here trying to avoid paying, not seeking to repay. That makes you a rare bird."

"And you?" Stroud asked. "What kind of debt do you owe?"

The man laughed again.

"I'm sure my ex-wife could tell you more about that than I can. But I'm not a criminal on the run. My name is Mark Wilson. I'm a botanist. I'm studying the flora in this region."

"You work for a university?"

"Used to. Not any more. Freelancing for pharmaceutical companies is a lot more lucrative, especially if you can get a shaman to show you how to concoct some of their healing and hallucinogenic formulas."

"Having much luck?"

"A little." The botanist shrugged. "Most of what the Shuar cook up is for killing or getting stoned. Sickness is a poisoning of the spirit, and healing is more a matter of eliminating spirit poison in magical ways not connected to chemistry. Oddly, the killing concoctions have more pharmaceutical possibilities, at least as far as the chemists can tell. Anyway, the ones that get you stoned are mostly illegal back home. One formula I sent in yielded a compound the researchers think might aid patients in recovery from surgery, and it's in the trial stages now. That's my biggest find yet."

He rose from the stool, approached Stroud, and looked down at him.

"It'll be dark soon," he said. "The question now is what to do with you."

"You could untie me now that you know I'm not a danger."

"Every man in this forest is dangerous," Wilson said. "Otherwise, they wouldn't be here."

"What then? You just going to leave me tied to this tree all night?"

"I think that would be best for now."

Wilson went to his tent, crawled inside, then emerged with a blanket. He went back to Stroud, tossed the blanket to him, then checked his bindings after throwing a couple more loops of rope around him and the tree, tying them off in back, out of reach.

"Yell out if any predators look like they're going to bother you."

"That's it?"

"What more do you want? You say you spent the last five days without food or shelter. I've given you both. We'll talk about more in the morning."

Wilson went over to his tent and puttered around for an hour before slipping inside and closing the flap, leaving Stroud to his thoughts and the sound of the forest. The first thing he did was try to loosen the ropes that held him, but the knots that were within reach were complex and tight. Resigning himself, he shrugged the blanket over him. If he thought he might have trouble sleeping, he was mistaken.

Stroud had been ravenous before he'd run across Wilson's camp, but the food he'd eaten from the pack only seemed to heighten his hunger. That was what woke him just as dawn and the morning twitter of birds filtered through the foliage overhead. That and the unmistakable sound of a gunshot. It sounded like it had come from less than half a mile away, somewhere off behind him.

He sat upright from where he'd slumped against the bole of the tree, listening, but he heard nothing else. He glanced at the tent. The flap was down, and it didn't seem that Wilson had heard the shot. Should he wake the botanist and warn him? Try to get Wilson to untie him if danger approached?

Then he heard the unmistakable rustle of a heavy body moving through the foliage, off his rear left quadrant. Twist though he might, he couldn't stretch his bindings enough to look clearly in that direction. Footsteps came up behind him.

"Wilson!" he yelled. "We have an intruder!"

"No," came a voice from behind him. "We have food."

The footsteps rounded the tree, and Stroud saw it was Wilson, the carcass of a peccary slung across his shoulder.

"You ate most of my meat yesterday," the botanist said. "Thought I'd get in a little early hunting. It's going to take most of the day to butcher this fellow and start drying the meat."

He took the wild pig over to another tree, where he tied a rope around its rear ankles, threw the rope over a limb, and hoisted the carcass off the ground. After tying off the rope, he came over to Stroud.

"I'm going to have to trust you. Up to a point. I'm going to un-tie you so you can help me. But don't fuck with me, don't get be-hind me, and stay away from the tent. And by the way, I hid your guns out there somewhere." He waved with his hand, taking in the forest. "Just remember," he said as circled the tree trunk and began working on the knots back there. "I don't have to kill you. I just have turn you out without your guns or anything else. You'll be dead in a week. You don't know where you are and you don't know shit about surviving out here. You need me, but I don't need you."

"I won't try anything," Stroud promised.

Wilson finished undoing the ropes binding Stroud to the tree, then he loosened the end looped around Stroud's left wrist and stood back, letting Stroud free himself and stand up. Stroud glanced at the peccary, then back at Wilson.

"What do you want me to do?"

"Gather firewood. A lot of it. It's going to take a couple of days to completely smoke this fellow. And while the meat is smoking, we'll go look for some edible plants. How does a nice pork roast for dinner sound?" Wilson gave a big smile.

Stroud went for the firewood, leaving Wilson to butcher the pig. By the time he'd amassed a fairly large pile, Wilson had strips of flesh laid out on a crosshatched rack made of green sticks and a haunch pierced by a spit ready to set over the fire.

"All right, then," Wilson said. "Let's go look for our veggies."

He handed Stroud a bag crudely woven from grasses then led them off into the forest, his eyes darting here and there over the fo-liage. Occasionally, he'd find something edible, and he'd point it out to Stroud before hacking it off with his knife or digging it up. Gradually, the bag Stroud carried filled.

"What about those?" Stroud said after they'd been foraging for an hour or so. He pointed to a clump of blade-like leaves jutting from the ground. "My guide told me about them. That's about all I could find to eat until I ran across you."

"Yep. Those tubers are good." Wilson pulled out his knife and threw it at the ground, where it embedded to the hilt next to the spiky leaves. "Go on and dig it up."

Stroud glanced at him, then knelt, pulled the knife from the earth, and dug up the tubers beneath. When he finished, he stood and passed the knife back to Wilson

Wilson stared thoughtfully at Stroud as he stowed the knife in its sheath.

"You sure you haven't been here before?"

"The Amazon? Never."

"You don't seem bothered by the forest. Most people who aren't from around here start to feel hemmed in. Antsy. You seem pretty comfortable."

"I grew up in southern Louisiana," Stroud replied. "Nothing but forest all around me my whole life."

The botanist nodded.

"Yeah, Some folks are like that." He jerked his head. "Let's go back to camp and cook up that roast."

That night, Wilson gave Stroud the blanket, but he didn't tie him up.

"Go back to your tree," the botanist ordered. "If you have to take a piss or shit during the night, don't do it near camp."

*   *   *

In the morning, they ate breakfast, consuming the same fare they'd eaten the night before.

"We need to get a few things straight," Wilson said when they were done. "First, you can't stay here. Not for long, at least. I have work to do, and I can't do that and take care of you at the same time. But I'm not just going to turn you out, either. I may be living among savages—and I don't mean the Shuar—but I'm not one yet. I'll put my research aside for two weeks. That should give you time to recover and give me time to teach you a few survival skills."

"I appreciate it," Stroud said. "I'll work hard."

"You'd better. You have a lot to learn about the people, plants, and animals. We're going to start with language."

"My guide taught me a few words of Shuar," Stroud said.

"He did? Show me."

Stroud spoke a little, sometimes pointing to objects that he named.

"Pretty good," Wilson said. "I can teach you a little more, and maybe a smattering of Portuguese. That'll serve you well enough around here and farther east. Most of the tribes around here speak a variant of Shuar, so if you can speak to some, you can speak to almost all. We'll start with this." He indicated the remains of the peccary they'd been eating. "This is a yugkipik. I killed it with this." He tapped his shotgun. "My akaru."

And so it went through the day and those that followed, until Stroud's head was spinning with strange words and his tongue was twisted by unfamiliar syllables. But gradually, as he and Wilson foraged, hunted, fished, and puttered around the camp, he began to understand, at least a little.

Hell, he thought. If the manin-pasuk can learn English, I can learn its language. It sure will be surprised when I get back and talk to it in Shuar.

"There's no way I can teach you every thing about Shuar," Wilson said one night as they sat around the campfire before bedtime. "The Indians have names for literally thousands of birds and even more kinds of plants. And some of the shamans know what most of those plants are good for, be it food, medicine, or hallucinogenic drugs. Hell, I've been here ten years, and I only know a little. But I've been learning."

"It's all so different than I expected," Stroud admitted.

"You thought it would be primitive tribesmen living the pristine forest life?" Wilson laughed a little sadly. "Maybe once, but not now."

"The only people I've seen in this godforsaken place except you and my guide, have been dead natives and slave labor camps."

"That'll be about all you will see anymore. Almost all the tribes have been domesticated. Every once in a while, some lost tribe emerges from the deep forest, and that'll probably go on for a few decades longer, but that'll be it. Most of the ones still out there stay lost out of fear. But once they get a taste of civilization—clothes and tools and other stuff—then all they want is more."

"Too bad they don't know that civilization is probably worse."

"Some don't, but some are clued in. It might seem strange for a Ph.D. in biochemistry to be saying this, but it's been a real privilege working with some of the shamans around here. They might seem primitive by American standards, but don't let either their lifestyle or stature fool you; the shamans are some of the sharpest minds around and they know a hell of a lot about the nature of reality as well as about the properties of the plants that grow here."

After the first week, Wilson disappeared into the forest, emerging half an hour later with Stroud's weapons.

"I figure you're safe enough since you still need me to teach you," Wilson said, handing them to Stroud. "Besides," he laughed, "you still haven't the faintest clue about where you are or which direction to go."

That was true enough. Stroud had become familiar with the immediate environs of the camp, but that was the extent of his geographic knowledge other than that he was somewhere in the western part of the Amazon Basin. He could wander for weeks before getting his bearings, if ever. Or run into more miners.

During the nights of the following week, Wilson showed Stroud how to weave a bag of grass stalks like the one he carried during their foraging trips. By the end of the week, the bag was done, and Wilson told him to fill it with whatever food he wanted from their stores.

"Time for you to leave, John. You're strong, now, and you've learned enough Shuar to get by. You'll pick up more as you go along. I have a contract to fulfill, and you have Tuchaua to find."

"I wish I knew which way to go."

"Maybe I can help you with that. Like I told you, he left before my time, but he's legendary in these parts. People say he went in the direction of Pavayacu. That's a village to the northeast, on the other side of the Rio Pastanze. About two weeks by foot. But there's no telling if he actually arrived there."

"It's something. You want to point out northwest to me?"

"Here," Wilson said, digging in his pocket then stretching out his hand. In it was a compass. "You need this more than I do. So you don't lose your way."

"Thanks."

Stroud was sorry to be leaving the temporary haven of Wilson's camp, but Wilson was right. Both of them had work to do. He left right after breakfast the next morning.

"Good luck, John. Hope you find what you're looking for."

"And you, too," Stroud replied. Then he shouldered his newly woven bag, picked up his shotgun—his akaru—and consulted his compass.

Northwest was that way, and he followed. Within a minute, the camp was out of sight, and by late afternoon, the territory around him was completely unfamiliar. But the compass gave him direction amid the tangled disorientation of the forest.

As Wilson promised, Pavayacu was about two weeks away, but Stroud arrived in good condition thanks to his mentor. He arrived to disappointment, though. Using his smattering of Shuar and Portuguese, he learned that Tuchaua had been in the village some years earlier but had left for Marsella, another village farther north. At Marsella, he learned that the shaman had moved on again.

With a sigh, Stroud pulled out the compass that Wilson had given him, and followed its lead through the forest and through the years.

14: TUCHAUA

I'M TOO OLD for this shit, Stroud thought as he stalked along the winding, root-infested trail. If I never see another jungle again, it'll be too damn soon.

But the truth was, he didn't feel old—at least, not as old as he really was. He still had plenty of vitality, as he'd proved with that little slut back in the last village. If nothing else, more than a quarter of a century of tramping around the Amazon, chasing Tuchaua, had kept him in pretty good shape. But enough was enough. He was weary to death of the tramping and humidity and seeing nothing but little naked brown people and a million shades of green. But what else could he do? He'd been away from the States for so long that he couldn't return without the formula.

And, even if he didn't want to admit it, he was growing old. He needed that fucking formula.

But Tuchaua had proved elusive. Stroud long suspected that the old bastard had heard Stroud was looking for him and was deliberately keeping one step ahead, laughing. Then he met Jimmy-Boy, a young man with an Irish father and Achuar mother who'd been raised in these parts. With a sour thought, Stroud realized that Jimmy-Boy had been born years after Stroud came to the Amazon.

Jimmy-Boy told Stroud that Tuchaua was living in an abandoned village nearby. Or, rather, dying. From what Jimmy-Boy had heard, Tuchaua looked ancient as hell and could no longer leave his hut. That puzzled Stroud, who expected to find the old shaman as hale and fit as Joe had described him. Given the shaman's knowledge,

Stroud couldn't understand why he'd become old and feeble. Why didn't he just use the powder to revitalize himself? Maybe he'd just given up now that his tribe's land was gone and his people decimated. But Stroud didn't give a damn about Tuchaua or his tribe. All he wanted was the formula. Joe had been a fool to settle for bags of the powder. Stroud was determined to wrest the secret of their formulation from Tuchaua, even if he had finish his miserable life for him.

The village—if eight decrepit huts swarming with vermin could be called a village—began with the first signs that advertised the presence of any Amazon settlement: a widening of the trail and then the increasing presence of numerous other trails crossing and intersecting until the village came into sight through the foliage. He'd met no one on the trail, and the village looked miserable and just as deserted. Plants were springing up through the tramped earth around many of the huts, and most of the structures had caved in.

He didn't know if it was this damn forest or just the wrenching despair that lay over most of the villages he'd passed through lately. When he'd come to this damn place nearly thirty years ago, it hadn't been like this, but the last few years had wrought devastating changes to these backwater communities. Some of that devastation has been wrought by Stroud's own hand.

Fuck 'em, he thought. It was Darwinism in action. The forest people were just too ignorant to go on much longer. Natural selection, which once had created a niche for them in this damp, leafy vastness, now had introduced modernity, and the little brown people with their primitive weapons and simple lifestyles were no match for determined men armed with guns and disease and hungry to pillage the region's natural resources.

The only person he happened on was a shrunken old hag sitting on a rotten log in front of one of the decaying huts, repairing a basket. Stroud stopped in front of her. Her decrepit bare breasts hung like loose bags above a wrinkled belly. She probably was forty-five, and Stroud, who was nearly twice her age, looked better than she did. Of course, he'd had help, but even if things had progressed normally for him, he'd still have looked better.

"I'm looking for a man named Tuchaua," Stroud demanded in the local dialect as he stopped in front of her. "Do you know him?"

Her fingers stopped their complex movements, and she glanced up sidelong at him. Was that wariness in her eyes? Hostility? Or just plain weariness? Stroud couldn't tell. He never had been able to read these jungle folk. Their beady black eyes held nothing he could understand. They were just too primitive, too removed from rational thinking.

She simply stared at him.

"Tuchaua," he repeated. "Is he here? In this village?"

Still she did not answer, and Stroud felt rage building in his gut. Twenty-eight fucking years, he thought, and it's come down to this: dealing with some old fucking bitch who is either deaf or too stupid to answer a simple question.

"Tuchaua!" he snarled, brutally sweeping the basket from her grasp. "Tell me about Tuchaua!"

"There," she said, cowering back and pointing with a shaking hand. "In the hut at the edge of the forest."

Without another word, Stroud straightened, turned in the direction she'd indicated, and walked off. Behind him, the old woman rose awkwardly from the log and went to retrieve her basket, glancing at the madman's retreating back. She knew she'd never see Tuchaua again, and she felt like crying, but her tears had dried up long ago.

Three huts sat on the edge of the forest, but Stroud had no trouble determining which was the right one. It had about it the aura of death. Stroud knew about that. He'd spent too much time in this godforsaken jungle, and a man who lived here—a white man, especially—had better know about such things or he wouldn't last long. And Stroud had lasted a long time.

But it wasn't the aura of death that hung around the miserable hut that stayed his hand just as it was about to grip the rotted woven grass curtain masking the doorway. It was the sudden, unexpected sensation of completion, the end of decades of bone-wearying search and danger and blind hope. Was the end of all that really behind that curtain?

He flung it back and stepped into the gloom. Inside, the miserable hovel reeked of feces, urine, and old age. An old man reclined weakly on a pallet of rotting animal skins. He was so ancient, shriveled, and diminutive that Stroud suddenly thought of the manin-pasuk.

Tuchaua looked up, wincing at the bright light streaming in. He couldn't see the features of the man who threw back the door flap. He was too backlit. But Tuchaua noted the hunch of the shoulders, the predatory step into the hut, the big, meaty hands. Hands that had killed. The stink of it was all over them.

"I do not know you," he said.

"But I know you," Stroud replied, letting the flap fall back over the doorway and stepping forward into the gloom. "My friend, Joe, told me all about you."

"Joe." Tuchaua let his eyes drop. "Your friend. Once he was my friend. I trusted him, and he betrayed me. He betrayed my people."

"He's dead, if that's any consolation."

"Death is never a consolation," Tuchaua said. "Just inevitable."

"Maybe for you," Stroud said. "I've been all over this god-forsaken jungle looking for you, old man. And I mean every damn where. For twenty-eight fucking years. I could write a fucking encyclopedia about this shitty jungle and the primitive assholes like you who live here."

"You've been here a lifetime," Tuchaua lisped over toothless gums. "I guess you're one of the assholes who live here, too."

"You're going to regret that, old man."

"I already regret our meeting. What is it that brings you so far for so long?"

"You know damn well who I am, and you probably guessed a long time ago what I want. That's why you've kept one step ahead of me. The manin-pasuk is why I'm here. To take to him what is rightfully his."

"I do not know what you mean."

"The powder, old man. Give me the fucking powder for longer life and to give life to the manin-pasuk."

"The powder." Tuchaua laughed. "You traveled all this way for a handful of dust?"

"And its formula. I want to know how to make it for myself. Remember, old man, I have the manin-pasuk. It's mine to command, and it won't give a shit if you're the one I send it to kill."

"Almost certainly," Tuchaua said. After what he'd done to the warrior who'd become the manin-pasuk, it probably hungered to come after him.

310

"It's gone," Stroud went on, "and your people are gone. Pretty soon, you'll be gone, too. You might as well give me the formula."

The shaman looked up at Stroud, lips wrinkling sarcastically. "You wish to become my apprentice?"

"That's right. I've learned something about the plants and animals in the time I've been here. I want to know how to make the powder, and you're going to tell me."

Tuchaua laughed again, his toothless gums hideous in the gloom.

Stroud stepped in predatorily and cuffed the side of the old shaman's head with a meaty palm.

"You're going to tell me, or you're going to suffer."

Tuchaua just looked up at him, a void in his dark eyes.

"That is something I cannot do."

"Can't, or won't?"

"You have been to my village?"

"Nothing left of it," Stroud said.

"Yes," Tuchaua nodded sadly. "It is gone. Ukunchkit and I are the last."

"Ukunchkit?"

"You met her." Tuchaua gestured toward the tent flap. "She's the only other person here."

"That old hag out there weaving that basket? That's the girl Joe was all hot as a pepper over?" Stroud snorted a laugh. "I don't see what all the bother was about."

"Of course you don't," Tuchaua said.

"You were telling me why you won't teach me the formula," Stroud said impatiently.

"The men who now live where our people lived drove us off and destroyed our forest."

"Well, tough shit for you and your stinking village. One hellhole in this jungle is as good as another."

"You should care," Tuchaua said. "The plants you need for your precious formula have no names beyond those in my memory, so I cannot tell you what they are, only show you. But they are all gone now. The white men destroyed them by fire and ax when they cleared the forest for their mine and huts." He peered at Stroud. "That is why I cannot help you."

"Don't fuck with me," Stroud said, grabbing Tuchaua by his neck and squeezing.

The old man's eyes widened, not in fear but with surprise.

"You have learned the Jaguar Hand," he choked out.

"I've learned many things in the god-forsaken place. You know that if I extend my spirit claws into your flesh, you will die."

"I am too near to death to care about your threats," Tuchaua rasped.

"Gone?" Stroud, let go of Tuchaua, who slumped back to his pallet. All these years in this hellhole for nothing. Worse than nothing: He'd given up everything he had in Oakdale on a wild goose chase.

"If I'd had the manin-pasuk," Tuchaua breathed hoarsely, "I could have stopped them."

"Why didn't you just make another? I thought your teacher showed you how to do that."

"He did, but I couldn't bring myself to do what was necessary to imprison another man in such a state."

Tuchaua's eyes grew distant, as if remembering deeds done and promises unkempt. Then they refocused on Stroud.

"I still have some of the rejuvenation powder. It's all that's left."

"Where?" Stroud demanded, jaw tightening as he leaned forward, shoulders tense, hands ready to grasp and wring the old man's wrinkled neck.

Tuchaua didn't shrink back in fear. He just turned and crawled to half-a-dozen rotting baskets piled against the wall to the left of the pallet. After digging through the pile for a moment, he pulled out a tattered woven grass tote. He started to crawl back to his pallet, but Stroud lunged forward, snatched the tote from him hand, and shoved him aside.

Tuchaua fell into the pile of baskets, sending up a cloud of rank, moldy dust, and he lay there, watching as Stroud opened the tote and peered inside. Four fat pouches were there. Stroud opened one and the familiar pungent odor of the rejuvenation powder wafted into his nostrils. Four pouches, he thought. It would have to do. Then suspicion flooded his mind.

"Why haven't you used this?" he asked. "Fuck. Look at you. You're nothing but an old, shriveled piece of leather."

"Death is inevitable," Tuchaua said. "He comes for all men, and the rejuvenation powder can only hold him off for so long. For you, the contents of those pouches will bring many centuries, but for me it is no longer effective. I've lived the lives of many men. I have seen entire peoples come and go. And I have grown weary. I still have my three spirits intact, but my people are all dead, and I am ready to join them. Besides, look at me. Do you think longer life in this state is preferable to death?"

Stroud cinched the pouch and dropped it back into the tote.

"Things might have been different," Tuchaua said.

"Different? How?"

"I still keep two secrets. One is my last and most powerful tsentsak."

"And the other?" Stroud didn't give a shit about some mythical magic darts.

"Remember when I said that death was inevitable?" Tuchaua was staring up at him, a secret gleaming in his eyes. "That's not really true."

"What do you mean?" Stroud felt a sudden, irrational surge of hope.

"There is another formula," Tuchaua said slyly. "I have it here with me. Enough for one dose."

"One dose? That won't add much to my life."

"This is a different formula. It confers immortality on the user."

"Immortality? Bullshit. You'd have used it long ago."

"I might have, but Joe took away that possibility when he stole the manin-pasuk."

"You need the doll to make it work?"

Tuchaua nodded.

"Where?"

Tuchaua indicated the pile of molding baskets.

"In there. In another pouch. A much larger one."

Stroud hastily rummaged through the pile, holding his breath to keep from breathing in the dust that blossomed up. Then he found it: a pouch nearly the size of a softball, greasy and dark with age. He plucked at the knot of the drawstring and opened it. Inside was a brown powder heavily laced with black specks like so much pepper. The odor it gave off was sharp and metallic—completely unlike that of the rejuvenation powder.

"This is it?" he demanded.

"Yes, but beware. Using it requires a sacrifice." Tuchaua levered himself into a sitting position. "Two sacrifices. One is the manin-pasuk. It must be destroyed during the ritual."

That took Stroud by surprise. He looked at Tuchaua, unsure what to think. The doll was the basis of Stroud's power. It was the means to destroy his enemies and subdue his allies and bend them to his will. But what use was it, anyway, if he didn't have the reani-mation powder? It was just an ugly, useless artifact. But immortality! After a lifetime of trading the lives of others for his own gain, yes, he could easily trade the manin-pasuk for immorality. He already had money and power, and with immortality, he would have them for a long, long time. What did he need with that decrepit old doll? He could hire hitmen, if he needed to.

"And the other sacrifice?"

"You will need human blood."

"Blood?" Stroud wasn't shocked. He'd seen too much blood shed, some of it spilled by himself. During his years in the forest, he'd killed nine men. Some had tried to rob or kill him, others had just gotten in his way. And he'd used enough of his own blood rean-imating the manin-pasuk, so he wasn't surprised.

"My blood?"

"From an infant," Tuchaua amplified. "The baby must drained and its blood mixed with the powder to make a paste."

"Why an infant?"

"A baby's blood is filled with a lifetime of vitality."

"What do I do with this paste?"

"You stand naked and smear it all over your body. You must be careful to cover every part of yourself. Then you must burn the manin-pasuk in a fire and breathe in the smoke."

"I have to destroy it?"

"You must choose between giving temporary life to the manin-pasuk or giving yourself eternal life."

"What else?"

"Nothing else. That is all. Within moments, you will begin to feel the effects. Your body will feel completely rejuvenated—young again. Power will course through your veins. You will have the strength of ten men. You have seen how quickly the manin-pasuk heals?"

"I've seen."

"You will heal just as quickly. And you will live forever."

"This," Stroud held up the bag, "is enough? I won't need to do it again?"

"How can one add to eternity? But think carefully before you use it. You believe you want eternal life, but really you'll discover eternal death. If you remain trapped in this body on this earth, your wakani can never become one with the great spirit creator, and your muisak will rise, dominant. I didn't understand this before, but I do now."

"Rationalize it however you want," Stroud said, "but I don't intend to let death get the upper hand over me." He bounced the bag on his palm. "You sure this is the stuff that'll make me live forever?" he demanded.

"Yes," Tuchaua said. "It will make you live forever."

Suddenly the old man made a throwing gesture toward Stroud.

"My final tsentsak," he said, and he burst into bloodcurdling laughter.

The laughter that cut into Stroud in a way he could not abide. He loomed over the old man, bent, and grabbed the scrawny old neck again. The thin flesh and brittle bones gave easily beneath the power of the Jaguar Hand, and in moments, Tuchaua was a lifeless rag.

Stroud straightened, wiped his palm against his pants leg, then pushed through the door flap. Outside, Ukunchkit stood, bent and aged, watching Stroud emerge from the hut.

"You do not take his tsantsa?" she asked.

Unwilling to touch her decrepit flesh or leave her, Stroud drew his revolver and shot her through the head. As her body slumped to the ground, Stroud turned and headed out of the village.

Home, which had remained elusive for so long, was still a long way off, but no matter. He now had plenty of time. In fact, he practically felt reborn.

**End of
Effigy: Book I**

Phosphene Publishing Company
publishes books and DVDs relating to literature,
history, the paranormal, film, spirituality, and the
martial arts.

For other great titles, visit
phosphenepublishing.com

www.ingramcontent.com/pod-product-compliance
Lightning Source LLC
Chambersburg PA
CBHW060523180626
46817CB00002B/470